The God Whom Moses Knew

A Novel

To Clint, a wise and gentle man whose friendship and help will always be deeply appreciated —

Roger Nelson

J. Roger Nelson, M.D.

WestBow
PRESS

WestBow Press books may be ordered through booksellers or by contacting:

WestBow Press
A Division of Thomas Nelson
1663 Liberty Drive
Bloomington, IN 47403
www.westbowpress.com
1-(866) 928-1240

Because of the dynamic nature of the Internet, any Web addresses or links contained in this book may have changed since publication and may no longer be valid. The views expressed in this work are solely those of the author and do not necessarily reflect the views of the publisher, and the publisher hereby disclaims any responsibility for them.

ISBN: 978-1-4497-0221-2 (sc)
ISBN: 978-1-4497-0222-9 (dj)
ISBN: 978-1-4497-0220-5 (e)

Library of Congress Control Number: 2010932290

"Scripture taken from the NEW AMERICAN STANDARD BIBLE®, ©Copyright 1960, 1962, 1963, 1968, 1971, 1972, 1973, 1975, 1977 by The Lockman Foundation Used by permission." (www.Lockman.org)

Printed in the United States of America

WestBow Press rev. date: 11/19/2010

Contents

Introduction

Believing that there is great drama in the early pages of the Bible that is not available to the vast readership, but that is of considerable value in trying to understand God and His relationship to us, I have taken a portion of the revered text and fleshed it out, all the while being careful not to alter the biblical facts.

In this book, we walk with Moses as he is propelled by a God who is— at first— new and strange to him. But God perseveres, encouraging Moses' vacillating, and often tried, trust in Him. As Moses leads the Israelites from Egypt to Canaan, he encounters challenges from the pharaoh, his own family, his aides, and tribal leaders, and conflicts with enemy armies. He deals with the common Hebrews in dynamic, often contentious, ways as he confronts their recurrent rebelliousness. Dialogue and actions bring to life characters whom the Bible leaves to our imagination.

In each event, God discloses more of Himself to us, providing exciting, valuable, and possibly life-changing insights into His Being. To get to know God is, according to Dr. J. I. Packer, the main reason for which we are on earth. [1]

When gaps are present in Scripture, I have tried to fill them in with considered reasonableness. For example, when Moses kills the foreman of the Hebrew slave gang and the Bible says of the event, he "looked this way and that" before doing it, an explanation for his premeditated action and its consequences is offered. As another example, in describing the thirty-seven years wandering in the wilderness, I have taken what facts are present in the Bible and tried to construct a credible, though largely fictitious, account of those years. I have given Moses a military role as suggested by the historian Josephus. [2] That occupation, although not so stated in the Bible, seems appropriate to his life. The biographical sketches in the boxes—of the leaders and Balaam—are from my imagination.

Two biblical quotations deserve special mention:

In Deuteronomy 4:2, Moses said, "You shall not add to the word that I am commanding you, nor take away from it, that you may keep the commandments of the LORD your God which I command you."

Proverbs 30:5–6: "Every word of God is tested .... Do not add to His words lest He reprove you and you be proved a liar."

It is not my purpose to "add," replace, or write new scripture, but rather, to offer the readers a narrative that will engage them and re-acquaint them with the vibrant details of this portion of the Bible. They may wish to return to the original Scriptures with fresh interest and insights, more familiar with the individuals and their roles in unfolding this trying but divinely influenced journey.

Although I have tried otherwise, some ideas gleaned from books read over the years may have been inadvertently incorporated without referencing them. To those authors, I apologize and offer my sincere appreciation for their fine works.

Quotations from God are referenced adjacently. Others' conversations directly quoted from the Bible or closely paraphrased are noted by an asterisk *. Superscript numbers identify words or phrases referenced in each chapter's endnotes.

One final note: It must be presumed that the topography of the Sinai Peninsula was different 3,500 years ago than it is today. The Israelites were able to drive large herds of animals across the land with adequate supplies of water to drink, and perhaps grass to eat; a difficult feat, considering my understanding of today's terrain. Mention is made in the Bible of passing through "the great and terrible wilderness, with its fiery serpents and scorpions" (Deut. 8:15) and through "wilderness, through a land of deserts and pits ... a land of deep darkness ... a land that no one crossed" (Jer. 2:6). Such descriptions are utilized in the book.

On the journey, forests with adequate wood for the building of dwellings were found at several sites. Since then, God may have destroyed the fruitfulness of the peninsula as He did in the Jordan River Valley, Sodom, and Gomorrah, and as He threatened to do elsewhere if the people remained rebellious.

The exact site of many locations (i.e., Mount Sinai) is unknown, but is approximated in the book.

The book is fully referenced so the reader can easily find and confirm the described events. Most references are to the *New American Standard Bible* (Reuben Olson, ed., La Habra, California: Foundation Press Publications, publisher for the Lockman Foundation, 1971) as found in the *Ryrie Study Bible, New American Standard Translation*, Charles Caldwell Ryrie, Th.D., Ph.D., Dallas Theological Seminary. Moody Press, Chicago, 1977. A few biblical references are from other translations, and these are noted in the text.

My heartfelt thanks go to Sharon Miller and Carol Shaffer for their seemingly endless typing of the manuscripts; to Catherine Rankovic for her thorough, painstaking, and surgeon-like editing; to Arthur Harter, Jr., the late Reverend Lewis Thomas, Mrs. Dale Griffin, my daughter Julie Manuele and Dr. Bernhard Asen, for reading the manuscripts and for their encouragement; to Dr. Clint McCann, Dr. George Robertson, and Bernadette Snyder for their welcome encouragement and gracious endorsements; and to George for his vital, helpful, theological input; and to my dear wife Jan for her valuable corrections and suggestions and for graciously allowing me the time to write. My thanks also go to Randy Elliott for his friendship, and to Judy Bauer and Dayle Ferguson for editorial suggestions. Thanks also to Tibor Nagy and Don Curran for the patient (and repeated) revisions of our illustrations.

Endnote
1. "Main reason," *Knowing God,* J.I. Packer. 1973, p. 29.
2. Josephus, Flavius. *The Antiquities of the Jews,* translated by William Whiston, A. M., 1987, book 2, chapter 10.

Map copyright by
Hammond World Atlas Corp.—used with permission.

Photography by David Stradal.

Tribe	Leader
Asher	Pagiel (painter)
Benjamin	Abidan (historian)
Dan	Ahiezer
Ephraim	Bershama (archer)
Gad	Eliasaph (stone mason)
Issachar	Nethanel (bricklayer)
Judah	Nahshon (jeweler)
Levi	Aaron
Manasseh	Gamaliel (bricklayer)
Naphtali	Ahira (soldier)
Reuben	Elizur
Simeon	Shelumiel (carpenter)
Zebulun	Eliab

From Book of Numbers, Chapter 1

Section I
Egypt—Circa 1560 BC to 1480 BC

Chapter 1

A Prince of Egypt Dethroned

"Here he comes," a tall peasant shouted from the midst of the throng lining the street in the city of Rameses, as the commander led his victorious army up to the palace. [1] Two forty-year-old men stood in the crowd. One leaned on a crutch, supporting his only leg. The other stared through his disfigured countenance; a scar slashed his face from nose to ear through an empty eye socket.

They both grimaced as Moses proudly passed by on his large, black horse, riding erect, wearing a purple robe thrown over his uniform. Following him in procession were his regal guard on horseback, a group of manned horse-pulled chariots, a marching detachment of Egyptian troops, and a selected regiment of slave-soldiers. The wounded, carried in chariots or on handheld stretchers, had already been delivered to their own homes.

"Look at him! Pompous as ever, and even his horse. Not a scratch on either," grunted the one-eyed man. "You'd think they wore invisible armor. I hope one day, he'll get what he deserves."

"He's no different from the other officers who expect so much," said his companion. "I'll never forget those long, hard, hot marches Moses ordered to 'toughen us up.'"

"He's simply mean," the first man sneered. "Granted, if we deserted or fought with hesitancy or fear, we deserved to be punished, but I have seen

Moses whip a poor slave-soldier himself, then have food withheld from his family for a week."

An old man kneeling next to them chimed in, "But men, give him credit; he usually wins the battles. Once, when I fought with unusual courage, my family received several pieces of furniture for our small home and my brother was given a week off from work."

"A small recompense, old man, and one that I never saw," said the one-legged man. "He has it in for us Israelites, and it's not just because most of our people are shepherds."

As Moses came to the palace gates, he halted his troops. They stood at attention, receiving the adulation of the mixed crowd of Egyptians and slave families, while women showered the soldiers with fragrant flowers. Many ran up to foot soldiers and fed handfuls of fresh-baked pastries into their hungry mouths, at times embracing the men.

Moses permitted this display for a while, basking in his commanding position. Then he left his troops and approached a large group of women who had been corralled by his lieutenants. Some were sobbing. Moses addressed them somberly from his horse, in Egyptian first, then in Hebrew. "Your sons fought and died valiantly under my leadership. They are honored by me and by the gods of war." He made a small salute to them and returned to his position at the head of the column.

He led this representative force through the palace gates into the spacious arena, to the waiting dignitaries gathered in Pharaoh's reviewing stand. Despite moderate cheering, this reception was more reserved. Pharaoh—accustomed to success in the victories that expanded the southern borders of Egypt and in the skirmishes that quelled riots against his harsh rule—was nevertheless elated over this latest major victory over Nubia. He stood and congratulated the soldiers on their valor, loyalty, and skill.

After the brief speech, Moses dismounted, climbed the steps toward Pharaoh, and bowed. With set jaw, he grimly gave a tally of the land conquered, the slaves captured, and of his own troops lost. Two of the ladies seated near Pharaoh eyed him flirtatiously. Moses bowed once more to Pharaoh and begged his leave.

In the solitude of his large sleeping quarters, Moses' suppressed anger erupted. He threw off his outer garments and stormed into his study. Wheeling around to the array of statues lining one wall, he strode to the quarter-sized image of Re,[2] the sun god, picked it up, and hurled it across the room. It shattered against the wall into several pieces. "You have failed me!" His eyes scanned his other idols, lifeless representations of gods, some of wood, others of ceramic or bronze. Picking up the lion-headed Anuke,[2] the goddess of war, in both hands, he raised it over his head, and then fell to his knees. The bronze figure slipped from his grasp as he dropped his head into his hands and wept aloud. "You, Anuke, allowed them to die. Arthius and Rexor, my generals, friends from my youth. We arose in the ranks together, fighting side by side. I loved them as no others. We reveled together, even cried together. And you let them be killed in one battle, by the shafts of two cruelly aimed arrows. And now you leave me to live—alone."

Many minutes passed before he arose and looked at his collection of graven images. *Was Nubia—the land of vicious warriors—worth such a price?* he wondered. Exhausted, he fell into his bed and slept until early evening.

A familiar set of knocks on the door of his living quarters roused him. "Come in," he said, looking at the disarrayed statues with no remorse.

His twelve-year-old aide, Joshua, entered to dress his master for the banquet honoring him that night. Without a word, Joshua returned Anuke and carefully collected the broken pieces of Re.

While Moses walked to the feast provided by Pharaoh, he felt his energy return, recalling the public display and the homage paid him that day. Entering the great hall, he acknowledged the many greetings. He then seated himself to the left of Pharaoh, knowing that his younger cousin would occupy the seat to Pharaoh's right.

Moses looked out over the gathered assemblage, smugly savoring his self-importance, enhanced by his latest victory. He did indeed live a charmed life. He had been raised as an only child and enjoyed all of the privileges of the palace with his cousins. His education had been supervised by his mother. Always obedient and conscientious, he surpassed all others in learning—including mastering mathematics, astronomy, debate, science, literature, the arts, and the martial disciplines. He became proficient in interpreting hieroglyphics, and became adept at the newer straight-line hieratic writings. He excelled in physical games, and became an accomplished equestrian. In his teens, he showed his mettle in battle and became commander of a regiment at sixteen and of the entire army by twenty-five. And now, fifteen years later, as he surveyed the revelers, he knew that the glory and accolades afforded him were well-deserved.

That night, after drinking and watching the erotic moves of female dancers, he climbed the stairs to his quiet chambers, where a dark-skinned girl awaited him. Known to have pleased Moses before, she had been chosen from the slaves for the night by Joshua to distract Moses and assuage his grief.

Moses had never married. He could find no woman to please him, except for a night or two, nor could he find a permanent consort to challenge his ever-active mind.

In the morning, he donned his regal attire and met with aides to assure that no detail was overlooked in honoring his fallen generals. Their bodies would lie in state for three days for the masses to mourn before the florid eulogies would be delivered, followed by the long, hot funeral processions.

During those days, Moses provided detailed reports and accountings to Pharaoh and his staff, visited wounded officers, accepted the final tally of his own casualties, interrogated several of his prized captives, and attended another banquet in his honor, while low-level officers relegated captives to various slave gangs.

After the burials of his generals, Moses entered his study to plan for his next campaign in the south. A tireless worker and master strategist, he carefully weighed every detail before making a decision. He consulted with his many Egyptian gods, seeking the only wisdom he lacked, but usually fell back on his own trusted intuition. With the exception of his two dead friends, Moses spurned the opinions of most of his human advisors.

Later that morning, he sat in the assembly next to his grandfather, the pharaoh, as each cabinet member filed in, giving his weekly report. On receiving the news that twenty-seven slaves had died working in the pits during the past month, Moses interrupted, "There have been worse months! They are replaceable. Besides, we have too many." Pharaoh nodded in silent assent.

That evening, in a small, one-room adobe home in the Hebrew enclave, two figures sat facing each other, heads bent forward in intimate conversation. "I am old and frail, my son," confided the once-robust woman, Jochabed. "The sufferings of our people have become intolerable. Our God promised that we would be freed after 430 years of slavery. That time is now.

"I know that Moses' authority has somehow been given by God. Apart from a few in the palace, our family of four and your wife are the only ones who know his true identity. We must enlist his help now. God has even prodded your sister Miriam to act."

"If we do, we must be secretive," said Aaron. "If it becomes known that Pharaoh has permitted one of us to rise to such power, Moses would be in great danger."

"Aaron, you must get a message to him," insisted Jochabed, "an obscure message should it somehow be intercepted. Put it into your father's box. Who in the palace is most trusted and loyal to Moses?"

"It is his servant boy, Joshua," said Aaron. After thinking for a moment, he added, "He shops for Moses at the marketplace early every mid-week morning."

The following mid-week morning, Aaron, his face shrouded, jostled into Joshua at the Hebrew market. Thrusting the small box into the boy's hands, Aaron said, "Pardon me, I have a confidential message for your master." He quickly turned and was lost in the crowd.

The boy stared at the container in surprise. The guard who accompanied Joshua made a delayed move toward the bold messenger, but the man had disappeared.

Anonymous requests for leniency toward a slave had been slipped to Joshua on a few occasions before, but never in a box. He walked to his usual booths, purchased required items, and returned to the palace, where he found Moses in the library. He entered with a short bow, and told of his encounter in the Hebrew market before presenting the box to his master.

Moses examined the item in his hand and then walked to his desk. He removed an identical box from a drawer and laid them side by side. A carved mahogany inlaid elephant adorned the flat top of each teak box, its feet and tusks bejeweled with small broken bits of multi-colored glass. The colors of the aged woods in both boxes were the same; the only difference was a small brass lock through the hasp of Joshua's box.

"Have the blacksmith break the lock, then return it to me—unopened," Moses ordered.

A sharp blow from the smith's hammer broke the lock, and Joshua returned the box to Moses, who eagerly opened it. He removed the papyrus, and read it:

"Our ancestor Joseph lives in you. Know our God."

It was unsigned. Puzzled, Moses asked, "What did the man look like who gave this to you?"

"He was a bit shorter than you—stockier, agile. His face was partly covered," replied Joshua. "He probably was Hebrew."

"Accent?"

"He spoke clear Egyptian."

"Nothing more?"

"No, sir."

"Tell me if you remember anything more about him. If you see him again, invite him to see me, but do not let him get away. Now go."

Moses sat on his bed, thinking. *Where could this box have come from?* The matched pair was obviously made by the same person, probably at the same time. He had owned his box all of his life, having played with it as a child. Its mate had sat someplace for many years. But where? In the Hebrew ghetto? And why was someone—a person who knew how to write Egyptian script—relinquishing it now? He pondered the note: *"Our ancestor Joseph lives in you."* He knew only vaguely of a Joseph in the history of the Israelite slaves. How could he have any bearing on Moses? If this note was from a slave in the market, was he suggesting that Moses was related to them? Absurd. Moses' mother was the oldest of three sisters. His father had also been Egyptian.

Was this some sort of a hoax from a malcontent? The ornate box refuted that idea. And why should Moses bother to "know their God"? He had plenty of his own. Curiosity pricked his mind, and he ordered Joshua to summon his long-time Hebrew mentor.

As the evening sun was setting, the heavily bearded, hooded, middle-aged priest entered the palace and was escorted to the library.

Moses said, "Wise counselor, you who know the history of the Israelites, sit down and tell me of the man, Joseph." Moses had been taught the verbal Hebrew language of the Israelites in order to command them effectively.

The priest sat on a cushioned acacia chair and cleared his throat. "All right. Our patriarch, Abraham—you've heard of him?"

"Yes," said Moses.

"This story begins over five hundred years ago. Abraham became blessed after courageously and faithfully responding to an invitation from God, moving his family from the east to the land of Canaan. One blessing was that, at about one hundred years of age, he sired a son by his barren wife, Sarah, and named him Isaac. Isaac became a wealthy farmer and had twin sons, Esau and Jacob. By devious means, Jacob gained ascendancy through a ruse that greatly angered his brother. Jacob, in fear, fled to the east, to Mesopotamia, and raised a family. He was renamed 'Israel' by God after successfully wrestling with an angel one night."[3]

"He physically wrestled with an angel and his god renamed him?" asked Moses.

"Indeed. Israel eventually returned to Canaan, forgiven by Esau. His favorite son, Joseph, was sold into slavery by his eleven jealous brothers and taken to Egypt. There, after suffering in dungeons for years, he rose to become the prime minister of Egypt, thanks to a God-given gift of being able to interpret dreams, even the king's dreams.[4] He became a man of great power, although he was an Israelite, a Hebrew. Through his wisdom during seven plentiful years, and then seven of drought, Egypt became a great nation, and it remained so until his death years later."

"He was a man of great power, although an Israelite," Moses repeated to himself. Then he said to the priest, "I am grateful for your information that will enable me to lead wisely. That will be enough," and he bade him goodbye.

Someone was trying to shake Moses' confidence in who he was. Why? Try as he might to ignore it, the annoying message repeatedly occupied his mind. He became more sullen, enjoying the luxuries of nobility less.

A week later, Joshua made his morning visit to the Hebrew slave market, accompanied by his guard. He was shopping for a supply of the special halvah candy made from sesame seeds and honey, the sweet treat baked by the Israelite women—and relished by Moses. Alert to each person he passed, he walked up to his customary vendor's stand in the pastry tent and handed the man his leather bag. "The usual pastries, please." As he handed the money to the clerk, he added casually, "Where is Otman today?"

"He had urgent business to attend to," said the vendor, opening the bag into which a woman carefully deposited the pastries. He caught Joshua's gaze as he took his money. Joshua was suddenly suspicious. Otman was always there to sell his wife's bakery items. The items were there, but neither Otman nor his wife was.

"And what is the nature of his business?" Joshua asked.

"He only told me that it had to do with their son's illness. I know no more, sir."

Joshua knew nothing of Otman's children but, seeing nothing else amiss, he accepted the explanation. He said, "Tell him I was sorry to miss him."

"I will."

The boy purchased a colored cloth at another vendor's stand. Then, upon returning to the palace kitchen, he emptied the bag. A small piece of papyrus fell out with the pastries, and Joshua recognized the name "Moses" on it. He hurried to his master.

Moses held it up and read to himself.

"Moses, you are Ephraim and Manasseh. Let our God guide you."

It was signed, "Your brother," in the same script as the first message.

Aroused, Moses asked, "Where did you get this?"

"At the pastry tent. But Otman was not there today."

"What did the person look like who gave it to you?"

"The only unusual features were his eyes, bright olive green." Looking at Moses he remarked, "They were like yours." Although curious, he dared not ask the contents of the message. "And, O master, I remember now. His voice sounded like the one who gave me the box."

Immediately Moses' eyes blazed. "We must go back to the market at once."

Arriving at the stand, Joshua was surprised to find Otman there. "Where is the man who worked your stand this morning?" Joshua asked.

"I do not know. A woman approached me late yesterday with a half-shekel of silver and asked if she could occupy my stand early this morning. She said she must give a present to Joshua—in private. I am poor and could not refuse the offer. She picked up a few bakery goods this morning and paid me for them also. Have I brought you harm?"

"Who was this woman who bribed you?" Moses demanded.

"I had never seen her," the vendor from Aaron's tribe lied.

Moses advanced, grabbed the vendor's shirt, and pulled him close. "If I find that you have lied to me, my guard will return to deal with you. And what happened to the man who took your place?"

"If there was a man, he abandoned the stand before I returned."

Releasing his grip, Moses stepped back, saying, "I must find them. There is a large reward for anyone who can bring me that man and his woman, or even their names. Search your memory, vendor!"

"And why do you want to find him?" the vendor braved.

"Because he sent a gift to me and I want to reward him for it."

"I know no more, but I will inquire."

"See that you do," said Moses. He turned to Joshua. "We can learn no more here."

They returned to the palace, frustrated. Moses knew only that Ephraim and Manasseh were names of Israelite tribes, but he knew nothing of their origins.

Summoned once again, the Hebrew mentor bowed in respect. "You wish to know more of Israel?"

"No," replied Moses. "I wish to learn more history so I can better— serve you Israelites. Tell me about Ephraim and Manasseh."

The priest began his tale. "All right. Last time, I told you that Israel's favorite son, Joseph, had become prime minister of Egypt. During that time, he fathered two sons, Ephraim and Manasseh[5], who were brought up in the luxury and protection of the Egyptian court.

"When the sons were still young, their grandfather Israel and his sons migrated from Canaan to Egypt with their animals, during a prolonged drought. They were established in the fertile Nile Delta by Joseph and Pharaoh. Years later, near the end of Joseph's life, Ephraim and Manasseh faced a grave decision: should they continue in their palatial lifestyle or forfeit their regal status to follow the God of their ancestor, Abraham and of their deceased grandfather, Israel—the God whom Joseph still worshipped— to live as shepherds with their relatives? They chose the latter course. That decision proved costly when, as you know, O wise Moses, sixteen years later, Egypt was invaded by a consortium of eastern powers, including Assyria[6]. A new king, assuming the Egyptian title of Pharaoh, arose over Egypt who did not know Joseph[7], and all Israel's descendants were enslaved—and so they remain today. Because of Israel's love for Joseph and because of their courageous decision for God, Israel appointed Ephraim and Manasseh to inherit Joseph's honored place along with his brothers as tribal leaders of the Israelites."

"Stop," Moses said. So, he reasoned, Ephraim and Manasseh— Hebrews, Israelites—were sons of Joseph and, until they chose otherwise, were fully accepted in Egyptian court. How could he, Moses, "be" Ephraim and Manasseh unless ... unless he was Hebrew himself? An Israelite? Impossible! His whole identity revolved around the palace, his Egyptian mother and grandfather, the pharaoh. Moses' father had died when he was young. As he dwelt on the message, doubts of his parentage gnawed inwardly. If he were a Hebrew, who were his real parents?

His systematic mind convolved this startling information through a sleepless night. Ephraim and Manasseh, Israelites, had great status in the palace. He himself had such status. They sacrificed their luxury for the cause of their god, who must be very powerful and convincing, a god about whom Moses knew little. No god he knew would cause Moses to leave the palace. Was the sender of the messages trying to enlist him in a cause? *"Let our God guide you."* Why?

For a short time, Moses ceased to enjoy the passing pleasures of sin,[8] abstaining from alcohol and sexual activity, hoping to curry favor with this annoying god of the Hebrews and perhaps even hear more from him.

The message had come from a man with unusual eyes, from the midst of the Hebrew market, and was signed "Brother." Moses had no siblings. He resolved to try to locate that man. But how? He could not question his Israelite soldiers; they might suspect that he sought a relative among them. Israelite blood in their commander? No, that was too great a risk.

He sent Joshua and his guard back to the market to find the man with olive green eyes. After a diligent search, Joshua failed to find anyone who was acquainted with such an individual; olive green eyes were rare in an Israelite. He reminded the market vendors of the reward, and most of them promised to cooperate.

Six days later, Moses heard a tap on his door. As he opened it, Joshua stood waiting, hesitant to speak.

"What brings you here?" asked Moses.

"Strange Miriam asks to see you today with an important message."

"I will see her after breakfast," said Moses.

Strange Miriam, the fifty-one-year-old Hebrew who swaggered with a feigned air of dignity, had been tolerated in the palace by the skeptical pharaoh for more than forty years, only because the princess accepted her as handmaiden and counselor. The princess was only one of a few who listened to her often-sage advice, advice that Miriam claimed came from her "God of Abraham, Isaac, and Jacob," advice that marked her as a prophetess among her own people.

Joshua ushered Miriam into the room, and she performed a perfunctory bow before Moses. When invited to speak, she said, "I have received a sacred word that I can share only with you, O mighty Moses."

"And your message?" asked Moses.

"Forgive me, sir, I do not understand it. Perhaps you will. It is: *'God saved child Ephraim to rescue the slaves.'"* She repeated the bow and turned to leave.

Perplexed, Moses called after her, "Wait, Miriam. When did you hear this?"

"Three days ago. I was hesitant to tell you."

"Have you ever heard a message like that for me before?"

"No, my lord, I haven't. If not driven by my God to tell you, I would not have. Excuse me, please."

"How did you hear it?"

"It came as I was sewing the princess' gown."

"Do you know a man with olive green eyes?" he blurted out.

"I have seen one or two, but you are the only one I am acquainted with, sir," she quickly answered.

Moses, stunned by the similarity of the messages, demanded, "Strange Miriam, you must tell me more of this god of yours."

"I can only say that He is a God of His word, and He occasionally talks to me. I can say no more. But, sir, if I have brought you any useful information, may I speak on behalf of my ailing father, dear Amram?"

"Speak," Moses said.

"He still works in the brickyards, although he is sixty-nine years old. It is because—if you will forgive my brashness—his guard hates him and our esteemed pharaoh requires slaves to work until they bow down to him or die. Forgive me, O Moses, but my father is stubborn—and so feeble."

"We will investigate this," answered Moses. He turned to Joshua. "Go and find out where this Amram works and try to arrange for him to be relieved from his duties."

"Bless you, O mighty Moses." Miriam bowed low and scurried out with Joshua.

Alone, Moses slumped into a soft chair. *"God saved child Ephraim to rescue the slaves,"* he repeated. The second message had identified him as Ephraim. But why did it use the word *saved?* Saved in battle? And why would anyone want to rescue the slaves? The idea, at first absurd, began to challenge his military mind. He would need to be sympathetic to their cause. How could this happen? Only through pity, unless … he was an Israelite, a Hebrew, himself! Why was he suddenly concerned about Amram, just another slave? Was Miriam's god working on his mind? If these revelations held any truth and he was not the grandson of Pharaoh, who was he? Who else knew about this matter? And could this be the answer to Moses' long-slumbering doubts about himself?

Escalating concerns that he might somehow be an Israelite preoccupied his days and ravaged his sleep. He took progressively longer walks in the slave market with Joshua to acquaint himself with the Israelites' ways,[9] and to familiarize himself with their beliefs. But he was not readily welcomed, being a royal reminder of their enforced servitude. When word reached the palace of his forays, they were considered as disgraceful. To relieve his mounting stress, Moses spent himself physically with enforced exercise and honed his archery and hatchet-throwing skills.

The sweltering mid-afternoon sun assaulted the small blacksmith's shop in the rear of the palace grounds. The perspiring, dark-skinned smith stood over the hot furnace, his prominent neck muscles blending with those of his upper chest and bulging granite-like arms. He ran a calloused fingertip along the edge of the battle axe in his hands.

"Would that I owned this one," he said to Joshua. "I'd venture that Moses took it off a dead Philistine in the war."

"It seems that you have ground the edge well, for my master had dulled it by frequent practice," answered Joshua.

"I have done only as instructed. I would give ten of our bronze hatchets for this. See the width of the blade, twice that of our bronze ones, the setting of the handle into its eye, the balanced weight of it. On the rare times I can work such iron, I see it respond to the furnace and feel its lingering warmth. It gives me even greater pleasure than the breasts of a harlot. Joshua, you are wise. Who, besides the Philistines, has an implement to match it?"

"I have heard that the tall king of Bashan has a very long iron bedstead[10], his prize possession," recalled Joshua.

The smith shuffled tongs that rested on an anvil and then stared at the boy. "Joshua, what is going on with your master? He came to me in bad humor, demanding a sharper edge than ever before." The smith looked away briefly. "I have heard that he is caustic with his younger cousin. Ha, that man, he is nothing but a young pampered Jacob; but Moses—"

"Careful with your tongue, smithy, we are only Israelite slaves."

"You know better than I the tales surrounding Moses. He in no way resembles his family. Who was his father?"

"Why, the princess's husband."

"The husband was able to sire but one child, eh?"

"Give me the hatchet that I may take it to my master," Joshua said curtly.

The heavy wooden door echoed with the firm, measured knocks. Joshua entered, carrying the hatchet cradled in a twice-folded, thick, red muslin cloth. He bowed and presented the weapon to his master. Moses' finger gently touched the honed edge and found it to his liking. He dismissed his aide absently. Turning the weapon over, he shifted it from hand to hand, checking its balance, vaguely distracted. A cold dew of anxiety moistened his forehead. If only his problem would leave him for even a few nights. His whole life, all he had worked to become— an esteemed prince and honored commander—was now at stake. In frustration, he called out, "Oh, god of theirs, new to me, if you exist, what will you have me do?"

Moses finally decided to confront Pharaoh. Since the pharaoh regarded many gods highly, Moses would approach him through them. He did not wish to incriminate Miriam.

"Grandfather, I must speak with you," Moses said one morning.

"Yes, what is it, Moses?"

"I have had several disturbing dreams lately," he lied. "I actually have one recurring dream from the supernatural that has bound my thoughts like a tightening net. A god has called to me persistently over the last two weeks telling me to stop harassing the slaves."

"You have had dreams before, Moses."

"Yes, but never ones like this. A fierce flaming god accosts me with threatening words. He laughs and shouts to me that I am, in reality, not Egyptian."

Pharaoh calmly asked, "And which god is it that has visited you at night? Some are not to be trusted, making up tales to draw us away from competing gods."

"I do not know his name, but he speaks with authority. The dreams torment me with questions of who I am. They suggest that I am not born of royalty but that my true parents were … Israelites."

"Nonsense! Look at you, Moses. You are my grandson, my finest grandson, born to my daughter forty years ago. There can be no doubt about your lineage. You are a prince, a commander. Perhaps your next dream will suggest that I too am Hebrew. Ha! You are wise enough to know that no one can interpret dreams. Let us talk about the Philistine threat on our eastern border."

"Sir, this god will not let me go. I must know who I am. Lately, I weary of the false life I am leading."

Moses walked to the far side of the room and turned. "I had wondered about my olive green eyes, my lack of resemblance to anyone in our family, and about my circumcision. As boys, we swam naked in the Nile, and I saw an occasional boy with the same mark. They told me it was done to decrease their sexual appetite in later years. Mother denied that, saying that it was performed on me to correct a birth defect. I chose to believe her until—these revelations. Please, sir, if you give me confirmation, I will not have to confront her."

"I believe that you had ... abundant foreskin."

"I, alone, in our family?" Moses said with a glare.

"Has someone talked to you about this?"

"No one," he lied again.

Pharaoh drew himself to his full height, looked into Moses' intense eyes, and sighed deeply. "Moses, Moses, must we do this? I have prayed that this day would never come, but your resolve tears at me. You force me to break a pledge of many years." Sinking onto a nearby chair, he continued, "I dearly love my daughter, and when she found you floating in a basket in the Nile, she begged me for your life. Reluctantly, I spared you, a Hebrew baby. Many times I thought of destroying you. Several times when you were young and in the army, I even ordered that you be placed at the head of our charging army, but you seemed to be protected by a god of war. You proved to be a tenacious fighter, a great leader, and you have the courage of six men. I have grown to respect you and to love you as my own."

Moses was disturbed, yet relieved, by this final confirmation. "Then I am Hebrew, set adrift by my Israelite parents, at a time—" He paused. "Grandfather, I know that this must be as difficult for you as it is for me. Do you know my real parents?"

"I do not know them. That was forty years ago. They are probably dead by now."

Moses' heart leapt within. *They may be alive,* he thought. Perhaps one was trying to contact him. "Grandfather, I must search somehow."

"Consider carefully any action you may take and let me know of it beforehand," Pharaoh advised. "You must not allow this revelation to become public—that I have knowingly, willingly raised an Israelite as my grandson these many years. It would be too great an embarrassment."

Moses continued to entertain thoughts of the Hebrew god. He remembered occasions when a Hebrew man's beliefs would not allow him to bow down to Pharaoh, a disobedience unaltered by whippings or even death. Moses had never seen such absolute faith before. He began to yield. "If this is the god who is to guide me, I must know more about him."

His Hebrew mentor supplied him with information: the Hebrew story of the seven days of creation by their God, contrasting it with the Egyptian myths of their gods, Atum, Amon, or the Phoenix,[11] each having created itself in the beginning, or of eight other gods who got together and created the world. The Hebrew spoke of a few of God's miracles: the deathless ascension of Enoch, the pregnancy of Sarah at one hundred years of age, the safeguarding of Noah during the flood, the divine intervention for Isaac on the pyre, and the providential use of Joseph. He told Moses that intermittent words from their God to his prophets and prophetesses had continued for the last four hundred years or more.

The next day, Moses summoned Strange Miriam. "I discovered that the message you gave me was for another person," he said, to quiet her suspicions. "But you have pricked my curiosity. What other messages does your god give to you?"

"He tells me to warn the Egyptians to stop harassing the Israelite slaves. A great tribulation may come if they continue. Meanwhile, we Israelites are to suffer patiently."

"No other communiqués, nothing else for me?" Moses asked.

"No."

Moses excused her. He was beginning to believe that this god of hers was alive and active, more so than any of his array of gods.

To learn more of the Israelites and their god, the next morning, he accompanied Joshua to one of the barracks. The guard was surprised to see him. "Master Moses, what are you about, sir?" Moses raised his hand abruptly and walked on. Soldiers in various degrees of dress were lounging about. Some were playing small games, but when they saw Moses, they stood up. These were men he'd fought alongside and he addressed a few by name as he walked through.

"Which are the slave barracks?" he asked the guard.

"Across the grounds, but you aren't going there, are you, sir? It might not be appropriate."

"Lead us there, soldier," said Moses. The uniformed man led Moses and Joshua across a field and into one of the guarded slave barracks. The din of voices ceased as the soldiers recognized their visitor. Various objects were quickly hidden under their cots as all struggled to their feet. Moses noted that uniforms were stacked loosely on a table to his right. There was silence.

The guard called out, "Everyone line up!" As Moses walked before the men, focusing quickly on each one's eyes, he observed that they appeared well-fed, each man's small bay was relatively neat, but that their few articles of clothing hung on nails on the wall or were strewn on cots. Three men could not rise from the floor, and two had open, angry, red, pus-filled wounds.

"Get a doctor in here to bandage and clean the wounds, and get hooks for their clothes," Moses barked to the guard.

He addressed the men. "Soldiers, you have fought well for me, especially in this last campaign. A small token of my appreciation will be given to each of your families." He turned to the man next to him and asked, "What is your name?"

The man awkwardly answered, "Shihon, sir."

"Have you a wife?"

"No."

"And who are you?" Moses addressed the next man.

"Mizrah," he answered.

"Have you family?"

"Yes, a wife."

"Children?"

"Two."

"When was the last time you were home?"

"Two months ago."

"Are you well?" Moses asked.

Stunned, the man said, "Uh, yes."

"Good," said Moses as he turned to the guard. "Have this man taken to his home today and give him two days' leave." With that, Moses turned and left the stunned group. He had seen no olive green eyes.

He visited only once more, four days later, but the encounter was stilted and brought little information.

Communications passed swiftly between slave-soldiers and their families. One of them, Nadab, the son of Aaron, reported these strange events to his father.

Aaron shared the information with his mother. "Thank God, our prayers are being answered," exclaimed Jochabed. "Your brother is developing concern for us. It is risky, but perhaps it is time for you to confront him. Let us formulate a plan."

That same day, Moses walked through the slave marketplace with Joshua and a guard, determined to find his mysterious "brother." He noticed the physical weakness of many people—some old, some malnourished with prominent cheekbones and sunken eyes. He saw the shabby dress of the peddlers who were selling pastries, broken pieces of wood, threadbare clothing, homemade pieces of pottery, healing balms and potions, and drinks of some liquids served from a wineskin. Many were barefoot, while some wore sandals made of a flat, thin strip of wood or occasionally, leather, secured over the foot with a lace thong. Walking sticks were simply stripped tree branches. Moses had looked at these wretches before, but had never really *seen* them. An unfamiliar feeling of pity overwhelmed him. A blood-stained whipping post stood at the far end of the market, close to the main thoroughfare. Moses turned to the guard. "I want to be notified if anyone is to be beaten."

The surprised guard replied, "Yes, my lord."

His visit produced no clues concerning his "brother." However, his loyalties were changing; any reward[12] he might earn from this Israelite god would outweigh Pharaoh's possible resulting anger.

The next day, Moses and Joshua mounted their horses for a ride to the Nile.

In a small house on the outskirts of the city, Mannel pulled his smock over his head, tightened his leggings, and tied on his sandals. He brushed the black hair back from his tanned forehead. Sturdy arms, with a bronze bracelet encircling each bicep and wrist, easily lifted the club decorated with a carving of Isis on its small end. He turned to his wife, Rovann, as she rinsed the pottery dishes. "I am assigned to those slimy Israelite slaves again today. By the god Amon, what a duty! They work well, but so many are scrawny and tire easily, not like the black slaves from the south."

"Are they a worry to you, Mannel?" she asked.

"They are more numerous than we Egyptians," he answered, tucking a whip into his belt at his back. "I'll take my cudgel with me, just in case."

"Some saw Moses walking near the brickyards yesterday. They say that he has recently shown an interest in the Hebrew slaves. Beware of him."

"Don't worry. I will be home for dinner."

During the hot morning, Mannel joined another guard to oversee his slaves. They whipped an occasional indolent one and shackled two contrary ones together, laughing as they fell while treading in the brick vats. But the afternoon did not go well for Mannel.

"You, Mannel!" shouted the head man. "Your Hebrews are working today as if it were a holiday! They are short of their quota again. Make it up."

Mannel's whip encouraged action, as all picked up their pace except for an old man, who swore softly to himself and glanced bitterly at the guard. Near day's end, Mannel's cudgel to his mid-back sent him sprawling to the ground. Another blow to the side of his hip evoked a scream. "Now, by the gods, you will work faster," growled Mannel.

The action was observed from a small hill overlooking the brickyards where Moses and Joshua had paused on their ride to the Nile. Moses wore his prized iron hatchet in the waistband sheath of his short tunic. He watched with newfound compassion. Joshua pointed out Mannel. "I am told that he is the guard most hated; 'Mannel the asp' he is called. He is said to smile whenever he beats a slave, and often gives his bloodstained rod to the slave to wash with his own saliva. If it is not returned to him spotless, others are punished. That old man is Miriam's father!"

Moses saw Amram struggle to his feet and hobble away from Mannel. "That vicious coward!" spat Moses angrily. "The old man was supposed to be relieved of his duties. Did you not deliver the order?"

"I did, sir. It must have been delayed."

Moses dismounted. "Take the horses back to the palace."

Moses watched Mannel's continued ruthlessness from a distance, his frustration and anger intensifying. When the guard left his post and walked to a secluded bank overlooking a dry creek bed, Moses followed. As Mannel began to relieve himself, Moses looked this way and that.[13] Sensing they were unobserved, he crept up to within twelve paces of the guard and, with a steady hand, hurled his axe at the upper part of Mannel's back. At that very moment, Mannel leaned forward slightly and the axe struck the lower part of his skull, splitting it open and propelling the unconscious man forward over the sandy bank. Moses leaped over the edge to the body, and bracing his foot on the neck, he pried out the hatchet. He rolled the body over and buried his hatchet into the neck, almost decapitating the guard. He quickly pulled a linen cloth from his belt to soak up the spurting blood.

Some had splattered on Moses' left arm and soiled his tunic sleeve. He stared at the body, feeling only a sense of relief, convinced that he had pleased the uninvited power that drove him. He had erased one of the greatest offenders of the Israelites, although they might never learn who their benefactor was. Surely, by this act, he had begun to help them.

Moses scooped out a hollow in the bank, put the bloody cloth with the body, and hid him in the sand.[14] Then he rubbed the blood off of the hatchet and his arm with sand, and scaled the bank. Taking a back route, he encountered no one on the two-mile walk back to the palace. There, he slipped past the guards without any of them detecting his bloodstained sleeve. In the secrecy of his room, he washed the blood from his garment.

The next morning, Mannel's wife reported her husband's absence, and soldiers were dispatched to the brickyard. Two Hebrew slaves remembered the direction he had taken when last seen, and one admitted seeing Moses follow him. By noon, Mannel's body was discovered, and reports of the incident reached the palace.

In the late morning, the war minister informed the eighty-four-year-old pharaoh of Mannel's death, and of the growing suspicion by Hebrews and guards that Moses was the murderer. The pharaoh walked to the window in silence and looked out. His worst fear had been realized. He turned to the minister. "It appears that it is my grandson who committed this crime, not simply against a guard but against the throne." He drew himself up. "Although I have loved him and treated him with great respect, I believe that he has become a threat to us, an insurrectionist. Kill Moses[15] before he stirs up a revolt."

The shocked but secretly pleased minister hastily summoned the captain of the guards, who dispatched twenty men from the palace guard to find Moses and then sent runners to the city gates.

The news spread rapidly among the slaves. Although they did not understand why the powerful Moses, esteemed by the palace, was being hunted down simply for killing a lowly guard, many were eager to see him captured and executed. To them, Moses was not the hero-liberator he had hoped to be, but simply one of the despised powers behind their prolonged suffering.

Earlier that morning, Moses had ridden into town alone, drawing no more attention than usual. Curious, he rode out toward the brickyards after a midday meal and on the way, saw two Hebrews fighting. When he dismounted to break up the quarrel, the two slaves stopped fighting and glared.

"Who made you a prince or a judge over us?" one snarled. "Are you intending to kill me as you killed the Egyptian?" *

Breathing heavily, the other warned him. "Soldiers are after you, Moses. Run!"

Moses said nothing, but—thinking his crime had been discovered—mounted his horse and rode off. "Pharaoh would not stalk me for killing a guard. I have such authority," he told himself. "He knows that I have defected. Although I do not fear him,[16] I am an embarrassment to him; his alleged grandson, a loathsome Hebrew."

He trotted calmly toward the city gates, stopping briefly at a market to buy a skin of water and bags of seeds, nuts, and fruit. As he rode past a small crowd of people huddled over a body, someone yelled, "The king's messenger was running and has fallen and broken his leg. He seems in much pain."

Sensing the messenger's intention, Moses spurred his horse on, wondering, *Could this be more of their god's work?*

At the eastern city gates, he said to the guard, "My friend left the city to attend to his dying mother. I must go to him." The guard waved him through as Moses exhaled in relief.

He followed the trade route southeast toward Midian, abandoning his wealth, authority, power, and his compelling mission to help the Israelite slaves. "Speak again to me, god," he pleaded in vain. "I must see you who are invisible."[17]

He rode all day, discarding a royal jacket while following signs of the recent passage of a caravan. He slept uncomfortably outside, and in the early morning, spurred his horse and overtook the caravan. Making his way to a fat man under an umbrella, a man who was riding on the finest camel, Moses asked, "You, sir, are you the caravan master?"

The toothless man growled as he fingered the hilt of a saber hung from his belt. "What have you to do with me?"

"We are traveling the same route. My horse and I are hungry and wish to join you," said Moses.

Sizing Moses up, he said in a guttural voice, "You are welcome to our protection and provisions. For a fee, of course."

"I can pay."

Two other armed caravaners with coarse, weathered features rode up beside the master.

"You ride a fine stallion. Stolen, I presume?" said the master to Moses.

"No, I am in the army."

"Your animal would ennoble me," he spit out. "You may ride on one of our camels—until you leave us."

"I can pay you—" countered Moses.

"The horse or nothing."

Having little choice, Moses reluctantly agreed to the exchange. He traveled with them four more days into the land of Midian, where, in the distance, he could see the Horeb mountain range, with Sinai as its highest peak. Passing through a village, he finally abandoned the caravan and walked on alone until, tired and thirsty, he rested by a well.

Seven girls, ranging in age from four to fifteen, came with their father's flock of sheep to draw water.[18] As they approached the well, three blustery shepherds appeared from bushes nearby and tauntingly laughed as they blocked the girls' way. Moses was angered as the girls recoiled. He arose, and brandishing his hatchet, drove the assailants away. Later, when the girls told their father, Jethro, a Midianite priest, of the Egyptian who had come to their aid, Moses was invited to dine with them.

"I am deeply appreciative to you for protecting my daughters today," said Jethro, bowing his plump body and balding head to the tall stranger. "You are most welcome in my house. May I ask your name?"

"I am Moses," he stated respectfully to the priest, looking into his placid eyes.

"Moses, the Egyptian commander?"

"Yes. But I come as a refugee, not as a leader." Not wishing to disclose more, Moses avoided more questions. "Have you work that I may perform in order to find a haven with you?"

Respecting the obvious diversion, Jethro sighed. "I am overburdened, having only seven young daughters to help me. My eldest is only now developing a measure of strength. I notice that your hands are not those of a laborer, but that is all I have for you to do. You may stay if you do not shy away from hard work and some danger."

"I am used to danger," said Moses. "I will do my best."

The next day, Jethro took Moses to his sheep pen. "My shepherd was killed two weeks ago, and I have no one to herd my sheep. I know you are of high position, but if you stay, that must be your duty. I will hire an experienced herder to teach you."

Moses had to strain to hide his disgust as he looked at the large number of loud, smelly animals before him. He was repulsed at the assignment, because all Egyptians had been raised to believe that every shepherd is loathsome,[19] the lowest of all occupations. But the priest and his daughters were hospitable and he had nowhere else to go. As he considered his task, he realized how far the commander of the Egyptian army had fallen.

He hated the job, initially feeling a deep humiliation, but with determination as the months passed, he persevered. He was safe, protected by oceans of sand and many days of hard travel from Egypt.

One night, having proven himself to be conscientious and reliable, Moses spoke to Jethro. "As you have guessed, I am a fugitive from Egypt," he confessed. "I was raised and educated in her courts. However, I committed a crime that cost me my position."

"And what was that?" asked Jethro.

"I murdered a man."

Jethro looked him in the eyes. "Should we be worried for our safety?"

"No, it was a singular act of passion. I killed a guard who was harassing Hebrew slaves."

"And why should that have been a concern of yours?"

"Who understands motivation? Was it compassion or pity? Perhaps I was finally driven to it because of the guard's brutal treatment of them, far beyond acceptable levels. I lashed out at one of the worst."

"An occasional slave who escapes to us confirms the harsh treatment they receive," said Jethro. "We still wish you to stay with us."

Moses was gone for a month, pasturing the flock on distant hills. When he returned, he enjoyed dinner with Jethro's family and the attention paid to him by the seven daughters. He was a delightful novelty.

"I have developed the greatest respect for you and admire the way you and your wife raise your fine daughters," he said to Jethro after the meal. "However, a question has arisen in my mind. Some shepherds I have befriended speak somewhat warily of you and your priesthood. I notice that few men come to seek your counsel. Why is that?"

"Many do not approve of me," answered Jethro. "Along with our other gods, I also worship the God of Abraham, because twice I have seen His hand in my own life. Most other priests have rejected Him, being loyal only to Midianite gods."

Moses was surprised. "This god of Abraham has caused my trouble. But I thought he was the god of the Israelites? How can you know him?"

"We revere Abraham, but not through either his wife, Sarah, or his concubine, Hagar. After Sarah died, he took another woman into his tent, the younger Keturah,[20] who bore him six more sons, the fourth of whom was our Midian. When strife arose in the family over five hundred years ago, Abraham dispatched Keturah and her sons eastward with many gifts. Midian moved into this area, and his descendants populate our nation today.

"Although Abraham's God established His covenant only with Isaac, leaving the majority of his inheritance to him,[21] some of us still worship Him."

Moses spread his hands and said, "If your god has more for me to do, he must tell me."

"Perhaps He will," said Jethro.

Several weeks later, Moses returned home unexpectedly, his left forearm wrapped in a bloody sheepskin. "A wolf tore it open," he said, as Zipporah, one of Jethro's daughters, began to gently remove the covering. The gash was moderately deep and would require repeated bathing, rewrapping with fresh sheepskin, and then binding with leather thongs. As Moses lay on a table, he spoke to Zipporah and Jethro. "You have welcomed me into your home, yet I have not been honest with you. You deserve to know the truth. I am neither an Egyptian nor Pharaoh's grandson."

"You are not Pharaoh's grandson?" repeated the worldly, wise Jethro, eyebrows raised.

"No, as I recently discovered, I am Hebrew, merely a slave who has masqueraded as a prince. I never knew my true parents—Israelites who abandoned me to the Nile and to Pharaoh's daughter as a baby. I have been wrestling with that revelation for many weeks, a predicament involving your god of Abraham. I must know more about this god. Can you contact him for me?"

"No, He speaks when He wishes, and then, only rarely," replied Jethro. "If you wish to learn more of Him, I suggest you pray to Him for guidance."

"I will."

"What do you know about Him?" asked Jethro.

"In truth, only stories of the Hebrew past. I am aware that their slavery was somehow foretold by this god. A visitor to our courts, Strange Miriam, claiming to speak on his behalf, issued dire warnings to our Egyptian rulers if we continued to harass the Israelites. We ignored her threats, of course.

"And there is another curious claim they make—that their god gives them divine protection from many of the diseases[22] the Egyptians suffer. If their god were truly benevolent, they wouldn't have been in slavery in the first place, would they?"

"You are searching, aren't you? God will reveal Himself to you in time," said Jethro.

Moses had learned from others that Jethro had always yearned for a son. However, his wife produced only four daughters. In frustration, Jethro took another wife, a woman from the Cush area of Nubia[23] whom he had wooed away from a caravan traveling from Nubia to Syria. She was beautiful, but birthed only three more daughters, to Jethro's distress. The next to youngest, Zipporah, had seemed to Moses to be the most attractive.

A number of years passed and Moses, his hair now graying, approached Zipporah as she sat outside on a stool, spinning wool.

"Zipporah," said Moses as he stood uneasily before her.

"Yes, Moses?" She paused to tighten a loose sandal strap. She was tall for a woman, and her skin was smooth, the color of burnt umber. A blanket of long, wavy black hair cascaded over her white full-length gown to the middle of her back, and over her covered breasts.

"I am but your father's shepherd," Moses began. "I have shared many hours with him and we know each other well. I have—waited patiently for you to grow up."

Zipporah seemed somewhat confused. "You have been with us ten years and I greatly respect you. But, what do you mean? You have waited for me to grow up? This I do not understand."

Moses' heart was bursting with affection. "Zipporah, you are the finest of the daughters, and I have great love for you."

She gasped, catching the full impact of what he was suggesting. "Moses, we have had many good conversations together, but would not one of my older sisters be more suitable for you? Besides, as you know, I do not share your faith in the Hebrew god."

"Jethro has given me permission to marry you," he persisted.

She looked away in silence. Finally she said, "Well, if you are sure and Father decrees it, then yes, Moses, I will—marry you."

Moses and Zipporah lived in a house next to Jethro and his family. Zipporah ran an efficient home, while Moses continued shepherding Jethro's growing flock. After a time, Moses' hopes for a child began to wane, until one day, he joyfully learned that his wife was pregnant. The pregnancy went well, and on the second day after their son was born, Moses entered their sleeping quarters.

"After all these years," said Zipporah, "we finally have a child, Moses, but why must you call him Gershom, which you say in Hebrew means 'a stranger here'?"[24]

"I am made to feel welcome in your homeland," he replied, "but yet I feel like a foreigner. My people, my true family, are in Egypt."

"But he is such a handsome boy, and he looks like you. Perhaps he will become a priest, like Father," she said.

"His name is Gershom," pronounced Moses.

A week later, holding the crying baby, Zipporah confronted Moses. "You have circumcised him, Moses! I did not agree."

"It is the law of the god whom I am trying to serve, and I will obey what little I know of him. Perhaps he will bless us with another son."

"It is *your* law!" she retorted angrily.

The couple shared the joy of watching Gershom grow. Although wishing otherwise, Zipporah had not become pregnant again. Many years passed before she announced their long-awaited news. "I am again with child; perhaps a brother for twelve-year-old Gershom!"

"Zipporah, we are indeed fortunate."

"We are," she smiled.

"If it is a boy," Moses said, "he'll be called Eliezer. It means, in Hebrew, 'the god of my father was my help.'"[25]

"Still *your* god. All right, but he will not be circumcised!"

For four decades, Moses and his family lived near Jethro in Midian. Fit and healthy at the age of eighty, Moses knew every sheep path, every hill, every valley, wadi, and oasis over the wilderness to the east and to the west, even as far as Mount Sinai. Many were the days he subsisted on biscuits and water, always with an ear listening at night for a straying sheep or a marauder threatening the flock. His arms were scarred from battles with predators, and his palms callused from brandishing his rod.

He surprised Semitic merchants traveling in caravans to and from the northeast with his knowledge of Hebrew. For hundreds of years, Hebrew had only been a spoken language, but from the merchants of the caravans, he learned to read and write the newly developed Hebrew alphabet[26] that had arisen in the countries east of the Great Sea. Always, he inquired about a man with olive green eyes from Rameses, but the answer was always no.

The rest of his learning and early training lay useless. His life was as if a king's lead horse had been relegated to the plow. He often regretted that his crime had deprived him of his chance to help the Israelites; if they were ever to be freed, their god would have to appoint another.

Although he increasingly included the Hebrew god among those he prayed to, his knowledge of that god remained rudimentary. Time was molding him into a humble man[27] and, as he surveyed his flock at the first glow of sunrise, he felt at last content to live out his life in Midian.

Endnotes

1. Josephus, Flavius. *The Antiquities of the Jews*, translated by William Whiston, A. M., 1987, book 2, chapter 10.
2. "Anuke, Re" *Gods and Mythology of Ancient Egypt*. http://tourgegypt. net/godsofegypt.
3. "wrestling with an angel," Gen. 32:24.
4. "interpret dreams," Gen. 40:1.
5. "Ephraim, Manasseh," Gen. 41:51-52
6. "Assyria," Isaiah 52:4.
7. "arose over Egypt," Ex. 1:18.
8. "passing pleasures of sin," Heb. 11:25.
9. "visit the Israelites," Acts 7:23 NIV.
10. "iron bedstead," Deut. 3:11.
11. "Atum, Amon, Phoenix," Egypt: Gods of Ancient Egypt—*Egyptian Mythology http://touregypt.net/gods1.htm pp 1–3.*
12. "reward," Heb. 11:26.
13. "looked this way and that," Ex. 2:12.
14. "hid him in the sand," Ex. 2:12.
15. "Kill Moses," Ex. 2:15.

16. "fear him," Heb. 11:27.
17. "invisible," Heb.22:17 NIV.
18. Jethro story from Ex. 2:16f.
19. "every shepherd is loathsome," Gen. 46:34.
20. "Keturah," Gen. 25:1-2.
21. "inheritance," Gen. 25:5-6.
22. "many of the diseases," Ex. 15:26.
23. "Cush," Ex. 12:1.
24. "A stranger here": referenced in footnote for Exodus 2:22 in *Ryrie Study Bible.*
25. "god of my father was my help," Ex.18:4.
26. "New Hebrew alphabet" Angel Saenz-Badillos, *A History of the Hebrew Language,* 1993, pp. 16–17. See also Edward Horowitz, MA., DRE. *How the Hebrew Language Grew,* 1960, pp. 12ff and George Rawlinson, *Moses, His Life and Times,* 1887, New York, pp. 29, 30.
27. "humble man," Num. 12:3.

Chapter 2

Turmoil in the Grain Storage Cities

The sun rose over the horizon in the cloudless sky, slowly illuminating the thriving city of Pithom[1]—ten miles east of the Nile and a day's leisurely journey by carriage south of the Great Sea—progressively coalescing the generic darkness beyond into identifiable shadows of the many public buildings, the treasure house and the fort. A seven-foot wall surrounding the city briefly shaded the slave community on the eastern edge of town. Four timbered guard posts overlooked its large collections of huts.

The fort was at attention. Shiny weapons intermittently caught and reflected the rays of the sun into Pharaoh's eyes as he made his official inspection of the three groups of military personnel arrayed in front of him. The first set was a line of forty men of varying skin color facing him, with nine parallel lines of men behind. Each soldier in the first six rows held a two-foot sword or shorter battle axe against his left chest as he stood at attention. Soldiers in the four rear rows held longer spears.

The tanned and slender thirty-year-old pharaoh slowly walked in front of the soldiers, hands clasped behind his back. He wore the official black shoulder-length headdress, a white robe over an orange and black knee-length skirt, leather sandals, and three gold bracelets encircling his left wrist. The only softness about him was the crop that dangled loosely from his right hand. By his side was the proud, self-assured company commander, and to the rear strode the paunchy vizier of northern Egypt.

Pharaoh's focused, discerning eyes missed nothing. Occasionally he would rivet his gaze on a soldier, like a hawk on a mouse. Woe to he who met his stare.

The second group, the archers, separated from the first by three spear lengths, maintained a kneeling position, shoulders back, left arms thrust forward, their hands firmly gripping vertically held, polished wooden bows. A quiver with twelve arrows was strapped to the back of each archer by a single thong that encircled the chest, attached at the left waistband and arching over the base of the right side of the neck. None moved in this bronze tableau.

As Pharaoh walked, he turned slightly toward the commander and spoke in clipped tones. "How does your slave population serve you?"

"The blacks we have brought up from Nubia are compliant and know their place," the commander replied. "The exceptions are the few that come from Cush in northern Nubia. They are the better educated but weaker, often arrogant, and occasionally unruly. We deal with them appropriately."

"The Israelites?" asked Pharaoh.

"The ones we have in the military make adequate fighters, but they tend to be an independent, surly lot—and argumentative. When properly dealt with, they can be controlled," said the commander, confident in his knowledge of these details.

"They proliferate like rabbits, you know," said Pharaoh. "My grandfather once decreed that all of their male babies be cast into the Nile.[2] The Israelites created such a commotion that eventually he rescinded the order. Someday, I may have to re-institute it."

The last contingent was of thirty war chariots, each pulled by two brown horses harnessed together, their manes adorned with orange and black ribbons. Each chariot had two bronze-rimmed wooden wheels and a three-foot-high orange-painted oval carriage with an open back. One charioteer stood on the platform of each, reins in one hand and a longbow in the other, an arrow-filled quiver over his shoulder. An almost imperceptible nod of Pharaoh's head signaled approval.

As he approached the middle of the line, Pharaoh paused and spoke again to the commander. "I am informed of the recent war exercises of the Philistines[3] on our eastern border. God Re, we lost many good men when they drove us out of the Sinai four years ago with their blasted iron chariots. My father died shortly afterwards, you know, I believe partly from sorrow. But I hear that for the present, they seem to have no further designs on Egypt, wanting to conquer Canaan, a land I would give the southern half of our country to repossess. But with the Philistine army interposed over the northern route, those chances seem slim. We will bide our time. Besides, Canaan is becoming a power in her own right under the coalition rule of the six kings. Perhaps the Philistines represent a welcome buffer after all. Our division at Rameses is battle-ready, and I am satisfied that your garrison is also."

"Of course," responded the commander.

Pharaoh continued the review, the final item on the agenda of his annual four-day visit. During that time, his aides from Rameses met with the local governor and his cabinet, reviewing the need for greater taxation, further measures to control the slave horde, the accounting of the year's grain harvest, and plans for enlarging the irrigation canals.

Pharaoh mounted his waiting chariot. He half-smiled as he inhaled the rich, warm, earthy smell of the two black Syrian stallions that drew it, each bedecked with a black blanket interwoven with splashes of orange, the color of glowing coals. Their manes were adorned with a long row of tightly tied orange ribbons. Pharaoh sat on the cushioned bench in the back of the black, four-wheeled chariot. His rod-straight charioteer flicked the horses with his whip, and the chariot sprang forward, swirling dust. Pharaoh preferred to be near the front of his caravan, following the king's guard of horsemen. The chariots of the vizier and Pharaoh's fellow dignitaries wheeled in behind as they rolled out of the low-walled compound, followed closely by six warrior-manned chariots.

Approaching the city gates, Pharaoh observed masons building a brick watchtower near the left gate. Ten paces before the tower, he heard the *thwap, thwap* of the guard's whip striking a lighter-skinned slave on his knees, blood seeping down into his left eye. Nearby, his hod lay on the ground, its brick load scattered, two of the bricks broken. "Clumsy Hebrew," Pharaoh muttered with disgust.

Beyond the gates, Pharaoh turned to view Pithom. How proud his father would have been of him for his dogged perseverance in enlarging and prospering that city. All of Egypt was rightfully his!

They traveled northward onto the double-lane dirt road heading toward the city of Rameses, not far from the Great Sea, where his grandfather had relocated the capital forty years earlier, renaming it after himself. As far as the eye could see, primarily to the west, sizable collections of small houses and tents sprawled over higher ground. This fertile area was the land of

Goshen[4], to which the Hebrews had been assigned when they arrived from Canaan centuries earlier and where many still lived, supplying a labor force, as easily gathered as grapes from a vineyard. As natural shepherds, many of them continued to watch over large herds of cattle, sheep, and goats, most belonging to Pharaoh; the Hebrews had been permitted to keep a number for their own use. A short distance farther on, they passed by guards patrolling a line of men marching in lock-step as they headed from the villages to the brickyards of Pithom, their shackles clanking.

Pharaoh looked to the east and saw the vague outlines of the city of Succoth above the horizon on the road to the highly productive copper mines. Scattered potholes irritated Pharaoh, and the thick cushion helped little to ease his plight when he grew tired of standing.

The road wound to the northwest and crested the hills overlooking the low floodplains that extended to the Nile. Each spring, water flowed from the mountains in the south, flooding the bottomlands with eroded, nutritious soils to produce the luxurious crops that fed many nations.

It was mid-autumn and slaves were tilling the fields, planting, or mucking out the accumulated silt from the labyrinth of irrigation ditches. Some of the workers were adequately paid Egyptian laborers, but the wealthy landowners were mainly dependent on the Israelite slaves.

Five miles north of Pithom, a road branched off to the right to one of the area's large limestone quarries. Limestone was found in abundance in the hills of the east bank of the Nile, but only a few sites yielded stone of construction quality. The majestic, thousand-year-old pyramids to the south, many built with native limestone, had weathered the desert winds well.

About halfway to Rameses, the caravan entered a village and halted in front of a small, one-story brick building. Pharaoh and his leaders climbed down from their chariots, entered, and reclined at the tables, grateful for the respite. Two barefoot young girls in white dresses brought in trays holding several pottery mugs of beer and fresh, sweet pastries.

"We have had two consecutive subnormal harvests," the pharaoh said to his minister of waters and agriculture. "You are my authority on such matters. What is the cause of this?"

The hunchbacked minister nervously stroked his long, swept-back black hair. He answered defensively, "Some years, the god of the Nile, Hapi,[5] gives us good crop yields, and in some years, they are less, depending, as you know, O Pharaoh, on the volume of our annual flooding. Why the river has been miserly lately, I do not know. Each spring, Hapi causes the

Nile to swell upstream to the south, well into the land of Nubia, cascading down to us, but we know nothing about what the gods do in the hills and mountains above Nubia."

"Have you any suggestions?" asked Pharaoh.

"Perhaps, mighty Pharaoh," stammered the minister, "we should sacrifice more animals to Hapi, and his goddess, Anuket."[5]

"I'll consider it," snapped Pharaoh.

More mugs of beer were quaffed before the troupe's thirst was slaked, and they continued on their journey.

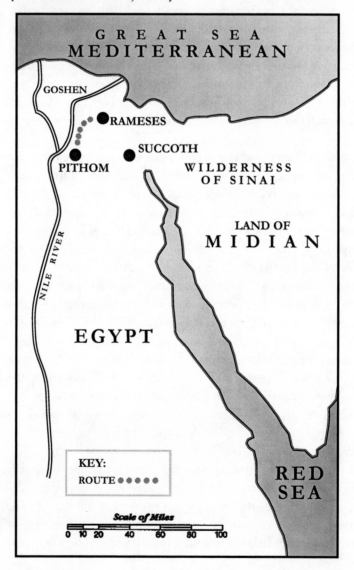

As the Nile flowed northward, it terminated into two main branches, creating the fertile delta near the Great Sea. The city of Rameses lay south of the sea, near the easternmost branch. The approaching caravan caught glimpses of ships between the clumps of palm trees lining the banks. Small pleasure boats with pointed ends and brightly painted sails scudded past barges carrying exports of grain, vegetables, limestone, gold, copper, and papyrus. Others were bound for Nubia to exchange their cargos for spices, ivory, slaves, and well-bred cattle; some were cruising into port with Syrian horses and cedar logs from Lebanon.

The chariots rumbled on, past a string of oxen-pulled carts that had pulled over to allow the entourage to pass. They carried high-quality clay, a bane to the Israelite slaves who were forced to dig it up day after day and transport it under the broiling sun to the nearby brickyards.

A short distance beyond, Pharaoh observed a flurry of activity at the brickyard, a yard several times larger than the one at Pithom. Under the prodding of Egyptian guards, thousands of slaves shuttled their burdens in weaving lines between mountains of straw, great heaps of clay, and the large trenches of water where the two were mixed to make bricks. The tons of straw—dried stems of wheat, rye, and barley—had been gleaned from the fields, mainly by hired Egyptian laborers. Masses of milling, sunburned men hoed or churned the viscid, gummy, maroon mixture in the trenches with their bare feet. Other slaves shoveled the final mixture into molds of different sizes to be sun-dried or baked in bronze ovens to satisfy Pharaoh's expansive plans to enlarge his cities. The smaller, finished bricks were loaded onto wooden troughs carried on men's shoulders, while the larger ones were piled onto wooden-wheeled carts to be rolled to construction sites. Most of these slaves were Hebrews, with fewer darker-skinned ones who had been captured in conquests of other countries.

Pharaoh smiled when he saw Egyptian guards strutting on the periphery of the lines, encouraging laggards with whips and rods. When the pace of a worker flagged, harsh words punctuated by the sting or cut of a whip temporarily revived fatigued muscles. The perspiring workers moaned long, spontaneous, singsong chants while an infrequent tree cast a morsel of shade toward them.

The royal cohort approached the bridge over the stagnant moat guarding the five-meter-high walls surrounding the city. Two guards on horseback galloped through the city gates and clattered toward the royal cohort over a wide wooden bridge. They saluted Pharaoh, who briefly raised a hand, and then turned to escort the caravan into the bustling fortress city. Two larger-than-life sculpted granite tigers flanked the city gates. Most of the larger buildings of the city were of limestone, the smaller of brick, many adorned with columns and ornate facades of carved animals.

Pharaoh prized this city. As a fortress, garrisoned by over 100,000 soldiers, archers, and charioteers, it could protect Egypt from enemy forces coming overland from the east. The garrison counted more than 600 chariots among its military assets. The royal navy, moored to the south where the Nile branched, was positioned to repel forces coming up the Nile.

As Pharaoh and his chariots rode through the busy streets to the palace, wealthy and poor alike fell to their knees in worship, because he was more than a king; like all pharaohs before him, he was believed to be the embodiment of the god Horus, king of the gods of the earth.[5]

The horses ambled as Pharaoh's chariot led the others through an archway and into the courtyard of the palace. Servants brought wine and sweet cakes, and court magicians and priests greeted Pharaoh with deep bows as he entered his royal home.

The calm of Pharaoh and his court was, however, superficial. Moral decadence simmered beneath the peaceful surface of the land, and its insidious influence was increasing. Though the Egyptians worshipped and sacrificed to their many gods, diseases spread and the number of graves multiplied. Even the wealth of this mighty country could not buy cures from her ill-equipped physicians, magicians, and soothsayers.

The masses of the tyrannized Israelite slaves, living in the city's poorer western section, were bowed to the breaking point, full of anger and revulsion. Generation after generation had known nothing but poverty and fear. Year after year of working for the cruel powers of the empire, the slaves—men, women, and children—were nothing but human beasts of burden to be used and discarded, always at the mercy of their taskmasters. Others, conscripted as soldiers, died valiantly in the wars of the aggressive Egyptians. The only immediate meaning life held for most was found in their tight-knit communities and the size and closeness of their treasured families as they multiplied. Although they suffered, they seemed curiously less susceptible to many of the deadly diseases that afflicted the Egyptians.

Occasionally, a talented artisan slave would be recognized and become employed in a semiskilled or skilled position. These more fortunate ones were treated moderately well and were less enthusiastic when they occasionally joined in the prayers for freedom.

But the great majority had ceased outward resistance and desperately cried out for relief from a supernatural power. Some prayed to the Egyptian gods, but growing numbers turned to Abraham's familiar "God Most High, Possessor of Heaven and Earth"[6], even though such prayers over the centuries had produced only occasional visions through his few prophets and prophetesses.

Large numbers of Israelites met secretly in the evenings in crowded homes and tents, claiming the ancient promise of Abraham's God to liberate them after 430 years of slavery in a foreign land. That time had arrived. Even as they prayed, they wondered what He could possibly do. They were so closely guarded that a rebellion would quickly be squelched. Could God—with stealth—arm them with superior weapons to overthrow the Egyptians, or perhaps cause the deaths of the Egyptian leaders? They even yearned for a foreign power to conquer Egypt and set them free.

"God, can you find a way to rescue us?" they cried.

Endnotes

1. "Pithom" and "Rameses," Nicholas Reeves, *Ancient Egypt: The Great Discoveries*, 2000, pp. 189, 198. See also David Daiches, *Moses: Man and His Vision*. 1975, p. 84.
2. "cast into the Nile," Ex. 1:22.
3. "Philistines," Avnr Raban and Tobert R. Stieglitz, "The Sea Peoples and Their Contributions to Civilization." *Biblical Archeology Review*, Nov.-Dec. 1991, pp. 40–42.
4. "land of Goshen," Gen. 45:10.
5. "Hapi" "Anuket" "Horus": *Gods and Mythology of Ancient Egypt*. http:// www.touregypt.net/godsofegypt/ page 1.
6. "God Most High…," Gen. 14:19, 22.

Chapter 3

A Sheepherder to Lead?

For four centuries, God had minimally intervened while the Egyptians oppressed the Israelites, and the Israelites, likewise, had distanced themselves from Him. When at last they cried out to the God of Abraham en masse, He finally responded, initiating the surprising, wrenching process of liberating them.

His first need was for a leader, a trained man who sought Him and was willing to learn obedience. Such a captain was not to be found in Egypt. Although the Hebrew elders believed in God, their leadership qualities had been suppressed by the subjugation of slavery and intimidation of their masters. However, just as God had allowed Joseph to stew in prison until his time to lead arrived, so also God had kept sequestered His chosen one—a spry, eighty-year-old Israelite refugee.

One day, while Moses was out pasturing Jethro's flock near Mount Sinai, he saw before him a lone bush with flames leaping from it.[1] He drew closer to investigate, amazed that its leaves and even its fruit were not even singed. As he approached, the bush spoke to him.

"Moses ... Moses ..."

He stepped back in wonderment. Then, mystified by who might be behind the bush, he answered, "Here I am." *

But walking toward the flaming shrub, it rebuked him. *"Do not come near here; remove your sandals from your feet, for the place on which you are standing is holy ground"* (Ex. 3:5). The bush demanded obeisance! He took his sandals off and moved three steps to the side. There was no one behind the bush. The voice had come from the fire!

Moses was apprehensive. "Who is here commanding me?"

At that, the voice identified itself. *"I am the God of your father, of Abraham, the God of Isaac, and the God of Jacob"* (Ex. 3:6).

Although Moses had long sought Him, now he was awestricken to be in the presence of this God who was also the God of his own father, whoever he was. Moses hid his face in his cupped hands.

"I have surely seen the affliction of My people ..." said God, *"and have given heed to their cry ... and have come down to deliver them from the power of the Egyptians ... and to bring them ... to a land flowing with milk and honey, to the place of the Canaanite"* (Ex. 3:7–8).

Why does He tell me this? wondered Moses.

"Therefore, come now," God said, expecting immediate compliance, *"and I will send you to Pharaoh, so that you may bring My people, the sons of Israel, out of Egypt"* (Ex. 3:10).

Would I know the new pharaoh? wondered Moses. *Maybe I could have influenced a pharaoh forty years ago, but now I am so old.*

"Who am I that I should go to Pharaoh and bring your people out of Egypt?" * he asked God.

Because what was Egypt to him but remorse, disillusionment, buried hope, and, worst of all, his arrest and probable execution? If he agreed, how many of the Hebrews would actually come with him and where would they go? Free the people? Lead them? All he led was sheep.

"Certainly, I will be with you and this shall be the sign to you that it is I who have sent you," God said. *"When you have brought the people out of Egypt, you shall worship God at this mountain"* (Ex. 3:12).

Moses' mind was racing. Any leadership qualities he had were all dried up. Yet God seemed to assume that he could succeed. "Even if I did get to Egypt," Moses said, "and explained to the elders of Israel that their God had appeared to me, would they not surely doubt me and ask, 'What is His name?' What shall I say to them?" *

"I AM who I AM," God responded. *"Thus you are to say to the sons of Israel, 'I AM has sent me to you'"* (Ex. 3:14).

I AM? Names had specific meanings, but this God must be beyond definition, His qualities too great to be captured by a name. Moses realized that the name I AM was given to him to convince the Hebrew elders.

"Go and gather the elders of Israel together and say to them," the voice of God continued, *"the LORD, the God of your fathers, of Abraham, Isaac, and Jacob, has appeared to you saying, 'I will bring you up out of the affliction of Egypt to the land of the Canaanite'"* (Ex. 3:17).

The chief afflicter, Pharaoh, might not know Abraham, but he certainly knew the Hebrews, so God added, *"Say to* [Pharaoh] *'the LORD, the God of the Hebrews has met with us. So now, please, let us go a three days' journey into the wilderness, that we may sacrifice to the LORD our God'"* (Ex. 3:18).

Moses knew that Pharaoh would never even consider such a preposterous request. Sure enough, God confirmed this, admitting to Moses that Pharaoh would indeed refuse to issue this three-day leave. In response, He would *"strike Egypt with all My miracles which I shall do in the midst of it; and after that* [Pharaoh] *will let you go"* (Ex. 3:20). But God told Moses that the Israelites would find sudden favor in the sight of the Egyptians before they left; the Egyptians would give them of their wealth: *"Thus you will plunder the Egyptians"* (Ex. 3:22). God clearly proclaimed His authority over the Egyptians while revealing the framework of His plan as its Master Strategist.

Moses remained unconvinced for some time. "What if they will not believe that the God of Abraham actually appeared to me, an eighty-year-old fugitive, a sheep herder?" he asked. "'Ha,' they'll laugh, 'prove it to us.'"

Moses' wooden staff suddenly squirmed in his hand. Stunned, he dropped it to the ground and watched it slither away.

"Grasp it by its tail" (Ex. 4:4), commanded God.

As Moses tentatively approached and grabbed the snake, the staff's hard texture returned. "It's a staff again but now, deep painful sores of leprosy consume my other hand."

"Now, put your hand into your bosom" (Ex. 4:6).

In fear, Moses again obeyed and, withdrawing it, exclaimed, "It is restored like the rest of my flesh!"

"If they will not believe even these two signs ... take some water from the Nile and pour it on the dry ground; and ... [it] *will become blood on the dry ground"* (Ex. 4:9).

Moses was relatively sure that these three miracles might convince the elders. But he pushed God's patience to the limit. "I am not eloquent, but slow of speech and tongue," * he whined.

"Who has made man's mouth? Is it not I, the LORD?" God rebuked him. Then He added, *"I will ... teach you what you are to say"* (Ex. 4:11–12).

Moses crumbled. "Please, LORD, now send the message by some other person, anyone but me," he begged.

God became angry. *"Is there not your brother Aaron, the Levite? I know that he speaks fluently. And, moreover, behold, he is coming out to meet you ... I will be with your mouth and his mouth and I will teach you what you are to do. Moreover, he shall speak for you to the people"* (Ex. 4:14–16). God also reminded Moses to take with him his staff with which to perform the signs. As the fire subsided, Moses felt God's insistence.

"My brother Aaron? So I am one of the tribe of Levi," Moses acknowledged.

Alone, bewildered, and unsure of himself, Moses herded the sheep toward home, preoccupied with his mysterious encounter but resigned to obey. He sought support for what could be a long and trying mission and decided to bring his family along with him. He doubted that Jethro would permit that, so when he arrived home, he presented his plan to his father-in-law, veiling its true purpose with a lie. "Please let me go that I may return to my brethren who are in Egypt and see if they are still alive."*

To Moses' surprise, Jethro said simply, "Go in peace."*

With that permission, Moses described to Zipporah the excitement of his encounter with God at the burning bush and of God's commission for him.

"Go to Egypt?" she blurted out. "Are you not afraid to return to your people?" Then, anxiously, she added, "And for me, forty-seven years I have lived in one place, now I am to be suddenly uprooted with our children?" Regaining her composure, she touched his arm. "Moses, if you must go, our sons and I will go with you."

Later that day, while organizing his few selected goods, Moses was startled when the voice of God spoke to him again, telling him that the Egyptian leaders who had sought his death had all since died. He also warned Moses that, in spite of the three miracles Moses would perform, Pharaoh would not let the Hebrews go. In fact, God would harden Pharaoh's heart against Moses' pleas. *"Then you shall say to Pharaoh, 'Israel is my son, my first-born.... Let my son go, that he may serve me; but you have refused to let him go. Behold, I will kill your son, your first-born'"* (Ex. 4:22–23), said God. And with that, God departed, giving no further information.

Moses sat on his bed, shoulders slack, as he struggled to make sense out of God's puzzling, conflicting revelations. Inexplicably, God would harden Pharaoh's heart, purposely making him unyielding, and thereby denying the success of Moses' first assignment—the release of the Israelites. Was God totally on his side or was He testing him by making his task almost impossible? Moses wanted counsel, but who could he ask? The burden must be his alone, he acknowledged, as he finished preparing for the trip.

After bidding goodbye to Jethro's family, Moses proceeded westward with Zipporah, who rode a donkey, and their two sons, Gershom, twenty-one years old, and Eliezer, eight. They crossed deserts and grassy plains between stark limestone hills and made camp at the end of the first day near an oasis. As they prepared for bed, Moses said to his wife, "God must have great love for us. He won me over by—"

"Moses!" God angrily called out, interrupting Moses' reflection.

Zipporah, jumping up in terror, could see light through the wall of the tent. "Is that your god, Moses? He has come back here!" she cried.

God roared that He would put Moses *"to death"* (Ex. 4:24).

Zipporah grabbed Moses' arm. "What does he want?"

Moses understood. "The circumcision," he said slowly.

"No!"

"We must or he will kill me," Moses said, leading Eliezer out of the tent.

Shaken by concern for her husband, Zipporah grabbed a sharp piece of flint, bolted out ahead of the two saying, "I will do it."

"Lie down," she told her son. She raised Eliezer's robe and straddled his legs. To the sound of his muffled cries, she cut off his foreskin and threw it at Moses' feet. "Because of the circumcision," she hissed, "you are not a husband of love, but a bridegroom of blood to me."*

Moses stood still, staring at the piece of flesh that had been a chronic source of marital conflict.

"Zipporah," said Moses, "my love for you is boundless, but our sin covered us with filth. By removing it, you saved us from this God who demands total obedience." Then God left them alone; the light contracted and disappeared.

Later that night, Moses confided to his wife, "Zipporah, the enormous task of convincing the Israelites to leave Egypt with me may be made more difficult if you are with me. They have laws against intermarriage. It is best if you and our sons return to your father's home for the present."

"If we are more of a hindrance than a help," said Zipporah, relieved but acting resigned, "then we shall go. Your trust in this god far exceeds mine. I shall be greatly concerned for your safety, my dear Moses," she said, and kissed him. "Come back soon."

The family journey, launched with a lie to Jethro, had run aground. The next morning, Zipporah and their sons returned home with the donkey, while Moses proceeded on foot toward Egypt.

And toward his older brother.

One morning in Rameses, as Aaron came in for a morning meal, his wife remarked, "Aaron, I hope that look is not for me. You seem troubled."

"I am. God spoke to me this morning—oh, it was not a dream, but clear words, and He gave me a mission."

She stared in disbelief. "God actually spoke to you?"

"Yes."

"And what did He tell you?"

"He wants me to go to my brother and meet him in the wilderness in Midian—and accompany him back here. He promised to lead me to him." He paused. "Moses has been selected to help us all gain our freedom."

"Moses?" she asked. "We have not heard from him or spoken his name in almost forty years." She thought a few moments. "If God has finally decided to act on our behalf, couldn't He find a leader from among us? How about you, you who are a spokesman in the council? You have stayed here in bondage while your brother ran away."

"Elisheba, it is God's choice, not mine."

"Will you go?"

"I must."

"How did God say that He would free us?"

"He didn't say, only that I should go. It's not that I want to go; I certainly do not know the desert."

"What will people think when they learn where you have gone? Only Miriam, Father, you, and I know that you and Moses are brothers."

"Do not tell the people that," Aaron warned. "Just say that God has sent me on a mission and that you do not know any more."

"Aaron," she asked, "how do you feel toward your brother?"

"In truth," he replied, "I still harbor some resentment. What privileges were his in his acquired life while we had such a meager existence! All four of our sons and even our two daughters work hard, and for what? For food, clothing, and a shabby hut. Our roles could have been reversed but by the fate of birth. You could have been my queen."

"You wouldn't have met me."

Ignoring her comment, Aaron added, "These last forty years he probably has been enjoying himself sumptuously in his freedom while we labor under arrogant masters."

"How right you are. But Aaron, when will you go?"

"Day after tomorrow, there is a caravan leaving for the east. I know the right people and can smuggle myself into it. Before that, I must explain to our sons. Should the soldiers come looking for me, plead ignorance. I hope to return within ten days."

Aaron mingled with the members of the caravan and, using his influence, hired on and secured his escape. He endured long days of travel but was convinced that if God had called him, he would find Moses. Under God's direction, he eventually left the caravan when it turned north, and continued on foot toward the southeast. In the afternoon of the second day after he had left the caravan, he came upon a man walking toward him in shepherd's clothes. He approached cautiously and thought he recognized him. "I am Aaron. Are you Moses?"

"Aaron!" Moses exclaimed. "So you are my brother?" They embraced and kissed. Moses looked into his face. "Your eyes, they are as mine. It was you who sent me those messages."

"Yes, but to little avail. Our relationship had been guarded by a pledge until Mother decided to ... bend it."

Moses noticed that Aaron was a head shorter than he, with prominent ears, curly white hair, and a trim beard. His face was smoother than Moses' weather-wrinkled one. Aaron entwined his long, slender fingers uneasily as they spoke.

"I am grateful to her," Moses said softly. "We wouldn't be here without the messages. You know, Aaron, I do remember you. On several occasions, I heard you plead the case for the Israelites. With your logical arguments, you marshaled support for your causes. Now, God has told me that you are to be instrumental in accomplishing His task for us."

"I will help as He sees fit," said Aaron.

"Aaron, how did you have the elephant box?"

"Our father was a skilled carpenter, though his talents were little used in Egypt. He made the pair of boxes with stolen wood, and since you loved to play with them as a child, he sent one back to the palace with you."

"And you kept the other?"

"Yes. We sent it thinking that it would cause you to believe more in the messages."

"It did. Now, my brother, listen to what God has done here." Moses detailed the events of the past weeks. When he told Aaron of the three miracles, Aaron gave his interpretation. "Moses, first, I believe that you are to overcome the snake that is the national symbol of Egypt with your simple shepherd's staff. I suppose that God will heal the Israelites, leprous in His eyes through their worship of other gods. As for the third, God will also control, perhaps destroy, the life-giving, sacred Nile."[2]

"You are as wise as God has said," reflected Moses. "Once I accepted his persistent offer, He revealed his plan, disciplined my wife Zipporah and me, and now He has sent you to me. He overlooks nothing."

Aaron fought back the lingering pride of the older brother and responded hoarsely. "Had I talked with you forty years ago, I could have taught you Hebrew cunning and wisdom; you could have been patient, harnessed your efforts, formed alliances, tested waters, and saved us then. But instead, you impulsively struck and did us no good. I hope that you have cooled during these forty years."

Moses returned the gaze. "I have matured as a protector of sheep as I never would have as a ruler of persons. And now, I must depend on you. I know few in Egypt but, as God implied, you are highly respected. Will you be able to obtain an audience with our people?"

"I can," Aaron answered. "Now, let's be on our way. It is a long journey."

There was little conversation as the brothers walked the road during the heat of the day but, refreshed by the cooler evening and a meal of rationed food and water, talk came more easily.

"Aaron," said Moses, "I have told you what God did with me. Now, tell me what has happened in your life."

"I have a devoted wife, Elisheba and four strong sons. Nadab, the oldest, was conscripted to become a soldier, and Abihu, the second boy, who idolizes Nadab, serves as an oarsman on a naval ship. The two younger boys, Eleazar and Ithamar, are brick-makers. Nadab and Abihu have always been high-spirited, but the younger ones are quieter, more thoughtful boys.

I have two daughters who are both talented with their hands. One cards and spins wool and the other is a seamstress."

Moses smiled. "And you seem strong yourself."

"After I'd been digging clay for five years, the potter's assistant became ill one day. Being nearby and respected by the guards, I was thrust into that position. I developed a skill at that trade, and in two years, began to produce vases that were appreciated. I learned to paint bright, variegated birds and fish on them, and have done that ever since."

"Had I known sooner who I was, I could have spared you and your sons," said Moses.

"And risked exposure—maybe death? No, you were safe only as an Egyptian grandson to the king. What has your life been like, Moses?"

"I married in Midian and have two fine sons, twenty-one and eight years old. My family started out with me on this journey, but at my request, returned home. I have a kind father-in-law who is a priest to his people. Life has been as peaceful as a shepherd can have."

"We followed your successful military exploits," Aaron said. "But what of your years growing up? It must have been an easy life."

"My clearest memories are those after the age of about seven. I did enjoy the many luxuries of the palace, where I received a broad education and mastered the Hebrew language without difficulty, though that should not surprise you. In the military, I must have accounted myself well because I became commander when I was twenty-five."

"I quietly took some pride in your victories."

Two nights later, Moses and Aaron sat talking. "I know the story of my parents placing me in the basket in the Nile to save me and of the princess finding me," said Moses. "But I have often wondered who my—our—parents were."

"Our father is still alive, and he is 109 years old. Our mother, Jochabed, died eight years ago. She was a fine woman who provided well for us with what she had. She tried to instill into us her unwavering faith in our God with endless stories of our ancestors. She made us swear we would never reveal that you were a member of our family, an oath we kept."

"I am in great debt to her and to our father."

As they approached Rameses, Moses said, "Aaron, were you ever jealous or angry of my good fortune?"

"No, I was glad that you lived and that your life had been favored."

"I'm not sure I would have been able to see it that way."

"It is just maturity," said Aaron.

Entry into Rameses was not tightly monitored, and they passed through the gates, hiding their faces, while pretending to help a merchant with his donkeys. Aaron took Moses to his house where his still beautiful wife, Elisheba, greeted him warmly. At the house next door, they were met by a tall, pleasantly stout, erect woman with long braided hair and dark eyes. "Moses, this is your sister, Miriam," said Aaron.

"Stran—" Moses caught himself. "Miriam! My sister!" as he looked warily at her. "In truth! The very Miriam, the princess's maid, the woman I barely tolerated. Had I known that you were my sister and a true prophetess,[3] I would have listened to you more often."

Miriam moved toward Moses with the grace of a young dancer, belying the wrinkles of her forehead and corners of her eyes, and briefly embraced him. "My brother, it is good to see you again. I wondered if you would ever know. How many times I wanted to tell you."

"Forgive my past brashness," Moses said. "I was a proud and callous young man. How I must have disturbed you and your God. I hope to redress my past with you."

Miriam responded coolly, "I look forward to that."

She took Moses to an old man seated in a shadow in the corner of the room. "Moses, this is your father, Amram." As Moses reached out to touch his shoulder, he saw a faint smile cross the deep lines of a face sculpted by affliction. Drooping lids draped dark eyes. Moses looked at Miriam in wonderment. "The Amram who was your father was also my father!"

Moses leaned toward the old man, "Father."

"He has difficulty hearing," Miriam said.

"Father," he repeated louder, "it is so good to finally meet you."

The answer came in a hoarse whisper from the man. "To be able to see and talk to you, my son—" Tears formed in his eyes, as he reached out a withered hand, "and to touch you."

Moses kneeled before his father. "I am profoundly indebted to you for my life. It must have been agonizing for mother and you to watch me live as I did and not to be able to communicate with me." Then Moses remembered. "How you suffered at the hands of the guards. Did you finally gain relief from the pits?"

"Yes. Months after you killed Mannel, I became ill and was finally relieved. I recovered, but never had to return to the pits. I am grateful for your act."

"Had I only known. I am so sorry, my father, that we were such heartless rulers, but thank God that you are still alive."

"I have lived for this moment," Amram said with a dry throat, as Moses leaned forward and kissed him on both cheeks.

Moses turned toward his sister. "Miriam, how did our mother feel toward me?"

"She saw that you were special. From the time she began to nurse you, after we brought you home, until she finally had to relinquish you at the age of three, she filled you with stories of our patriarchs in Hebrew, while still being careful to teach you Egyptian. On visits to the palace, when you would use Hebrew words, the princess would scold you. Even at three years of age, you learned which words to use at our home and which ones to use at the palace."

"Some of her stories must still be in my mind. An amazing woman," said Moses.

"She was," replied Miriam. "Now, you must be tired. Elisheba and I will prepare a meal for you and we will share the past. Will your stay be long?"

"I do not know. I am on a mission ordered by the same God who communed with you."

"He still does," corrected Miriam.

The four sat on stools around the small, unpainted wooden table and ate the last few bites of their meal.

"Miriam, your purple tunic came from the east," observed Moses.

"A gift from an emir whose caravan was saved from highwaymen by my advice. But tell us, Moses, how will you proceed with your ambitious task?"

Moses began slowly. "Aaron and I are to go to Pharaoh and plead for the release of the slaves. God has miracles with which He will strike Egypt, so that they will finally drive us out. The details are His."

Miriam pondered a moment. "God has revealed nothing of your mission to me. As Aaron may have told you, I have a moderate following among our people. What role shall I play in this venture?"

"I know no more. He asks for our blind trust."

"Of course," Miriam said, but she looked disappointed.

The thirty-nine Hebrew men—two elders and the leader from each tribe—assembled at Aaron's invitation in the large secret room dug beneath the house of an Israelite. Most squatted, some were seated on the ground, and a number stood. In the front of the room, four white candles burned on a waist-high wooden table, painting shadows of the standing men on the opposite wall. Aaron introduced Moses and many greeted his presence with surprise. Filmy threads of his past had been preserved and handed down by venerable elders, tales of his royal upbringing and of his flight from Pharaoh many years before. Caravan travelers had added to the mystery, bringing occasional rumors of his residence as a shepherd in the east. Yet here he was standing before them, but not as Aaron's brother, because fear of Moses' fugitive status had convinced Aaron not to reveal their kinship yet. There would be time for that later. The midwife and Jochabed had carried the secret to their graves.

One of the leaders addressed Aaron. "You are a trusted, proven one among us. Why have you brought this Moses into our midst?"

"God sent me to bring him to you and sent Moses to obtain our freedom," Aaron replied.

"And how does he plan to do that?"

"The details have not as yet been revealed," said Aaron.

The elders mumbled among themselves. Finally one asked, "What is the name of this God of ours, Moses?"

Moses rose and spoke, "The God of your fathers, the God who identified Himself with two names: one simply 'I AM' and the other, 'The God of Abraham, Isaac, and Jacob.'[4] He told me of His keen concern for your plight and He supplied me with proof of His powers."

"And what proof is that, Moses?" they asked.

"Will you watch what His power can do?" He tentatively dropped his staff before them, and watched as God transformed it; then Moses demonstrated the healing of his suddenly leprous hand. He picked up a pitcher of water, drawn from the Nile, and it poured out as blood. The amazed elders became quiet and, one by one, bowed their heads in worship of God.

On the evening of the new moon, the leaders of the Israelite tribes of Issachar, Benjamin, and Gad gathered in the Benjaminite's house, talking together before their monthly meeting with the leaders of the other ten tribes.

Issachar's Nethanel was the youngest leader at thirty-three years of age. His body had been hardened from years of brick-making. "If we are to believe these two old men, one a stranger to me, then the God of Abraham is acting for us. But," he asked the age-old question, "Why has He waited so long? Have we been degraded all these years for a purpose? Was it only a coincidence that our ancestors migrated here from Canaan, only to become enslaved?"

Eliasaph, from Gad, the oldest leader, spoke deliberately. "Nethanel, perhaps God has kept us here to mature, to become less contentious, since we come from a quarrelsome and jealous stock. You know the stories as well as I; Cain killed Abel out of jealousy; Hagar, the maid, when she bore Abraham's son, was banished to the desert by his barren wife, Sarah. Then Jacob coveted Esau's birthright and stole it. Even Joseph's brothers sold him out of jealousy. Perhaps God hoped that the poverty of slavery would bond us. After all, doesn't envy dissolve when there is little to envy? As for this Moses, I will tentatively support him."

"If God truly orchestrated all of this," offered the Benjaminite, Abidan, massaging one of his deformed knuckles, "slavery might have been the only way we would stay together and multiply. Left to our own, our people would have scattered as chaff blown by the winds. Look again at our history. Abraham and Isaac were nomads, and when strife arose between them, they split up and lived separately. Jacob ran off to Mesopotamia after his argument with Esau. And even Esau, when he married outside of our tribes, moved south to the land of Edom. Joseph was shipped to Egypt. God's hand has been in our awful servitude." He paused and then continued slowly, "And now, as for me, I too believe that Moses carries God's credentials."

As other leaders began to arrive, Nethanel said, "Your arguments are wise, but I think that our slavery was to subdue us, to make us humble and willing to follow God when, where, and if He wished."

Eliasaph, rubbing his calloused hands together, replied thoughtfully, "Consider that the fault lies with us. Perhaps we have relied too long upon our many gods. It seems that Abraham's God has waited for our allegiance."

Nethanel;

Nethanel, youngest of the tribal leaders, had grown up in Goshen with three older brothers and two sisters. Although he tried in vain to succeed, he had difficulty absorbing the basic schooling lessons that his rather simple but canny mother tried to teach him, formal schooling being denied to the Israelites. Teased by his siblings, he strove to excel in every physical endeavor he undertook. He even endured his mother's cooking lessons, as he attempted to please a father who made it clear that his birth had been a mistake, and wore his resentment of him like a garment. Continually rebuffed, Nethanel sought acceptance in three male friends who shared his passion for novelty. He was the first to try beer, to ride a "borrowed" horse, and to seduce a girl, Nara, one night behind the remote hut of the tanner. The hot, tangy smell of leather always reminded him of her.

He developed a taste for beer, wine, and fighting. When he was sixteen, his father enlisted him in the army as a foot soldier because he was felt to be incorrigible. As the new recruit in a barracks stocked with hostile, testing veterans, his physical prowess enabled him to win fights and slowly won him not only their acceptance but also their respect.

He soon came to resent his senior officer, believing him to be tactically inadequate in battle. During his second campaign, Nethanel and four other young soldiers drank too much date wine and, by stealth at night, captured an outpost manned by a dozen Assyrians. When his senior officer angrily tried to discipline him for disobedience, Nethanel attacked him with his fists. He was punished, discharged from the army, and put on permanent brick-making duty. His rebelliousness was often met with beatings, until he donned a cloak of submission, keeping his wild spirit chained.

Nara remained his one true female friend, tolerating his bouts of anger and slowly tempering his impulsive, confrontational nature. She encouraged his qualities of trustworthiness and perseverance. They were married when he was nineteen and she bore him a son and a daughter, whom they cherished.

Though shunned by the Egyptians, he gained approval from his tribe of Issachar for his wisdom in council and his adeptness at carrying out acts of resistance. Eventually he rose to become the tribe's leader at the age of twenty-eight, simply by assuming the position with tacit approval of the tribe.

Endnotes;

1. The recounting of Moses' meeting with God is told in chapters 3 and 4 of Exodus.
2. "Snake, leprous hand, Nile," Alfred Edersheim, *Bible History: Old Testament,* "The Exodus." 1949, pp. 50, 51.
3. "prophetess," Ex. 15:20.
4. "God of your fathers," Ex. 3:14-15.

Chapter 4

The Day of Reckoning

Armed with the support of the elders, yet harboring apprehension of Pharaoh's rejection, Moses and Aaron approached the palace gate.

"Who goes there and for what purpose?" challenged the guard, wearing the familiar orange and black.

Aaron responded boldly. "I am Aaron, spokesman for the Hebrew tribe of Levi. I bring with me Moses, a man from Midian, with news from the east for the highly esteemed Pharaoh."

"Wait here," the guard ordered.

Pharaoh was puzzled at the news.[1] "I have heard once of the eloquent Aaron, one of the Israelites. But Moses? Many years ago there was a Moses in my grandfather's court, I believe. Is he an old man?"

"Yes, but lively," said the guard. "He says he has come from Midian and promises important news for you from that land."

"Bring them in—and remain with us." The guard bowed and departed.

Moses and Aaron gazed in awe at the grandeur of the palace as they were marched through the gate to the courtyard and into the Great Hall, its high ceiling supported by six marble columns equally spaced around its perimeter and one in the center. A line of six gray sepulchers stood in the rear of the hall. At the front, eight rows of benches faced a slightly elevated wide platform. A black-armed throne, padded in the familiar burnt-orange fabric, was on the center of the platform; to its left, a rostrum hung with a delicately embroidered cloth, and to its right, a small table holding a purple vase. A slender female attendant, decked with gold and copper bracelets, anklets, and necklaces, poured liquid into the vase. A large ornate tapestry of men in battle hung behind the throne. Moses was familiar with the halls and rooms, but not its furnishings. "Who produces this artwork?" he asked the guard.

"Most is by our Egyptian craftsmen," he answered. "But the more talented Hebrew slaves have also been trained to make them."

Moses remembered the favored slaves of his time, but was anxious for current information. "What skills have the slaves acquired?" he asked.

"Some of the more clever ones have learned to do all sorts of work as carpenters, potters, stonemasons, metalsmiths, and jewelers. Some even design the patterns. Pharaoh uses them well to keep our nation proud and prosperous. Come, Pharaoh waits."

Moses wondered if indeed all slaves yearned for freedom. "Are the craftsmen treated better than the slaves?" he asked.

The guard laughed. "Pharaoh is wise; he has a soft hand toward the artisans."

He ushered them through a doorway and into the library. The highly polished dark wooden floor of the library, covered with an exquisite Eastern rug, caught Moses' attention. He halted momentarily as memories washed over him. As a youth, his surroundings were taken for granted and had seemed important to him, but in the intervening years, his simple lifestyle and the dominant importance of his family had eroded their value. Still, they were magnificent. And now he had returned. Apprehensively, silently, he wondered, *Will I be welcome? Was the murder truly forgotten? God, prove Yourself again!*

Pharaoh sat in a raised black velvet chair at the far end of the carpet. As they approached, Moses glanced at the ornate fabric coverings on three walls and the dark, wooden shelves filled with scrolls on the fourth. Limestone pedestals bearing busts of winged gods and warriors were evenly spaced about the periphery of the room. Light was admitted from windows on one side of the room.

The brothers came forward and dropped to their knees.

"Oh, great Pharaoh, I present to you Aaron and Moses," the guard announced.

"You may stand," said Pharaoh. "Moses, I have heard of you— occasional whispers, rumors when I was young. You would have known my father, the crown prince when you were here, and my grandparents, the pharaoh of your time. For years, it was forbidden to speak your name within these walls after you left. I myself bear you no ill will, having no interest in pursuing the reasons for your departure." Then, curtly, "Now what news do you bring? I am quite busy."

In the lavish surroundings, Moses felt humbled. He bowed again and spoke self-consciously. "I have been sent to speak on behalf of the Israelite slaves. This is what the LORD, the God of Israel says, *'Let my people go that they may celebrate a feast to Me in the wilderness'*" (Ex. 5:1).

"What kind of strange news is that?" parried a surprised Pharaoh. "Who is this lord that I should obey him? * I do not know him. And let the slaves go anywhere? Ha!" he laughed. "You fools have bizarre ideas." Then slowly, scornfully, he said, "Who are you to bother me with such a request?"

"The God of the Hebrews has met with us!" Moses replied. He paused, but Pharaoh was unmoved. Then Moses pleaded, "Please let us go a three days' journey into the wilderness that we may sacrifice to the LORD our God—" he hesitated, "lest He fall upon us all with pestilence or with the sword". *

"If I halfway believed this 'meeting with a god' tale, I would still not consider getting by without the slaves for even one day. Now leave!" barked Pharaoh.

The brief encounter was over.

Word of Moses' intervention spread among the Israelites. "Freedom is imminent; forget the bricks," the Hebrew slaves joyously said to one another. But a different order came from the enraged Pharaoh: "Maintain your quotas but—get your own straw!" * Moses' visit with Pharaoh had worsened their plight.

Having to forage for their own straw doubled the slaves' work and, as the production of bricks diminished, the Israelite foremen were beaten. Those men angrily confronted Moses and Aaron. "May the LORD look upon you and judge you, for Pharaoh and his servants will kill us." *

The brothers retreated to their home, dispirited by the reproach. Their resumed responsibility for the success of the mission burdened them. In the evening, as Moses walked alone outside, he raised his eyes heavenward and cried out. "God, why did you ever send me? I've only brought suffering and You have not delivered Your people at all". *

"Now you shall see what I will do to Pharaoh," answered the voice of God, *"for under compulsion, he shall let them go, and ... shall drive them out of his land"* (Ex. 6:1–2). Sensing Moses' discouragement, God stayed with him, reminding him that He had steadfastly been the God of Abraham and of his descendants, even while they suffered in Egypt. Moses' flagging spirits gradually lifted.

"I will deliver [the sons of Israel] *out of their bondage,"* God reconfirmed. *"I will also redeem* [them] *with an outstretched arm and with great judgments ... .I will be* [their] *God ... .I will bring* [them] *to the land which I swore to give to Abraham, Isaac and Jacob and I will give it to* [them] *for a possession; I am the LORD"* (Ex. 6:6–8).

Moses listened carefully, later relaying this conversation to the disillusioned leaders, who scoffed. "Get away from us, Moses; we do not listen to you anymore."

God soon reappeared to Moses, telling him to plead again with Pharaoh for his people. "I am proving to be unskilled in speech," Moses replied dejectedly.

God encouraged him: *"See, I make you as God to Pharaoh, and your brother Aaron shall be your prophet"* (Ex. 7:1). God explained that He would prevent Pharaoh from releasing the Hebrews so *"that I may multiply My signs and My wonders in the land of Egypt.... And the Egyptians shall know that I am the LORD"* (Ex. 7:3–5).

With renewed spirit, Moses and Aaron returned to Pharaoh. He grudgingly heard them in the presence of eight council members. The brothers again requested release of the slaves.

"If your God is so powerful, show me a miracle," said the pharaoh. At God's instruction, Aaron cast down his staff and it became a serpent. Not to be outdone, the court magicians threw down their staffs next to Aaron's and they were also transformed into serpents. Aaron watched in astonishment as his serpent swallowed up the others.

"I am not impressed by your little games," said Pharaoh with a sneer. His attendants quickly hustled the brothers out of the palace.

Perplexed, Aaron said, "Could Pharaoh not see that the powers of our Hebrew God far exceed the black powers of his court magicians? What will it take?"

"We must wait for God's next move," said Moses.

God soon disclosed to the brothers the next piece of his plan. Neither by war nor insurrection would He pry His people out of Egypt, but through a series of plagues—predicted, precise disasters—that would also show the Egyptians that the one true God was at work in their midst, seeking their recognition of His sovereignty.

It was early summer[2] and time for the first plague. God gave instructions to Moses and Aaron.

Pharaoh made the brothers wait another week before again admitting them to his chambers. "What is it that you want this time? I don't know why I keep allowing you in here," he said.

When permitted to speak, Moses said to Pharaoh, "God tells you to let His people go or He will turn all water in the land into blood."

"Are you trying to intimidate me?" Pharaoh retorted. "We are accustomed to seeing red-brown Nile waters every spring with the floods, without consequence. So what?"

"Tomorrow morning," asked Moses, "will you come to the Nile and see a miracle happen?"

"A miracle?" scoffed the pharaoh. "I will enjoy your embarrassment."

"Oh, God, help your servant not to fail," said Aaron as he raised his staff before the small gathered royal crowd on the banks of the Nile the next day. Then, when he obediently struck the Nile, all water above ground in Egypt—wide rivers, small streams, and pools—was changed suddenly into viscous blood.

The court magicians at the pharaoh's side, by trickery or by the sorcerous power manifest in them, also changed some water they had brought with them into what looked like blood. The relieved Pharaoh mounted his chariot. "I have no concern for this inconvenience," he said as he departed.

A generalized stench arose as all of the putrefying fish of Egypt, killed by the bloody liquid, floated on the waters. The people were forced to brave the rancid odors and dig down around the rivers to find potable water. After three days, God cleansed the waters.

When seven days had passed, God sent another message to Pharaoh through the brothers. "God warns that another plague will descend upon you and your people, one of frogs filling the land, if you still refuse to let the slaves go."

"Ha," said Pharaoh, "we are used to frogs, as they come up out of the Nile after the rains. Besides, they are representations of the gods to us."

"When God sends them, they will engulf you, and you will suffer," said Moses.

"Leave!" ordered Pharaoh.

Once again, Aaron was chosen by God, and when he lifted his staff toward the waters of the Nile, invading armies of slimy green frogs inundated the cities—each home, each living area, leaping seas of them everywhere. In the midst of the plague, one of Pharaoh's daughters composed a whimsical poem:

> Frogs dangle from my spoon of soup,
> squirming oil 'tween my feet in bed,
> powdered beasts from my flour bowl spring,
> under my cap they soil my head;
> carpets jerking green, squash as I step.
> Oh, oceans of toads, must I to thee be wed?

Although the court magicians were able to duplicate the feat with their powers on a small scale, Pharaoh finally called for Moses. "Entreat the LORD to remove the frogs and I will let the people go, that they may sacrifice to your god." *

Moses cried out to God, and the frogs died. They were shoveled out, piled in heaps, and the land became foul.[3] But Pharaoh again revoked his promise to Moses.

Several weeks passed before God said to Aaron, *"Stretch out your staff and strike the dust of the earth"* (Ex. 8:16).

As he did so, dust particles throughout Egypt were transformed into gnats, the air a heavy fog, creatures flying into eyes, crawling into ears, nostrils, and mouths of men and beasts, swarming on the skin, taxing the sanity of all.

"It's their god's act!" admitted the frustrated magicians, unable to vivify a single grain of dirt.

"Hmmmph," responded Pharaoh, trying to ignore these transient afflictions.

Days later, God dispelled the gnats.

God continued to torment Pharaoh with a succession of temporary plagues, each separated by a long enough period of time to allow Pharaoh serious cogitation.

Pharaoh had never known of a god who both warned of events and reliably executed them on time. And why should this god punish him? He provided well for his family, conscripted a strong army, and expanded the empire. The slaves had houses and he had improved their nutrition. And, if they only worked harder, they would not require discipline.

Why doesn't this god honor him and consult with him directly rather than through these underlings?

When the LORD next sent Moses and Aaron to Pharaoh, they bowed low, failing to kneel, and then confronted him. "God said, *'Let My people go that they may serve Me.* [If not], *I will send swarms of insects on you and on your servants and on your people … in order that you may know that I, the LORD, am in the midst of the land.'*" They added God's new dispatch: *"And I will put a division between my people and your people"* (Ex. 8:20–23).

"I cannot understand why I remain curious about and receptive to your visits," said Pharaoh. "Havoc is your ever-present companion, and Aaron's staff is my bane. No, the Hebrews must stay!"

The next day, God acted without using Aaron's staff, sending great swarms of biting, chewing insects, infesting the houses and laying waste the land, but this time, completely sparing the Israelites. Moses was summoned to Pharaoh, who spat out his orders. "Go, you and your people, and sacrifice to your god. But do not leave Rameses."

"If we sacrifice animals here, the Egyptians—who consider them sacred—will attack us," said Moses. "We must go a three-day journey into the wilderness and sacrifice to the LORD our God as He commands us."*

"All right, if you can manage to dispel these horrible insects. But do not go far away."

Obtaining the promise he sought, Moses fell to his knees for the first time and prayed to God. The insects vanished—but once again the crafty Pharaoh revoked his promise.

Two weeks later, the Egyptians began their planting season of barley and wheat.

Days broiled on and the Israelites continued to struggle under their taskmasters. After five more weeks had passed, Moses, with increasing trust in God's power, boldly carried a new communication into Pharaoh's library one morning. He warned him that God would send a fifth plague of death that would attack every animal left out in the field if the Hebrews were not freed. Pharaoh was irritated by the message but not enough to make him yield. Except for the fish kill, the plagues had been mainly nuisances. His attendants, however, spread the warning quickly to the populace.

On the next day, God's punishment of this oppressive ruler's nation suddenly intensified. Every Egyptian cow, horse, donkey, camel, sheep, and goat that was left outside, unprotected by their doubting owners, developed rigors, sapping fevers, seizures, and breathlessness. They then collapsed to the ground and died, while the Hebrew animals grazed peacefully. When this plague finally ended, it left in its wake the destruction of much of the Egyptian milk and meat supply. The pharaoh countered by confiscating many of the smaller Israelite herds to partially satisfy his needs and those of his people.

"Pharaoh, my God has more agony in store for you if you remain stubborn. Let the people go," warned Moses a month later, as he and Aaron stood again before Pharaoh, omitting the bow.

"I loathe you and the mounting burdens our nation must bear because of you and your insane requests," Pharaoh fumed from his throne. "If you control this vexatious god, stop Him! You are gradually destroying us. But greater disaster would occur if I release the slaves. My answer is still *no!*"

On this occasion, God chose Moses to execute the plague. He invited Pharaoh outside, and then walked to a kiln, gathered handfuls of soot, and threw them into the air. Painful pus-filled boils broke out on all of the Egyptian people and their animals throughout the land, the innocent as well as the flagrant persecutors—but the Israelites were again spared.

"My magicians! Where are my magicians?" called Pharaoh. "You and your ruthless god have jeopardized the health of my people. Have you no pity?" His magicians gave no answer, for they had retreated into their own wounds.

More than a month later, long after the sores of the last plague had subsided, God prompted Moses to rise up early and meet Pharaoh and his aides at the river where he bathed.

Moses said to Pharaoh, "God has told me that He could have easily killed all Egyptians with pestilence, but He has allowed them to live to witness that there is no power like His in all the earth, so that His name may be proclaimed everywhere. Can't you understand?" Moses pleaded, touched with pity, "He wants you to know Him, Pharaoh. Abandon the gods you worship, your fertility gods, the gods of the skies, nature, war, and more, so that all people may worship Him as the only God. If you do not heed me, a greater disaster for your people is even at this time in the offing."

"Give up my gods?" Pharaoh shouted. "You suggest that I turn my back on the ancient gods who give us life, who sustain us, who provide wealth and power? It is you who must give up your god. Do you dare think that I—a god by birth, a god by reputation, experience, and by my own wisdom—should give credence to this … this evil power? Your mind deserts you, Moses. And these plagues you usher in have become lethal weapons cast wantonly from your staffs," Pharaoh replied with anger. "Don't you think you have afflicted us enough?"

"Were it but mine to control," said Moses solemnly. "Now behold, tomorrow He sends another plague of hail, and all people must seek shelter, along with their remaining livestock. Those who do not will die."

"Leave," commanded Pharaoh.

Moses grieved in frustration, regretting his impotent role as but a harbinger of harrowing hail. The announced ordeals were inevitable and his pleadings with Pharaoh were worthless by divine decree, as God Himself hardened Pharaoh's heart.[4] What could he do for the innocent? In anguish, Moses briskly walked the roads all day and into the night, spreading the warning, shouting to those who would listen, "Drive your animals into barns! Seek shelter! Death is on the way!" Those heeding the word brought their slaves and livestock inside and spread the word to others. In the morning light, Moses stumbled home.

The sky blackened and winds roared through the land, vanguards of a great storm. The people leaned into it, running for cover.

"Stay inside!" wailed the fortunate.

In moments, bolts of lightning and fire exploded out of heaven; large hailstones struck every ripe plant and shattered every tree of the field. All the exposed and their innocent animals were killed, while the storm parted around the Israelite dwellings and fields. After two hours, the winds calmed and the sky lightened.

Pharaoh was deeply embroiled in these disasters. His dwindling grain stores could barely satisfy a restless nation, hungry from loss of the vegetable and barley harvests, all destroyed by the hailstorm. Desperately, Pharaoh promised relief to his people, since a bumper crop of wheat would ripen in five weeks.

There was quiet in Egypt for awhile. Moses continued his pose as a stranger befriended by Aaron. He had little interchange with Miriam, a satisfactory arrangement with her, since sight of him often reminded her of the past. She was proud that her reputation had put her in the household of the princess, allowing her to save her brother's life and secure the temporary bond between her mother and the baby. In the palace, she had learned to play the timbrel and lyre and become a skilled seamstress, devoting hours to entertaining the child and making clothes for him. Although their mother was barred from the palace by the fearful Pharaoh when Moses was three years old, Miriam stayed on. As Moses grew, her pleasure gradually turned into a deep-seated resentment of the unwarranted advantages he enjoyed and of his ignorance of her crucial role in obtaining them. After Moses fled Egypt, palace life no longer held her interest and she returned to her people.

One afternoon, God's voice came clearly to Moses. It was time to visit the pharaoh again. "Yes, God, and the message?" Moses asked.

God said to him, *"Go to Pharaoh, for I have hardened his heart and the heart of his servants, that I may perform these signs of Mine among them. Thus says the* LORD, *the God of the Hebrews, 'How long will you refuse to humble yourself before Me? Let My people go that they may serve me. For if you refuse to let my people go, behold tomorrow I will bring locusts into your territory. And they shall cover the surface of the land ... [to] eat the rest of what has escaped ... from the hail ... every tree that sprouts .... Then your houses shall be filled and the houses of all your servants ... something which neither your fathers nor your grandfathers have seen ... until this day'"* (Ex. 10:1–6).

Then God emphasized his enduring motives: *"That you may tell in the hearing of your son and of your grandson how I made a mockery of the Egyptians and how I performed My signs among them; that you may know that I am the* LORD" (Ex. 10:2).

Moses and Aaron were ushered into the Great Hall.

"I had not heard from you for quite a while," Pharaoh began. His hard-soled sandal heels clicked on the floor as he paced before the throne. "I was hoping that perhaps the hail had brought an end to your visits and, with good fortune, your lives as well. What do you want now?"

When Moses advised him curtly of God's threat that locusts would destroy anything green, including the late-ripening wheat, Pharaoh's advisors pleaded with him, "Let the slaves go; do you not realize that Egypt is destroyed?" *

"All right, go," said Pharaoh to Moses, "but, who are the ones that are going?" *

"All go, young and old, and our flocks and our herds," insisted Moses.

"The young must stay," said Pharaoh. God had bolstered Pharaoh's defiance, having determined that His entire course of punishment must be completed.

"All or none," said Moses resolutely. "Otherwise, we shall all stay to observe what God will do next to you and your people."

"Who are you to threaten my empire? Get out of my courts! Guards, throw them into the street."

"Moses, stretch out your hand over the land of Egypt" (Ex. 10:12), God commanded. As he did so an east wind blew in, carrying clouds of voracious locusts and grasshoppers. Soon nothing green was left, and the entire anticipated life-preserving wheat crop was decimated, except in the spared Hebrew fields.

"I have sinned against the LORD, your God, and you," * admitted Pharaoh the next day. "Remove this death from me."

Moses agreed, went outside, and raised his staff again. For many hours, a strong west wind took up the locusts and drove them into the Red Sea.

Then Pharaoh sent word to Moses that the slaves would not be allowed to leave.

The ninth plague arrived unannounced. *"Stretch out your hand toward the sky, Moses"* (Ex. 10:22), said God. Complete and terrifying darkness covered the land for seventy-two hours, a darkness which was felt.[5] No Egyptian stirred from his house, while God amazingly provided light for the Israelite dwellings in Goshen. As light gradually returned to the Egyptians, Pharaoh, agitated at his slipping command over his exploited empire, ordered Moses to court.

"Moses," the pharaoh announced, "I must have some kind of accord with this vengeful God of yours. He manipulates not just water, earth, and the heavens, but also dispatches the creatures of the water, earth, and the air to inflict his plagues as he wills. Yet, how he protects the slaves!" He took a step toward Moses. "If I permit them to go, will he leave us alone?"

Moses was silent.

"Yes, go, but since our animals have been slaughtered, leave your flocks and herds behind."

Moses countered confidently, "Not a hoof will be left behind, because until we get out into the wilderness, we ourselves do not know with what we shall serve the LORD. * We are like a feather in His wind."

"Then stay!" Pharaoh said. "Now, get away from me! Be sure that I do not see your face again or you will die."

The end of winter arrived, marking more than ten months of the intermittent plagues.[6] Moses sat down to eat the morning meal with Aaron. "Brother, God spoke to me again last night," said an intent Moses.

"Whenever He does, I know that trouble is coming," observed Aaron with a shake of his head.

"Yes. But after that, God has said, Pharaoh will not just let us go but will surely drive us out from Egypt completely." Each visit from God seemed to energize Moses.

"What will He do?" Aaron asked.

"I don't know yet, but we will not leave empty-handed. It may sound absurd, but we are to tell each Israelite to ask his Egyptian neighbors for articles of silver and of gold and of clothing as a free gift. I can't imagine that they will comply, but seemingly God can bring about anything He wishes."

"Would He transform me into the pharaoh?" mused Aaron.

The Hebrews hesitantly but obediently solicited their neighbors and were surprised because once again God changed the hearts of those who oppressed His people. The Egyptians looked with favor on their slaves and gave generously of their riches, including gold and silver jewelry, dishes, and bowls. Even Moses, the perpetual deliverer of bad news and the archenemy of Pharaoh, had risen to be "greatly esteemed in the land of Egypt."[7]

God's voice came to the brothers that same day with details about the coming plague—a scourge of death to all Egyptian firstborn males.

In a flash of illumination, Moses understood what God had told him at the burning bush: *"Because Pharaoh would not let my first-born go,"* referring to the Israelites, *"I will kill his first-born"* (Ex. 4:22–23).

But first, God added, a feast must be celebrated. The Israelites must mark that day as the first day of the first month of the year henceforth and, on the tenth day of that month, each family, or two families together if they are poor, must select an unblemished lamb or goat and care for it.

Then on the morning of the fourteenth, every home must be cleansed of all leaven. All bread made during the following week will thus be unraised, unleavened; and the week should be celebrated as the Feast of Unleavened Bread because God said, *"On this very day, I brought your hosts out of the land of Egypt"* (Ex. 12:17).

At twilight on that fourteenth day, they were to slaughter their lambs by bleeding, being careful not to break any of their bones, and were to collect the blood and paint some of it on their doorposts and lintels to signal God to pass over them later that night. They would then roast the lamb and eat all of it, garnished with bitter herbs;[8] whatever meat was left over must be incinerated by the next morning. They must do this while dressed and prepared for travel, with loins girded, wearing sandals, and with staff in hand.

Moses summoned the elders and informed them of God's plan.

"We will hold a feast to celebrate the coming of a plague, indeed the worst one?" asked one elder. "We have never done that before. Are we so crass?"

"We are to celebrate God's protective and liberating power over us," replied Moses. "It is a wise plan, and He seems assured of its success."

On the morning of the fourteenth day, Moses and Aaron arrived at the palace and were ushered in. The chief servant met them. "Oh, great Moses," he cried, "bring no more sadness to our master. He is no longer himself. We cringe at his anger. Sometimes he speaks in riddles. Dinner trays return hardly touched. Some days, he scarcely moves from his room, yet his sandals scuff the marble halls in the depths of night."

"I grieve for you all," said Moses, "but greater sorrow comes tonight, this time in the form of a death that you cannot escape. Now, please let me see him."

With wide, red eyes, a rumpled cloak over his unbuttoned shirt, and only a single sandal, Pharaoh met Moses.

"Bring me good news. How can I hate yet," Pharaoh said, voicing God's implanted perception, "respect you as you burden us with evil? Haven't you something better to do than to plead for the lowly, mindless slaves?"

"No, Pharaoh, I haven't," Moses paused. "But now, your time has arrived. There will be no more frogs, insects, darkness, disease, or hail to do God's work. Tonight at midnight, He Himself will come to kill all firstborn. A loud wailing cry will be heard throughout the land such as there has not been heard before and such as shall never be again. Your precious gods will be destroyed." His voice rose as he said, "And yet, O Pharaoh, against any of the sons of Israel, 'a dog shall not even bark.'[9] Then your servants will call to us and insist that we leave." Trying to control his frustration, Moses added, "Pharaoh, O Pharaoh, what a great calamity you have brought upon Egypt!"

"Get out, get out! I'll decide—tomorrow," said Pharaoh.

"It's too late! God help you for what you and your people have done!" Moses stormed out of the palace and walked down the street, filled with the same uncontrollable anger as on the day he had murdered the Egyptian guard forty years earlier.

As evening approached, the fearfully apprehensive Israelites reasoned among themselves. "Moses' predictions have been accurate, so we must do what he says. The stakes are enormous. So smear plenty of blood on the doorposts so that God, if He does come, will be sure to see it."

They roasted their lambs, and later that night, obediently dressed for travel, ate the meat and herbs while waiting—anxiously waiting. At midnight, God struck, accompanied by a band of destroying angels,[10] visiting their terror house by house, field by field. Death vacuumed the breath from her selected Egyptian victims, as every firstborn died, from the house of Pharaoh to the smelly dungeons, including the firstborn of all animals. There was no home where there was not someone dead.[11]

God executed His vengeance against all the gods of Egypt, pulverizing every one of their statues and idols and destroying their places of worship. "There is only one God," the devastation cried out, one God whose long-standing chastening of the Egyptians abruptly escalated that black night. But on that night, even His consuming wrath was overshadowed by His pure protective love for the unscathed Israelites. "Remember this Passover, remember."

An hour before dawn, Pharaoh hastily summoned Moses and Aaron. As they walked toward the palace, cries from the sobbing Egyptians filled their ears. "Go quickly," one called to them, "before we are all killed."

The brothers were brought into the library, where a barefooted Pharaoh sat on the floor, leaning against his chair, defeated yet tearless as his oldest son lay dead on the rug near his feet. His sleepless eyes stared through them as he said, "Rise up, get out from among my people, both you and the sons of Israel; and go, worship the LORD as you have said. Take both your flocks and your herds as you have said and go." Then Pharaoh pitiably held out his hands and begged, "Bless me also," * but received no answer.

Moses and Aaron hurried into the night and to their homes, collected Elisheba and Miriam, and alerted Aaron's sons. They gathered their small bags of belongings and bags of food before hastening toward the city gates. News of Pharaoh's order spread rapidly, shouted from house to house, and thousands of Israelites streamed out of their homes and fell in behind Moses and Aaron. Most of them, reveling in their release from slavery, strode pridefully and defiantly[12] in victory, contemptuous of the state of their stricken masters. They carried with them all of their recently acquired silver and gold, as well as swords, bows, and arrows. Another promise of God to Abraham had come to fruition: that when His people left the foreign land, they would come out with many possessions.[13]

Accompanying the Israelites were a mixed multitude of people from Egypt and other lands, some disenchanted, others disenfranchised, and a number who chose to leave their homes to follow this powerful God.

As the suddenly emancipated masses jubilantly surged forward, many singing and chanting familiar ballads of long-coveted freedom and shouting to Moses words of praise and thanksgiving, two men accosted Moses.

The first to speak was Javell, of the tribe of Dan, a talented lyre player in Pharaoh's court. His cold eyes looked at Moses accusingly from behind long lashes.

"Moses, I swear by the gods that you will regret what you have done to our families, you and your foolish mission! We are being disgorged, the vomit of the Egyptians, dispatched as refugees. The home that I built was not luxurious, but it was decent. My family lived an adequate life with plenty of good food. We were safe. And now you have driven us out toward the desert with only what we can strap on our cow. I would not want to be in your shoes if anything goes wrong."

His fellow tribesman, the large-chested Hasor, panted from walking briskly to catch up. "You have greatly troubled us, Moses," he huffed. "The gold and silver given us by our neighbors do not make up for what we left behind. I am a metalsmith. What is to build out here? Man, do you know what you are doing?"

Nahshon, a plump jeweler and leader of the tribe of Judah, dressed in his hallmark white robe, was walking near Moses and overheard the remarks. "Moses, you warned us that to be free, we must travel to the land of Canaan, which you described as a near-paradise. Surely, we welcome freedom, but I am hesitant to go there. I know from the stories our historian

Abidan relates that Noah angrily swore that his grandson, Canaan, would live under a curse. Later, father Abraham forbade his son Isaac from marrying a Canaanite woman. Isaac barred his sons Jacob and Esau from similar entanglements. Abidan hints that the Canaanites have become a highly contaminated, poisonous people."

Moses tried to defend the goal. "God says that Canaan is a good place for us, the land and its fruits, if not its people. I realize that, for some of you, this departure represents a very difficult change, but see what miracles have already occurred—we are a chosen people in the tenacious hands of the living God.[14] Trust that He will take us there safely and that the land and our new freedom will be worth the trip."

Javell grumbled. "We seem to have no choice now but to go with you. Don't you and your God let us down."

"Canaan may prove too great a task even for your God," said Nahshon as he lagged back from the striding Moses.

Nahshon

Nahshon the jeweler was born into the tribe of Judah. His father, a soldier, had been killed in battle when the boy was ten years old. As the oldest son, Nahshon soon began working, gathering straw for the brickyards. One day, as he walked past the jewelry shop in Rameses, he found a tiny fragment of an opal on the ground, and holding it up, was fascinated by the colors as light bent through it. He looked into the shop window and was dazzled by the colors of the lapis lazuli and jasper stones he saw there. He spoke with the benevolent jeweler and was soon invited to observe his skills. On Nahshon's rare days off, he visited the shop and his new friend.

He treasured the dust of the fashioned gold and bronze and the minute discarded chips of fitted stones. When he came into the shop one day and proudly showed a narrow ring of bronze with a rosette of tiny fragments of stones, the jeweler recognized his talent and invited him to become his assistant. The foreman of the straw gatherers grudgingly approved, and when the jeweler died after twenty-three years, Nahshon, though still a slave, was appointed chief jeweler of that shop.

He stood tall and totally straight like a spear, an anomaly among the browbeaten slaves, a posture that gave him a regal bearing. Coupled with an innate shrewdness from his youth, he often found himself in minor positions of Hebrew authority, and was eventually elected the prince, or leader, of Judah, the largest Hebrew tribe.

His external confidence hid an inchoate anxiety that plagued him with bouts of insomnia and periodic insatiable gluttony— causing him to buy a series of progressively longer belts. His insecurity was tempered by his physical appearance, his wily dealings with Egyptians and fellow Israelites, and by a modest cache of cuttings and stone chips pilfered from the shop over the years. He wore a long white robe with a white, square, flat headpiece, gifts given out of respect by his peers. Convinced of his own wisdom, he enjoyed authority and grew publicly stubborn and self-important, though privately more subdued by a wise wife.

In truth, he was more tin than bronze.

The Israelites were all suddenly uprooted, and even the hesitant departed. They walked to freedom past the torrents of tears of the heartbroken Egyptians. They drove their healthy herds down roads of despair, past barns and fields littered with carcasses of less fortunate animals, as they left the city and headed southeast.

The time that the sons of Israel lived in Egypt was 430 years—to the very day.[15]

When word of Pharaoh's decision reached the similarly devastated city of Pithom and other smaller towns, their Israelite slaves were also freed. The throngs from the cities met and made their first camp at the town of Succoth. Celebration was blended with apprehension; sleep was fretful for many. The next morning, still reeling from the sudden change in their status and their destiny, the tribal leaders heard Moses relate new directives from God. Because their firstborn had been spared last night, in the future, all Hebrews must sanctify to God every firstborn,[16] both of man and beast, for they belong to Him. The firstborn animals were to be sacrificed on an altar, while each firstborn son of Israel must serve God and be redeemed for five shekels.

God told Moses that He despised the triumphant, haughty attitude of many Israelites as they had walked away from the Passover devastation. He decreed that a Passover feast must be observed every year in remembrance of His liberation and that it must be celebrated with pious and humble thanksgiving.

God also permitted two other groups of men to celebrate Passover, each having received the irrevocable brand of a believer in God by being circumcised—first, the Hebrews' male slaves (for Hebrews could have their own slaves, indentured for unpaid debts) and the second, the non-Hebrew sojourners who had lived with them continually. In order to celebrate Passover, a sojourner first must convince all male members of his family to be circumcised. Errors that had occurred during the first Passover were not to be repeated.

Three women of the tribe of Benjamin were baking bread in a small oven on that first morning at Succoth.

"Didn't anyone bring dough that rose overnight? All bread that leaves these fires today is flat," observed Ruth, the heavyset eldest, a mother of four. "It is cursed by this God, just as the Egyptians were last night. I feel sad. How often I had wished, even prayed, that those who mistreated us would suffer as we have. But for the last few weeks, we have been almost respected. A demanding Egyptian lady I worked for suddenly gave us gold and silver items and silks. I tried to forgive her previous abuse, and truly, I began to enjoy her company. Then her fine son Gorin, who secretly liked our daughter Lethra, died suddenly last night, as did his father. I wept last night, a few tears of joy for us yet more of sorrow for them. But of what use are my tears? They won't even raise any of this bread."

"As soon as Moses' message came," said Shum, the young, dark wife of a laborer, "we moved quickly. I didn't think about the Egyptians; I was just glad to get out." She paused. "As for the dough I brought along, I cannot remember if I seeded it or not. I did bring the leaven batch with me."

Slender Chaletra fondled her recently acquired dangling gold earrings. "I was too busy yesterday to prepare dough for the trip. I also feel guilt; so many Egyptians had to die for our freedom. God must have a great mission for us."

Ruth said, "God told us to eat only unleavened bread for this week. We will—but it is not because we were obedient; we just forgot the leaven or were too rushed. He seems to have satisfied His requirements in His own way."

"Ha!" chimed in Shum. "He expected us to rid our homes of all leaven yesterday morning. What a waste. Once I left a batch of dough outside for a whole week before the gods put the leavening agent into it. I sold some of it for a nice profit. But Moses insists that we are to burn it or to crumble it and throw it to the wind.[17] If I did that, how could I replenish my supply?"

"Buy some from a gentile pagan among us," said Chaletra, "or else leave your dough outside and wait. Today my husband warned me that we must never break this law again; leaven represents imperfection to this God."

"So we shall," Ruth acknowledged, "at least for a while."

Endnotes
1. The encounters with Pharaoh are told in Exodus, chapters 5 to 11.
2. "early summer," Alfred Edersheim, *Bible History: Old Testament*, "The Exodus." 1949, p. 70.
3. "piled in heaps," Ex. 8:13.
4. "hardened Pharaoh's heart," Ex. 9:12.
5. "a darkness which was felt," Ex. 10:21.
6. "ten months," Alfred Edersheim, *Bible History: Old Testament*, "The Exodus." 1949, p. 70.
7. "greatly esteemed," Ex. 11:3.
8. "bitter herbs," Ex. 12:8.
9. "a dog shall not even bark," Ex. 11:6-7.
10. "band of destroying angels," Ps. 78:49.
11. "there was no home," Ex. 12:30.
12. "defiantly," Ex. 14:8 RSV.
13. "with many possessions," Ex. 15:14.
14. "hands of the living God," Heb. 10:31.
15. "430 years," Ex. 12:14.
16. "first born," Ex. 13:2f.
17. "burn leaven or crumble it," Jacob_Neuser, *The Mishnah, A New Translation*. "Pesahin 2:1, 2, 3," 1988, p.232.

Chapter 5

Slaughtering Their Enemies, Gaining Their Trust

After several days of rest at Succoth, Moses and Aaron led the horde of people, numerous as the stars of heaven,[1] in their march eastward.[2] They were assisted by the leaders of the thirteen tribes, who quickly organized the crowd with their animals into a marching order, preventing a confused flight. Safely in the midst of the crowd were two honored Israelites, selected by Moses, to carry a purple-draped chest. It contained the bones of Joseph, satisfying a pledge made by his sons to have his remains returned to his homeland for proper burial when at last they migrated to Canaan.

As evening approached, a moving, whirling white pillar of cloud[3] suddenly appeared before Moses. Hearing God's voice from the cloud, Moses was startled, realizing that God had amazingly materialized, wrapping Himself in that vapor and transforming His purely verbal captaincy into a visible one. The cloud was just one more marvel to the people who followed as it preceded them to Etham, their next campsite. Thereafter, the cloud led them each day, becoming a pillar of fire[4] by night, to allow travel after dark. The fire held vigil as they slept; the cloud reappeared as the Israelites awakened.

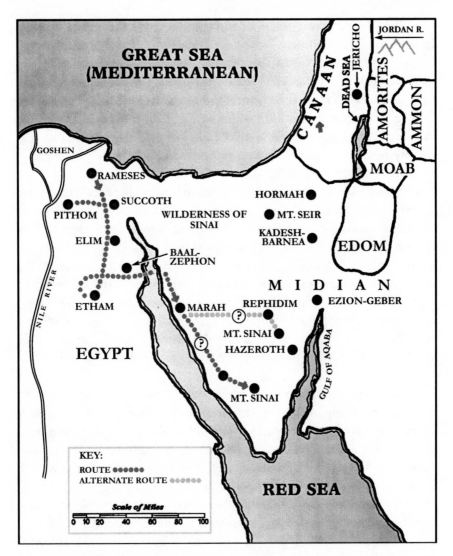

In the morning, the throng broke camp and the cloud led them southward. There was a vibrancy among them. Shouts of excitement and encouragement, mixed with occasional songs and chants, bounced from group to group.

Young Nethanel, the brickmaker, walked next to Moses. "Moses, why are you not leading us toward the early sun? We know now that Canaan lies there."

"True, but you also know of the tenuous truce that exists between Egypt and the Philistines. Troops are stationed at Egypt's northeastern border," said Moses. "God tells us that the southern route is safer."[5]

Overhearing them was the archer, Bershama, the slender leader of the tribe of Ephraim. He was in his mid-forties, as were most of the leaders. "I fought in the southern campaigns and still limp from an injury," he interjected, "but know little of the Philistines and the weapons of iron that we hear they possess. You are experienced in the east, Moses; tell us of them."

"Stories blow like the sands through the caravans of the Sinai," said Moses. "Many have I heard in the land of Midian where I lived, and their reliability may be no better than the camel-drivers themselves. I have learned that the Philistines originally lived in the islands of Caphtor[6] and Cyprus in the Great Sea. They developed a highly trained but restless army. Twenty years ago, they sailed northward to attack the armies of the Hittite empire[7], an empire that encompassed the land extending far beyond the northern shores of the Great Sea, a land rich in iron ore. The Hittites had developed a method of extracting the iron[8] and forging it into tools, weapons, and chariots, far stronger and more durable than the bronze ones of Egypt.

"God may have intervened in that battle,[9] providing the Philistines with victory. Many of the Hittites escaped into Canaan, where they live today. Four years ago, equipped with iron weapons, the Philistines invaded the Egyptian mainland,[10] driving back the army of Pharaoh's father, and occupying part of Egypt and lands farther to the east and north. We will skirt around that area on our way to Canaan."

"We may avoid the Philistines, but if we invade Canaan, we should have a relatively easy victory," said Abidan, emphasizing his point with a raised crooked index finger. "Remember the curse that the Canaanites live under?"

"I have heard of the curse. Tell us the d-d-d-details," stammered quick-speaking Pagiel, the painter, stroking his short black goatee.

"I'll tell you as I remember it," said the historian Abidan, proud of his knowledge. "Long ago, after Noah finally landed on dry ground, he planted a vineyard.[11] Later, he drank excessively of the nectar of the grapes, lay down naked in his tent, and fell asleep. One of his three sons, Ham, came upon him, stared at him with contempt, then brought his own son, Canaan, to similarly look at him with disrespect. Ham sought out his brothers to ridicule Noah. The brothers, however, were dismayed, went to their sleeping father, and covered him with a blanket. When Noah awoke and learned what Ham had done, he was filled with disgust. This son of his—one of only eight people in the world whom God had spared from the rising waters—was, he now realized, tainted. He swore a curse on Canaan that his descendants would eventually be slaves of their brothers." Abidan laughed as he reached down to rub a sore knee. "Perhaps we can bring that curse to fruition and make them our slaves also, eh?"

"That is not our mission," Moses sternly reminded them. "We are to organize an army and defeat the nation of Canaan, to kill or disperse them totally, and to occupy their land. In addition to the displaced Hittites, there are large communities from other nations that also live there, peoples descended from Canaan: the Amorites, the Hivites, and the Jebusites.[12] Fortunately, the Philistines, descendants of another of Ham's sons, the youngest and favored son, Mizraim,[13] have not moved into that area. With God's help, we shall be victorious."

Abidan

Because of diffuse arthritis beginning at age twelve, the Benjaminite Abidan had been excused from brick-making. The sun provided him with some relief from his joint pains and long hours outside had turned his skin the color of mahogany. In his mid-thirties, the inflammation and pain gradually subsided, leaving him misshapen hands with prominent, deformed knuckles, deviated fingers, bulbous knees, splayed feet, and gnarled toes. He walked without pain, but his gait was slow and choppy. At age forty-four, when he left Egypt with Moses, he was carried out on a donkey.

His mind dwarfed his misshapen body. Even as a child, he had sought answers for problems, some of which only he perceived. He was an incessant questioner of experts: those knowledgeable in architecture, medicine, politics, history, navigation, and even techniques of papyrus production. With his intense interest in the past and his physical limitations, he was assigned to the library, where he learned to read, becoming an avid historian, eventually committing large portions of the written Egyptian and oral Israelite history to memory. He was especially intrigued with the hidden mysteries of the hieroglyphs.

His disabilities developed in him a tenderhearted, empathetic concern for others, rejoicing with the fortunate as easily as he sought to lessen the burdens of the grieving. The community saw him as a totally selfless person, but, in truth, an intense need for approval drove his life. Rejection and criticism were received defensively. In his early years, failure to solve a problem or help others when he could was intolerable. As he matured, his actions remained the same, but a growing self-confidence changed his motives, and his kindness to others became more genuine. His clothes were often threadbare, worn as an example of his frugality.

Fortunately, his fun-loving wife kept the atmosphere light at home. She was physically suited to perform the heavy work of a household while rearing their four sons.

His compassion made him beloved by most, easing him into the role of the leader of the tribe of Benjamin. However, skeptical of others' motives, his trust in Moses would require day-to-day reinforcement.

God directed Moses to pitch two more camps before heading east toward the Red Sea. Having abandoned their accustomed, though compromised, life of slavery to follow God into the mysterious and unfamiliar desert, many Hebrews became anxious and fearful. Their conversations often were rebellious, many already wanting to desert this enforced march. God, observing them, became disturbed.

He had failed to win them over by His protections from the sufferings of the plagues. Certainly He could have altered their minds and turned them into obedient puppets—as He had with the Egyptians, parting with their wealth—but that was not His method with the Israelites. He zealously courted them, desiring His people to come to Him of their own free will.

Another miracle appeared to be necessary to deepen their trust in Him. So, assigning His angel to stay in the cloud and fire before the Israelites, God returned to Pharaoh to prick his soul.

Pharaoh was suddenly overwhelmed by the enormity of his decision. "What is this that we have done, that we have let Israel go from serving us?" * he exploded. "Half our population is gone! We have no one to do our work, to serve us." Energized out of his lethargy by his God-generated agitation, he called up his own chariot and rallied every available one in northern Egypt, including the six hundred select chariots of his army. "We must bring them back!" he declared. His soldiers and horsemen assembled for battle; in the morning, he would set out in pursuit.

That night, the Israelites pitched camp and rested a fifth time. Next afternoon, as they approached the Red Sea at Baal-Zephon, with the cloud before them, they saw behind them on the distant horizon chariots churning up a storm of sand and dust. Terrified, they realized Pharaoh and his armed legions were in pursuit. They were trapped; behind them was the army and in front of them was a wide, pounding sea, with no boats or barges in sight. Surely they would be slaughtered like animals or recaptured and marched back, beaten and humiliated.

They cried out. "God help us! God save us!" Hearing no reply, they turned on Moses. "Is it because there were no graves in Egypt that you have taken us away to die in the wilderness? Why have you dealt with us in this way?" With mounting anger, they reminded Moses, "Is this not the word we spoke to you in Egypt, saying 'Leave us alone that we may serve the Egyptians?' For it would have been better than to die in the wilderness." *

Moses raised his hands and shouted his message from God to the panicky Israelites. "Do not fear, stand firm and watch how the LORD will save you today. He will fight for you, and you have only to be still. The soldiers whom you see today, you shall never see again." * His voice lowered as the prattle of the crowd lessened. "Word of this battle will reach Egypt and, therefore, as God has said, *'The Egyptians will know that I am the LORD when I am honored'"* (Ex. 14:18). Then Moses added, "And perhaps even our trust will ripen as a result."

Moses separated himself from the crowd, his own fragile faith faltering, and he sought God for direction.

A disappointed God returned to him, chiding him, *"Why are you crying out to Me? Tell the sons of Israel to go forward. And as for you, lift up your staff and stretch out your hand over the sea and divide it and the sons of Israel shall go through the midst of the sea on dry land"* (Ex. 14:15–16).

The cloud pillar withdrew and settled behind them, expanding, and blanketing the Egyptians in heavy darkness. Pharaoh, riding in the lead chariot, ordered his legions to halt until daylight. Although he was becoming resigned to God's series of antagonistic miracles, he was perplexed by the sudden intrusion of the night and commanded his forces to simply, "Light torches and make camp." The troops hastily set up their tents and settled in.

Moses, meanwhile, enjoying God's favor and continuing sunlight, thrust his staff above the sea, generating wild winds from the east that wedged the waters and desiccated the sea's sodden floor as the people braced their backs against the blowing force. When the winds subsided, the Israelites and their livestock cautiously followed Moses and Aaron onto the sea bottom. Finding it firm, they began to cross between two widely separated, menacing walls of water. The threat of the pent-up water, restrained by an unseen fence, seemed less than that of Pharaoh's legions. While the Egyptians slept, the Hebrews descended the sloping floor to the center of the sea, a depth of five hundred feet and then climbed up the far side.

Dawn awakened Pharaoh from a fitful sleep. After a brief meal, he chose to mount his royal steed, feeling more in charge with the powerful horse beneath him. He led his army to the Red Sea shore, where they halted in astonishment. In the distance, the Israelites were walking between the parted waters. Driven into a rage by frustration, Pharaoh shouted to his commanders, "Follow them! Destroy them all! Don't let them get away! Our gods will protect you." When his army hesitated, he whipped his wide-eyed horse, causing it to rear on its hind legs and snort in fear. Pharaoh dug his heels into the animal until it shared Pharaoh's frenzy, and they recklessly bolted onto the wide expanse of the sea bed. His troops obediently followed, led by the phalanx of chariots, followed by the army of trotting, orderly soldiers. Once the entire army was committed, God released rivulets of water that moistened the sea floor, and their chariot wheels became clogged in a sodden, gooey mass. Horses' hooves pawed into the muck and, too late, the Egyptians discerned God's hand.

When the last Israelite climbed safely onto the opposite shore, Moses raised his staff again, removing the invisible dam. The released waters roiled and crashed down, drowning the enmeshed, screaming army. None survived. Even Pharaoh and his horse perished.

A number of the Israelites lined the shores, awed by the sight of corpses as they bobbed to the surface of the restored, white-capped waters. Women sobbed from a mixture of terror and relief; men stood in stunned silence; many of the adults embraced children. However, at a distance further inland, a greater number of people danced with joy, reveling at their rescue from the feared army.

Chaletra buried her face in her hands. Between sobs, she said, "I am so frightened—it could have been us at the bottom of the sea."

Ruth put an arm around her. "God acts with ferocious power, but He seems precise in His protection of us."

"It wasn't enough," said Chaletra, "to kill the firstborn but now, a whole army—drowned for us?"

"Remember the stories that we heard of Pharaoh's drowning the babies in the Nile?" Ruth reminded her. "This could be God's harsh retribution."

"Harsh? No, *ruthless* is a better word," said Shum. "But we are safe. One day surrounded, the next free. God destroys our enemies like the bloody Nile her fish."

Gratitude soon became the common emotion. Moses and the people composed a song to the LORD and sang it enthusiastically.

I will sing to the LORD for He is highly exalted.
The horse and its rider He has hurled into the sea.
The LORD is my strength and song,
And He has become my salvation;
This is my God and I will praise Him [and] … extol Him.
Thou dost send forth Thy burning anger, and it consumes them as chaff.
And at the blast of Thy nostrils, the waters were piled up.
The enemy said, 'I will pursue, I will overtake, I will divide the spoil;'
Thou didst blow with Thy wind, the sea covered them;
Who is like Thee, majestic in holiness,
Awesome in praises, working wonders?
The peoples have heard, they tremble;
Anguish has gripped the inhabitants of Philistia.
Then the chiefs of Edom will be dismayed;
The leaders of Moab; trembling grips them;
All the inhabitants of Canaan have melted away.
Terror and dread fall upon them;
Until the people pass over whom You have purchased.
Thou wilt bring them and plant them in the mountain of Thine inheritance,
The sanctuary, O LORD, which Thy hands have established.
The LORD will reign forever and ever.[14]

Miriam picked up a tambourine, waved it vigorously, and began to dance in a high-stepping march, calling on all of the women to join her. When she looked back at the throng of women who followed her, slapping other tambourines and singing, she was filled with pride. She climbed up on the bed of a small cart and led them as they repeated the words, "Sing to the LORD for He is highly exalted; the horse and the rider he has hurled into the sea."

They confidently understood that God would carry them, His special children, safely to Canaan. All they had to do was to watch Him perform His miracles.

The evidence pointed to this God as the most powerful of all gods, but not, however, the only god to be worshipped. They believed that other gods had also previously produced such events as drought, rain in its season, and the quieting of storms. Yet, the attraction of this tenacious, materialized God was compelling.

"We will trust You forever!" the Israelites said.

Really? wondered Moses.

The cloud floated southeastward, tracking the Red Sea down the coastal lowlands of the Sinai Peninsula. The Israelites followed day after day, resting only at night. One morning, the cloud ascended and turned east. The people, driving their livestock before them, climbed up the seven-hundred-foot slope that led onto a vast limestone and granite plateau. When Aaron, in the forefront with Moses, surveyed the expanse, he asked his brother, "Are you familiar with this area? Are we likely to encounter settlements along the way?"

Moses said, "Probably. I know of small villages and towns, some near the copper and tin mines."

"The area looks too dry for all of use to survive."

"I have been here twice, once even during an infrequent rainstorm. The water pours off this limestone and is carried away into long, sandy-bottomed wadis, some shallow, others quite deep, holding water even in dry seasons. We will probably pass by many of them. There are also natural springs scattered along the way that provide oases with grass for the animals."

"The heat here is stifling," complained Aaron, "and it is so quiet, except for the sounds of the people behind us. The occasional shriek of a distant bird[15] is so loud, it could be perched on my shoulder. I hope God knows where He is going."

"I believe He does."

Midway through the first day on the plateau, they came to a large, deep wadi with abundant water. Plants grew through the cracks in the rocks, and green and blue flowers and vines sprang from the earth. After a welcome refreshment, the caravan departed with bags full of water.

The cloud drifted to the east. A loose rectangle of marchers and animals followed, advancing across a long front up to fifty people abreast and extending several miles to the rear. They traveled with unaccustomed freedom, expecting no major problems as God's chosen, protected people. They remembered only the victory of the Red Sea and not their preceding panic. However, since a lasting trust in God needed adversity to grow, another time of testing approached.

Five days after leaving the wadi, the travelers' water stores ran out and they began to thirst. Finding another wadi, they eagerly knelt to drink, but instantly spat the water out.

"Moses, we are parched in this heat and now this water is foul-tasting," the people complained. "Have camels been here first?"

Nethanel shouldered his way through to the water, knelt, cupped his hands, and drank without showing his distress. "Though it is bitter, it at least quenches my thirst," he muttered. "Boil some, you who are so spoiled."

Several near Moses wailed pitifully. "Why have you led us here to suffer so?"

Moses shuddered when he too sipped the water. "They are complaining of thirst and the water is bitter," he moaned to God. "What shall they drink?"

God indicated to Moses a particular tree that would sweeten the waters.[16] Moses instructed two of the complainers to put an axe to the appointed tree, and as it toppled into the wadi, the water immediately became sweet and fresh. They drank their fill, convinced that they deserved it.

"Another miracle. How God loves us," they said.

Moses was dismayed at their response to the bitter water. "Do not displease God further with your complaining," Moses told them. "We have all personally witnessed His terrible anger while in Egypt. Let it not fall on us."

And, in truth, God was sorely disappointed with them and their grumbling. Had four hundred years of slavery produced a band of whiners rather than the trial-hardened, committed company He sought? The next day, He sternly warned them again through Moses. *"If you will give earnest heed to the voice of the* LORD *your God, and do what is right in His sight, and give ear to His commandments … I will put none of the diseases on you which I have put on the Egyptians"* (Ex. 15:26). The people listened attentively to Moses' words, words that explained their apparent resistance to certain diseases. After that exhortation, the cloud led them a half-day's journey to a large oasis called Elim. The people rejoiced, set up camp, and drank luxuriously from the cool, clear, fresh waters of twelve bubbling springs. Scattered over the oasis was a stand of seventy tall, stately date palms, their high palm fronds forming a canopy overhead to shade them from the hot sun. Young boys easily scaled the trees and returned with arms full of fruit savored by the travelers.

After resting a while, the caravan left Elim and continued eastward. Physically refreshed, their stores of water replenished, many of the people were enthusiastic, embarking with light-hearted joy. Others advanced with caution, realizing that God's blessings had become conditional, dependent upon their obedience.

Fifty-five days after leaving Rameses, and seventeen days after leaving Elim, they camped at Ahush, their food supplies exhausted. Four tribal leaders confronted Moses and Aaron on the people's behalf: the jeweler Nahshon, young Nethanel, Ahira of the tribe of Naphtali, and Shelumiel from Simeon.

Shelumiel spoke up first. "We are starving, Moses. We have rationed our food for several days, and now it is gone. The people are hungry and angry."

Nahshon, one hand in the pocket of his robe, added, "If the LORD wanted to kill us, why didn't He do it in Egypt, where we had pots of meat and bread to the full, rather than to let you lead us out in the wilderness to die of hunger?" *

Ahira, a military man, considered their stand and then interposed, "Moses, I believe I can see to it that the tribe of Naphtali will not falter or complain."

Moses sympathized. "Thank you, Ahira, but this is a problem we all share. I am as hungry as you, but have come to believe that God will not abandon us. Perhaps we are being tested again. Let me go away a distance and see if He will provide a solution."

"I suggest that you do," Shelumiel said. "By evening, the people may begin to slaughter their own animals, the stock we may need later."

As Moses and Aaron separated themselves from the others, God gave them a message for the people.

When the congregation had assembled, Moses stood before the Israelites. "The LORD told us that He is wearied by your complaining. He says that He will provide you with meat and bread but He will test you severely."

Even as Moses spoke, the attention of all was drawn to the desert, where they saw the familiar cloud rapidly approaching. But this time, its appearance was different. From its center shone a white light of such brilliance, they had to look away.

God called to Moses from the cloud. *"I have heard the grumblings of the sons of Israel; speak to them, saying, 'At twilight, you shall eat meat, and in the morning you shall be filled with bread and you shall know that I am the LORD your God'"* (Ex. 16:12). The glory of the LORD had come visibly to punctuate His message for the people. The cloud and its brilliance faded as swiftly as it had come.

Moses relayed this new message to the people, adding God's order to *"Gather a day's portion every day that I may test them, whether or not they will walk in My instruction. And it will come about on the sixth day, when they prepare what they bring in, it will be twice as much as they gather daily"* (Ex. 16:4–5). Shelumiel allowed himself a doubting chuckle as he considered this unlikely feast.

Shelumiel

Shelumiel, the carpenter, leader of the tribe of Simeon, had shiny black hair and a slender body as hard as the handle of his hammer. He wore sleeveless shirts that emphasized his taut muscles and a balled-up left biceps, like an egg in the midst of a rope. He was agile and strong, lifting and balancing heavy beams with relative ease. He was meticulous and skilled, able to create perfect, freehand mitered joints. Raised with eight siblings, he was devastated as a child by the deaths of the sister who was closest to him, and his mother, victims of the "blooded pneumonia." He retreated into a lifelong emotional shell to protect himself from further hurt, but remained sensitive and a keen listener. He was pragmatic and reserved in speech, though given to issuing occasional frank and sometimes caustic opinions.

He repeatedly resisted the normal infatuations with women until, at age thirty-three, he fell under the spell of a soft-spoken, bright, attractive and nurturing woman of twenty-two. She was the youngest of four and had lost her father in combat. Just being in her presence brought him great satisfaction, and—though searching for flaws as was his custom—he found no reason to avoid her. After two years, they were wed, a relationship he was to guard with an uncommon jealousy. A son and daughter were eventually born to them.

Perfection was his goal, and he expected no less from others. With the perseverance of a tiger, he gained great respect from his peers—becoming leader of the tribe of Simeon—but, eschewing emotional involvement with others, made few friends.

Early the next morning, Lashinar, a herdsman from the tribe of Manasseh, arose full of expectation. Departing his tent, he met fellow tribesman Sorin, the weaver.

Lashinar said, as his sandals kicked at the moist ground, "Moses promised us food but I see only heavy dew."

"Another ruse to keep us quiet," answered Sorin as they walked about, puzzled and discouraged. Others joined them in their fruitless hunt for the promised bread. They were about to give up their search, but as the dew evaporated in the warming sun, they noticed it left an unfamiliar residue. Lashinar bent over, scooped up a handful of it, and sniffed it. He gingerly put a little into his mouth.

Startled, he said, "Try some, Sorin! This white, odorless grain is not bad; it is somewhat tasty, almost like wafers and honey."[17]

"Yes, and the ground is thick with it," said Sorin, sharing Lashinar's excitement. "Get a bag and we will fill it."

Returning from their tents, they began to scoop it up. "Why such a large bag, Lashinar? We were told to gather only one day's worth each morning."

"Foolish Sorin! How sure are you that this will be here tomorrow? I will gather plenty for my family."

"My friend, you refuse again to obey. Testing God?" challenged Sorin. "I have all I need. I will see you again tomorrow—if you are still here."

Lashinar reached down for the final few handfuls, and then brought the bag into the cool of his tent.

"What have you there?" asked Coresha, his wife.

"Food from the sky, I suppose. We had to gather it from the ground," said Lashinar, as he poured a portion out into a large bowl.

Coresha allowed some to run through her fingers and then licked them. "Lashinar, what a surprise. It is fine and flaky and even tastes good raw. I will grind and bake some into cakes and boil another part of it. We shall have enough for a week for us and our daughter."

When she opened her bin the next morning, she reached for a cake then dropped it quickly. "Holy Sikkuth, it is crawling with slimy worms. Where did they come from? I baked it well."

"It's that God's doing," said Lashinar, and he carried the bin to the door and threw the remainder outside. But, looking down, there was a thick field of new white flakes as far as he could see. "Give me my bag, Coresha, I'll collect some before the heat of the day. And, to avoid God's slimy crawlers, only today's portion."

"Tomorrow is the Sabbath, and you are not to gather then. Should you not collect enough for two days?" she asked.

"One day at a time," he insisted.

The following morning, he and many others arrogantly defied God and carried their bags out, but found only grass on the ground.

God saw them searching about, and His growing frustration mounted. He challenged Moses. *"How long* [will these people] *refuse to keep My commandments and instructions?"* (Ex. 16:28). Moses relayed God's condemnation to the people.

There were some men, however, like Sorin, who were learning to trust God. On the Sabbath, they refrained from searching for their food, their *manna* they called it, a word meaning "what" or "what is this?"[18] The one-day's portion, baked the day before, miraculously doubled in size, providing enough for the Sabbath, and it did not become wormy.

God told Moses to keep a portion of the manna in a sealed jar to show to the coming generations the bread He fed them in the wilderness—and it would maintain its unchanging form in the jar thereafter.

That evening, a number of quail flew over, dropped into the camp, and were captured as God continued to woo the people, providing a welcome and bountiful addition for dinner.

Aaron assisted Moses in many ways, but Moses soon realized that he required extra help in his many duties, so he sought a person who trusted in God to carry his messages to the leaders and the people. The choice was an easy one, as he re-appointed his former assistant, Joshua, son of Nun, from the tribe of Ephraim, as his aide.

Joshua

When Moses fled Egypt, Joshua returned to his family. He joined the army as soon as he reached the age of twenty and was almost immediately sent south, where he fought in the successful campaigns against Nubia. Battle turned this meek, allegiant soldier into a canny, vicious, and tenacious fighter. However, his meekness returned after each engagement, when the fire within him would temporarily subside. He had been promoted twice, and four years previously, led a battalion against the invading Philistines. Although fighting courageously, his overmatched unit was driven back until the Philistines halted, having accomplished their goals to the south and west. When a peace treaty followed, Joshua remained in the army until God's liberation of the Israelites.

Moses appreciated this man who, at fifty-two, kept his body firm with self-imposed long marches. Joshua had a crooked, battle-damaged nose, long, red hair that was often windblown, and soft eyes that hid an inner passion. Those eyes missed nothing, and he methodically analyzed every impression from them. His learning was instinctual, gained more from life experiences than from the Hebrew teachings.

He shared the same reputation Moses had at that age—being God-respecting, honest, and intensely loyal to those men whom he held in esteem.

Joshua was assigned to walk next to Moses and Aaron in the lead when the cloud moved off to the east after their stay at Ahush. After several more stops along the way, in the third month after leaving Egypt, a series of mountains became visible beyond the plateau. As they progressed closer, they could see some very high, barren peaks that blended with lower mountain ranges stretching north to south as far as they could see, territory familiar to Moses.

"The Horeb Range," Moses pointed out to Joshua, "and the highest is Mount Sinai. The closest mountain is Rephidim. We shall make camp at its base, where there is a nearby oasis."

Joshua squinted his eyes. "We should reach it in about two days," he calculated. "It will be welcome because our water stores have about run out."

When they pitched camp that night, Moses paid a visit to Miriam's tent, concerned by her continual unexpected reticence whenever he was with her. "Miriam, how were you able to keep the secret of my birth?" he asked.

She sighed thoughtfully. "Pharaoh had three children when you were found: the one who adopted you, age eighteen, and two other daughters, three and two years old. I was aide to the oldest. She knew immediately that you were Hebrew, but prevailed on her doting father to let you live because she had been married three years and was barren. I asked her, 'Shall I go and call a nurse for you from the Hebrew women, that she may nurse the child for you?' She agreed and I returned with our mother. To add to the deception of your regal birth, we kept the princess sequestered for a few weeks. Her husband died several years later, Pharaoh's daughters forgot, so the only ones who remembered your real identity were the princess, her parents, and an aide, sworn to secrecy."

"That finally explains why grandfather arbitrarily appointed my younger cousin," said Moses, "ten years younger than I, to be the next crown prince. That was a source of great resentment to me then. I was to lead the army, he to follow his father as the next pharaoh.

"Miriam, life must have been difficult for you and the family when I was born and they had to hide me. Can you remember much of that time?"

"Yes, some of it," Miriam responded. "I was about twelve years old and already a prophetess. I stayed mostly in the palace but made occasional brief visits home. No one ever followed me or cared where I lived. Because of Pharaoh's edict to drown the male babies, no pregnancies were planned, although obviously some developed. When you were born, Mother and Father distrusted everyone except the midwives."

"Why were they trusted?" asked Moses.

"Before the decree, they had thwarted Pharaoh's previous order to kill every newborn male as it was being born, saying that Hebrew births were so vigorous and so fast that the babies arrived before the midwife could get there."[19]

Moses was intrigued. "Where did the midwives get such courage?"

"From God," she answered simply. "They feared and trusted Him. Births seemed easier with them present, and their deliveries, fortunately, produced a surprising predominance of females. The midwife would often arrive under cover of night and stay until the baby was delivered, all the while encouraging the parents to trust in God. Some parents were persuaded by their messages. While an occasional traitor divulged names of new parents to the Egyptians for money, a midwife could always be trusted to keep the secret.

"They would wait until dark to depart, and return eight days later if a circumcision was desired. Many families ignored the procedure, but since Mother and Father thought you would be sacrificed soon, they wanted to be sure that God would approve of you."

"Miriam, did you ever observe a drowning?" Moses asked.

"No, but during the months they hid you, Mother told me she walked to the river several times to see if any babies were being spared. She said there were always armed soldiers present to assure the drowning. She once saw a woman scream as she was forced to hold the head of her struggling month-old son underwater with one hand, pinioning his arms in front of him with the other until air bubbles ceased to surface. She saw a father, with his wife at his side, wade out into the water, cradling his trusting baby in one arm, holding a stone manacled by a piece of rope to the child's ankle in the other. Glances were exchanged between the parents before the father swung his arms to the right then hurled the silent child and the rock as far as he could into the Nile. The body struck the water then submerged, after thrashing for an instant. She saw a woman wrap a thin, worn, woolen shawl around a baby sucking at her breast, and walk out into the water, her legs struggling against the current. The baby sucked as its head disappeared beneath the water, then, choosing to share the watery grave, the mother exhaled and walked on, her head silently disappearing beneath the surface.

"Mother said it happened every day. Some babies were pushed out into that river on blankets or fragile rafts, or simply laid on cherished cloths to struggle and sink."

"And I was to have the same end?" asked Moses.

"Yes, until I helped to procure your survival."

"I owe you a debt I cannot repay, Miriam."

"Perhaps someday, you will be able to," she said.

"I will look forward to that opportunity," Moses said.

After a night's rest, the mass of people traveled toward the mountains. The morning sun bore down on them. Lashinar groaned, "Yesterday, my daughter suffered bites on her leg from a stinging scorpion. Today, the wound looks angry and red. I hate this infernal trip to—only God knows where."

"I am sorry about your Shenra, but if she is no worse than you say, she should recover. But don't complain," said Sorin. "You are not stomping in clay pits today, are you? And this God does not carry a cudgel in that cloud of his. Today my feet carry me in my own honor, buoyed above the ground by a God who provides all I need: food, water, and shelter for my family."

Lashinar answered wryly. "Come now, my martyr friend, tell me you do not miss that fruit, vegetables, garlic[20] and all of that tasty seafood! Do you prefer your own home, or the one you must carry on your back?"

"Lashinar," said Sorin, "the air is sweeter on this side of the sea, the ground softer, and the sun that sapped our strength in Egypt nourishes my soul now; even the cattle seem joyous. I'll trade fish and fruits for freedom any day."

"Don't you wonder what will happen if we run out of water or food or when your sandals wear out?"

"There are some of us who are willing to leave that up to God. Look ahead, we are to camp at the foot of the mountain tonight."

At Rephidim, a din of voices arose, punctuated by occasional shouted orders and the pounding of hammers, as the people set up their tenth campsite since leaving Rameses. Joshua dispatched scouts in different directions to locate the oasis, but the last ones returned two hours later, saying that no oasis existed. With parched throats, and urged by their complaining tribes, ten of the leaders approached Moses.

Nethanel said, "We speak on behalf of our tribes. There is no oasis, no wadi, no water at all anywhere around. Do something!"

Pagiel, the painter, staring bug-eyed, demanded, "Give us water that we may drink." *

Moses surveyed them carefully. "You have all come, except Gamaliel and Eliasaph. Where are they?"

"They thirst in silence," said the carpenter, Shelumiel. "They try to remind us that God has provided in the past and will do so again. That bit of rhetoric fails to moisten our lips."

"Why are you blaming me? The cloud brought us here. Trust Him if you can, but do not complain," snapped Moses.

However, with rising anger, they all blamed Moses. Bershama whined, "Why now have you brought us up from Egypt to kill us and our children and our livestock with thirst?" *

Peevishly, Abidan raised his gnarled hand. "Can't you get water from your god, who wants to be our principal god?"

Some men nearby, pushed to the limit by their thirst and feeling betrayed, gathered rocks in their callused hands and strode menacingly toward Moses.

Moses suddenly felt alone and cried out, "God, help me! What shall I do, for they seek to kill me?"

God answered him, *"Pass before the people and take with you some of the elders of Israel; and take in your hand your staff with which you struck the Nile, and go. Behold, I will stand before you there on the rock at Horeb; and you shall strike the rock and water will come out of it, that the people may drink"* (Ex. 17:5–6).

A rock: to the men a missile;
to Him, a fountain?

The cloud-pillar then hovered over a huge boulder at the base of the mountain, some distance away. While Moses and Aaron walked toward the stone, they sent Joshua back to summon the elders and leaders. They followed Joshua across a large field and gathered around the cloud-topped boulder. Moses raised his rod, and with growing confidence, struck the rock. To the surprise of the leaders, the rock split open at a seam, and cool, clear water gushed from it. The larger body of the Israelites, unable to see Moses' act, saw the gurgling stream and rushed headlong to it, gulping the fresh water to satisfy their thirst. When they discovered its origin, they stared at Moses, dumbfounded; many offered praise in recognition of his supernatural power. One man said Moses learned his trick from Pharaoh's magicians. All quenched their thirst and filled their water bags before watering their livestock.

The frail Javell spoke excitedly to his friend and fellow tribesman. "Hasor, I know that your breathing prevents you from walking distances, but I searched all about that large rock Moses struck—even around the hill behind it. There was no water on any side of it."

"It's a miracle, all right," said Hasor, "but why does this God wait until we are suffering so to satisfy us? Wouldn't it be much easier if He would anticipate our needs?"

"I agree," said Javell, "considering the long years in Egypt and these impositions of foul water, hunger, and now thirst. This God only acts when we are in dire need of Him. I don't understand."

"Maybe this is all part of the testing that Moses told us to expect," grumbled Hasor.

God was deeply disturbed by the Israelites' recurrent murmurings against Him and their failure to understand the trials He imposed. As their discontent increased, God's responses went from warnings to worms. But, when they threatened to stone His servant, He was incensed.

After resting a few days at their camp at Rephidim, the cloud moved out. The Israelites followed, marching toward the highest mountain on the distant horizon. At the end of the day's long march, the tribes were a long, confluent mass, with stragglers spread out in the rear. Suddenly, a host of men with horses and chariots, brandishing swords and axes, swooped down on the laggards in a vicious attack, quickly overwhelming the few armed sentries. With unintelligible whoops and shrieks, they killed many Hebrews, gathered up the possessions from those who fled, and took many captives. A large, hastily formed band of armed men from the Hebrew legion confronted and then drove back the attackers, who fought briefly before retreating over the hills. One of their horses stumbled, throwing its rider to the ground. Joshua and several of his men brought their injured prisoner to Moses.

"Who are you?" Moses demanded.

"A member of the army of Amalek,"[21] he answered defiantly in broken Egyptian.

"Do you live here, and if not, where have you come from?"

"We have come from the land of Arabia, to the south and east of here," he said, appearing unafraid.

"Why are you here now?"

"We were powerful at home and ruled the country for many years. However, strange diseases have weakened us, and the Assyrian army attacked us and drove us out. We have been traveling north and west with our herds and flocks for four months and settled but a short distance away. Our lookouts have been observing you for days."

"Why have you attacked us?" asked Moses.

"Our leaders were threatened by your huge throng, marching toward our best lands. We see also that you have many fine possessions that we shall have soon."

"What will your army do now?"

"You will see. Tomorrow, you will be annihilated!" the captive said. "We are part of a powerful army, and you look to be but a motley band of refugees."

"Do we?" asked Moses. He ordered two of Joshua's men to remove and guard the prisoner. Then he addressed the remainder. "We lost over three hundred travelers when they swept in as a whirlwind. They gathered us as leaves. The number of men in their full army is probably several times our force. Their arms are superior, and they drive swift chariots. They will surely return tomorrow.

"Joshua, choose men tonight and prepare to defend our company. I am too old to fight, but since God has brought us this far, I will climb to the top of that hill over there with the staff of God in my hand and entreat Him to help us."

"Moses, my master," replied Joshua, "God has protected us since we left Rameses. If He is really in charge, why did He allow this bloody attack? Has our repeated complaining angered Him?"

Moses placed his hand on Joshua's shoulder. "You have the understanding that escapes many. God's blessings please us, but we must learn from His discipline."

The next morning, before sunrise, Moses, Aaron, and Hur,[22] a highly respected elder of the tribe of Judah, ascended the hill overlooking the valley of the Hebrews. Joshua positioned his armed, hand-picked men in a frontal array across the valley, with three other rows of recruits behind them. Some of these former slaves were also trained foot soldiers and archers. Bershama joined the archers stationed behind small hills and bushes on the left flank, while the soldier Ahira commanded the right flank.

Joshua's faith and outrageous courage sustained the motley band as they waited, some fervently praying that the enemy would not appear. As the sun rose in the eastern sky, just as the captive had predicted, the entire well-equipped Amalekite army charged at the Hebrews from over a distant hill. Joshua, with flowing hair, bravely led the outnumbered Israelites into battle.

As they clashed, Moses raised his staff toward heaven and the Hebrews accounted themselves well, suffering few casualties as they drove their foe backward. After a time, Moses lowered his staff, his aching shoulders crying for rest. The tide of battle turned instantly, and the Hebrew line of soldiers gave way. Perceiving the bloody rout inevitable, Moses raised his hands and the rod again, beseeching God. To his amazement, the retreat ceased, the Hebrews held, and soon went on the offensive again.

It is the staff, held up to God, which brings success, Moses realized. After another hour, fatigued, he said, "God honors me but does not give me strength. I cannot hold my hands up any longer." As he lowered them, the Amalekites surged forward.

Aaron and Hur, observing the tides of battle, rallied to his side. "Sit down; we'll hold them up for you." As Moses sat on a rock, they stood beside him and cradled his outstretched arms in theirs. The clang of metal against metal, the occasional shrieks of impaled men, and the snorting of horses rose above the battle lines. The tiring Hebrews, stumbling over dying horses and around overturned chariots, routed their foes under the late afternoon sun, the survivors retreating beyond the hills.

A grateful Moses turned to Aaron and Hur. "Whatever the conflict, even against heavy odds, we must trust in God, for the battle is His."

"We did not pray but merely supported you," admitted Aaron.

"Just as those brave warriors down there in the valley, Aaron, we need each other to complete God's work. Today, I was physically too weak to fulfill even my part alone," answered Moses.

As the three descended the hill, the victors gathered up their plunder amid the stench of blood and entrails. The surviving horses were corralled. A tired but jubilant Joshua surveyed the battlefield where he and his men had fought. His unaccustomed pride quickly passed when Moses told how the course of battle had followed his raised staff, and Joshua's respect for Moses and his faith in God grew.

Moses directed a stone altar to be built in thanksgiving for God's victory and named it "The LORD Is My Banner."[23]

Meanwhile, over the hills, the bloodied camp of the Amalekites bound up the wounded and buried their dead. "We have been humiliated by a band of ex-serfs!" growled Medor, their king. "Spread the word and warn the caravans. There was something almost supernatural in their fighting. We were defeated today, but I vow that we shall yet have our day with them."

As if in response to Medor's vow of vengeance, God promised His retribution for the cowardly attack on the stragglers the previous day. *"Write this in a book as a memorial,"* He told Moses, *"and recite it to Joshua, that I will utterly blot out the memory of Amalek from under heaven."* Despite the promise, the obliteration would be long delayed, as God added, *"The* Lord *will have war against Amalek from generation to generation"* (Ex. 17:14, 16).

Moses dutifully recorded God's promise on his papyrus pages, writing in the Semitic alphabet he had learned in Midian. He read God's message to Joshua, who spoke Hebrew but, although tutored by Moses, was not yet able to read it.

Endnotes

1. "stars in heaven," Deut. 1:10.
2. The story of the trip from Egypt to Mount Sinai is told in chapters 12 through 19 of Exodus.
3. "pillar of cloud," Ex. 13:21.
4. "pillar of fire," Ex. 13:21.
5. "southern route," Ex. 13:17-18.
6. "The Philistines came from the Islands of Caphtor." See Exodus 13:17, Jeremiah 47:4, and *Interpreter's Dictionary of the Bible, Supplementary Volume,* "Philistines," Keith Crim, ed., 1991, pp. 666ff.
7. "the armies of the Hittite empire," *See Interpreter's Dictionary,* ibid. p. 412.
8. "The Hittites developed a method of extracting the iron": See Dr. Werner Keller, *The Bible as History: A Confirmation of the Book of Books.* Translated by Dr. William Neil, 1964, p. 83.
9. "God intervened," Amos 9:7.
10. "the Philistines came south and invaded the Egyptian mainland": See Exodus 13:17 and Bryant G. Wood, "The Philistines Enter Canaan: Were They Egyptian Lackeys or Invading conquerors?" *Biblical Archaelogy Review,* Nov.-Dec. 1991, pp. 44–52. See also Immanuel Velikovsky, *Ages in Chaos,* Vol. I., 1952, pp.59–90.
11. "Noah," Gen. 9:20-27.
12. "Amorites, Hivites, Jebusites," Ex. 3:8.
13. "Mizraim," Gen. 10:6, 13-14.
14. Moses' song consists of selected phrases from Exodus 15:1–18. Lyrics adapted from the New American Standard Bible. ©Copyright 1960,

1962, 1963, 1968, 1971, 1972, 1973, 1975, 1977 by The Lockman Foundation. Used by permission. (www.Lockman.org)

15. Adapted from Alfred Edersheim, *Bible History: Old Testament,* "Wanderings in the Wilderness," 1949, pg. 91.

16. "sweeten the waters," Ex. 15:25.

17. "wafers and honey," Ex. 16:31.

18. "manna; a word meaning 'what' or 'what is this?'" according to the footnote for Exodus 16:15 in the *Ryrie Study Bible.*

19. "midwife," Ex. 1:17,20.

20. fruit, vegetables, garlic, Num.11:5.

21. "Amalek": See Immanuel Velikovsky, *Ages in Chaos,* Vol. I., 1952, pp. 59–90. Also, following story from Exodus 17:8f). See also George Rawlinson, *Moses, His Life and Times,* p. 136.

22. Story from Ex. 17:8f.

23. "LORD is my banner," Ex. 17:15.

Section II
Indoctrination at Sinai

Chapter 6

Transforming Slaves into Priests

Three days after their victory, Moses followed the cloud, leading the Hebrews to the mountain named Sinai in the southeastern part of the Sinai Peninsula, 150 miles from Rameses. As they approached, the travelers were surprised to see the lushness of the area and the forests to the east and south.

"In this whole valley," exclaimed Miriam to Moses, "the grass is so thick and green that my feet hide in it![1] The trees are laden with fruit. There must be many oases nearby and higher rainfall than anywhere we have been since leaving Egypt. Are these God's fields?"

"Perhaps, but it is always this way," said Moses. "I have pastured sheep here occasionally, though I do not remember so many nearby trees. By bringing us here, God has kept yet another promise to me. He says that we are to make a more permanent camp and stay for a while, probably to be prepared for Canaan, though that land is still more than two weeks' journey away."[2]

"I will be in no hurry to leave this garden spot. God has led us here." She hesitated and then added, "through you. He speaks to you so much more often than to Aaron and—" She looked down at her feet. "Never to me anymore, since you arrived in Rameses."

"He loves you just as He loves Aaron and me," Moses said gently. "I just happen to be His appointed leader."

"Yes, I suppose that is so," she conceded.

God's plan, one that He had only partially revealed to Moses, was to park them all at Sinai for the next eleven months, tutoring them and trying to mold them into a well-organized, cohesive community with a steadfast trust in Him. He would then move them into Canaan, overpower the inhabitants, and establish a principled nation there.

The next morning, God called Moses to the mountain that towered two thousand feet high over their camp. As Moses walked to its base, he passed by the white cloud and assumed that God had left one of His angels in it. Moses began ascending the rocky slope, seeking worn paths, wondering why God wanted him on the mountain. He had never had any difficulty hearing God's word from thin air or from the cloud or fire before.

Halfway up, God spoke to him from the summit. *"Thus you shall say to* [the people] *'You yourselves have seen what I did to the Egyptians,"* God's voice then softened, *"and how I bore you on eagle's wings and brought you to Myself. Now then, if you will indeed obey My voice, and keep My covenant, then you shall be My own possession among all the peoples, for all the earth is Mine; and you shall be to me a kingdom of priests and a holy nation'"* (Ex. 19:4–6).

Moses sat down, trying to understand the message. God was promising more and more, in spite of their persistent lack of trust in Him; the Israelites would be a kingdom of priests! But with obedience as the price tag, could they comply? With doubts, he descended the mountain, assembled the thirteen leaders, and conveyed God's message: "Consider God's offer and take it to the people."

The council of leaders, one from each tribe, met together just outside the village as the sun was setting. They discussed God's offer before placing it before their people.

Bershama—nicknamed Barley—from the tribe of Ephraim, stood to speak. "This God asks us to follow Him who knows where, and to obey Him, no matter what He demands of us. Are we making too great a commitment to Him if we recommend to our people that we all agree?"

"In effect," said Ahira, "He wants us to yield our wills to His. We would become His servants."

"Yes," replied Eliasaph, "He asks those things of us, but, consider what He has already done for us! The plagues, the division of the Red Sea, the manna, the victory at Rephidim, water from a rock. Fellow travelers, He has my vote."

"He says he will make us all holy. Can you see me as a priest?" jeered Nethanel.

"Perhaps," answered Pagiel, "even you. Then you would have direct access to God, to pray to Him and even to intercede with Him on behalf of others. Quite a p … p … p … privilege, but quite a responsibility."

"If we refuse, might He just leave us out here to fend for ourselves?" asked Ahira.

Gamaliel, from the tribe of Manasseh, spoke up. "That is unlikely. He seems to desire the best for us. I believe that He will ask no more from us than we can give, and command no more than we can obey. As for me, I'll side with Eliasaph. Hasn't He already answered the prayers of more than the last four generations? Let us accept. We have much to gain!"

After a short silence, Eliasaph inquired, "Are there other dissenting views?"

"I have but one question," said Bershama. "When we present these offers to our people, will the foreigners have a vote in this?"

"No," said Eliasaph. "This is God's offer only to the Israelites. We are all in one accord then?" he asked.

"Yes," they answered.

Gamaliel and Eliasaph

Gamaliel was a large and handsome man, with dark eyes, dark complexion, a boxlike jaw, and broad shoulders. He was, along with Eliasaph of Gad, a spiritual leader among the tribes.

The mothers of each of these two men strongly believed in the God of Abraham, beliefs borne from answered prayers, and they instilled that faith into their sons, naming them with His name, El.[3] Neither mother would worship any of the many Egyptian gods. In contrast to most families, they would not allow even one idol in their houses. Their sons were elected tribal elders when in their late twenties, serving for five to seven years before being honored as princes and leaders of their respective tribes. Their mothers soon became fast friends, and remained so until Gamaliel's mother died four years later.

To Gamaliel, success came easily and early. His stamina and physical skill promoted a self-assurance that persisted. In his teens, he was assigned as a bricklayer, rising to foreman three years later. An excellent swimmer, he was routinely stationed on the Nile shores for special events and saved three people from drowning.

Behind his roughness, this idealistic man had a woman's quick intuition. His plans often succeeded through hard work and by humorously cajoling fellow workers. "Gamaliel the wise bull" he was called. He was also intensely loyal to any who befriended him. His strong belief in God, nurtured by his mother, afforded him a forbearing love, and as many believed, was the true basis for his persistent confidence. These qualities assured his election as leader of Manasseh. He and his wife, a woman of matching quiet confidence, had seven children, and he was truly his family's shepherd.

Gad's Eliasaph, the eldest of the leaders, was three years older than Gamaliel. He was heavyset and shorter than his friend. In contrast to Gamaliel's boundless energy, this bald man was sleepy-eyed and deliberate. As a boy, with the secret help of a scholarly Hebrew priest, he taught himself to decipher not only the hieroglyphs, but some of the newer hieratic straight-line writings. He occasionally stole word-filled papyrus sheets from Egyptian teachers, but would always secretly return them after reading them.

Eliasaph was a quiet yet sincere worrier, always ruminating on possible tragedies, believing in some measure that his worrying affected the outcome of events. Although he wore a façade of sympathy, the problems of others only added an additional burden to his already overloaded mind.

He worried also about his wife, who was frail and of a complaining nature. Her frequent illnesses had spared her the task of bearing children. As she gradually adopted the status of an invalid, Eliasaph assumed her household chores; at first, with a helpful, almost prideful attitude. But as the years passed, a hint of resentment clouded his love for her.

He worked the brickyards, finally reaching the position of assistant stonemason. Slow and deliberate in life, his large hands moved quickly laying brick, and his heavy wrists and forearms settled their share of disputes. Coupled with knowledge gained from his voracious reading, he became the natural leader of his tribe.

Because of his faith, he often led group prayers to Abraham's God. However, he hedged his bets, secretly carrying a small amulet of the god Re.

Their leaders took God's proposition to the people, whose reply was unanimous: "All that the LORD has spoken, we will do!"

Moses climbed back up the mountain to give God the good news, setting God's special plan afoot. God told Him, *"Go to the people and consecrate them today and tomorrow and let them wash their garments ... For on the third day, the LORD will come down on Mount Sinai in the sight of all the people"* (Ex. 19:10–11). Moses was instructed to set stakes around the mountain so that neither man nor beast would climb up or even touch the border of the mountain. Those who dared to would be stoned or shot through with arrows. *"When the ram's horn sounds a long blast, they shall come up to the mountain"* (Ex. 19:13), God said.

The people prepared as commanded and were told to refrain from sexual intercourse for those days.

Everyone arose on the third morning to barrages of thunder and shattering flashes of lightning that illuminated a thick, black cloud covering Mount Sinai. The stentorian blare of a ram's-horn trumpet, heard even above the claps of thunder and the lightning, cowed the people until Moses alone stepped forward. "Follow me!" he shouted and led the frightened people to the foot of the mountain.

What had appeared at a distance to be a dark cloud was now clearly seen to be an intense fire discharging smoke as from a furnace. God had descended onto Mount Sinai. As if the atmosphere were not terrifying enough, the entire mountain and the very earth on which they stood shook violently, scattering the people.

Assuming a cloak of bravery, Moses raised his staff. "Come, trust in God!" he commanded.

When the quaking ceased, calm returned to them. As the sounds of the trumpet grew louder, Moses called out to God, who answered him with further peals of thunder and an invitation to climb the mountain, this time all the way to the top.

Leaving the assembly, Moses disappeared into the rolling smoke and ascended toward the fire. After more than an hour, he reached the top of the mountain unharmed.

Again, God's voice came to him. *"Go down, warn the people, lest they break through to the LORD to gaze, and many of them perish. And also let the priests who come near to the LORD consecrate themselves"* (Ex. 19:21–22). Several men from each tribe had been elected to the role of "priest" to represent them in worship to their gods, to hear problems, and to sacrifice animals when necessary.

After his long climb, Moses had to turn around and go back down to simply repeat a warning he had been given previously. Up the mountain, down the mountain, up, down, up, down. How was Moses responding to his training as an eighty-year-old errand boy? Not a whimper, not an argument, no "Why again, LORD?" was recorded; Moses' maturing meekness was confirmed.

Before descending, Moses assured God that the people would obey; the mountain would be untouched. God told Moses that when he returned to the people, He would deliver His message to the assembled throng. Afterward, He wanted Moses to return to the mountain, this time accompanied to its base by Aaron.

When Moses rejoined the people, the thunder, the lightning, and the trumpet sounds all ceased. A portentous silence followed. No one dared move beyond the appointed boundaries at the foot of the mountain. Many wondered what God would say. Would He pronounce a dreadful sentence on them for their lack of trust, their lack of obedience to Him? Trembling, they listened attentively.

GOD

God created humans for fellowship with Him, placing them into a perfect environment that they might enjoy it fully. However, when He allowed Adam and Eve to be tested, they succumbed, falling from that ideal state.

They multiplied, and generations later, their descendants had become so evil that God decided to destroy the world with a flood, sparing faithful Noah's family. At the same time, He reduced man's lifespan from the previous eight to nine hundred years to a paltry one hundred twenty years. Sadly, God's hope that man would follow Him and His precepts was short-lived, as man descended again into lustful self-centeredness.

Eventually, God implemented another strategy: He would create a nation of priests to minister to the world and to save it. He began with another man who listened and obeyed: Abraham. God guided Abraham's progeny, the thousands of his descendants, for more than five hundred years, finally bringing them to this very mountain. What would He say to them in these, His first words to such a multitude, having spoken only to individuals through the ages before? How could He convey to them the glorious, totally satisfying, joy-filled, and successful lives that He desired for them with all His Being—lives of service born of His love for them? Only He knew the true path that they must walk, the path that wound safely through the jungle of distracting obstacles and worldly temptations. Here, at Mount Sinai, He had gathered His people to tell them.

Breaking the stillness, God's voice boomed out clearly through the surging smoke into the valley below.

"I am the LORD your God, who brought you out of the land of Egypt, out of the house of slavery." Let there be no doubt that their powerful God, who knew their past suffering, was speaking.

"You shall have no other gods before Me." None: not wealth, power, possessions, or any other.

"You shall not make for yourself an idol, or any likeness of what is in heaven above or on the earth beneath or in the water under the earth. You shall not worship them or serve them"—His imageless Spirit would satisfy—*"for I, the LORD your God, am a jealous God, visiting the iniquity of the fathers on the children, on the third and fourth generations of those who hate Me, but showing loving kindness to thousands, to those who love Me and keep My commandments."* In the first minute of His presentation, He warned the people that their descendants would either continue to suffer for their rebelliousness or would revel in the fruits of their obedience.

"You shall not take the name of the LORD your God in vain, for the LORD will not leave him unpunished who takes His name in vain." A dire warning for such sacrilege.

"Remember the Sabbath day, to keep it holy. Six days you shall labor and do all your work, but the seventh day is a Sabbath of the LORD your God; in

it you shall not do any work …." And the reason for this precept was given: *"The LORD … rested the seventh day."* The seventh day belonged entirely to God.

He next commanded respect for parents, who stood just below God. *"Honor your father and mother."* However, with this law came a valuable reward. *"That your days may be prolonged in the land which the LORD your God gives you."*

God continued, forbidding certain behaviors that would be deadly to the development of His intended holy nation:

"You shall not murder.

"You shall not commit adultery.

"You shall not steal.

"You shall not bear false witness against your neighbor."

There was no discussion. God had spoken.

The most important matter—that which dealt not with actions but with the mind, not with the tinder but the spark—was left for last. The only way to assure that God's laws would not be broken was to corral envious thoughts.

"You shall not covet your neighbor's house; you shall not covet your neighbor's wife or his male servant or his female servant or his ox or his donkey or anything that belongs to your neighbor" (Ex. 20:1–17). Don't even think about them, the urges, the cravings, the lustful thoughts; but if you do, do not dwell on them, nurture them, or rationalize why you deserve them.

These laws emphasized the survival and vitality of the community as pre-eminent. The transient desires of each individual must be subordinated to the well-being of the community. Remind them, remind them.

After the Ten Commandments were issued, thunder, lightning, and the wail of heavenly trumpets burst forth again. God's first words to the people had not been greetings or promises, but a stern message. "God has come in order to test you," Moses told the people, "that the fear of Him may remain with you, so that you may not sin." *

Tradition told the frightened people that they would all die if God persisted in instructing them directly, so they entreated Moses to go forth and communicate with Him alone, on their behalf, while they withdrew. As Moses approached the mountain base, God told him to remind the people that although the fire and smoke were on the mountaintop, His message was from heaven and carried that authority.

The Israelites had been released from the crushing burdens imposed by harsh Egyptian laws, but God knew that the absence of law would breed tumult. He now began to issue His own new set of statutes, laws that defined the behaviors of individuals, and by which Moses could judge the people. God would give the people the option to accept or reject His laws. If they accepted them, Moses was to build a large altar and sacrifice sheep and oxen to God in burnt and peace offerings, ceremonies already familiar to the Israelites, rituals engaged in since the time of Cain and Abel. When all of this was accomplished, then God would bless His people.

God prefixed His other laws by repeating the second commandment, *"You shall not make other gods besides Me; gods of silver or gods of gold, you shall not make for yourselves"* (Ex. 20:23). Why? Did He peer into their hearts as He emphasized this prohibition—this ban on making gods of gold?

Next, He reconfirmed two things that he had told Abraham: his people would receive great blessings in all that they did if they believed and remained obedient to His commandments. The condition was equally clear, however, that if His chosen people broke His laws, God would punish them just as harshly as He would their enemies.[5]

He issued many other laws, including a simple, straightforward one regarding personal injury: if a person caused the loss of another's eye, hand, or life, he himself must submit to the removal of his own eye, hand, or life; likewise, fracture for fracture, burn for burn. No greater or lesser penalty could be exacted, although a surviving victim might angrily seek more.

Other laws given to Moses detailed care of indentured servants, widows, and orphans—and even that one must help an enemy's donkey in distress (could they love God's laws more than they disliked their enemy?); laws concerning borrowing and usury; penalties for stealing animals and for the owner of an ox that gored another person—the ox must die, and if it had gored before, the owner must also be killed; and further laws concerning the firstborn and the Sabbath.

God decreed that they must also allow their fields to lie fallow every sabbatical (or seventh) year, because rest for the soil was important. God would triple the yield from the year prior to the Sabbath year to feed them for three years without spoilage.[6]

"Three times a year, all your males shall appear before the LORD *God"* (Ex. 23:17), He said, at a place to be specified by Him—at the Feast of Unleavened Bread, at the feasts of the celebration of the first and of the last day of the year's harvest.

God promised to play a powerful role in the inevitable battles they would have on their way to Canaan. He would send an angel who would guard them along the way and bring them safely to Canaan and completely destroy their enemies there. If they truly obeyed the angel, God would *"be an enemy to* [their] *enemies and an adversary to* [their] *adversaries"* (Ex. 23:22). However, God warned: if His people disobeyed, the promise would not hold.

After his long audience with God, Moses returned to inform the elders of the covenant. Would the people still stand by their approval of it?

The leaders reconvened without Moses at the home of Abidan that evening.

Gamaliel opened the meeting. "Now that Moses has informed us of God's many laws and of the great protection and the provisions He offers—only if we obey—shall we respond any differently? God wants us to consider our acceptance once again."

"If we are to judge from the laws that He has given us, they seem practical enough and not too difficult to follow," said Shelumiel. "One I particularly like, Nethanel, is that our cattle are to graze only our own fields. Yours, in Goshen, wandered too often onto my small pasture."

"Oh, really?" retorted Nethanel. "Well, keep that daughter of yours away from Pagiel, for God tells us not to seduce or be seduced by a virgin, and I trust she qualifies."

"Gentlemen, we have important business before us," interrupted Gamaliel. "Consider the advantages God promises us: no more sickness, no miscarriages, and no barrenness. In battle, He will send His own terror into the enemy ranks. It will not be like Rephidim again. What do you say, Nahshon? You are the representative of the lead tribe of Judah? Six weeks ago, you were the most outspoken against this journey."

Nahshon, smoothing his white robe, rose deliberately. "I came out of Egypt objecting, bitter, and doubting, as did some of you, although you were more reserved. But now, our newfound freedom goes down well into my soul. I walk and do as I please and I like it. However, that freedom may become bound by a new set of laws, some of which seem strange to me and invade my privacy. He is asking us to cast our future into His hands." He paused. "Into hands that, I admit, have performed an impressive series of tasks. I have weighed the evidence and it seems proper to accept His offer." He paused again and then added, "But if we do, we must not break His laws."

"Surely we can do that," said Pagiel, siding with Nahshon. "I too left Egypt reluctantly. But I believe God does treasure us. We can follow the laws, although I won't like not charging interest to a fellow Israelite."

Eliasaph added, "Do you see how privileged we are? God has seen fit to honor us with laws concerning the smallest details of our lives. I doubt that any other nation has these."

"You speak wisdom," said Gamaliel. "We seem to be together then. Is there anyone who disagrees?"

After a silence, Nahshon said, "No; let us recommend to our people that they accept His offer."

Pagiel

He was once called "Pagiel the Peculiar" by his early playmates, who taunted him because of his stuttering. Self-conscious as a child, he abhorred the resulting isolation and decided early to become so likable that he would be accepted. At that he succeeded, developing a sense of humor that allowed him to laugh at himself. He easily became the butt of his own stories, with his protruding eyes and, later, a short black goatee. He learned to treat his stuttering as a disease, rather than as a personal deficiency, and with determination, was able to speak with assurance, stumbling doggedly through occasional difficult sentences without embarrassment. He developed the habit of speaking quickly to avoid the self-analysis that often provoked his stuttering. As years passed, his affliction lessened and was bothersome only when he became angry, tired, or at rare times, deeply frustrated.

He was thrifty, perhaps somewhat miserly, keeping frequent and accurate account of his own modest holdings, and naturally became treasurer of his tribe's common purse. His stinginess may have accounted for his remaining a bachelor.

The Egyptians disliked his quick, insightful, cutting humor, and he never rose above being a house painter for them. However, he was immensely popular among the Hebrews. Throughout his teens and well into his adult life, he cherished the role as the tribal comic. His sharp-witted adlib satires of Egyptian royalty and even of the caustic guards provided laughter and temporary relief from their drudgery for his fellow slaves. He could effortlessly sway audiences to his wise ways of thinking, a skill that led to his eventual leadership of his tribe of Asher.

When the leaders had circulated details of Moses' message among the people, the congregation reiterated, "All that the LORD has spoken, we will do." Moses painstakingly penned in Hebrew all of the words of these laws and promises of the LORD into his papyrus scroll, calling it the Book of the Covenant.[7]

Early the next morning, Moses conscripted eight young men to construct an altar with twelve pillars at the foot of Mount Sinai, each pillar representing one of the original tribes of Israel. He gathered the people there to celebrate the ratification of this new covenant. Selected young men brought several young bulls to the altar to be bled and sacrificed. Profoundly aware of the magnitude of this occasion, Moses took half of the blood and poured it on the altar, signifying God's dedication to the people and to the covenant. One more time, he read God's words from the Book of the Covenant for all to hear.

The people chanted once again, "All that the LORD has spoken we will do," and this time added, "and we will be obedient." *

Hearing those words, Moses walked slowly among them, sprinkling the remainder of the blood randomly on them, saying, "Behold the blood of the covenant which the LORD has made with you, in accordance with all these words" *

The tribal leaders were seated in two rows in the front of the congregation as Moses passed them. "Three times God has asked, three times we accepted," said the puzzled Ahira. "Then an altar, commanded animal sacrifices, blood doused on the altar and on us. This is no ordinary covenant. God has forged a strong bond with us."

"This ceremony was a moving one; I shivered when the blood splashed on me," said Nahshon. "It seems to me we have become enrolled as willing vassals to a beneficent master."

"You interpret it as if we've become slaves?" offered Shelumiel, looking quizzically at Nahshon. "Do you think that He would celebrate our entry into bondage? I believe He cares for us too much for that. It seems more like being adopted as His children."

"Such a ceremony Moses enacts at God's bidding! Almost like being married," said the slender Bershama.

"Certainly, we must not consider ourselves the equals of Him," cautioned Ahira.

"When Moses sealed our acceptance with blood, did we know that our commitment would be as words engraved into gold?" asked Shelumiel. "We must take seriously this sacred agreement."

Gamaliel said, "I believe this to be another step in His plan to make of us—what did He say—*'His holy nation of priests.'* But priests for whom?"

Following the ceremony, Moses invited chosen men of the Israelites—Joshua, Aaron, Aaron's older two sons Nadab and Abihu, and seventy of the elders, including Hur—to accompany him to the mountain as God had commanded. As they were walking toward the mountain, their new, personal God, now Master/Father/Husband, materialized before them, not in the form of a cloud, but this time as a Man whose only discernible features were His feet. The rest of Him was covered, and "under His feet there appeared to be a pavement of sapphire, as clear as the sky itself."[8]

Startled at this unexpected manifestation of God, they feared greatly for their lives. But they were not harmed. Instead, a surprising peace filled them, accompanied by a thirst and hunger that were satisfied as they drank water and ate portions of the recently sacrificed bulls placed before them. Suddenly, He was not a God just to fear and obey, but they recognized Him as a God of love, One who enjoyed their fellowship and radiated a calming peace. These were His qualities the men would carry back to share with the assemblage.

Endnotes

1. "the grass is so thick" Edward Henry Palmer, *Desert of the Exodus,* Vol. 1, 1872, page 117.
2. "two weeks' journey," Deut. 1:2.
3. "naming them with His name, El," Edersheim, "The Exodus," *Bible History: Old Testament,* 1949, page 30.
4. This retelling of the gift of the Ten Commandments is taken from chapter 20 of Exodus.
5. "blessings…, punishment," Deut. 28.
6. "triple the yield," Lev. 25:21.
7. "Book of the Covenant," Ex. 24:7.
8. "pavement of sapphire," Ex. 24:10.

Chapter 7

The Panic of Abandonment

God then singled Moses out of the group and said, *"Come up to Me on the mountain and remain there, and I will give you the stone tablets with the law and the commandment which I have written for their instruction"* (Ex. 24:12).

Moses' previous ascents to hear God's messages had been trips lasting half a day. This time, although he was simply to go up for the tablets, he had been told to remain there, indicating a stay of at least several days.

Moses spoke to his brother privately. "While I am gone, it is most important that you act as God's leader in my stead, handling disputes with Hur's help. Will you do it?"

"Of course," said Aaron. "Will you be back in a few days?"

"I hope so," said Moses as he prepared to leave.

Joshua accompanied Moses as far as the base of the mountain, while the others returned to the camp. Moses climbed alone but soon was stopped by a heavy cloud cover as the glory of the LORD rested on Mount Sinai. To the people below, it appeared that Moses was ascending into a raging fire. They feared that his death was imminent.

Moses stayed where he was for six days, unable to move in the obscuring darkness. The eerie silence was unbroken. Deprived of most sensory cues, Moses felt an initial uneasiness and apprehension that was soon washed away in an all-pervading tranquility, in which physical hunger and thirst were nonexistent. On the seventh day, God's voice called out to him, the darkness lessened, and he climbed onward until he reached the summit, where he fell asleep, exhausted.

The next morning, he was awakened under a light haze by a familiar voice. God informed Moses that for His creation to achieve its greatest joy, peace, and satisfaction, He must be the primary object of their worship and, in the performance of the worship services, there must be a sacred place, a sacred person, and a sacred time.

First, the *place*. God gave long, precise instructions for the building of a tabernacle in which He was to reside and be worshipped: its size, its rooms, the composition of its walls, roof and doorway, its furniture, and even the size and makeup of the surrounding courtyard. He constructed a scale model for Moses, with exact measurements.[1]

The days stretched into weeks as God continued His instructions. He had decided to appoint a high priest as the *person* to provide the worship on behalf of the people, and He chose Aaron for that consecrated position. Moses was to anoint him and his four sons as assistant priests in a special ceremony.

Back at the camp, the people kept themselves busy, engaging in their usual daily chores the first week. However, the cool nights were becoming disquieting. Moses was still absent, perhaps dead, and no word had been received from God.

The second week brought growing doubts. Although the manna continued and fresh water was available, restlessness was setting in. Why had they not heard from God? Had He abandoned them?

At the end of the third week, Abidan, Pagiel, and Gamaliel called for a meeting of the council of leaders.

Pagiel began, "We had put our hopes in that man who b-b-b-brought us up out of Egypt[2]. It has been twenty silent days since he entered the mountain fire. He may be dead, for all we know, or else he has abandoned us. Friends, in re … re … re … reality, who was he? What do we really know of him?"

Ahira added, "Little, in truth. Before he left for the mountain, he told us that Aaron was his brother and Miriam, the prophetess, was his sister. Many of us knew Miriam for her talents; others knew Aaron, although he was a stranger to me."

"There were the stories of Moses' ambush and murder of an Egyptian guard almost a half century ago," said Abidan, "and of his escape from justice. Rumors placed him in Midian after that."

Nahshon stood thoughtfully. "Then he returned, 'sent by God,' so he said. He convinced me with those three miracles, or tricks, and so, after the plagues, we followed him. New marvels were enacted, leading us on, but we never knew him well."

Ahira tapped his fingers nervously on his thigh. "God even spoke to him in front of us. The persistent absence of those two smells of a concocted scheme. Our family is growing leery of Moses, and my people wonder if all of this was just some ruse to get us out of Egypt."

"I understand all of your concerns," interrupted Gamaliel. "We are all uneasy in this remote land, but I call for patience. God and Moses have both been true to their goals for us in the past. Let us give them another two weeks, and then we shall reconvene."

They conversed awhile longer. "All right, fourteen days," concluded Ahira.

Ahira

Ahira was a soldier, a tireless worker, and a resourceful leader of men. His long, hooked nose seemed to peer into a small mouth, largely hidden by his unkempt beard. Fidgety fingers constantly tugged at the bushy growth.

His father had been a highly respected breeder and trainer of Pharaoh's horses, who was permitted, on rare days off, to take his six-year-old son on scouting rides with him. They did this many times until he was nine years old, when he was conscripted by the Egyptians to carry water to their soldiers, often bivouacked near the front lines. During military withdrawals, he occasionally became embroiled in the battle scene. Amazingly, he survived battle after battle, whether by God's providence or by the pity of opposing soldiers when they encountered his unarmed, skinny frame. His agility proved invaluable as he wove between charging horses and chariots, and more than once, he ducked under a slashing sword.

In his teens, he was promoted to foot soldier and accounted himself well in battle, with his bronze hatchet and a captured sword. He was promoted to corporal at age fifteen and assigned a horse, developing a reputation as a man of great bravery—although secretly, he remained intensely fearful before each battle. By age twenty, he had gained another promotion.

In the early months as a corporal, he was overly sensitive and sought approval both from the men under him and his superiors, enabling him to attribute blame elsewhere for any failure. A lieutenant once scolded him, embarrassing him before his men: "Going to nursemaid them? By the goddess Isis, you are soft, too tender with those men. Trying to be popular will get you and all of us killed!" Shaken by that encounter, Ahira became stricter, putting distance between his men and himself.

He was often resourceful. One time, when the Philistine war was going badly, Ahira led twenty-five Egyptian soldiers as they crept within bowshot range of a group of Philistine chariots and began to rain arrows on them. They felled a horse and wounded a charioteer, and then escaped, leading their Philistine pursuers into a lethal ambush.

On another occasion, with his regiment surrounded, Ahira and two others entered the enemy camp at night and kidnapped a senior officer. He was coerced to reveal the Philistines' most vulnerable point. Ahira's entire force was able to attack it at dawn and battle through to safety.

As a long-standing member of Naphtali's council, when its leader died, Ahira became his obvious successor, earning the pride of his wife and six children.

On the mountain, God again put special emphasis on the Fourth Commandment, the Sabbath day, the *time* for worship. Its observance as a mandatory day of rest was to be more than just a day for refreshment; it was to act as a *"sign ... that you may know that I am the LORD who sanctifies you."* Whoever profanes the Sabbath *"shall surely be put to death"* (Ex. 31:13–14), said God. He seldom decreed death as a penalty, and that only for egregious errors. The Sabbath was to be holy.

Then He gave Moses two stone tablets containing *"the law and the commandment which I have written for their instruction"* (Ex. 24:12, and Ex. 32:15–16). The tablets were engraved on both sides by the finger of God.[3]

Four Sabbaths dragged by for those waiting in the Israelite camp. Anxiety had penetrated their wavering commitment. They had put their faith in a god who seemed to ignore them, though that strange non-consuming fire continued to burn on the mountain.

The council met.

Nethanel was the first to speak. "Where is this Moses? If he is not dead, he has run off with his God someplace—perhaps enjoying the luxury of His company on that smoky mountain. What do you wish to do?"

"I join with many of my people," said Shelumiel. "We'll never see Moses again, or God. We are ready to leave this place. But where should we go?"

Ahira absently picked at a scar on his cheek. "We could go on toward Canaan. It must be straight north and cannot be more than another week's march. Or we could return to Egypt—if we could find our way."

Bershama rose, his clothes now hanging loosely on his slender frame. "I have been secretly constructing maps of our journey at the end of each day, plotted by the position of the sun and the Dog Star. I believe I would be able to lead us back."

"But how would we be treated in Egypt?" asked Ahira. "Probably slaughtered, after the trouble we caused. I wonder who rules, without Pharaoh or his army?"

Pagiel's quick speech had slowed markedly. "Who knows? What a ripe grape she must be for an outside power to pl ... pl ... pl ... pluck. No matter, she is still home to me. I'm also ready to go, forward or back—even tonight, since I cannot s ... s ... s ... sleep anyway."

Abidan stood on aching feet. "My wife questions me every day. She taunts me that if we must stay here for the rest of our days, we should build houses and plant crops. The children, who seem to sense our anxiety, argue continuously."

Nethanel added, "I have lost interest, even to collecting the manna. And our people, they have turned to their trinket idols for worship."

"As I originally predicted, this march has failed," Nahshon said, "and now we are on our own."

Bershama nodded. "Ephraim is grumbling that we should make a sacred god for the whole congregation's benefit, one that provided for us in the past, before this one took over."

Gamaliel, working the muscles of his square jaw back and forth, stood up. "God has proven His faithfulness repeatedly. Surely He knows our plight. Besides, He specifically forbade idol worship. Ten more days; if he or Moses do not return, then we make other plans."

Shelumiel concurred. "Our last ten days, then?"

Bershama

Bershama led the descendants of Ephraim, Joseph's other son and Manasseh's brother. An accomplished archer, Bershama kept his skill well-honed with a bow and a few arrows stolen from the armory and secretly replenished through the years. He still limped from damaged muscles in his left thigh, torn by a Nubian arrow years earlier, and scarred and deformed by infections.

When Bershama was an infant, his father was cudgeled to death after accidentally spilling muddy water on a guard. He and a brother were raised by a loving, doting mother who had (he felt) slovenly habits. Overreacting to a messy house that embarrassed him as a child, he became obsessively tidy and organized.

At age eight, he was sent to the fields daily to gather hay and stubble for brick-making. He and other children were transported in wagons miles away and were required to fill them by sunset or receive the bite of a whip. At twelve, he became a hod carrier, and at nineteen, became foreman, a promotion that brought out the disciplinarian in him. He insisted that the men under his command comply with their Egyptian masters' orders, act courteously to one another, refrain from swearing, and wear clean clothes weekly. His industrious, fierce determination and his zeal for power and order brought him progressive leadership roles.

A teasing girl nicknamed him "Barley" because of his long narrow face and neatly groomed short-cropped, wiry hair. That same girl later became his wife, managing to keep the house of their three sons and two daughters in tolerable order under his close scrutiny.

By well into the sixth week of Moses' absence, the gloom of hopeless abandonment swallowed the camp. The depressed sought isolation, some considering suicide; the fearful cringed; the defiant raged at their betrayal by God and Moses; and the contentious erupted in fistfights and stealing. Sexual promiscuity flourished. Increasing numbers of the people, driven by ineffable anxieties, clamored, "Aaron, make a god who will go before us" *.

Leaving the murmurings outside, Miriam walked into Aaron's large tent, where he sat at the table with Elisheba and his four sons. "Our problem magnifies daily," Miriam said. "Moses must be dead or else he has deserted us again." Turning to Aaron, she said, "You and Hur are in charge, appointed to rule in Moses' stead. You must do something to quiet this camp. It will reach the boiling point in a day or two."

Aaron answered, "I am torn within trying to satisfy God's law while the leaders demand some—almost *any*—action. But what?"

"Our prayers to God and our other gods go unanswered," she said. "A public idol is demanded by many. When God was with us, He prohibited the making of such an idol—but God has quit us."

Shouts from outside, calling for action, erupted around Aaron's tent. Miriam said, "God may never return, nor our exalted brother who has abdicated his authority. Besides, God will never know what we do."

Aaron's son Abihu interjected, "We cannot go on much longer, Father. I will back whatever you do."

Nadab added, "We are only human, Father. God will understand. After all, His absence caused this dissension."

"There is now no one here who disagrees," said Elisheba.

Drawing himself up, Aaron took a deep breath. "I am the one who must satisfy this mob."

As Aaron began to leave, Miriam prodded, "Make it of gold."

Aaron walked out among them and shouted. "Tear off the gold rings that are in the ears of your wives, your sons, and your daughters and bring them to me!" *

"Finally!" the mob cried, as they ripped the jewelry off and rushed it to Aaron in blood-tinged hands.

Aaron took the accumulated metal, melted it in a cauldron, and, using a graving tool, fashioned it into what to him was a natural representation of this powerful God, a small bull calf. Unveiling it the next day to roars of approval, he shouted, "This is your God, O Israel, who brought you up out of the land of Egypt." *

The shiny yellow beast so filled Aaron with pride that he had an altar built before it, proclaimed a feast for the next day, and called for animal sacrifices to be made to the calf. In a burst of relief, the people exploded into celebration and dancing—merriment that soon slid into wild drinking, debauchery, and even dancing naked before the beast.

God was watching. He ordered a surprised Moses, *"Go down at once, for your people, whom you brought up from the land of Egypt, have corrupted themselves. They have quickly turned aside from the way which I commanded them. They have made for themselves a molten calf, and have worshipped it, and have sacrificed to it and said, 'This is your God, O Israel, who brought you up from the land of Egypt'* (Ex. 32:7–8).

"Now, then, let Me alone, that My anger may burn against them, and that I may destroy them, and I will make of you [Moses] *a great nation"* (Ex. 32:10). God was angry enough with Aaron to even kill His priest-elect.

At ease in God's presence, Moses first ignored God's offer to gather glory to himself at the expense of his wards, and then reminded Him that this idolatrous people were His, not Moses'. Then Moses said, "If You kill them, the Egyptians will say, 'With evil intent, He brought them out to kill them in the mountains and to destroy them from the face of the earth.' * Please change Your mind. Remember Abraham, Isaac, and Israel, Your servants to whom You did swear: *'I will multiply your descendants as the stars of the heavens, and all this land of which I have spoken I will give to your descendants, and they shall inherit it forever'"* (Ex. 32:13, Gen. 12:7).

God listened and was persuaded, resolving not to destroy the entire contrary mob, but to judge harshly only the most shameless of the people.

Moses apprehensively descended Mount Sinai, carefully guarding the stone tablets. *Had the people really constructed a calf and sacrificed to it?* he wondered. Twice they had heard God's specific command not to do exactly that. Near the base of the mountain, he came upon Joshua, who had been protecting the mountain against interlopers. He also had been sustained by God for forty days without food. As they approached the village, Joshua was alarmed as he heard shouting but Moses assured him that it was only singing.

As they burst into the midst of the crowd, Moses, who had lived forty days with consummate righteousness and absolute purity, became so disgusted, so filled with uncontrollable anger at their devilish reveling, that he willfully raised God's sacred tablets above his head. "You do not deserve these!" he shouted as he smashed them on the ground before the people. In his fiery rage, he lifted the calf, flung it into the fire, scorching it, and then grabbed a nearby mallet and pounded it into powder. He scooped up handfuls of the gold dust, threw them into a nearby brook, and demanded of the people, "Go, drink of it!" *

Then Moses turned upon Aaron, who had done nothing to stop the demonstration. Moses demanded, "What did this people do to you that you have brought such great sin upon them?" *

Aaron retorted, "You know the people yourself. They are prone to evil. They said to me, 'Make a god for us who will go before us.' I said to them, 'Whoever has any gold, let him tear it off.' So they gave it to me, and I threw it into the fire, and out came this calf." *

Moses had seen many of God's miracles, but doubted that this was one of them. Moses stared at Aaron suspiciously for a moment. Then he turned to the crowd, many of whom were still wildly dancing.

Moses called out to the people, "Whoever is for the LORD, come to me." * No trials would be held, no arguments entertained. Moses had watched God seethe at the people with an exterminatory anger that could only be appeased by the death of the flagrant violators. Moses implored, "Reuben, Simeon, Levi, Judah, Gad, Asher, Benjamin … " All thirteen tribes were encouraged to come forth.

Aged, stooped Zuriel, one of the elders of the tribe of Levi, quickly gathered a number of his younger tribesmen together, and spoke to them. "Look! No one goes forth to answer Moses' call! If you Levites can have courage, this may be the opportunity for which we have waited five hundred years, years deprived of leadership because of Simeon and Levi's violent sin."

Hamal, a Levite soldier, said, "Simeon and Levi should have been considered heroes by God for avenging the rape of their sister, not criminals."

Zuriel said, "You call hacking to death King Shechem[5] and his men the day after their circumcisions heroic? But now, perhaps, we can atone for that and regain God's approval. Will you answer His summons?"

Hamal raised his sword and shouted, "For the tribe of Levi!" and walked toward Moses with swarms of Levitical soldiers falling in behind him.

Moses angrily shouted, "This is what the LORD, the God of Israel, says, 'Go back and forth from gate to gate in the camp, and kill every man, his brother, his friend, and his neighbor!'" *

How much easier their task would have been had Moses instead called the worshippers of the golden calf "heinous sinners." However, the Levites thrust swords into the naked, swung hatchets across the fornicators, buried arrows into the drunk, and beat senseless the stupefied, slaughtering in all three thousand of the brazen offenders that day, including some members of their own tribe.

That evening, a tired, remorseful, and sober Zuriel sat and wrote in his diary.

Brothers of slavery, kindred of mine,
Dined at my table, drank of my wine.
But naked and drunk, you worshipped the calf,
As you pierced God's heart, scribed your own epitaph.
Executioner? Friend, we assume that façade,
Strange to us, but ordered by God.
I harvest you my neighbor like sun-ripened wheat,
Scythe the blade from the beard—see, it bleeds!

The next day, Moses walked between two long rows of newly mounded graves. *Had I returned sooner, these might not be dead,* he thought. *Why was I up there so long? It did bolster my commitment to Him. I used to speak to God as one person to another; now I want to bow before Him.*

He knelt beside a grave. *Was it to test the people? If so, they failed, betraying God's trust. That set off my anger, the same anger I had toward Mannel and toward Pharaoh's hard-heartedness.* When his mind calmed, he realized that he was angry, in part, because the people had flouted his leadership, breaking the rules he had brought to them from God: *"You shall have no other gods before Me (Ex. 20:3)."*

He cringed when he remembered that he had broken God's tablets in his rage, the most holy items he had ever held. His feelings of guilt widened as he admitted to himself that, early on, when the Levites began slashing the offenders to death, he felt a certain satisfaction, a feeling that abated as the numbers of slain grew.

As he walked back to camp, the cloud joined him for a short while to comfort him. Then God assigned him a new task, a more joyous one, to reward the obedient tribe.

At God's bidding, Moses assembled the Levites with their blood-stained swords. "Dedicate yourselves today to the LORD, in order that He may bestow a blessing on you," * Moses exhorted them.

"You Levites, because you alone stepped forward to execute God's judgment, you are designated by God to become the priestly tribe among all of the sons of Israel. After the high priest is ordained, you will assist him and his family in the religious and spiritual life of the community."

"That is supposed to be our reward," asked a Levite in puzzlement, "for being the only tribe to kill our brothers?"

"So God says," answered Moses.

"Who will become this high priest?" asked another.

"God has appointed Aaron, my brother."

The crowd fell silent for a few moments. "But Moses," said one, "Aaron fashioned the golden calf himself. And he gets honored?"

Moses answered solemnly. "If he did as you say, he must have been driven to it. God will deal wisely with him. He and his sons will be the priests."

"All we have is your word for it?" they asked.

"Yes, unless God confirms it."

Thus, out of the dust of the golden calf did the flower of Levi finally sprout, while its powder grew only painful remorse for Aaron. Had he not weakened, the calf would not have existed. But he lost a second chance; had he admitted his deed to Moses, he alone may have been punished—losing his newly coveted priesthood, but perhaps saving three thousand lives.

Three days after the mass killings, a downhearted Moses told the people he would intercede with God on their behalf. "Perhaps I can make atonement for your sin," * he said, including Aaron's lie to him about the spontaneous creation of the calf, a lie confirmed to him later by a man who had overheard the conversation between the brothers. Moses had not spoken further of it to Aaron.

Moses returned to the broken tablets, picked up a few pieces as his chosen symbols of repentance, and walked toward the mountain. He sighed. As he looked up, he saw that a large white cloud had replaced the smoking fire.

When Moses attained the barren summit, the brisk wind billowed his shirt while leaving the cloud overhead motionless. He spoke to the cloud, knowing that God would hear. He readily admitted the great sin that the people had committed and accepted God's punishment. "But now, if Thou wilt, forgive their sin," he begged. He appealed for divine mercy, adding that if God would not forgive their sin, "then blot me out from Thy book which Thou hast written"[5]

God did not forgive the people and rejected Moses' self-sacrificial offer. He simply told Moses to lead the people north and claim the land He had promised to them. *"I will send the angel before you and I will drive out the* [inhabitants of Canaan] *before you,"* said God. *"However, I will not go up in your midst because you are an obstinate people, lest I destroy you on the way"* (Ex. 33:2–3).[6]

God commanded the people to take off their fine jewelry so that He *"will know what to do with* [them]*"* (Ex. 33:5).

When Moses descended and told the people of God's decision, they took off their ornaments but stubbornly refused to budge. Accustomed to having the real presence of God in their midst, they found His angel an unsatisfactory substitute.

Moses returned to the foot of the mountain, carrying this despondent mood of the people. He climbed up a short way, and then repeated his request. "God, please forgive them for having broken their covenant with You by the golden calf." Then he made a second request. "Your angel is inadequate for the Israelites. If You do not go with us, do not lead us up from here" *

God responded that, only because of His profound love for Moses, He would change His mind and lead them Himself.

Buoyed by God's strong affirmation, Moses brazenly made a third request. "If I have found favor in Your sight, let me know Your ways that I might know You" * His growing devotion to God included the desire to know His intimate thoughts.

Moses even made a fourth request. To that end, he continued, "I pray that You will show me Your glory." *

God considered this bold plea. *"I, Myself, will make all My goodness pass before you."* Then He added, *"I will be gracious to whom I will be gracious, and will show compassion on whom I will show compassion"* (Ex. 33:19). By His mercy and grace, He might redeem even an obstinate people.

Back on level ground, God set Moses in the cleft of a rock, placed His hand over his face, but removed His hand as His "glory" passed by. *"You shall see My back, but My face shall not be seen"* (Ex. 33:23).

Moses never described what he observed. Would he remember this experience and always be obedient? Would he now be perfect, mature in all things? God hoped He had a man who was capable of such permanent loyalty.

After two days, God called Moses to return alone onto the mountain a fifth time. Chafing because Moses had shattered the first tablets, God told Moses to cut out two stone tablets himself and bring them up for Him to rewrite the Ten Commandments.

Because God had not formally forgiven the people of their sins, Moses was still deeply concerned that He might destroy them.[7] Therefore, when Moses reached the sunlit mountain peak carrying the two tablets, he prostrated himself in desperate submission for many days.[8]

Finally, one day, God descended as a cloud and hovered near him. Moses was still unaccustomed to these manifestations, and rose only at God's invitation. Moses had asked to "know God's ways" and God chose to answer him. *"The LORD God, compassionate and gracious, slow to anger, and abounding in loving kindness and truth Who keeps loving kindness for thousands, who forgives iniquity, transgression, and sin; yet He will by no means leave the guilty unpunished, visiting the iniquity of the fathers on the children and on the grandchildren to the third and fourth generations"* (Ex. 34:6–7).

Moses was humbled by God's graciousness, bowing low to the earth. Of his four requests, three had been promptly granted. Only one request remained unanswered, perhaps the most difficult of all. Therefore, he called out to the LORD again, "Pardon our iniquity and sin and take us again as your possession." *

God did not specifically forgive their sins, but responded, *"Behold, I am going to make a* [new] *covenant"* (Ex. 34:10). Trained in law, Moses welcomed a second covenant to replace the broken first one.

The new covenant: *"Before all your people, I will perform miracles which have not been produced in all the earth, nor among any of the nations; and all the people among whom you live will see the working of the LORD, for it is a fearful thing that I am going to perform with you. Be sure to observe what I am commanding you this day: behold,"* God repeated, *"I am going to drive out* [the inhabitants of Canaan] *before you. Watch yourselves that you make no covenant with* [them] … *lest it become a snare in your midst. But rather tear down their altars and smash their sacred pillars and cut down their Asherim* [symbols to the mother of their god, Baal] *for you shall not worship any other god, for the LORD, whose name is Jealous, is a jealous God"* (Ex. 34:10–14).

The covenant also required them to remember to celebrate all festivals, have their males gather before the LORD three times a year, and rest on the Sabbath. He also emphasized a warning that their sons must not play the harlot with Canaanite gods or sacrifice to them. God reiterated a number of old laws and told Moses to record all of these words.[9] Moses opened his lengthening papyrus scroll and did so.

Moses gathered these writings and the two rewritten stone tablets and descended the mountain. Growing hungry, he realized that God had sustained him without food or drink for a second forty days. As he reached the camp, he found that no significant disobedience had occurred in his absence. There was no golden calf. He placed the stone tablets into his tent for safekeeping.

When Moses summoned Aaron and the leaders so that he could convey the terms of God's new covenant, he was surprised at their reluctance to approach him. Aaron said, "Moses, the skin of your face glows so brightly that we are afraid."[10] Hearing that, Moses realized that some of the glory of God had been transferred to him while he was in God's presence. His altered appearance would strengthen his role as God's messenger among this doubting people.

Moses insisted that they come near to him and they fearfully obeyed. He transmitted all the words that God had given to him, knowing that they would listen more intently and be convinced of their authenticity because of his shining face.

Afterwords, he gathered the entire congregation, who also were reverent because of his appearance, and reiterated all of God's words. They knew that this was not just Moses speaking but that the power of God was behind his message and that they must obey.

Moses placed a veil over his face and asked the leaders to consider the terms of God's new covenant.

That night, some of the tribal leaders met privately.

"The slaughter by those opportunistic Levites seems to have satisfied God," said Shelumiel. "He will accompany us to provide easier victories, if we can believe Moses."

Gamaliel said, "His shining face convinced me."

"If we see God going before us, we can believe them both," remarked Ahira. "However, I for one am losing my zeal for fighting."

Bershama leaned on his bowed leg. "The battle should be easier since God said He would send swarms of hornets[11] into the enemy ranks, an attack that would drive a man mad. He promised, *I will drive out the* [enemies] *before you*" (Ex. 33:2).

Ahira said, "I presume that God can supply us with superior weaponry and wise tactics before the battles. Hornets? We'll see."

"If you doubt the hornet promise, Ahira," said Gamaliel, "weren't you surprised when God promised, *'No man shall covet your land when you go up before the LORD three times a year?'* (Ex. 34:24) God will even extinguish any envy our neighbors might have."

Shelumiel said, "He alters the minds of others to our advantage but leaves me to decide matters on my own."

Ahira said, "That's free will; get used to it."

"But my will may get me into trouble," said Shelumiel. "Moses reminded us that God will afflict our next three or four generations for sins that we commit. That seems vicious and unjust."

Gamaliel responded as they adjourned, "His loving kindness, kept for thousands of generations for those who obey, so far overwhelms His judgment on three or four generations that it stupefies."[12]

The meeting ended, and each sought his own home, a sometimes difficult task in the vast fields of shelters, extending for several miles in each direction. There were tents, a few small wooden houses, and many little more than boughs and branches arranged around central posts. The leaders had tried to keep their own tribes together but with only marginal success, because friends tended to congregate, often intermixing tribes. Lacking an overall housing plan, the Israelites lived with disorder.

Disordered also was the mind of Shelumiel as he addressed the six-member council of Simeon six days later. "The tribe of Levi was restored by their boldness while we still walk in disgrace. Had I acted, we too might have answered Moses' call and been honored. It is best that you replace me."

"I have been told," said one, "that it was old Zuriel and not the tribal leader who challenged their young men while we all delayed. We're all to be blamed. Stay, Shelumiel, you serve us well."

Another man stood up. "I did not volunteer because I had favored Aaron's golden calf, as did many of those hypocritical Levites. Remain, Shelumiel."

Other heads nodded in agreement.

"If you feel that way, I will stay, but with a burdened heart," Shelumiel said solemnly. "We must learn from this."

As he left the meeting, Shelumiel met his friend, Dathan, a council member of the tribe of Reuben. "Why so glum, Shelumiel? The burials are over. We must go on."

Shelumiel sighed. "The matter I discussed with you earlier has been settled. I have been retained as tribal leader."

"Your tribe was disgraced because of a slaughter, mine from Reuben's sexual lust," said Dathan. "Believe me, we will not miss another opportunity like this one."

"Agreed. Keep alert."

As the glow of Moses' face began to decrease, he kept the veil on before the people so that they could not see its diminution[13]. However, whenever he went in to talk to God, he removed the veil, perhaps hoping to have the fading brightness replenished. In time, as the glow subsided, so did the people's awe for Moses and the veil was soon discarded.

But Moses' commitment was not lessened. His six-week engrossment with God had transformed him. He would continue to speak, cry out, or pray to God as before but, when under intense stress, he would unhesitatingly fall on his face before God in public supplication[14].

Endnotes

1. exact measurements, Ex. 25:9, Acts 7:44, Heb. 8:5.
2. "man," Ex. 32:1.
3. "finger of God," Ex. 31:18.
4. Story of King Shechem, Gen. 34.
5. Moses' plea was one with two possible meanings: If Moses meant for God to destroy his earthly body, he would head the elite list of the courageous men who sacrificed themselves to save the lives of others, the shepherd giving his life for his sheep. But, more likely, if Moses offered to relinquish his life after death, his very soul, it would be the most astonishing gift anyone had ever offered.
6. Author's note: Might even God become unable to control His righteous wrath or was He further testing Moses?
7. "He might destroy them." Deut. 9:25.
8. "prostrated himself," Deut. 9:18 NIV.
9. "Record all these words," Ex. 34:27.
10. "veil," Ex. 34:30.
11. "hornets," Ex. 23:28.
12. "His loving kindness kept … stupefies." Quotation from written letter from the Reverend George W. Robertson, Ph.D., senior minister, First Presbyterian Church (PCA), Augusta, Georgia.
13. diminution, 2Cor. 3:13.
14. supplication, Num. 16:4.

Chapter 8

His Sanctuary in Their Midst

One day, a traveler advised Moses that Jethro was bringing his family to join them.[1] So when Moses heard from the northern outpost that a party of four was approaching on donkeys, leading several sheep, he left his tent and broke into an easy trot to meet them on legs well-conditioned by the march.

"It is good that you have come. I have greatly missed you!" Moses exclaimed as he reached up to kiss Zipporah, who was riding the lead donkey. The smell of her unique perfume was not wasted. "My role with God and the people is more assured than a year ago, and I believe they will welcome you." Zipporah smiled back at him, still gently holding on to his offered hand.

"And you two, how good it is to see you," he said, turning to his sons, who were walking at her side. Dust puffed from their shirts as Moses embraced each briefly. "You look healthy," admired Moses. "We will find plenty for you to do to earn your keep. Gershom, you were always good with an axe. You and Eliezer might build a little home for us." They nodded absently, their eyes bewildered by the mass of people nearby.

Moses turned and bowed down before his father-in-law as he dismounted. Then Moses rose and kissed Jethro on both cheeks. "Tell me," Moses began, "how you have been during my absence. Have you missed your shepherd?"

"Your sons and my other growing grandsons tended to your tasks," Jethro said. "Since you have returned to Sinai, I felt it proper to reunite your family. Moses, word fills the land of God's actions through you and of His deliverance of the Israelite slaves. I want to hear more."

"Come into my tent and rest and I will tell you." Moses signaled to a nearby attendant. "Show my wife and sons to a cool bath."

"It is our God's work," Moses began as they sat, and he detailed God's wonders over the last year. Jethro listened carefully. "Now I know that the LORD is greater than all the gods," * he finally said. "Come, bring Aaron and the elders, and I will offer sacrifices of my sheep to Him. We will all share a meal."

That evening, there was a great feast and celebration. The months of separation brought a crowning reunion of Moses and Zipporah.

Jethro remained ten days with them. He observed that Moses spent most of each day listening to and judging disputes, petty ones and grave ones, employing the recently revealed laws of God. "If you continue, you will surely wear out. I shall give you counsel and God be with you," Jethro told Moses. "Choose men to judge the people. Every great matter they shall bring to you, but any small matter they shall decide themselves. The judges should have three basic characteristics: they should be able men who fear God, men of truth, and those who hate dishonest gain. If you do this thing," he bowed to divine authority, "and if God so commands you, then you will be able to endure." *

Moses agreed and selected capable men to act as judges, some to judge over groups of ten people, others over fifty, some over hundreds, and the most capable men to judge over thousands, leaving him freer to serve God.

His task completed, Jethro departed to begin his solitary journey back home.

That same evening, several leaders were eating a light meal together. "Moses has invited us again to join him tomorrow as he goes out from the camp to speak with the cloud—I mean with God," said Abidan.

Eliasaph's eyes lit up. "What a unique opportunity we have! Moses told us that anyone who seeks to worship God may go. I borrowed Shelumiel's extra tent and went four days ago, and I'll go tomorrow also."

"It is certainly handy now," said Nahshon. "I suppose that Moses finally proved his loyalty to God by all his trips up the mountain, so now

God will meet with us nearby. I'll join you tomorrow." Nahshon only admitted to himself that it was purely curiosity that drew him away from the camp.

"I'm not interested," said Nethanel.

Pagiel voiced the thoughts of several. "Eliasaph, can you hear what they talk about? We pitch our te … te … te … tents near Moses', but when the cloud comes to his, he won't let us get close enough to hear their conversation."

Eliasaph said, "Nethanel, you should go. It's extraordinary. It is only after Moses and Joshua enter the special tent they've erected—the tent of meeting, they call it—and leave the flap open that the cloud suddenly appears. Moses stands there inside, the cloud outside, and they talk face to face, as I might talk to you. When I am bowed down in front of my own tent, as we have been told to do, I cannot make out the words either. How lucky Moses is."

"We are there only to honor and to worship Him," said Gamaliel, "and to ask for His bene—"

"It's eerie," interrupted Abidan, "how I feel tingly while the cloud is there. Then when it disappears, I feel normal again, as Moses silently leads us back to the camp."

"All except Joshua," replied Gamaliel, "who stays in the tent overnight. It's out of reverence, he says."

"Only later does Moses tell us about their conversation," said Eliasaph.

"How about the rest of you, will you come with us?" asked Gamaliel.

"I will wait until the next time," said the cautious Ahira.

The simple tent of meeting proved useful for a while but soon outgrew its adequacy for God, who desired to dwell among the people in the midst of the camp. Having materialized in the vaporous form of a cloud, He was unable to walk among them, touch them, laugh with them, or dine with them; perhaps that day would come later. However, He still longed to be included as an integral part of the community. To that end, He had given Moses the precise, detailed plans for construction of His sanctuary, the tabernacle.[2]

God also appointed the workers. Twenty-four-year-old Bezalel, son of Uri, son of Hur, of the tribe of Judah, compulsive and stubborn, had been one of Pharaoh's most respected artisans. He had designed the tigers at the entrance to Rameses and supervised their production. His wood carvings, placed on pedestals throughout the palace, uniformly drew acclaim from visiting dignitaries. His creative, precise works in gold, silver, and bronze ranged from heavy commercial items to delicate artworks. Pharaoh had appreciated this man.

God knew well Bezalel's talents and appointed him to supervise the construction of the tabernacle, using Moses' plans. He endowed him with the rare, precious gift of His own Holy Spirit, thereby magnifying his skills, wisdom, and knowledge. God also gave special talents to the chief weaver and engraver, Oholiab of the tribe of Dan, and to all the workers for their appointed tasks.

Speaking through Moses, God asked for volunteers to contribute to His tabernacle. Let them bring *"gold, silver, and bronze, blue, purple and scarlet material, fine linen, goats' hair, and rams' skin dyed red, and porpoise skins, and acacia wood, and oil for lighting, and spices for the anointing oil, and for the fragrant incense, and onyx stones and setting stones for the ephod and for the breastpiece* [of the high priest]" (Ex. 35:5–9).

Once the specific needs were announced, the people donated their gifts, some being those received from the Egyptians on the eve of their flight from slavery. Some soldiers, who had stripped the fallen Amalekites, also brought their stolen booty to Moses. More goods were received than were necessary.

The craftsmen and craftswomen diligently set to work, using the tools they had either brought with them or fashioned in the desert. The settlement was abuzz with activity. The woodsmen hewed the hardwood acacia trees from the nearby forest and shaped them to the needed sizes. The weavers made curtains. Carpenters cut boards, made poles, and built furniture. The seamstresses cut, spun, and wove goats' hair, and made curtains of dyed porpoise and ram skins. Metalsmiths hammered and shaped intricate items of gold, silver, and bronze, and jewelers set them with precious stones. Small furnaces were built to cast bronze handles, bases, and tools; woodcarvers, embroiderers, and perfumers also worked tirelessly. In the middle of the ninth month at Sinai, the twelfth since leaving Egypt, the tabernacle was almost complete and the furniture installed—as God had commanded.

Moses gathered three foremen outside the courtyard on the day of the final inspection. He led them around the perimeter of the oblong courtyard fence, one hundred fifty by seventy-five feet. The lengths of its skeleton were formed by twenty vertical seven-and-a-half-foot-tall acacia pillars placed about six feet apart in a line, and the widths by ten similar pillars. Each pillar was anchored by two bronze sockets into long baseboards. As the men walked, they stepped carefully over bronze pegs driven into the ground to hold taut ropes attached to the tops of the pillars, securing them.

When they reached the east side, Moses drew apart the doorway of the courtyard, made of tightly interwoven purple, blue, and scarlet linens, and ushered the group inside. A continuous curtain, made of the same linens, hung all around the inside of the fence, completely shielding the courtyard from outside view.

The most prominent structure in the courtyard was the tabernacle in the west central area. In front of it stood the eight-by-eight-foot sacrificial altar, five feet high, made of acacia wood overlaid with bronze to withstand the heat of the fires within. Rising above each of its four corners was a wooden horn covered with bronze, to which the sacrificial carcasses could be secured. Pails, shovels, flesh hooks, and fire pans of bronze were kept near the altar.

Moses walked to a wooden stand, the laver, placed between the bronze altar and the tabernacle, and lifted a washing basin from its top. "God insists that all priests wash their hands and feet before entering the tabernacle, to cleanse themselves so that they would not die."³

The inspectors, sobered by that news, then walked with Moses up to the boxlike, gabled tabernacle, fifty feet in length and fifteen in width. The roof was composed of three layers: an inner one of woven goat's hair, a middle one of ram's skin, and a water-shedding outer layer of hand-sewn porpoise skins that overhung the sides of the tabernacle halfway down its seventeen-foot-high acacia walls. Below the covering, one could see the lower halves of the twenty vertical pillars that made up the walls on the north and south sides, the six on the west or back wall, and the five on the front. Each pillar, two feet wide and three inches thick, and separated from its neighbor by six inches, was covered with gold on all sides. They were attached by tenons to baseboards. Long horizontal poles of gilded acacia passed through gold rings on the outer face of each board, connecting them all together and stabilizing the walls. Between the pillars, drapery hanging on the inside of the tabernacle could be seen.

"Are we permitted to enter?" they asked apprehensively.

"Only this once, for the inspection," said Moses.

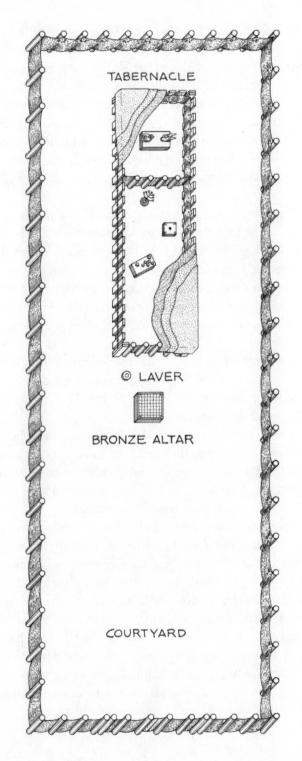

TABERNACLE

LAVER

BRONZE ALTAR

COURTYARD

Moses led them into the tabernacle by pushing aside the doorway curtain on the east, the only break in an otherwise continuous curtain woven of purple, scarlet, and blue material that hung from silver hooks on the inside of the boards, hugging the entire inner wall of the tabernacle.

As Moses watched, two workmen finished installing the final item, a thick tricolor curtain, two-thirds of the way toward the back of the room, dividing the tabernacle into a larger front anteroom, or holy room, facing east, and a smaller back room, the holy of holies, facing west. The curtain or veil was suspended from hooks on four vertical pillars of gilded acacia wood.

Moses inspected the three items in the holy room: the golden altar of incense, the table for holy bread, and the lamp stand. The altar was of wood overlain with gold, waist high and twenty inches square. Two golden horns were attached to opposite corners on the top of it, and a small golden cup stood between them. The second item, the rectangular table for holy bread, also gold-covered, was a hand shorter than the altar, with a top large enough to hold dishes, pans, bowls, and jars, all of the gold objects to be used in the ceremonies.

Moses momentarily picked up the loaf of bread from the table and sniffed it approvingly before fingering the gold rings on the sides of the two pieces of furniture, noting the poles on the floor nearby that were to be inserted through the rings to carry them.

He marveled at the lamp stand. Six parallel branches came out horizontally from the stand, three on each side, curving upward, each branch terminating in cups shaped like almond blossoms. Another branch, with cups, protruded from its top. The lamp stand had been hammered to perfection from one continuous seventy-pound piece of gold. Small golden lamps were made separately and installed on the ends of each branch to hold oil that, when lighted, would illuminate the anteroom.

Moses parted the veil and entered the sacrosanct holy of holies alone— reserved for the high priest and Moses—the room of the ark of the covenant and the mercy seat. The ark, about the size of a large writing desk, was made of acacia wood, overlaid inside and out with gold, and set on four cast-gold feet. Two rings were attached to each side of the ark, each pair holding a gilded pole of acacia for carrying. Those poles were never to be removed from their rings, allowing for its immediate emergency transportation. Inside a cabinet in the ark were placed the tablets containing the Ten Commandments and the jar with a portion of the manna.

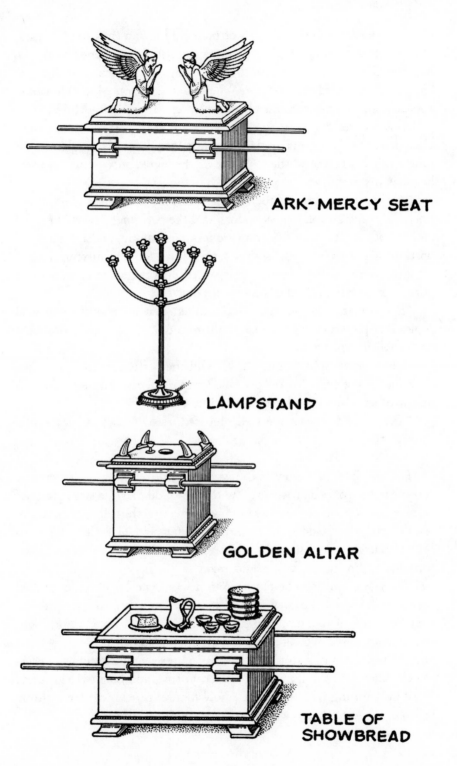

ARK-MERCY SEAT

LAMPSTAND

GOLDEN ALTAR

TABLE OF
SHOWBREAD

A thick, flat, rectangular slab of pure gold lay on the top of the ark, of its same width and length. Affixed on top, at opposite ends, were two hammered gold cherubim, angels with wings spread apart, facing one another. God called the structure "the mercy seat," on which He would appear as a cloud between the cherubim when He met with Moses.

As Moses returned through the veil, he paused before the golden altar. He touched the grainy material inside the golden cup and brought it to his nose, sniffed, and was satisfied. "What are the ingredients of this incense?" he asked his perfumer.

"At God's instruction, I took a measure of mussel shells and ground it finely, releasing a strong musky odor," said the perfumer. "Next, an equal amount of the bitter-tasting, aromatic resin, galbanum, and a third equal portion of the sweet spice, stacte, were added and the mixture beaten together into powdery incense. It is stored on the golden altar, a small portion to be burned in the lamps twice daily."

"Remember," said Moses, "God warned that anyone but you who copies that prescription shall be cut off from our people. And now, what of the holy anointing oil?"

"I have made sixty pounds of it," said the perfumer, "myrrh, cassia, cinnamon, cane, and olive oil, per God's requirements. Private concoction by any other is also prohibited, as you know."

"The oil and incense are well prepared," said Moses as they exited through the curtain into the daylight.

During the many months the workers were building the tabernacle and the masses of people were trying to learn God's laws, a large group of garment makers, empowered by God, were making the clothes that Aaron was to wear[4] when, God said, *"he may minister as priest to Me"* (Ex. 28:3). In spite of Aaron's demonstrated frailties, he was still God's designee. Given time and authority, his faith would grow.

The first garment to be put on Aaron was a checkered tunic, girdled with a sash. It was covered with a longer blue robe, and around the circumference of its hem, pomegranate-like balls of blue, scarlet, and purple cloth were sewn, alternating with small gold bells.

The next layer of Aaron's clothes, worn over the robe, was a sleeveless smock called an ephod, made of scarlet, purple, and blue twisted linen. Since his clothing was to assume a holy nature, threads cut from thinly hammered sheets of gold were interwoven with the others.

Aaron's ministerial representation of each tribe was carried in two ways. First, on the top of each shoulder was sewn an epaulet with a delicate setting of gold for an onyx stone. The names of six of the tribes of Israel who could go to war were inscribed onto one stone, the other six on the other stone.

Second, a square "breastplate of judgment," folded double to be nine-by-nine inches, was woven of the same materials and secured to the front of the ephod. Four rows of precious stones were attached to the breastplate, three stones per row, each bearing the name of one of the tribes. Among the stones were a ruby, an emerald, a blue sapphire, a diamond, a red-orange jacinth, and a purple amethyst.

A turban was made for Aaron with a small gold plate on its front bearing the engraved words "Holy to the LORD," empowered to remove any sinfulness from the Israelites' gifts and sacrifices. Linen breeches were made for all five priests, to be worn when serving God. Finally, tunics, sashes, and caps were sewn for the four sons.

"I went by the clothiers today," said Moses, "and your garments are nearly complete. You will be honored above all other men here."

"Except for you," Aaron added.

"Mine is a different calling. Be gracious and humble in your new role," advised Moses.

"I am told that there are bells sewn into the hem of my robe that will jingle as I walk. What are they for?"

"Of utmost importance," said Moses. "God says that His ear is carefully attuned to their soft tinkling sound, as a mother's ear to her baby's cry. He will hear and protect you whenever you enter or leave the holy of holies. If you try to enter that room without the bells on, or if an unauthorized person does, he will surely die."[5]

"By what means?" Aaron asked. "God cannot always be present at that veil. Even you see Him as a focused God who, as you said, 'rides the heavens to your help.'"[6]

"I'm not sure. Death seems automatic. There must be a lethal power guarding it, perhaps Death himself, or an angel, like the destroying ones at Passover. Warn your sons, who will wear no bells, that they are prohibited from ever entering that sacred room. Only I am permitted in there, when invited, without the bells."

God's desire to dwell among the Israelites was about to be satisfied. No longer would He hover as smoke on the nearby mountain or visit Moses' remote tent in the form of a cloud. His tabernacle was completed and all was ready.

Early the next morning, Moses and Aaron entered the courtyard. Moses walked alone into the tabernacle, lighted the oil in the lamps, placed incense in the cup on the golden altar, and then exited as God had ordered. The tabernacle was to be vacant. As the two brothers waited expectantly, the bright cloud soon hovered over the tabernacle and indwelt it. Even the curtains surrounding the tabernacle glowed from the inner light; the glory of God had occupied His home.[7]

That first day of His residence was to be a busy one. It was imperative that the vacillating Israelites comply with God's first commandment— *"You shall have no other gods before Me" (Ex. 20:3)*—or else their devotion would be milked away by the world's idolatrous enticements, destroying the perfect society that He sought for them.

Soon after the cloud had settled over the tabernacle, God called Moses into the holy of holies. He informed Moses that the primary way the priest and people were to worship Him was through sacrifices.

Moses knew that the Egyptians had worshipped their many gods with various sacrifices—animals, goods of many kinds, even children—but Moses wondered, what of value could these people sacrifice? They had proven skills as craftsmen and could make elegant goods to give to Him.

But that was not God's wish. The sacrifices must be the most highly prized animals that the people had bred and raised. The lesser animals would continue to provide for the Israelites as usual.

God had specific rituals of worship, designating the name and occasion for each sacrifice and the items required. The sacrificial animal must be a firstborn, perfect one-year-old. If chosen from the herd, it was to be a young bullock, a sheep, or a goat. To sacrifice *"an ox or a sheep which has a blemish or any defect, is a detestable thing to the* LORD *your God"* (Deut. 17:1), He warned. Sacrificial birds must be turtledoves or pigeons.

God named the first sacrifice a *burnt offering* (Lev. 1:1f). If the people wished to revere Him, to show Him great respect, they must bring an animal to the priest, kill it, and burn it up completely on the bronze altar.

A second type of sacrifice was the *thanksgiving (peace) offering* (Lev. 3:1f), made when a person wished to thank God for a remarkable blessing. The priest retained a portion of this slain animal's meat for his own family to eat, showing God's acceptance of it, and then returned the remainder to the person offering the sacrifice. This was the only time that a layperson could share in the consumption of a sacrifice. Since there would be a large amount of meat left over from a goat, lamb, or bull, the giver was encouraged to hold a banquet. Passover was this type of sacrifice.

If a man broke any of His laws, God—being absolutely holy and righteous—could not tolerate such sin, and the lawbreaker deserved to die. However, being merciful, God offered man a surrogate, an animal, to die in his stead. This *sin sacrifice* (Lev. 4:1f) would satisfy God, as long as the sinner was contrite. If the sinner were a common man or a low-level leader, although God abhorred the sin, He was eager to forgive him. God considered his animal to be holy, and therefore the priests must eat a portion of it. The remainder was to be burned on the bronze altar, its smoke ascending as a soothing, sweet odor to God.

However, the meat of the animal sacrificed for the sin of the most respected people, the priests or the congregation as a whole, was considered vile, and God ordered that animal to be taken outside of the camp in disgrace and burned up totally in a place designated as "clean."[8] Although the sinner was forgiven, God would not inhale the foul odor of that sacrifice. That ended God's message.

Moses met with the leaders and Zuriel outside the camp. He stood in the middle of the group, who were seated on a hillside under a late-afternoon sun.

Nethanel said, "Moses, we are puzzled. God issued His strict commandments for us but now He gives this sacrificial code, indicating—to me, at least—that He knows we cannot obey His laws."

Moses said, "We cannot by ourselves, and He knows it. By His mercy, the animal sacrifices are the only means to gain His forgiveness."

"All right, for the animals," added Abidan. "But you mentioned to us earlier that God prohibits child sacrifice. Think of the cultures that sacrifice a child to their gods to ward off evil or to add the vitality of the child to their gods."

"If God never condoned human sacrifice," said Ahira, "why did He tell Abraham to offer Isaac as a burnt offering?"

"He was but t … t … testing Abraham," said Pagiel.

"I believe that you are right, Pagiel," Moses said. Then he added, "child sacrifice is an abominable, cruel act to God. He knows that it would tear the heart out of a parent to sacrifice a child. There will be no child sacrifice, and that is God's final word.

"I have told you how to treat the meat of the animals. Now I must speak to you of life, as God has directed me, that essential force that God exhales into the nostrils of every living being. Powerful and sacred, it resides in the blood.[9] Therefore, it is an abominable thing for any man to ingest any of another being's lifeblood. The custom of other peoples, to consume the blood of specific animals to gain their strength—the deer for speed, the bull for strength—must never be done by us.

"Since all blood is God's, all animals must be bled to death before being prepared for a meal or a sacrifice. That blood contains strong sin-cleansing properties outside of the body, as it may also have within it. God has a special use for it.

"For example, if a man breaks a law," Moses explained, "that sin takes on a vitality of its own,[10] defiling the sinner with a pervasive guilt. That sin also pollutes God's holy items, sticking to them like scum; lesser sins befoul only the bronze altar, but the more serious ones invade the tabernacle.

"The precious blood collected from every sacrifice must be sprinkled about the bronze altar to symbolically soak up the individual sin that befouls it, like a sponge, cleansing the altar. However, only a portion of the blood collected from the animal sacrificed for the sin of a priest, or the congregation as a whole, whose meat has been rejected by God, should be spattered about the bronze altar. The remainder must be carried inside the tabernacle's holy room by the high priest and sprinkled before the golden altar to eradicate the sin that has invaded the tabernacle and to gain God's forgiveness."

Nahshon asked, "Moses, the sinner must bring his animal into the courtyard, right up to the bronze altar, give it to the priest, press his hand on the animal's head, transferring his guilt to it, and slay the animal himself in a bloody ceremony. Why not have the priest do the killing?"

"God's laws, not mine, Nahshon. I suppose that He wants the person to realize the seriousness of his crime." Moses continued, "I have told you what is to be done with the meat and the blood of the animals; now the fat. God says also that *all fat is the LORD's* (Lev. 3:16). Therefore, any animal killed for the sacrifice that is not burned up completely on the altar must have the fat of the intestines, the kidneys, and the liver removed by the priest and burned up on the altar. Thus, a portion of every animal is cremated."

Shelumiel was puzzled. "What benefits do we get for slaughtering our prized yearlings?"

"His blessings, I suppose," offered Abidan. "It's the only way that we can communicate with Him. Only Moses speaks directly to Him and, I suppose, Aaron and his sons will too when they are anointed."

"We will lose many animals," Shelumiel continued. "Moses tells us that the priest will kill a lamb every morning, one every evening, and an additional one on the first of each week. Seems a waste just to satisfy this God."

Eliasaph wagged a cautionary finger. "A waste to you, perhaps, but consider—God wants us to focus our worship on Him. We each have our failings. Gamaliel, you worship your athletic ability, winning almost all physical games we play. Bershema, the hours you spend maintaining your skill as an archer could be called worship. Abidan, your scrolls are to you the most important possessions you own. You pore over your history every spare moment you have. And Pagiel, how many times a day do you count your money? God wants our worship first; our own interests come second."

Gamaliel said, "Don't forget that we are to also burn some of our precious grain every day—the *grain offering* (Lev. 2:1f)—to acknowledge that all sustenance comes from Him."

"Gamaliel, will we not deplete our stores of grain by such daily sacrifices?" Ahira asked.

Moses answered, "Use only a portion of the grains you brought with you, Ahira, because God's manna will satisfy your hunger until we reach Canaan, where we will find fields ripe with grains."

As the meeting was drawing to a close, Moses said, "Another feature of the sacrifices: God stipulated that since leaven is considered to be a symbol of evil, it may never be offered on the altar."

Endnotes
1. The story of Jethro in this chapter is based on Exodus 18.
2. Chapters 25 to 31 of Exodus give details of God's plan for the tabernacle.
3. "not die," Ex. 30:20.
4. Aaron's clothes, Exodus chapter 28.
5. "surely die," Ex. 28:35.
6. "rides the heavens," Deut. 33:26.
7. "glory of the LORD," Ex. 40:34.
8. "clean," Lev. 4:12.
9. "resides in the blood," Lev. 17:11-14.
10. "that sin takes on a vitality of its own" *Interpreter's Dictionary of the Bible, Supplementary Volume*, "Atonement," Keith Crim, ed., 1991, p. 79.

Chapter 9

God Means What He Says

One day, a judge brought a girl before Moses.[1] With reddened eyes, she looked beseechingly at him. The judge began, "Moses, I have no law to decide this particular matter, and I need your help. This girl wants to be married tomorrow but made an oath to her father in anger several years ago never to marry. What can she do?"

Moses answered, "The law states that her father could have nullified the vow on the day she spoke it. However, her husband-to-be can nullify it, but only on the day of marriage. Otherwise she must live by it.

"Furthermore, a husband may nullify a vow that his wife makes and then rues. However, a man must keep any vow he makes. A widow or divorcee, having no man to intervene for her, is also bound by her vows."

"Are there no exceptions?" asked Eliab.

"You may try to bend those laws, but to me they seem clear and without variance," said Moses. "Any vow attracts God's attention, as do the bells on Aaron's robe. Or perhaps His angels hear the vows and bring them to Him. Beware, He requires their fulfillment."

On another day, Eliasaph and Pagiel confronted Moses. Eliasaph said, "This morning, soldiers stoned a man to death for practicing sorcery. One of the soldiers said that you condemned him."

"God says that the crime of practicing sorcery, like consulting spiritualists, cannot be forgiven. Two men overheard him in his tent, calling on a clay demon to kill Nethanel so that he could rule his tribe. If two witnesses agree, that is all God requires," Moses answered. "I have been given a set of commandments that I dare not alter. Ordering executions is the most difficult."

"It must be," Pagiel sighed as he sat down.

"God demands much!" said Eliasaph. "Moses, we know of His laws, but we should become wary of the penalties. Are there many other sins calling for execution?"

Moses answered grimly, "Although the animal sacrifices suffice for most of the confessed sins, God treats those of murder, beastiality, sodomy, sorcery, and adultery harshly.[2] The same brutal penalty applies to one who sacrifices a child to a god, one who blasphemes the name of the LORD, or one who seduces a person away from loyalty to the LORD.[3] In God's eyes, the extreme penalty is appropriate for such an abhorrent sin. Don't do it."

"Moses," said Pagiel, leaning forward, "let's be honest. Some people will not confess a sin they committed in secret, perhaps unwittingly, like gossiping, or even one committed hau ... hau ... hau ... haughtily—like a ... a ... a ... adultery. What are we to do about those?"

Moses answered, "Those unconfessed sins accumulate at the altar and will eventually seep into the tabernacle, contaminating it so much that God might not enter it.[4] To remove those sins, once a year, and only once a year, the high priest must carry some of a specific animal's blood into the holy of holies room and sprinkle it on the ark's mercy seat to cleanse it. That is the Day of Atonement. The three altars are therefore of graduated holiness: the bronze, then the golden, and, most sacred, the mercy seat.[5]

"After we satisfy Him by our sacrifices on the bronze altar, He also offers us another great gift, freedom from our feelings of guilt. That applies to our own lives also, doesn't it? Only when guilt is washed away by forgiveness can the opportunity for love return."

Pagiel said, "During our sacrifices before the tabernacle, we are permitted to physically come as close to God as possible."

Moses smiled. "That's His wisdom. He wants us to shed our bad habits, Pagiel. If we can turn to Him with all of our heart and soul, He will help us do so. We will talk some more tomorrow."

Moses was fatigued from the day's activities and slept well that night, awakening near dawn for another appointment with God. The cloud spoke above the mercy seat and told him that it was time for him to perform the sacred ceremony, ordaining Aaron and his sons as priests.[6] Moses invited a number of congregants into the courtyard for the ceremony but warned them to stand clear of the tabernacle and the bronze altar.

When the crowd gathered, Moses ushered Aaron and his four sons, clothed only in their breeches, to the doorway of the tabernacle. Moses carried a basket of unleavened bread. Ten strong Levites led two rams and a bull ox up to the altar.

Moses helped Aaron to dress in his full priestly outfit. Then Moses filled a small vase with anointing oil and, entering the tabernacle, dabbed a little on each item there. Once again outside, he anointed the bronze altar and its utensils, and finally Aaron's head, dedicating them all to the service of God.

Moses turned to Aaron. "Aaron, being sinful as we all are, your sins must be washed away before you can be invested into your holy office. Have your sin offering brought to me."

After Aaron and his sons placed their hands on the bull, transferring their sins to it, Levites exsanguinated the animal. Moses dipped his finger into the blood and rubbed some of it on the horns of the bronze altar and poured the remainder at its base, purifying it of any past sins of the priests. The excised fat of the bull was burned on the altar, while the remainder of it was taken outside the village and burned to ashes in the clean place.

Next, a ram was sacrificed, its blood sprinkled around the altar and the carcass incinerated on the altar, as a burnt offering for the five, a pleasing aroma arising to God.

Moses dabbed the blood of the second sacrficed ram, the ram of ordination, on the right earlobe, right thumb, and right great toe of each of them, symbolic of their being able to hear God, do His works, and walk with Him.[7]

Moses piled the fatty organs of the second ram, a piece of unleavened bread, and some oil onto their opened hands, as God gave authority over His sacrifices to the priests. After removing the items and burning them on the bronze altar, Moses anointed the sons.

The five roasted and ate some of the meat of the second ram and some of the unleavened bread in front of the tabernacle before entering into its holy room to be sequestered for seven days for God to finish their ordination.

The one prized bull, sacrificed for the sins of the priests-elect, was insufficient to set them apart in God's eyes. Therefore, during the week of their seclusion, Moses sacrificed another bull daily to acquire that holiness. In addition, Moses was told to begin the daily sacrifice of two lambs for the congregation.

As the crowd began to disperse, Moses detained the twelve tribal leaders. He said to them, "The tabernacle is reserved as the priests' private place of worship. The bronze altar, however, is for the people's worship. I dedicated the tabernacle, but it is you who have been honored to dedicate this altar.[8]

"Each tribe will be assigned one day in sequence to bring their offering. Even though tribes vary greatly in size, all will bring the same, so that none will expect greater blessings.

"Each leader on his appointed day will bring a large silver dish and bowl, each filled with flour and oil as a grain sacrifice, and a smaller gold pan filled with personal incense. The tableware will be put into the tabernacle. Also bring twenty-one animals—three bulls, six rams, six goats, and six lambs—to be sacrificed as burnt, peace, and sin offerings, because it is a sacred altar."

Whereas the smaller golden altar in the tabernacle was warmed only slightly by the oil that Aaron ignited in it twice a day, this larger bronze altar outside would be a hot and busy place. There the fires would smolder continuously, to be stoked into blazing heat as necessary to incinerate the parts of the carcasses thrown upon it by the priests.

God selected the tribe of Judah, Israel's (Jacob's) fourth son, to initiate the dedication of the bronze altar. In a society where the firstborn deserved all honor as the leader and a double portion of inheritance, Israel had rejected Judah's three older brothers: Reuben, the eldest, when Israel discovered him fornicating with the handmaiden, Bilhah, Israel's concubine; and Simeon and Levi for the vengeful slaughter of the Shechemites. Judah was the one chosen to lead. "Judah the lion" Israel called him more than 450 years earlier. "His brothers would bow down to him—the scepter shall not depart from Judah."[9] Although Judah would lead, Israel had long ago conferred the inheritance rights of the firstborn on Ephraim and Manassah, the offspring of his favorite son, Joseph.[10]

The following morning, Moses stood before the tabernacle and received the tableware (acquired from the Egyptians) and grain from

Judah's Nahshon, and with his many assistants, consummated the animal sacrifices. Then each day, a different tribe brought their offerings.

On the eighth morning, after Gamaliel had paid his tribute, Moses went to the tabernacle door and called to Aaron and his sons. They emerged solemnly, keeping to themselves whatever insights they had gained in God's presence during their period of seclusion. They would only rarely appear in public thereafter.

"While I anointed the items of the tabernacle," Moses said to them, "I was reminded to emphasize one particular law to you priests: since the golden altar is sacred, never place any strange incense or burnt offering or wine on it.[11] Also, now that you are ordained, you must make the daily sacrifices for the congregation. Sacrifices such as the ones Jethro made or that I have been making will no longer be acceptable."

Aaron addressed his brother solemnly. "Moses, I believe that I am changed. You had your time on the mountain with God, and we had ours, perhaps not so intimate, in the tabernacle."

"Good. Having been ordained, it is time to inaugurate you priests into service."[12]

Therefore, in the afternoon, Aaron, assisted by his sons, offered first his own personal animal burnt and sin sacrifices, and then the animals that the congregation had donated. Only the carcass of the congregation's goat—a holy sin offering for this occasion—was placed on the ground next to the altar, to remain there until cooked and partially eaten by the priests and their families.

When Aaron lifted up his hands and blessed the people, the glory of the LORD suddenly appeared before them. Tongues of fire leaped from the bright light and consumed the remains that were on the altar in a blazing show of God's approval. When the people saw it, they shouted and fell on their faces before God. Later, as the light gradually disappeared, everyone filed out of the courtyard.

Weary from assisting in the sacrifices, Nadab and Abihu, Aaron's sons, retired to Nadab's empty tent that evening. They flopped on a couch, passing a skin of wine back and forth between them.[13]

Nadab began, "I've had enough. I am tired of being ordered around by Aaron and his God. We spent most of our lives following the dictates of those Egyptians. And now, being free, no one is going to tell me what I can and cannot do. After all, we are priests.

"How can this God tell us, after all His work we do," as the pitch of his voice rose, "that we cannot go into the holy of holies, only Aaron can? Ha, Father with all of His faults. Well, by Osiris, we're important too."

"God cannot get by without our services," added Abihu.

"Miriam tells us that our old friends, who we used to drink and party with, taunt her whenever they see her, saying that we are no better than they," said Nadab.

As they drank more, Nadab said, "We'll show them. Let's do it. God won't be there at this time of night. Just in case, let's take our censers with us. I'll get some coals for them. But where can we get incense?"

"We can use some skin lotion. It won't make any difference. The smell is about the same," said Abihu.

They walked to the courtyard, swinging their smoking censers on cords, Nadab guzzling from his wine skin. They entered the tabernacle's holy room. Giggling, Nadab spilled some wine on the golden altar.

"All right, Abihu," said Nadab. "Let's see if God is in there or not."

"Bells or no bells ... " Abihu began as they parted the curtain and walked into the holy of holies. Before a further word was spoken, a sword of fire shot out from the mercy seat and consumed their flesh.

When they were noted to be missing, Moses, Aaron, and his other two sons set out to look for them. Inquiring about, a man recalled seeing them walking toward the tabernacle. The foursome hurried through the gate into the courtyard.

"Have you seen Nadab and Abihu?" Moses asked a Levite sitting on the ground near the fence. He pointed toward the tabernacle. As they entered the tabernacle, Moses held up his hand and ordered, "Stay here," and then parted the curtain and walked alone into the holy of holies. He stared in shock. Lying before him were the bodies of the two sons, with charred skin covering the skulls and the hand bones that protruded from their tunics. Aghast, he fell to one knee, gently touching the tunic of one.

Moses dragged their remains out through the veil, one at a time, and laid them down in front of Aaron, who buckled to his knees in grief and horror at the fearful sight of their blackened, featureless heads. Their brothers turned away, disgusted. Moses walked outside, called to the Levites, and told them to summon two of Aaron's male cousins.

When they arrived, Moses gave them a terse order: "Carry your relatives away from the front of the sanctuary and take them outside of the camp immediately."

One asked, as the cousins viewed the bodies, "What happened?"

"God," was the only answer that Aaron could murmur.

"Their bodies are burned but look, their tunics are intact," said one of the cousins as they picked up the bodies.

"God's aim is perfect," said the other.

Moses turned to Aaron, gently grasping his forearm. "God has said, *'By those who come near Me I will be treated as holy, and before all the people I will be honored'* (Lev. 10:3). No anointed one can expect sympathy when he willfully breaks God's laws. You must outlaw your own grief. Therefore, do not show your troubled faces to the people lest God become wrathful against all the congregation."[14] Aaron, fighting back tears, stumbled silently into Eleazar's arms as Moses consoled him. "All of the other Israelites will grieve in your stead for Nadab and Abihu."

God's cloud appeared and warned Aaron, *"Do not drink wine or strong drink, neither you nor your sons with you when you come into the* [tabernacle], *so that you may not die"* (Lev. 10:9).

As the cloud receded, Aaron said to Moses, "Could they have been drinking?"

Seeing the wineskin, Moses answered, "Perhaps. All I know is that God's word is reliable, either as warning or promised blessings." Moses left to check on the bodies.

An hour later, he returned to the courtyard to search for the carcass of the holy goat with its meat. Aaron and his sons were standing near the bronze altar.

Moses said, "I do not see the body of the holy goat. Have you eaten of it as commanded?"

"No," said Aaron.

Moses looked to the altar and saw flames consuming the carcass. His sympathy toward Aaron vanished. "Aaron, God put that goat into your hands! By failing to eat of it, the guilt of the congregation persists. Brother, these are not my laws, but God's! Dare you bring God's wrath on us all?"

Aaron answered defensively, "Because of the sins of my sons and their execution, if we had eaten a sin offering today, would it have been good in the sight of the LORD?" *

Moses' withering stare softened. He hesitatingly accepted Aaron's explanation and hoped that God would also. Dusk brought an end to the proceedings, and Moses left them.

Early the next morning, a haggard Aaron and his two sons faithfully dressed and entered through the courtyard gate to sacrifice the mandatory year-old lamb with oil, grain, and the newly ordered quart of wine, God's libation[15]

After that, Abidan and a cadre of men from Benjamin brought grain-filled tableware and their twenty-one animals into the courtyard, where Aaron methodically orchestrated their sacrifice. Moses entered the courtyard to bring God's reminder to Aaron that it was the ninth day of the month. The Israelites had been so busy dedicating the altar, and the priests so preoccupied with first their own ordination and then the tragedy, that all had forgotten to prepare for Passover, one year after leaving Egypt. *"Let the sons of Israel observe the Passover at its appointed time"* (Num. 9:2), said God. The next day, all families selected their lambs and prepared them.

Four days later, following the bronze altar sacrifices of Naphtali, the twelfth and final tribe, the entire company of people celebrated Passover. They stripped their houses of the last vestiges of leaven, killed the lambs at twilight, roasted them, and ate them quickly with unleavened bread and bitter herbs.[16]

"Why bitter herbs?" Nethanel had asked Nahshon.

The jeweler answered, "It was bitter living in Egypt. But it was also bitter, I'll wager, for God to kill all of those firstborn Egyptians. Perhaps we have some bitterness ahead of us. You decide."

Complete now was God's sacred circle: the sacrifices themselves, the fully ordained priests to administer them, and the dedication of the altar on which to proffer them.

Endnotes
1. The emphasis on vows is based on chapter 30 of Numbers.
2. "murder, beastiality, sodomy...," Lev. 18:19-31; 20:6, 10, 13, 27.
3. "seduces a person...," Lev. 20:2,27; 24:16; Deut. 13:10.
4. "sins accumulate" *Interpreter's Dictionary of the Bible, Supplementary Volume,* "Atonement," Keith Crim, ed., 1991, p. 79.
5. "altars of graduated holiness" J.H. Kurtz, *Offerings, Sacrifices, and Worship in the Old Testament,* 1998, p. 49.
6. Leviticus 8 describes the ordination ceremony.

7. "blood on right earlobe...," description of the rite: J.H.Hertz, ed., *The Pentateuch and Haftorahs;* Hebrew Text, English translation and commentary, 5 vols. 1929–1936.
8. altar dedication, Num.7:10ff.
9. "scepter shall not depart...," Gen. 49:8,9.
10. "rights of the first-born," 1Chron. 5:1.
11. "strange incense," Ex. 30:9.
12. Leviticus 9 describes inauguration ceremony.
13. Story of priests testing God told in Leviticus 10.
14. "wrathful against all the congregation," Lev. 10:6.
15. "libation," Ex. 29:40.
16. "bitter herbs," Ex. 12:8.

Chapter 10

God's Word: A Lamp Unto Their Feet
(Ps. 119:105)

Following passover and, at the conclusion of the Feast of Unleavened Bread, God called Moses again to the tabernacle and reminded him, *"Tell your brother Aaron that* [except for the annual Day of Atonement] *he shall not enter at any time into the holy place inside the veil, before the mercy seat ... lest he die"* (Lev. 16:2).

God continued with a list of directives for abundant living and for faithful and appropriate sexual activities. He exhorted them: *"You are to be holy to Me, for I the LORD am holy; and I have set you apart from the peoples to be Mine"* (Lev. 20:26).

The ownership of the land that sustained human existence was important to God. To guarantee that each family would always have their apportioned plot in Canaan, He established the Year of Jubilee, a time to be celebrated every fifty years, at which time all land deeds would revert back to their original owners at no cost. *"The land, moreover, shall not be sold permanently, for the land is Mine. You are but aliens and sojourners with Me"* (Lev. 25:23), God said. If, for some reason, one's land had to be sold, a kinsman must buy it and be prepared to sell it back to its original owner for its adjusted value. If a kinsman could not buy the land, another could purchase it under the same agreement.

God commanded them to love one another regardless of the behavior of a neighbor or stranger. They should not lie or swear falsely to him, and never slander him. They should settle their differences peacefully and not carry grudges. In consideration of the poor, they should leave the ends of the crop rows unharvested, and the fallen grapes in the vineyard for them to gather so they would not have to steal.

God accentuated these and other admonitions twenty separate times, reminding them that *"I am the LORD your God"* (Lev. 19).

Moses recorded all of God's orders on his scrolls and left the tabernacle.

Shepherds and scouts, away from camp for days, often killed and consumed the meat of wild dogs and boars, ravens, and even snakes. So also did other Israelites, determined to spare their own animals. Those men occasionally became seriously ill and some died. God sought to protect them, so He prohibited the eating of certain animals. He divided the creatures into edible ("clean") and inedible ("unclean"), with specific details about each group.[1]

"Animals with a divided hoof, and which chew their cud, are clean," Moses told the leaders at a meeting, "cows, sheep, and goats. Pigs do not chew their cud, and rabbits do not have a cloven hoof. Animals that walk on their paws are unclean. Only fish with both fins and scales are clean. Among birds, the carnivores are unclean."

"Eagles and seagulls," said Abidan.

Nethanel was relieved. "Good. We can still eat the quail and partridge. Any more, Moses?"

"One more. Of insects, only the four-footed ones with jointed legs for jumping are fit for human consumption."

"Ah, the locust and grasshopper," said a smiling Ahira.

Gamaliel said, "Gentlemen, by separating these foods, we are reminded daily how God has separated us from other nations, giving us a different calling, and obliging us not to be as they."[2]

Moses said, "I am told that some men are offering parts of even their slaughtered clean animals to strange gods, such as the goat demon.[3] To prevent this, all animals to be eaten must be brought up to the tabernacle and bled before the priest."

Moses added, "God also tells me that anyone, including undertakers and gravediggers, who touches a dead person or his grave or who enters his tent is unclean and must leave the camp for seven days to be certain he will not become ill. He may re-enter the camp, briefly on the third, and also on the seventh days, to receive purification by being sprinkled with sacred water that had been filtered through the ashes of a perfect red heifer[4]. Likewise, every open vessel in the dead man's tent without a covering tied down on it shall be unclean."

"Does death move from one body to the next?" asked Ahira.

"Or is death in the vapors arising from the deceased?" asked Nethanel. "I've heard that is so."

"I do not know," said Moses. "Just follow His laws. He wants to protect us."

God's new laws added to the burden of a people who needed help and encouragement in obeying. Moses brought his concerns to God, who promised that He would shower endless blessings on them if they maintained their allegiance to Him, giving to them rains in their season, fruitful trees, an abundance of food, protection from harmful beasts and enemies, and peace. The people would multiply greatly, and God would bless every phase of their lives.

But widespread disobedience was intolerable and would ruin their consummate future, as only He foresaw. Increasing curses would befall them if they were rebellious. First, it would be disease, fevers, and fears. They would flee at the sound of a driven leaf.[5] Then a famine would occur. Finally, many would be captured by enemies, and others would be scattered among other nations, suffering plagues. But in their absence, at least the land will enjoy its Sabbaths.[6]

God added, however, that if the suffering people could humble themselves and confess their waywardness, He would remember His covenants with Abraham, Isaac, Jacob, and with His people, and would not totally destroy them. He offered no other promises.

Moses sank to one knee and wiped the perspiration from his forehead. God's litany of curses for his wards, though only a threat, weakened him. He would have his leaders inform the people of these conditions.

One morning, Ahira was walking through the village with his two good friends, Gamaliel and Abidan. Ahira commented, "The continual bickering of my people exhausts me. There are days when I wish the Naphtalites would appoint a different leader."

"Why are you so irritable lately, Ahira?" asked Abidan. "There seems to be more to your anguish than just your people."

"Perhaps." Ahira paused a moment. "God has commanded us to love and care for our wives, but I often fail. They largely bless us, but at times they try us; is that not so?"

"My wife and I disagree," admitted Gamaliel. "Sometimes it is bronze against stone, if that's what you mean." He looked hard at Ahira. "Is it deeper?"

Seeming a bit uncomfortable, Ahira flicked an invisible bug from his left foot. "Safda takes good care of our family and has greatly satisfied me for twenty-three years," said Ahira. "It is only our conversations. It is a problem I have analyzed too much already."

"And that is?" asked Abidan.

"I evaluate everything, even conversations," said Ahira. "Growing up, I often felt foolish with what I would say to people, and I began judging myself. I gradually spoke less, and then more thoughtfully. As I grew older—and wiser, I hope—people began to listen to my ideas and I became confident. But this judging persists, no longer by choice. I even judge Safda's conversations, and sometimes they cause me discomfort. It is my own fault."

Gamaliel turned to Ahira. "You have spent much energy crafting your speech, but that is not a priority with Safda. It is obvious that she cares for us all. If we could but sample humility, we might put our wives' well-being ahead of our own."

"God will have to enlarge that virtue within me," said Ahira.

"Speech flows from our hearts," said Abidan regretfully, "and anxious hearts produce both anxious speech and anxious ears. Perhaps we need to calm our hearts first."

Ahira smiled. "Your wisdom helps. Maybe I will be able to treat Safda better, for I hate to lose her love, even for a day."

A few days later, after Aaron had completed the prayers of dedication, he and his sons were prepared to sacrifice the morning lamb for the congregation. While Ithamar held the lamb firmly, Aaron began cutting away the wool from the left side of its neck.

"Ithamar, the meal that your wife served us yesterday was fit for a pharaoh," said Aaron. "She is a magician in the kitchen."

"I'll thank her for you, Father."

"She is a beautiful woman. And the little jewelry she wears is simple but elegant," said Aaron.

"She chooses well."

"Her jacinth ring is also expensive." Aaron looked at his son sternly.

Ithamar was silent.

Aaron continued, "It looks like the ring that Sorin gave to the treasury a month ago in thanksgiving for God having brought his son through the high fevers."

Ithamar silently tightened his grip on the shoulders of the animal.

Aaron stopped his cutting. "If that is true, how did you get the ring?"

Ithamar finally met Aaron's searching eyes. "Our treasury is well stocked from the census and other gifts. I told her of the ring once, and her mind settled on it."

"You stole it?" asked Aaron. "God has forbidden such a thing! You may bring down His anger on us all!"

"I am sorry, Father." There was a pause before Ithamar continued, "Will I be burned as my brothers were?"

"No," answered Aaron. "But you must return the ring and offer a sacrifice. Ask the herdsman, Matalel, if he will sell you one of his bull calves."

"How can I pay for it?" asked Ithamar. "I have spent the little personal money I had."

"Good fortune is yours. In two weeks, the tribes must give their first tithe to the Levites, who must in turn give to us priests a tenth of their collected tithe. You shall have more than enough for Matalel."

The two weeks passed, and Ithamar received his share of the money and bought his bull calf. Matalel and his four helpers brought it to the perimeter of the Levite camp the next day, where Ithamar met him with his brother Eleazar.

"I will go with you," said Matalel, holding one of two ropes fastened around the animal's neck, "because this one has an element of trust in me." The animal had been fed a large portion of a tasty root that made it more compliant.

The seven men herded the animal down a wide path through the Levite grounds to the curtain around the courtyard. When they parted the curtain and walked through, the calf began to pull against its ropes. The perspiring men strained to wrestle the 250-pound animal up to the bronze altar.

"Tie its legs together, front to front and rear to rear," said Aaron. Two of the men shackled the limbs of the bull, allowing a hand's breadth distance between each leg pair, as the animal began to thrash. An additional rope was secured about its middle.

Ithamar knew the routine. He placed his hand briefly on the bull's bobbing head, identifying it as a substitute for himself.

"Now cut," commanded Aaron. Ithamar had never sacrificed a bull for himself. He quickly, nervously tested the edge of the knife blade, and then, following his father's pointing finger, stuck the knife into the right side of the bull's neck. The animal jerked its head in pain, and Ithamar's moist hand dropped the knife.

"Plunge and slice!" yelled Aaron. Ithamar picked up the knife, drove it into the fettered bull's neck again, and pulled hard toward himself. The life-filled blood shot toward the ground in a steady, pulsating stream. Eleazar, bucket in hand, tried to catch it by moving in synchrony with the jerking victim. The bull's bulging eyes followed Ithamar as he raced around the men, steadied himself, and sliced into the left side of the animal's neck. Other helpers with buckets caught as much of the blood as possible, as puddles of red stained the earth. Then, on his knees, Ithamar stabbed into each groin. Blood issued from the right side only, into a waiting bucket. The bull began to sway. After several minutes, its eyes rolled back, its breathing became shallow, and it sagged, being pushed onto a waiting cart. Shaking, Ithamar looked away as Aaron took the knife from his hand.

"See that you sin no more," Aaron warned his humiliated son. "Being an anointed one of God, your deed invades the very tabernacle, and the blood of your animal must not only be sprinkled on the bronze altar but also onto the golden one inside."

Addressing the Levites, Aaron ordered, "Haul the carcass of the bullock out of the camp and burn it to ashes in a clean place."

Endnotes:
1. "clean, unclean," Leviticus chapter 11.
2. Separation of the foods: J. H. Kurtz, *Offerings, Sacrifices and Worship in the Old Testament*, 1998, p. 26.
3. "goat demon," Lev.17:7.
4. "Red heifer," Numbers 19:18f.
5. "sound of a driven leaf," Lev.26:36.
6. "land will enjoy its Sabbaths," Lev. 26:34.

Section III
Preparation for Departure

Chapter 11

Organizing

The first day of the next month arrived, the tenth month at Sinai. Only God knew that in just three weeks, the Israelites would embark on the last leg of their journey to invade Canaan. Were they ready? God had devoted no time to battle plans but instead had groomed them by outlining the ways in which He should be worshipped, ways that would enable the Hebrews to spurn the licentiousness of Canaan's inhabitants.

On a more mundane level, practical matters needed to be accomplished before their departure. How many people were at Sinai and how strong an army could they muster? In what order would the mass of people march, set up future camps, and how were they to transport the tabernacle?

God summoned Moses into the holy of holies one day and called for a census of the people[1], both individually and by tribe. All men would be counted who were over the age of twenty, the age at which each would have to serve a stint as soldiers; excluded from the census were all females. As each man was counted, he was required to pay the priest a half-shekel of silver to make atonement for himself, the money to be stored in the tabernacle. Curiously, when the noncombatant Levites were counted, all males older than one month were included, making their tribe seem larger than it was.

God enlisted the help of Aaron and the same twelve leaders who had represented their tribes at the bronze altar dedication to assist Moses in the census.

The census concluded that the seventy persons of Jacob's family who had immigrated to Egypt had multiplied profusely. The men over the age of twenty now numbered 603,550. If those under twenty and the women were added, the figure would be at least 2 million.

The totals did not surprise Moses, who had been told by God that they outnumbered their Egyptian masters and that the land was filled with them,[2] Israel's family having grown into a mighty and populous nation[3] while in Egypt. Moses and Aaron pondered the figures, wondering how they could continue to feed such a large number.

The census completed, God's next two concerns were the formulation of a housing plan for the great company and the plan for an orderly marching formation when departing from Sinai.

During the months at Sinai, the village of the Israelites had consisted of a somewhat random—often confused—arrangement of families in their huts and tents. To organize them, God directed the people of each tribe to dwell around their own particular standard with its unique insignia. The tabernacle and the courtyard were always to be in the center of the encampment, with the Levites, the families descended from the three sons of the long-dead Levi—Gershon, Merari, and Kohath—camped immediately around it. Moses and Aaron's families, also Kohathites, were to be located on the east side.

The first tribe in the camping sequence after the Levites was Judah, just as it had been in the bronze altar dedication. Judah was to reside under its own standard to the east, flanked by the tribes of Issachar and Zebulun; on the south, Reuben, between Simeon and Gad; on the west, Ephraim in the center, with Manasseh and Benjamin on its sides; and on the north, Dan, with Asher and Naphtali on either side. The descendants of each mother, Leah, Rachel, and their maids, remained together, except for those of Zilpah.

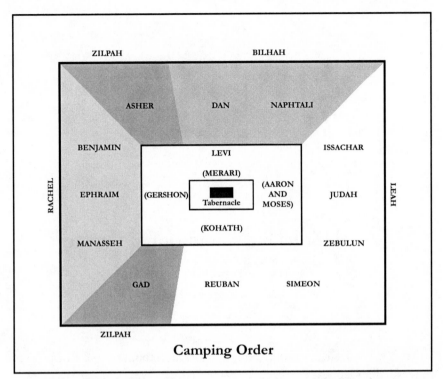

Camping Order

God told Moses that as each campsite was vacated, the tribes were to march in the same order as at the bronze altar dedication: Judah, Issachar, Zebulun, Reuben, and so on.

Endnote
1. "census," Numbers 1:1-46.
2. "land was filled with them," Ex. 1:7,9.
3. "mighty and populous nation," Deut. 26:5.

Chapter 12

A Glorious but Conditional Future

There had been a heavy rain the night before, and four men were inspecting a nearby flooded wadi.

Shelumiel stood with his hands on his hips. "This stream should not threaten our camp, but it will make the fruit trees produce. This Garden of Eden will be difficult to leave."

"Moses hints that our departure may be soon," Eliasaph said.

Shelumiel tossed a pebble into the stream. "Yes, to go up to Canaan to fight. I only hope that the conquest will be as easy as God says. The best we can hope for is that the enemy will be small in size and number, and their cities relatively unprotected."

"That battle is one problem," said Nahshon, "but God also ordered us to *'tear down their altars and smash their sacred pillars, and cut down the engraved images of their gods'*" (Deut. 12:3).

Eliasaph added, "I know. Our God says that we *'shall not follow other gods ... for the Lord your God in the midst of you is a jealous God'* (Deut. 6:14–15). That is why we are to destroy them."

"I feel uneasy about tearing down an altar to any god," said Shelumiel. "We've seen the wrath of this God of Abraham; dare we offend other gods and bring their vengeance on our whole camp?"

Nahshon nodded. "I share your concerns. Remember that the foreign kings who conquered Egypt and destroyed many temples were eventually driven out by vengeful Egyptians under the power of their degraded gods. No, my friends, it will take much more convincing before I'll put my axe to another god's shrine."

Eliasaph shook his head. "If this miracle-working God tells me to go into Canaan and destroy altars, I'll do so."

"Big talk, Eliasaph," said Nahshon. "We'll see how you do. But before we worry about others, let's look to ourselves. I'd be surprised if there isn't an idol of some other god or goddess—Anuke, Moloch, Rompha[1]—in most tents here."

"You are right," offered Pagiel. "We know that a moral rottenness exists in the village. For God's blessings to p-p-p-persist, we must consecrate ourselves, expelling those who are unclean, c-c-c-confessing our sins and performing required sacrifices."

Nahshon nodded solemnly. "I cannot remember banishing an unclean person, though they are known."

"There can be no exceptions," said Eliasaph. "We must enforce the laws. I am beginning to believe that God somehow sees into every tent, every bedroom."

Three days after Passover, Lashinar charged into Eleazar's tent, pulling a reluctant Coresha along with him. She was the same height as her husband, and her head was bowed. Lashinar blurted out, "Now, priest, what should I do with this insufferable wife of mine who has been unfaithful to me?"

Eleazar responded sternly, "On what grounds do you believe this?"

"I have seen her talk with the bachelor, Meelar, on several occasions," Lashinar spat out. "When we walk down between the tents, people titter to themselves and to each other behind cupped hands, evading my questioning stares. She keeps me at bay often, and I do not know why. She spends less time preparing meals, and their flavors have waned. She has been away when I come in at night—at least three times in the last month. I believe she is having an affair."

"When she came home late, where did she say she was?" asked Eleazar.

"At her sister's. She denies anything else."

Eleazar looked away for a moment. "And what does her sister say?"

Lashinar glowered. "Of course she wouldn't tell me the truth; you know how sisters stick together like dye to a cloth."

Eleazar turned to Coresha. "Go home, daughter Coresha. Let me talk with Lashinar alone." She raised her dark eyes to the priest, bowed quickly, turned, and glided away.

Eleazar carefully weighed his words. "If this is true," he said, "your anger is merited. I suspect that those deeds go on from time to time in our close quarters, although none have been caught in the act, thank goodness. The penalty is severe." He looked off in the distance. "Meelar has always been a trusted worker, but I admit, the ladies are attracted to him. He should be married."

"Trusted by you, maybe, but I would like to kill him."

"Have you lost your love for Coresha?"

Lashinar softened. "Priest, I still love her, perhaps too much. I hate what I think she has done with him."

"Does Coresha know how much you love her?"

"If I would tell her how much I love her and how important it is that she loves me and is true to me, wouldn't she think me a helpless child? I realize my love the most after we have been angry, and I try to show it then without words." He waited a moment, pondering. "But God, how I need her, how I ache in silence at the little attentions she gives to other men. I believe she would be better occupied if only she could have another child. Our only, Zessa, is twelve. But first, I must know if she is but mine—alone."

Sympathy welled up in Eleazar's heart. "God has laid out a ceremony for such an occasion and named it the Law of Jealousy[2] because He sympathizes with the agony you suffer. He himself is jealous for those who have committed themselves to Him. Tomorrow, bring Coresha to my father Aaron, along with three and a half quarts of barley meal as a grain offering to show your sincerity. God has promised that, in this ceremony, He would discern the truth and punish or reward her."

The next day, Lashinar and a compliant Coresha appeared in front of Aaron near the tabernacle with the required grain offering. She stood before the priest, loosened her hair, and accepted a cupful of grain the priest poured into her hands, the grain offering of jealousy. Aaron brought forth a container of holy water, adding dust from the ground to form a water of bitterness, empowered by God to produce a curse or blessing. Aaron wrote a curse on a small scroll and washed water over it into the water of bitterness, and then stirred. Over the water, Aaron spoke an oath that Coresha repeated, understanding thereby that, if she were guilty of adultery, the water would cause her abdomen to swell permanently and her left thigh to waste away. If innocent, she would be immune from the curse of the water and would not merely be exonerated, but blessed. If previously barren, she would become miraculously fertile. Then she slowly drank a mouthful of the water of bitterness and returned the cup to the priest, who took the grain offering from her hand and burned it on the altar.

"Why don't you punish Meelar also or put him to the test?" asked Lashinar.

"I do not know why God chose the woman. Is she more in control of the situation? Is she more capable of resisting such a relationship? Or is she more subject to loneliness and rejection, more susceptible to unfaithfulness? Only God knows," answered Aaron.

Coresha's embarrassment hid what little anger she felt toward Lashinar and the priest, and her quiet acceptance of the humiliation helped her endure the trial. As she and Lashinar walked from the tabernacle, she felt a deeper love for him. If he loved her enough to go through this ceremony, he must be jealous of her. She had not been sure of that before. Only she knew of her physical innocence; but would she be condemned for her occasional wayward thoughts?

Over the next two weeks, her thigh remained strong, her figure fine, and her love with her husband was gradually restored.

Lashinar happened upon Sorin, mending the flap of his tent.

"Sorin, my friend, how is your family, your fine son, Hanniel?"

"They are fine, thank you. But Lashinar, you have become a bounding rabbit with a new enthusiasm about you, a joy absent for the last months. I have been worried about you. But now I am happy to see you at home more."

"I have a secret relief, Sorin; and yes, life is good and I am well. My Coresha, we talk now as we haven't in years. We seem to hear each other better. But tell me about your son."

"He is fine, vigorous, and healthy," Sorin replied. "But lately, he has a restlessness within. Nothing satisfies him. And it is not girls. He is nineteen now and will serve in the army next year. However, he speaks of a different commitment after that. He is drawn to this God and His concern for us, and wishes somehow to serve Him. Several other young men feel the same, and have joined together to see what options are open to them."

"That seems strange," puzzled Lashinar. "Would God welcome him? What does the priest say?"

"They have learned of the Nazirite vow[3] that God told Moses about, a way to draw closer to Him. By it he may serve God through the Levites for as long as he wishes—months or years—spending each day with them, helping them, and as he puts it, learning of God's revelations."

"With all the work to be done around the camp and all of the pretty girls from whom to choose a wife, that seems a bit unusual," remarked Lashinar.

"I agree, but that is his feeling," said the weaver.

"To get in with the Levites, there must be a price to pay, no?"

"Eight shekels, to show sincerity, at the beginning," said Sorin. "Then he cannot shave his hair or beard during his commitment and cannot eat or use any of the products of the grapevine—the juice, the oil, the wine, vinegar, raisins—nothing."

"I hear that grapes are plentiful in Canaan. That will be quite a self-denial. What does Karrinen say?" asked Lashinar.

"She is a loving mother, and whatever Hanniel wants to do is all right with her. She will support him, as I will—and help him to scrape up the shekels."

"You are lucky to have a son, even one with peculiar ideas. Perhaps I will someday be similarly blessed," said Lashinar.

"Oh?" Sorin's eyes brightened mischievously. "Do you know something we do not?"

"We shall see," said Lashinar as they parted.

Having concluded the orders for the consecration of those on the lower rungs of His holiness ladder—the people, then the Nazirites—God turned His attention to the promoted sons of Levi. He called Moses to the tabernacle's holy of holies and said that the Levites must go through an ordination ceremony[4]—similar to that of the priests—to obtain their consecration as ministers. The details of that ceremony were laid out to Moses, so he gathered the Levites and the congregation.

During the service, the Levites shaved their entire bodies with a razor, put on recently washed clothes, and were sprinkled with water by Moses instead of being anointed with oil like the priests. Representatives of the congregation laid hands on the Levites who, in turn, placed their hands on the heads of the two bulls chosen for the sacrifice, and past sins were purged from them as the bulls were killed.

Their life plan was given to them by God.[5] In his first twenty-five years, a Levite would live a normal life, during which time he could marry and have children, but for the next twenty-five years, he was to serve God. He and his family would always live near the tabernacle, assisting with its care and with Aaron's ministries to the people, teaching them the laws he learned from Aaron. Prohibited from land ownership by God, he would be given ample land to use for his home, for gardening, and for grazing of the cattle that he was permitted to own. All of his other food and money needs were to be supplied as gifts from the other twelve tribes. At age fifty, he could retire and have his needs still met by the community.

The Levites, forgiven by God, were not, however, imbued with instant perfection. Though a step closer to God, they had been rewarded by relinquishing their rights to land ownership, and were forbidden to fight in wars. They were to serve their own cousin, Aaron—whose golden-calf debacle was remembered—and his two sons, merely their peers. They were promoted from independence to subjection. At least a few resented the arrangement, and they served reluctantly.

Most, however, began their chores dutifully, passing on to others the knowledge that Aaron gave them, and they found that most of the people received these teachings well. It became apparent, however, that many of the Simeonites resented the Levites' presence in their homes and even shunned them out in the village. The Levites soon ceased advising them.

A few days after the Levite ordination, God told Moses that when the cloud ascended out of the tabernacle and moved away, the people were to follow until it stopped, there to set up the tabernacle and their village again.

Moses would need to communicate orders to the camp, and as instructed by God, he assigned his trusted metalsmith, Bezalel, the task of casting two silver trumpets for that purpose.

Bezalel

Bezalel was underweight at birth, and as he grew, he remained short in stature, with a broad nose, large, often protruding tongue, and wide-set eyes. He was always last in foot races because of a lack of energy and soon gave up trying. His mother, Rohja, recognized early that his mind was duller than those of her other three children, so she paid him more attention, encouraging his limited capacity.

She was a frugal housewife and collected the bits of clay that her husband, Uri, brought home in his pockets or on his feet. She learned to make sun-dried pottery from them for her family and often gave finished pieces away to admiring friends. In time she produced dolls, urns, and figurines from the clay. These were stealthily placed next to bricks in the ovens by Uri's friends. When Bezalel showed interest in trying to mimic his mother's work, Uri—an ox of a man with a tender heart for his family—began to come home with muddier clothing and feet.

The boy found satisfaction in his work, and in time, amazed his parents with beautiful artifacts fashioned by his stubby fingers. Uri once gave one of his son's painted vases to a benevolent Egyptian foreman. Word spread, and soon an Egyptian craftsman and his assistants came to visit the boy. The Egyptian snickered at the ugly eleven-year-old boy, but when Bezalel formed a small but perfect running horse out of clay before them, they were impressed. He was eventually sent to artisan's school, primarily so Egypt could make some use of this freakish-looking child.

Through a bull-like perseverance, Bezalel devoted himself to his tasks single-mindedly, mastering the wheel and the kiln, then the forge by age thirteen, and the hammer and chisel soon after. His favorite enterprise was sculpting, which often elicited his high-pitched croaks of glee. He flourished under the growing recognition of his accomplishments and was twenty-three when Pharaoh released the slaves. On the journey, he doggedly kept up with the others, in spite of his shuffling gait.

When tapped to supervise the temple construction, Bezalel was amazed at—and gratefully appreciatively for—the new skills that God instilled in him. He was a beloved leader and now enthusiastically tackled his new assignment.

He drew two nuggets of pure silver from the bag he had brought from Rameses and added them to a silver dish that he melted down, providing enough metal for the trumpets. Traces of other metals hardened the soft silver, and for several days, he molded and hammered them into two forearm-length trumpets. The instruments had slightly different diameters, so that when blown, they produced different sounds.

Bezalel proudly presented the two lustrous instruments to Moses. "I am unable to blow hard enough to play them," he apologized, "but I have heard my father do so.

"When blown steadily, their tone is melodious. When a forceful, intermittent breath is applied, the sound of an alarm is produced. I hope God approves of them."

"I am sure that He will," said a pleased Moses. "There will be many occasions for their use. Their blast will summon leaders. They will usher in feast days and days of sacrifice, Bezalel, to remind the people that God is their LORD. God has even told me that, should an enemy attack us, Aaron's sons, the trumpeters, are to blow an alarm to alert God and the people, and to assure them that God will go before them. I believe that God's ear is attuned to their distinct sound, just as it is to the tinkling of the bells on Aaron's robe. Thank you, Bezalel."

With that, God's agenda for Sinai was concluded. Much had transpired at that place in a little more than a year. His worship by the priests, the Levites, and the Nazirites was assured. He had provided precise details of how He would guarantee victory in upcoming battles and had given instructions about consecration at all levels. Now it was time to leave Sinai and put those principles into practice.

To confirm His responsiveness to His priests, God told Aaron that His blessings would be given to the people only after the priests would publicly pray for them. As they all assembled ready for the journey to Canaan, Aaron prayed aloud:

"The LORD bless you and keep you.

The LORD make His face to shine on you and be gracious to you.

The LORD lift up His countenance on you and give you peace."[6]

Endnotes

1. "Anuke, Moloch, Rompha," Acts 7:43.
2. "Law of jealousy," Num. 5:29.
3. "Nazirite vow," Numbers 6:1-21.
4. Levite ordination, Numbers 8:5-22.
5. Levite life plan, Numbers 8:23-26.
6. Aaron's prayer, Num. 6:24-25.

Section IV
The Journey Resumes

Chapter 13

Dissension Abounds

Once the trumpets were ordered, Moses suspected they would be moving out soon. He was familiar with the lands to the east, west, and south through his years of shepherding, but knew little of the more rugged valley directly to the north, with its scrubby brush, low trees, and rocky soil, an area unfit for grazing. That, however, was the direct path to Canaan, and if God should lead them in that direction, Moses wanted to be prepared. So one morning, Moses and his son Gershom mounted two donkeys with a supply of food and water, bid good-bye to Zipporah, left the camp, and followed Jethro's path to the east. In four hours, they arrived at Jethro's home, where they were greeted warmly. Moses briefly explained his mission and sought out his brother-in-law, Hobab.

"Hobab, you are aware of the horde of people that have been thrust into my hands to lead to Canaan?" asked Moses. "It is time for us to depart, and I believe that we will go northward. I know it to be a 'land of deserts and pits ... of drought and of deep darkness.'[1] You know where we should camp in the wilderness, and you would be as eyes for us. Will you lead us to Canaan?"

Hobab shook his head. "Moses, I have no need to go north now. Besides, I do not believe in your God, and I would feel unwelcome among you."

"I give you my word that whatever good the LORD does for us, we will do for you," replied Moses. "God will honor you. We are told that Canaan is a wonderland and that the opportunities that lie there are limitless."

"So Jethro has told me, for he traveled there once with a caravan." Hobab thought for a minute. "I have little holding me here. Jethro has plenty of help to care for his animals. If he will permit his daughter and grandson to leave, we will lead you. We will bring two bags with us in case we decide to stay for a while."

"We will need to leave in the morning, if it is agreeable with you," said Moses.

"If the others in my family are willing, we will go."

At sunrise, the party left, returning to the Israelite camp at noon.

Three days later, at dawn on the twentieth day of the fourteenth month after leaving Egypt, one of the sentries excitedly awakened Ithamar. He arose, followed the sentry out of his tent, and, glancing at the tabernacle, ran to Aaron's tent, pushed the flap ajar, and called in, "The cloud is rising from the tabernacle!"

Aaron said, "Then it is time to leave! Tell Moses!"

The sentry took the message to Moses. The brothers left their tents and stood watching as the cloud moved rapidly toward the north and then stopped about thirty miles away. The heartbeat of the people quickened as they made preparations to break camp. There arose a general din of expectant excitement.

While their wives and families packed their belongings, Moses and Aaron set out on different missions.

Moses soon found Joshua and told him to alert the leaders of the tribes to assemble. He hurried on to Hobab's tent. "God has indeed set our course to the north," he told his brother-in-law. "Our people are ready to follow you. We will take the morning to prepare; then plan to leave after noon."

"If they are ready for it, so are we," replied Hobab. "We may be in for a few days of difficult travel."

Moses then met with the leaders and went over the final marching orders.

Meanwhile, Aaron, who was responsible for the maintenance of the tabernacle, its courtyard, and grounds, sent Ithamar to the Levites' tents. Since the journey to Canaan would require that the tabernacle be relocated often, the tribe of Levi had been assigned to transport it.

"Notify them to meet with us outside of the tabernacle as soon as possible and see that the trumpets are blown," Aaron said to Ithamar.

Aaron walked to the tabernacle, where he met his two sons and many Levitical men. "Let us get moving," he said to the throng.[2] No specific orders were necessary because Aaron had trained the men in their respective tasks. As the priests entered the tabernacle, the men of the three Levitical families began their rehearsed work—more than three hundred had gathered already. The family of Merari was in charge of all of the wooden objects, from the wallboards to the pegs, and the family of Gershon, the curtains, the roof, and the screens. They first disassembled the courtyard walls, its gate, and the bronze altar before tackling the tabernacle itself, packing the heavy items onto six carts pulled by twelve oxen, all donated by the other tribes.

Aaron and his sons, who were permitted in the holy of holies for this occasion, worked alone inside. They took the heavy veil that separated the holy room from the holy of holies from its hooks, folded it, and spread it over the ark-mercy seat. Each of the other holy objects was covered with a separate colored cloth, chosen from a small, neat pile kept in one corner of the room. Animal skins were carefully fitted over each object to protect it from the weather. Aaron covered the hallowed ark with a pure blue cloth in order to vividly identify it, per God's instructions, while his sons placed the carrying poles through the handles on each of the other holy items. Once the items were covered, they called the third Levite family, the Kohathites, the clan of Aaron's family, to carry them, for God had said that no one except the Aaronites could see the uncovered holy items even for a moment, lest they die.[3]

"Remember," Aaron cautioned the leader of the Kohathite contingent, "the ark must always be carried by hand. Never put it on a wagon!"[4]

By the time the men carrying the furniture led the way into the hot sun, the Levites were taking down the tabernacle itself. Each man had an assigned duty, be it the carrying of pegs, the loading of lumber and curtains, separating and loading the layers of roof, or carrying a holy item from one site to another, there to re-assemble it. With such a workforce, all was soon made ready.

At midday, the trumpets of Bezalel sounded and the tribe of Judah, captained by Nahshon, led them out, trailing only Hobab and the ark-carrying Levites. Moses prayed aloud for protection and rallied the people: "Rise up O LORD! And let Thine enemies be scattered, and let those who hate Thee flee before Thee."[5] Nethanel and his Issacharites were followed by Eliab's Zebulun.

The fourth group, the tribes of Gershon and Merari, were protected by the three tribes in front of them. They would arrive at the campsite soon enough to set up the courtyard and the tabernacle so that the holy items could be installed when they arrived.

Two of the men of Gershon and Merari, traveling together, were talking. "Where are the firstborn males when there is work to be done?" asked the Gershonite. "I thought God honored them as the first sign of fertility of the womb, so that they would serve Him for life. I am third-born Levite and honored only in that I am steadying this heavily laden wagon in the hot sun."

"Who can hear your complaining?" said the second. "I think God chose them to serve Him in Canaan, not here. Besides, how much easier it is for Him to use us, an organized tribe who can serve now, than to try to muster up all the firstborn from each camp?"

"Then what is with this firstborn business? Consider the poor, clean animals, the firstborn never to be yoked, those from the flock never shorn, but both must be sacrificed in a holy ceremony held once a year?"

"You know, as I do. It shows our understanding that all life belongs to God. But as for you, remember that you could be carrying some of that load without the wagons or oxen."

Ignoring his comment, the first continued. "The firstborn children still have to be redeemed for five shekels, but then what? There are plenty of them walking easily before and behind us. It doesn't seem right."

"Wait and see. There will be plenty for them to do in Canaan. Now look, a small guide-cloud remains in the distance, but the large cloud has returned overhead to provide shade for us. Seems that your complaints were heard."

The tribes of the south side of the tabernacle, Reuben, Simeon, and Gad, walked next, then the Kohathites, carrying the holy items and following several hours behind the other Levites. After them were the tribes of Benjamin, Manasseh, and Ephraim. Forming the rear guard were Dan, Asher, and Naphtali.

In three days, led by Hobab, the Israelites reached the guide-cloud and made their camp, still in the rugged wilderness. When the ark arrived into the camp, Moses proclaimed, "Return Thou, O LORD, to the myriad thousands of Israel,"[6] a ritual he was to follow at the end of each day's march.

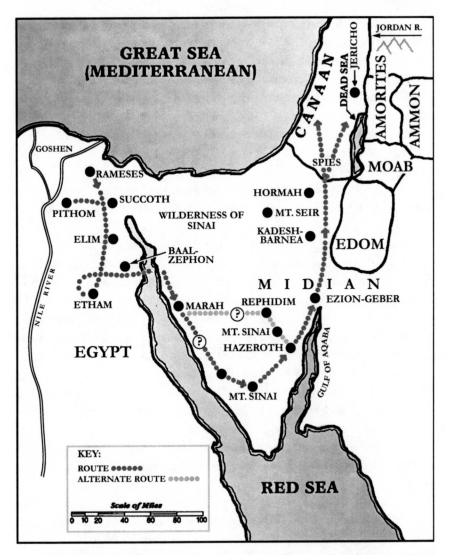

When the last of the travelers arrived, their weary shoulders and tired hands dropped their belongings. Others unloaded the wagons, pastured the oxen, arranged the baseboards for the tabernacle, erected the walls and curtains and drove in the individual tent pegs.

As personal tents were put up in the prescribed order and huts raised, occasional complaints turned into a din of sullen voices growing out of the temporary camp.

"Thirty miles in three days, across that wilderness. What does God expect from us?"

177

"I thought Hobab knew the best paths. Seems that we skidded off rocks every other step."

"Branches caught my hair."

"My arms were scratched by the shrubs."

"We should have stayed at Sinai. Why did God bring us here? No land can be worth this suffering."

"At this rate, my shoes will wear out in a few days. God better find me some new ones."

God listened to each murmur against Him and became deeply troubled again. His elaborate preparations had been for naught, the year at Sinai wasted.

Suddenly Moses, who was watching the completion of the tabernacle, heard shouts coming from the camping areas to the north, those of Dan, Naphtali, and Asher. Pagiel and Ahira arrived at the same time. "Moses," Ahira panted, "the camp is on fire. Flames began spouting out of several tents, and now they are spreading. Some people have been burned and goods destroyed. Even cattle are seared. It must be the fire of the LORD. Pray to God for us, Moses. We are sorry, so sorry, for complaining"[7]

Moses saw smoke rising from the entire northern edge of the camp. He fell on his knees before them, put his face on the ground, and pleaded, "God, forgive us. Quench the fires, the heat of your anger. We deserve what you have done, but forgive us once again."

The flames died out, the smoke blew away, and the ground cooled, leaving a perimeter of charred tents and belongings, and some minor skin burns.

"What a harsh god," Bershama complained to Abidan, as they stood with Gamaliel and Nethanel, surveying the damage. "To do this just because people grouse against Him!"

"It is much more than that," said Abidan. "This is at least the sixth time we have complained that God should have let us stay in Egypt. Each time His punishment escalates."

"We developed no trust at Sinai," said Gamaliel. "What little faith."

"Don't criticize, Gamaliel," said Nethanel. "You are so often in your prayers. Get your head out of the clouds and put your tongue on the grimy soil. Taste the tears of our people. They are resentful and afraid."

Gamaliel was undeterred. "Trust in the power of God, Nethanel. Look to yourself. Can you part even the stream of water that issues from your bull?"

As Abidan examined a piece of burnt tent cloth, he sought to calm them. "I'm sure God is justified. All He has done for us, only to be needled by complaints."

"More warnings and explanations for our people, correct?" said Nethanel.

"Yes, I'm afraid so," said Abidan.

They named the place "Taberah," which means "burning"[8] because the LORD's fire was vented there.

After the fire at Taberah, the Hebrew camp followed the cloud north for five more days through a great and terrible wilderness afflicted with fiery serpents and scorpions[9] before breaking out into the desert, where they established another camp.

God had continued to supply enough manna daily to fully nourish all, and He would continue to do so throughout the journey to Canaan. Although physiologically adequate, the monotonous menu left the travelers' taste buds wanting, and complaints were again lodged at the new campsite. The non-Hebrews, as well as the Israelites, wept for meat again: "We remember the fish which we used to eat free in Egypt, the cucumbers, the melons, and the leeks, and the onions and the garlic,[10] but now our appetite is gone. There is nothing at all to look at except this manna."

God became annoyed, and Moses, the middleman, grew frustrated and depressed. The people he represented were murmuring, and the God he served was angry. The embers of Taberah were hardly cool, and he feared greater punishment. He cried out to God, "Why have You been so hard on Your servant? And why have I not found favor in Your sight that you laid the burden of all this people on me? Was it I who conceived them? Was it I who brought them forth, that You should say to me, *'Carry them in your bosom as a nurse carries a nursing infant, to the land which You swore to their fathers?'* (Num. 11:12). Where am I to get meat to give to all this people? I alone am not able to carry them." Then, ready to give up, he pleaded, "So, if You are going to deal thus with me, please kill me at once—and do not let me see my wretchedness." * He had not spoken that way to God since Pharaoh had forced the Israelites to find their own straw.

"Gather for Me seventy men from the elders of Israel," God said, *"and I will take of the Spirit who is upon you and put Him upon them; and they*

shall bear the burden of the people with you, so that you shall not bear it all alone" (Num. 11:16–17).

Moses was anxious. If he yielded some of the precious Spirit to others, would he feel depleted, less powerful, less bound to his jealous Master? *Why must He take it from me?* he wondered. *Doesn't God have a limitless supply of Spirit?* Obediently, Moses hand-picked seventy elders, most of whom had accompanied him to the foot of Mount Sinai, and they joined him inside the courtyard near the tabernacle. As the men stood together, God took a portion of the Spirit from Moses and distributed it to the men. The Spirit-guided men then prophesied for a short time, giving witness to God, and a few even foretold future events. Joshua, standing at the gate, appreciated the precious gift God had given.

At the same time, two other men, Eldad and Medad, who had been selected by Moses but who had stayed back in camp, also had the Spirit placed upon them by God. Their families were shocked to hear them unexpectedly, uncontrollably prophesying, and a young man excitedly ran to tell Moses. He first encountered Joshua, who became angry when he heard his story. Believing that the two men were speaking presumptuously without intercession from Moses or from God, Joshua implored Moses, "Restrain them." *

"Are you jealous for my sake?" asked Moses. Then he added humbly, "Would that all of the LORD's people were prophets, that the LORD would put His Spirit upon them." * He was delighted, not jealous, to have the men elevated to a position near to his own.

Moses' mind soon returned to the problem facing him: how to feed the complaining people. He asked God, "Should flocks and herds be slaughtered—or all the fish in the sea be gathered together—for them to have sufficient food?" *

God's answer was withering. *"Is the LORD's power limited? Now you shall see whether My word will come true or not"* (Num. 11:23). Referring to the whining people, he announced they would get so much meat that it would *"come out of* [their] *nostrils and become loathsome to* [them], *because* [they] *have rejected the LORD who was among* [them] *and had wept before Him, saying 'Why did we ever leave Egypt?'"* (Num. 11:20).

"It is an orient wind that blows today," said Cheletra, looking up while she and two other women washed their clothes in a stream, "a gale that suddenly darkens the skies."

In a few moments, Shum pointed up into the sky. "Birds! They are birds. It is a plague of birds."

As they came closer, Ruth cried out, "They are quail with lungs full of sea breeze, blown off course! They are thick as brick-mud. Now look! They fall like rain!"

"They will engulf us. Get to shelter," Cheletra shouted.

While many people took cover, the quail fell exhausted, teeming on the earth so that little ground was visible. The people came out, many with bags, and began to gather them. The women built small fires to roast some of them. "Remember the law," Moses reminded them.

The people did not pick up simply one day's worth, as God had ordered, but ravenously collected for thirty-six continuous hours and began gorging themselves on the longed-for quail meat. Before many could swallow the meat, God's anger was kindled, unleashing a severe plague.[11]

Coresha was roasting three quail on a small fire next to a full bag and baking some manna into cakes, when the two men appeared at the doorway of her tent. Before they could say anything, she inquired of them, "Have you seen Lashinar? He has been out with the men all day."

The men went outside and brought the lifeless body into the tent and laid it at her feet. His stilled, cold mouth was full of meat.

"He is only one of many," they said. "We are so sorry."

"Oh, Lashinar, my love, my dear and only love," she cried as she knelt beside him, laying her head on his chest. "My love, oh my husband. And I had not even told you that I am with child, perhaps a son for you, the one you wished for, to teach, to hold, to love. Oh, Lashinar ...."

Wailing arose from each tribe, as grief and remorse seized the victims' families. They were stunned that a plague would be directed against them.

Abidan and Gamaliel were walking together the next day. Abidan said, "It is not as if Moses had not warned them about the quail. It seems that it is only when God's anger escalates into fury that He gets our full attention."

"God has many of the same emotions we have," said Gamaliel, "though not irrational or capricious, as ours are. I hope that He doesn't become so frustrated that He leaves us. We must change. Remember, it is only a twist of the wrist from the back of His hand to His outstretched palm."

"Would we listen better if He were a flesh-and-blood man?" asked Abidan.

"I doubt it. Our duty now is to keep our people obedient. The next punishment could be worse," cautioned Gamaliel.

The bodies of those consumed by the plague were buried and the campsite named Kibroth-hattavah, meaning "graves of the craving."[12] Moses could only hope that the vulgar gluttony of the people had been removed.

It was time to move again. Trumpets sounded and the march resumed. They journeyed several days farther north to a place named Hazeroth, where the cloud settled, the tabernacle was assembled, God invested Himself within, and the people camped.

A few days later, Miriam drew Aaron aside as they stood outside their neighboring tents. "God seems annoyed with Moses' leadership. Our brother broke the sacred tablets and brought a plague on us for the quail. Aaron, you and I are chosen leaders behind an incompetent man, and it is time for us to assume, or at least share, authority over these people."[13]

Aaron sighed. "Miriam, you are recognized as a leader. What more do you want?"

"God has gotten so wrapped up in Moses that He has cast me aside. But Moses is indebted to us, Aaron. Where would he have been without me? I saved him. Through the years, while we slogged in mud, he was carried in chariots and spoiled. We kept our promise to keep his birth a secret. But don't you see, Aaron? God has chosen us just as much as he chose Moses."

"God stirred me and, although I do not remember why, I walked to Moses readily," said Aaron. "I am older than he, and perhaps I should be leading instead of him."

Miriam's eyes glowed. "Of course. See what could be ours, a close, protected relationship with God, leaders of these people now and in the Promised Land of Canaan later. Great honor would be ours. Aaron, I have a plan. We'll use his marriage."

The two called a meeting of Moses and the tribal leaders in the courtyard. Miriam began. "You all know of God's statute that we must never marry outside of our own nation, don't you? Moses' wife is a non-Israelite woman, a Cushite, a marriage that makes him a sinner in God's eyes. He does not deserve to lead. Has the LORD indeed spoken only through Moses? Has He not spoken through us as well?"

Moses was surprised, but his meekness silenced his tongue. However, this was not so with God, who appeared as the cloud at the doorway of the tabernacle and called the three to Him. He spoke directly to Miriam and to Aaron, bristling. *"If there is a prophet among you, I, the LORD, shall make myself known to him in a vision. I shall speak to him in a dream. Not so with My servant, Moses. He is faithful in all My household; with him I speak mouth to mouth, even openly and not in dark sayings."* Then God questioned them. *"Why then were you not afraid to speak against my servant, against Moses?"* (Num. 12:6–8). In anger, God afflicted Miriam with leprosy, not the red rawness of active disease, but the scarred, deformed, total whiteness of the burned-out stage.

Aaron called on his brother, remembering how God had healed Moses' leprous hand. "Oh, my lord, I beg you, do not account this sin to us, in which we have acted foolishly and in which we have sinned," cried Aaron. "Do not let her be like one dead, whose flesh is half eaten away." *

Moses prayed for healing and God refused, answering only that she must leave the camp for seven days to be cleansed. She gathered some food, donned a shawl, and left in disgrace. At the end of the week, she returned, bearing her scars.

Although Miriam had been the one punished for challenging God's special servant, another of Aaron's weaknesses had become evident—envy of the only man closer to God than he.

Endnotes
1. "land of deserts and pits ," Jer. 2:6.
2. Moving the tabernacle, Numbers 3:17-28.
3. "lest they die," Num.4:20.
4. "Never put it on a wagon," Num.4:15.
5. "Rise up O LORD…," Num. 10:35.
6. "Return Thou O LORD…," Num. 10:36.
7. "complaining," Num. 11:1-4.
8. Taberah means "burning" according to Cheyne and Black, Encyclopedia Biblica. Wikipedia.
9. "great and terrible wilderness," Deut. 8:15.
10. "cucumbers, melons…," Num.11:5.
11. "plague," Numbers 11:33.

12. "Campsite named Kibroth-hattavah, meaning 'graves of the craving'" according to the footnote for Numbers 11:34 in the Ryrie Study Bible.

13. The story of Miriam's revolt is told in Numbers 12.

Chapter 14

Attack!

The congregation broke camp and traveled north from Hazeroth into the desert, following the cloud. They trudged through that dry wilderness for five more days, finally entering a well-watered valley between rolling hills south of Mount Sier and near the town of Kadesh-barnea, where they camped. Scouts were dispatched and they confirmed, as Hobab had said, that the Israelites were only a two-day march from Canaan.[1]

After a two-day rest, Moses called the leaders together at the northern boundary of the camp and addressed them. "Tomorrow you are to instruct your warriors to go north and begin the occupation of Canaan, the land which God has given us. Your army will leave at sunrise, and the support will follow immediately."

The leaders responded by fidgeting, looking down at shuffling feet, fingers rubbing dry lips. Ahira spoke up. "Moses, we have been observed by their sentries for the last two days, and word of our presence has certainly reached their captains. We know nothing firsthand about their fortifications or their weaponry— information we need to acquire and carefully evaluate before we act, as any army would."

Gamaliel said, "This is hilly country, Moses, and their troops may be scattered, hiding, ready to ambush us. We had better send men before us to see by which routes we should travel."

"I doubt that is necessary," Moses responded. "God told us that He or His angel would prepare the way for our victory. But if you insist, I shall take this to God."

Moses walked to the tabernacle and entered the holy of holies, saying, "Our people are hesitant to attack."

God granted their wish, repeating, *"I am going to give* [the land of Canaan] *to the sons of Israel. You shall send a leader from each of their father's tribes"* (Num. 13:1).

Moses returned to the meeting with God's approval. "Each of you, select an agile spy who is also a strong leader, and one who can learn dialects easily. Now, who will they be?"

Shelumiel of Simeon spoke first. "I suppose that Shaphat will be ours."

Nahshon of Judah added, "Who have I who would go except for Caleb, son of Jephunneh? He is strong in body, mind, and trust in God."

After a long pause, Bershama spoke softly. "I am loath to volunteer anyone on such a trip, but the best man from our tribe is Joshua, son of Nun. Moses, he is your assistant; will you allow him to go?"

"I can get by without him for a while. Yes, he may go for you."

Eliasaph, Pagiel, and Nethanel resisted assigning a man, but in the end, each leader appointed a representative, until there were twelve names.

Early the next morning, well before sunup, Moses spoke to the twelve before sending them out. "Go up beyond the desert into the hill country. Spread out to the Jordan River and to the sea, if possible. Gauge the strength of the defenses of their cities, the might of their men, the quality of their land, and bring back some of the fruit grown there, because it is time for the first grapes. Be back in forty days."

As the first streaks of dawn lightened the night sky, the men set out to the north with small bags of goods and money, spreading out in pairs. They pulled cowls over their hair and cinched light robes about themselves so they could mingle and observe. They brushed through gates into cities, where some took transient jobs to learn about the surroundings and earn money for their food, camouflaging their mission. They learned to converse sparingly in the local language. Several reached the Jordan River, nearly eighty miles to the north; and two others the Great Sea.

The spies returned safely to camp at Kadesh after forty days, bringing with them luxuriant fruits. There were pomegranates and figs. Two men brought a single cluster of grapes that was so heavy, it had to be carried on a pole between them. They told of a lush land, as God had foretold, that flows with milk and honey.[2]

The people eagerly listened to them. They accepted the report of a land of plenty lying ahead of them as confirmation of another of God's promises.

The spies revealed the whereabouts of the different tribes God had foretold. The Amorites, Hittites, and Jebusites occupied the hill country. Some of the Canaanites dwelt by the Great Sea and some along the banks of the Jordan. A new group of people had taken up residence nearby, in the land south of Canaan: the contentious Amalekites, in the desert of Negev. The spies also reported that their great and splendid cities were well fortified. The Israelites began to worry.

Moses tried to reassure them by reminding them of God's provision. "Do not be shocked, nor fear them. The LORD your God who goes before you will Himself fight on your behalf, just as He did for you in Egypt before your eyes, and in the wilderness, where you saw how the LORD your God carried you, just as a man carries his son." *

Joshua and Caleb also spoke up encouragingly. "We should by all means go up and take possession of it, for we shall surely overcome it," * said Caleb.

The other spies, however, reported that Canaan was a hostile land, and all the people whom they saw in it were men of great size. "There also we saw the Nephilim"[3], they said ominously, the giant sons of human mothers, with fallen gods from heaven as their fathers. "We seemed to ourselves no larger than grasshoppers."

Moses stepped forward, proclaiming, "Be strong; God will deliver a victory to us. Let us move out at sunrise the day after tomorrow."

The crowd dispersed, grumbling against the order. In the evening, Gamaliel and Eliasaph, among the last to retain a trust in God, conversed outside of Gamaliel's tent. Eliasaph said, "Moses asked us to attack an entrenched giant enemy, a cricket charging into a crocodile. I am feeling lost myself, Gamaliel, afraid, and worried for my family."

"Be patient, Eliasaph, and keep strong. We need a plan. Meet me here tomorrow evening."

Eliasaph did not appear for the meeting. Early before daybreak the next day, Gamaliel left his tent, and with a sudden sense of relief, blended quietly into the crowd that assembled with the leaders before Moses.

Nethanel spoke first. "Why is the LORD bringing us into this land, to fall by the sword? Our wives and our little ones will become plunder! Would that we had died in the land of Egypt or in this wilderness!"*

Shouts soon erupted from the crowd. "No, it will not be so! We will not go!"

Abidan said, "Moses, even we leaders are withdrawing our support for this senseless attack, hopeless even with the help of the ark and the priests."

"We are uncertain whether God will intercede for us," Ahira added. "And besides, we're not well enough trained or equipped to defeat the Nephilim. No, Moses, God must give us a more concrete guarantee that we can succeed in battle."

Gamaliel hesitantly said, "The people not only refuse to fight but they wish to go back to Egypt. At least in slavery, we will stay alive. We will retrace our steps, using the maps Bershama has made for us."

Nethanel said, "Let us appoint a leader and return to Egypt—now!" * Then, turning to Moses, he added, "Moses, you are on your own. You may come with us if you wish, but not as our leader, for we leave your God here."

Moses was stunned. Was this how the journey would end? Would God allow this? Then, for a moment, he considered his options. If the people left, his responsibility would end, the chaos in his life would be over. Or he could go back to Egypt, where his talents and reputation might again return riches and power to him, particularly since Pharaoh was dead.

However, just as quickly he remembered the love and power of God and realized that he preferred the reproach of [God] to the riches of Egypt.[4] He would follow God, with or without the people.

As he scanned his leaders, he held out his hands to them beseechingly. "Stay. Don't you realize that this is the goal for which all Israelites, each man, woman, and child, suffered for four hundred and thirty long years? Three times God told you in detail exactly what would happen here, and three times you vowed to follow Him. He has promised that He would deliver you from the enemy."

Nahshon interrupted. "Have we earned that deliverance?" As he turned to walk away, he said over his shoulder, "Your God is hard to please."

In frustration, Moses and Aaron fell on their faces in front of the crowd. Caleb and Joshua, distraught, passionately tore their clothes in frustration. Caleb shouted to the people that Canaan was an exceedingly good land! "If the LORD is pleased with us, He will bring us into this land

and give it to us. Only do not rebel against the LORD, and do not fear the people of the land, for they shall be our prey!"*

Joshua added, "God did not promise that He would deliver our enemies to us at Rephidim, but here, He does! Just believe Him."

Deep fear and perceived betrayal closed the ears of the congregation. Many armed themselves with stones, intent on eliminating the four troublesome men.

Suddenly the glory of the LORD rose up over the tabernacle for all to see, stopping the men where they stood. Moses hurried to it and God said, *"How long will this people spurn Me and not believe in Me, despite all the signs which I have performed in their midst?"* (Num. 14:11).

Immediately, God sent a plague that killed the ten spies who spread the bad report about the land, sparing Joshua and Caleb. He also warned through Moses that He would send pestilence to destroy everyone but Moses, Aaron, Caleb, and Joshua. He would begin anew, as with Noah, to make a great nation of the faithful four and their families.

It was an appealing offer to the struggling, dispirited Moses, to be rid of these ingrates, to have a fresh start with a community of believing, trusting families, to populate God's garden spot. But Moses was their appointed shepherd. These people were his responsibility. God was not just allowing them to return to Egypt as they planned; He would destroy them all.

Moses interceded again with God, as he had at Sinai. "If You slay them, the Egyptians will say, 'Because the LORD could not bring this people into the land which He promised them by oath, therefore He slaughtered them in the wilderness.'" * He repeated God's own words: *"'The LORD is slow to anger, and abundant in lovingkindness, forgiving iniquity and transgression; but He will by no means clear the guilty, visiting the iniquities of the fathers on the children to the third and the fourth generations'"* (Num. 14:18).

Moses continued, "Yes, LORD, they have committed a great iniquity, but pardon it, I pray, according to the greatness of Your lovingkindness, just as You also have forgiven this people from Egypt even until now." * This time Moses did not offer his own life for the people; his patience with them had run out.

God listened to Moses' pleas. *"I have pardoned them according to your word, but,"* He added, *"indeed, as I live, all the earth will be filled with the glory of the LORD. Surely, all the men who have seen My glory and My signs … in Egypt and the wilderness, yet have put Me to the test these ten times and have not listened to My voice, shall by no means see the land which I swore to their fathers"* (Num. 14:20–23).

The pardoned nation of Israel would survive. Their sin was forgiven but not its consequences. God had said that *"He will by no means leave the guilty unpunished"* (Ex. 34:7). All men who were over the age of twenty at the outset of the journey were condemned to die.

But the journey, originally planned to last only two years, would now be a forty-year ordeal, one year for each day of the ill-fated spying trip. God informed the condemned, *"And your sons shall be shepherds for forty years in the wilderness, and they shall suffer for your unfaithfulness, until your corpses lie in the wilderness.… I, the LORD have spoken; surely this I will do to all this evil congregation who are gathered together against Me"* (Num. 14:33, 35). Except for the faithful four, all had betrayed, and all deserted.

The irrevocable judgment was made by a brokenhearted God, redirecting His hopes to the younger men. He commanded the people to abandon their camp the next day, turn around, and return southeastward, by way of the Red Sea. They were not to encounter the nations of Canaan nor the Amalekites, for God would not be among them.

Many of the Israelite men could not accept the sentence of thirty-eight more years of wandering, suffering, and death without some action. They met and banded together, determined to exonerate themselves. Therefore, the next day, all of the soldiers armed themselves and marched north to attack the Amalekites and Canaanites, hoping to occupy Canaan and appease God. Perhaps He would have pity on them and change His mind. Neither Moses nor Aaron, nor the ark accompanied them to protect them.

Zuriel watched them depart from a hilltop nearby and penned these lines:

The Amalekites crouch before our haphazard charge,
wondering why we must again dispense the scourge of widowhood,
while Sinai's rills are still scarlet, her ravens sated with dead flesh.

The Israelites' power, however, had remained behind. The Amalekites fought zealously, killed many, and drove the surviving Israelites back south to Hormah, north of the village of Kadesh-barnea.

Zuriel wrote more as he observed the warriors return with the wounded:

Their flesh-tears profound, foes' blades scarlet, wet;
thirsty arrows lodged, all senselessly wrought.
Their wastage He'll mourn.
Know! His Word, with depths of wisdom, inscrutable,
once uttered cannot be retrieved,
but purifies, sears, or saves by its own execution.

"Set out ... by way of the Red Sea" (Deut. 1:40), God had ordered. As a result of the battle, the whole earth would soon know that the Israelites attacked without provocation but that they could be defeated. The beaten soldiers bivouacked at Hormah and its oasis.

Endnote
1. The events of this chapter are based on Numbers, chapters 13 and 14.
2. "that flows with milk and honey," Num.13:27.
3. "Nephilim," Num.13:33, Gen. 6:4.
4. "reproach of God," Heb. 11:26.

Chapter 15

Thirty-Eight Wasted Years

Moses brought the congregation up to Hormah, where the wounded could heal, and the people would rest and begin to deal with their botched future.

In the fourth month at Hormah, a vicious plague of cough, fever, chills, and mental confusion spread throughout the village, attacking the older men, and all who fell ill died. Eliasaph was one of the first persons to contract it, coughing uncontrollably from lung congestion, feeling the strength of his mighty arms ebb away. His tribe prayed fervently for his healing, many in gratitude for the prayers he had often offered for them, but to no avail. His self-absorbed wife remained tearless.

Along with the several thousand who also died of the illness was Ahiezar, leader of Dan, a quiet, deep thinker and tactful problem-solver. He died within five days of his first rigor, survived by a wife and three children.

Pagiel and Ahira happened upon Nahshon and Gamaliel at the edge of a large field that was being used as a cemetery. It was depressing watching wagonloads of bodies being deposited there.

"Have we witnessed the first of God's ravaging or was this just a random disease?" asked Ahira.

Nahshon said, "God will not destroy us all for a little hesitancy to fight. He needs us, as we need Him."

"Perhaps. At any rate, Eliasaph's wisdom will be sorely missed," said Pagiel. "None could match his faith in God, at least for most of the trip. Ahiezar's quiet, f ... f ... firm leadership will be difficult to replace. We must choose new leaders from the tribes of Gad and Dan."

"And young ones too," said Ahira, "those in their teen years when we left Egypt, who will have a chance to survive the trip, if God's decree holds up."

"The months ahead will tell," predicted Gamaliel.

It was one month later when Aaron confronted Moses on the first day in the seventh month of the year. "During this time, whether or not we are dying under God's punishment, we must celebrate the Day of Atonement," he advised. "We must be trying God's patience with the few sin sacrifices that have been made since we left Sinai. Perhaps Atonement will satisfy Him."

"Let's hope so," said Moses.

The tenth day of the seventh month arrived, and Aaron, after bathing and dressing, sacrificed a bull for himself and a goat for the people. He took some of the blood of each animal and entered the holiest room—the only time during the year that he could enter into that extraordinary room, into God's presence—and sprinkled it on the mercy seat, purging the tabernacle of any and all accumulated sins of his family and of the people.

Levite assistants took the remains of the animals outside the camp and burned them up at the clean place.

"Now bring me the second of the congregation's goats," he ordered his sons.

While Ithamar and Eleazar were untying and wrestling with a belligerent goat, they overheard two Hebrew men talking nearby, oblivious of the priests.

"I am here only because God commanded it. I am a Judahite and I do not sin, nor does my family," boasted the first. "But I know of many neighbors who need forgiving as much as a cow needs grass."

"It is too bad that you had to attend," said the man from Simeon. "If I were only that clean. My mouth ..."

"Some snakes I know," interrupted the first, "don't deserve forgiveness—you excepted, of course. Maybe Atonement will make better people out of them. I do hope this ceremony is brief, because I have other things I would rather be doing."

"Perhaps, for your sake," said the second, as the priests resumed pulling the goat to the altar.

"You delay so," chided Aaron to his sons, as they brought the animal to him.

"The knots were too tight," said Eleazar.

As the sons held the goat, Aaron grasped its horns and rapidly confessed all of the known and potential sins of the congregation over it, then sent it alive into the wilderness. "The blood purifies the temple; the scapegoat[1] carries the sins themselves away," he said.

Then Aaron concluded the ceremony by sacrificing his and the congregation's ram as burnt offerings, securing God's favor.

God's favor also fell upon Coresha's pregnancy. During the later stages, an uncommon energy filled her, perhaps, she reasoned, because the child was the only part of Lashinar she had been able to cling to. Be it daughter or son, it must look like Lashinar: the soft-lidded eyes, the wide mouth, the large hands. They were not the marks of beauty as such but they would bring him back, not in his death pose, but alive, loving, even self-willed. Would she be able to nurture this child's independence while keeping it close by and safe?

After twenty-three hours of labor, the midwife helped Coresha bring forth a normal, healthy, baby boy with a cry heard throughout the community of Manasseh. The cry was greeted with relief, then smiles, by those who heard it, a cry announcing that Lashinar's seed had sprouted, and a warning that the community should prepare to change. Little Machir had arrived.

The first males to see Coresha's jewel were Lashinar's good friend Sorin and his son Hanniel. They made a hesitant visit that first night. *Big cry, big mouth,* Hanniel thought when he first saw Machir. On his third daily visit, he was allowed to hold the baby, and Hanniel felt an affection unknown before. Thereafter, he treated Machir as a little brother and planned to take him to prayers with the Levites, carry him on hikes into the woods and hills, help with his schooling, and show him the ways of a shepherd.

Machir was six months old when the cloud moved away from Hormah in a westerly direction, drawing the camp with it, before settling fifteen miles away. During the year they had been at camp, 21,000 Israelites had died of another disease marked by progressive weakness and wasting[2] of the muscles, first of the legs, then the arms, and finally the chest. It had struck the older men, a lingering illness proving fatal. The people left large graveyards on the northern edge of the old camp. At the new site, they found the grass a bit more abundant, fruit trees nearby, and stands of other trees suitable for building simple dwellings.

After fourteen months at that new location, the cloud rose again and moved off, this time to the southwest. More graves had been filled, many people having died from strange accidents. God had not told Moses that the cloud would stay at this new site for five years so, anticipating departure at any moment, the people planted none of the few seeds they had. Without grain, no bread or cakes were baked. The people, sustained by manna, complained less.

In the fourth year there, another plague struck the camp, this one with symptoms of intense, persistent diarrhea and vomiting. It claimed 12,000 older men and women. Nahshon and Bershama were among those affected. Nahshon lost considerable weight with the disease, succumbing after ten days, while his wife Susken ministered to him. He was buried in his white robe. During his illness, he revealed the location of his hidden cache of jewels to her. After his death, disturbed by the booty, Susken retrieved the jewels and secretly left them outside Moses' tent one night, with a note to add them to the tabernacle treasury. In Nahshon's place, Caleb was chosen to lead the tribe of Judah. Although older, he had become a popular choice with a promised survival into Canaan.

On the eighth day of his illness, having lost much of his renowned "barley" hair, Bershama died, survived by his wife, three sons, and two daughters. Though he was industrious and hard-working, his secret mapmaking of the route back to Egypt had showed his lack of confidence in God's mission. When weakened by his condition, he entrusted the maps to Kemuel, son of Shiphtan, his personal choice to succeed him as tribal leader.

The dead were buried as quickly as possible, but the stench in the village was one reason God moved the camp out farther to the south, to a lightly wooded area where the grass was less abundant. The animals would require large supplements of manna to survive.

The pattern was established: set up camp, graze until the grass was eaten down and the burial grounds filled; then the cloud would move on and the people would follow, staying in each place for an average of three years. They moved from Rithmah to Rimmon-perez, to Libnah, to Rissah, to Kehelathah,[3] each of the campsites being about ten to twenty miles apart and arranged in a great meandering circle, keeping Mount Sier in the center. At each site, God provided a test for them and carefully observed their responses to determine if their faith in Him was maturing. Failures were growing less frequent.

Not all accepted their dismal fate. Forty-two older men organized themselves and, led by Kemuel, slipped away from the camp one night. Using Bershama's maps, they traveled southward, heading for Egypt. Before they had traveled thirty miles, seven died of snake bites and another five from an acute lung congestion. The remaining ones limped back into camp, humiliated.

A council meeting was called. "Are you prepared," asked Abidan, "to continue this course with God or will you abandon Him? Will any repeat Kemuel's disastrous escapade?" Kemuel silently bowed his head.

"No," said Shuham, the stonemason from Dan selected to replace Ahiezar. "We new leaders represent tribes who do see, hear, and remember. We may not always understand fully or always be right, but we talk among ourselves of this God often, seeking to please Him. Having a god in our camp is never allowed to be taken for granted."

Abidan said, "We have lost four of our original leaders. The survival of the community rests with you younger ones."

"They know their responsibilities," said Caleb.

"Turn your words into action and all will benefit," said Abidan.

The years of freedom passed faster and more pleasantly than those of slavery. God remained with them, filling their needs. Except for times of mourning following each plague, a growing peace, laughter, and humor found its way back into the community. Individual creativity returned in the form of plays, songfests, and small orchestras. Once a year, the priests and Levites publicly read all of God's laws to refresh the people's commitment.

In the seventeenth year, a heavy plank fell on the carpenter Shelumiel's leg. The bone fragments broke through the skin. Although it was bandaged and splinted, it became red, swollen, and pustular. Poultices were applied, but it gradually turned black. Shelumiel grew confused, shouting incoherently, until he finally fell into a coma and died, with Abidan at his bedside.

Abidan's trust in God's plan had grown during the trip from Egypt to Sinai. However, fearful and distrusting after the spies' report, he had sided with the deserters. Since then, however, his faith had been restored and he became again a steadying influence on his Benjaminites. When another plague of the dreaded lung disease with coughing, fevers, bloody sputum, and chest pain swept through the camp, he visited and ministered to the sick until he finally contracted the illness himself. Moses visited and comforted him often until his laborious breathing ceased.

Moses had found it difficult to completely forgive his leaders for their desertion. However, the rekindled loyalty of several leaders, including Abidan and Gamaliel, had been a source of encouragement while the people's trust in him dwindled. The majority of people resented him and blamed him for the plagues, the growing list of wailing widows and orphans, their nomadic existence, and their absence of any near-term destination, all the while pointlessly following the cloud. Their belligerence gave him occasional concern for his own safety. He also knew that his prayers to God for the plagues to cease, repeated by rote at the leaders' urging, could not be met. In spite of all these challenges, he doggedly maintained a civil, caring attitude toward the individual problems of his people.

Through the difficult years, he clung to the promises of conquest and of the plenteous life they would live in Canaan, when contention with his people would end and his family could thrive, with God at its center.

For the most part, Moses also had pleasure in his own family. In his earlier years, he enjoyed fatherhood, sharing his beliefs and ancestral tales with his growing sons and teaching them the skills of shepherding. Now that they were married and had their own families, he enjoyed grandfathering. His chronic concern was Gershom's future, because he had been twenty-one at the beginning of the march.

Moses appreciated Zipporah's growing trust in God and the gradual softening of her headstrong obstinacy, partly crediting his own patient, understanding way with her. She satisfied him and grew to be a valuable, trusted supporter, providing the glue of their mellowing marriage.

Eliab, Zebulun's leader, died two short days after contracting the same illness that claimed Abidan. A quiet, reserved person, he had retained leadership because of his steadfast support for all of his tribal members.

Moses and the surviving original leaders—Gamaliel, Pagiel, Ahira, Nethanel, and Elizur—called a meeting with the seven replacements.

Moses said, "Although we continue on this march of God-sent attrition, He continues to provide for us. Even though we walk daily in our sandals and shoes, they do not wear out; and your clothes, often washed, show no signs of wear even after twenty-five years."[4]

"Yes," Pagiel added, "and it may be a long time before we leave this mou … mou … mou … mountain, until God sees a different attitude."

Nethanel said in a tired voice, "I won't leave, ever. I hate worrying about when I will die."

"Trust Him, Nethanel," Caleb said. "I believe those who die are with God in some way, even the sacrificed animals. But meanwhile, we must mature into holy people. Joshua knows this, and so does Moses."

"There is one thing more," interjected Pagiel. "We now travel under no c … c … c … covenant with God, having broken His first at Si … Si … Sinai by the golden calf and the second by our desertion. Now there is none in force. Yet He stays with us. We must show Him our trust."

Nethanel's depression worsened. Nara often stayed up with him during his sleepless nights, listening to his ravings, trying to calm and reassure him. Occasional visits by his son and daughter did not help. He slowly descended into himself, becoming quieter. Pagiel spent seemingly useless hours talking and listening to him. Then one morning, Nethanel's joy returned. He spoke freely and pleasantly to Nara, even straightened up his sleeping area and changed his clothes. Nara arose the next morning to find him lying on his side in a pool of blood near the door, the handle of his knife protruding from the left side of his chest.

Hanniel was chosen to speak at the memorial gathering. He had concluded his voluntary ten-year service as a Nazirite by shaving his long hair and beard, throwing them on the altar fire, and sacrificing his appointed animals. He marked his return to secular life by drinking wine made from the previously forbidden grapes. His resolve to serve God persisted, and he accepted a role with the Levites. His father, Sorin, had died of the stomach plague, but Hanniel perpetuated his father's humility, honesty, and devotion to God. His friendship with Machir had remained strong.

"In Nethanel, we have buried another courageous leader," said Hanniel. "Before he became so ill, Nethanel used to say that if we cannot obey out of fear, let us do so out of gratitude for what God has done for us. He would encourage us to put aside our preoccupations with personal goals before the end of our days."

Nara and her two children embraced in silent tears next to his grave.

Council meetings continued, now every other month, as the troop was led from campsites at Mount Shepher and Haradah, to Makheloth, to Tahath, to Terah, and to Mithkah.[5] Local villagers were astounded to see this large mass of people seemingly following aimlessly after the strange white cloud. The Hebrews often told them about the God who led them and of their eventual goal of Canaan, while seldom mentioning their own desertion. They carried on a limited trade, and when the Israelites moved on, they left the villagers largely undisturbed.

God tested the Israelites from time to time with thirst, hunger, even temptations to worship other gods, including their formerly revered Moloch and Rompha. When they erred, He disciplined them but afterward always came to their rescue. Their murmuring slowly changed to gossiping, to soft grousing, and then to resigned silence, as their anticipation of miraculous deliveries grew.

In the thirtieth year, on a particularly hot, dry day, swarms of flying insects attacked the camp from the east, stinging and biting both man and beast; there seemed to be no escape from them. On the fourth and fifth day, thousands of the older men began to fall ill with fever, headache, and lethargy, each finally drifting into a coma. Death uniformly followed. After a week, the insects mercifully left, leaving a scattering of dead animals also in their wake.

Ahira had set up and supervised the many pots of animal dung that smoked over fires surrounding the village. He exposed himself to the insects, almost recklessly, trying to drive them away before finally falling ill on the fifth day. He died eight days later and was replaced as leader of his tribe by his aggressive but emotional son, Jazallun.

Elizur of Reuben and Gamaliel also contracted the fatal illness. On Gamaliel's last day, a small, respectful crowd gathered outside of his tent, while inside, Hanniel and Moses stood near his bed. A grieving Pagiel was holding his hand when he died.

Hanniel was invited to replace Gamaliel as leader of Manasseh, a large tribe that controlled great herds of cattle. He hesitated, realizing that he would have to relinquish some of his cherished duties assisting the Levites if he accepted the offer. He consulted long with Pagiel and Machir and only said yes after Machir agreed to be his advisor. And a good advisor he would be, for Machir had grown to be the independent thinker and actor his mother Coresha had envisioned, devoted to God and standing up repeatedly for Him.

The deaths of Ahira, Elizur, and Gamaliel left Pagiel as the lone survivor of the original leaders. He appreciated the fellowship of the younger men and of their council meetings. Although he was referred to as "the relic," his opinions were given great weight by the council members. He rued his generation's desertion and recommended a direct strike to the northwest to Canaan, toward the Jordan, should they be given the opportunity again. His devoted, steadfast support for God and Moses was evident to all.

At the beginning of the fortieth year, God brought them all back to Hormah, where the years of wandering had begun. Although they and the priests had not observed sacrifices regularly and circumcision had been abandoned,[6] God stayed. "For the LORD your God has blessed you in all that you have done," said Moses. "He has known your wanderings through this great wilderness. These forty years the LORD your God has been with you; you have not lacked a thing."[7]

Most of the men who were over twenty years of age at the beginning of the march had perished, totaling over 800,000. Children and grandchildren had grown to adulthood, some to assume leadership. Among the latter were Samuel of Simeon, replacing Shelumiel; Tasun of Benjamin for Abidan; Shuham of Dan for Ahiezar; Kemuel; Kenan; Shimron of Issachar for Nethanel; and Jazallun for Ahira.

It had been both a bitter and sweet period of time, as God exacted His lethal judgment on the fainthearted older men while nurturing the faith of the young and the women.

While they camped near the oasis of Hormah, God changed some requirements of the sacrifices. At Sinai, the limited supply of oil and wine was rationed to the mandatory sacrifice of morning and evening lambs. However, in Canaan, one to two quarts of oil, one to two quarts of wine, and three to six quarts of grain would have to be added to each burnt and peace offering. The oil would be produced by manually beating bushels of gathered olives, the wine processed by trampling troughs of picked grapes, and the grain hand-harvested, requiring countless hours of vigorous labor for sacrifices that were to be simply poured out onto the fire—true sacrifices and not mere donations.

Previously, the offering made for the unwitting sins of the entire congregation, or for groups of people, required only that a bull be sacrificed outside the camp. Now, however, the bull was to be burned to ashes on the bronze altar as a burnt offering, and a male goat added, to be killed outside the camp.[8]

In the first set of laws, the priests were more severely penalized than the leaders, and the leaders more than the common man. In the new law, all sinners were to be treated equally, and the less important animal, the female goat, was chosen as the common sacrifice.[9] God intimated that while His law would not change, the penalties would when He saw His people begin to mature or when situations changed.

God permitted the foreigners who traveled consistently with the Israelites, the sojourners, to worship and to sacrifice to Him, to be under the same laws, and to be judged just as the Hebrews were.

God instituted material reminders to help His people obey Him. He required each Israelite to wear tassels on the corners of his garments, tied by a cord of blue, *"to remember all the commandments of the LORD ... to do them and not follow after* [their] *own heart and eyes ... and be holy to* [their] *God"* (Num. 15:38–40). Tassels with blue cords; how could anyone miss them?

But Korah did.[10] He was a Levite, a member of the family of Kohath, those who carried the holy tabernacle items only after Aaron had covered them. While he grudgingly served his cousins, Moses and Aaron, his jealousy of them took root and became his master. He craved supremacy and secretly approached others, seeking accomplices.

God had assigned the tribe of Kohath to camp to the south, fifty paces away from the tabernacle courtyard. Korah had chosen to pitch his tent on the far southern perimeter of the marked area, next to the tents of the tribe of Reuben. (See drawing page 161). Adjacent to Korah's tent were those of Dathan, Abiram, and On, three sons of the tribe of Reuben, who were eager to restore the honor that had been removed by their ancestor's sexual misconduct. Korah induced the three to help him foment a rebellion.

The quartet found 250 prominent men from all the tribes to enroll in their cause, including the leader Shimron of Issachar. However, when this throng finally came to threaten God's two chosen men, the three schemers were absent—Dathan and Abiram cowered in their tents, while On had quit the insurrection altogether.

"You have gone far enough, Moses!" shouted Korah, who at sixty, was half the age of Moses. "All the congregation are holy, every one of them, and the LORD is in their midst." He raised his fist to Moses and Aaron. "Why do you exalt yourselves above the assembly of the LORD? " * Then he added, "Any of us, including me, is fit to lead." *

The accusations shocked Moses, who, in humility before Korah, fell face down and said, "Tomorrow morning the LORD will show who is His, who is holy." * He told Korah and his company to take censers, fill them with burning coals and incense, and bring them before God the next day. Aaron would to do the same. "And the man whom the LORD chooses shall be the one who is holy." *

Noting the sizeable contingent of Levites among the rebels, Moses echoed Korah's phrase in parting. "You have gone far enough, you sons of Levi! Hear now! Is it not enough that the God of Israel has separated you from the rest of the congregation, to bring you near to Himself, to do service in the tabernacle, and to minister to the congregation? And would you seek the priesthood also?" * There was no answer.

Moses dispatched an aide to summon the two conspirators, Dathan and Abiram. Dathan responded with a sarcastic message to Moses: "You have brought us up out of the land of Egypt that was flowing with milk and honey to have us die in this wilderness, as you lord it over us." *

Abiram also refused the summons, saying that Moses had not brought them to the glorious land he had promised and that he would probably put their eyes out if they came to him.,

Moses became angry, turned toward the tabernacle, and asked God to deal with this unruly mob, pointing out that he himself had done nothing to provoke them.

As they walked back to their tents, Aaron confided to Moses, "I am worried. A number of fine men have joined Korah. Since his uprising is against the LORD, if we are confirmed as the holy ones, will they all perish?"

"We will see tomorrow," said Moses.

The next morning, Korah and the 250 appeared in the courtyard with Moses and Aaron, each with a filled censer, hoping to be chosen. Dathan and Abiram had summoned up their courage and were present, but On was nowhere to be found. Korah was so confident that God would bless his followers and himself that he had assembled members of the congregation to observe the event.

The powerful, resplendent light once again suddenly appeared before the tabernacle, illuminating the skies. Moses and Aaron approached it cautiously as the people withdrew and God spoke from within it: *"Separate yourselves from among this congregation that I may consume them instantly"* (Num. 16:21).

When Moses relayed the message, Korah became agitated. "God must hear my side of this dispute! We have not joined all these men to us in this cause without just reason. We deserve an advocate and a trial, to argue on our behalf. Ask God to make His decision only after all the evidence has been presented."

God's ears were deaf to the pleadings of Korah. There would be no trial, just a simple annihilation. Moses sought clemency for the many innocent onlookers, asking God, "When one man sins, will You be angry with the entire congregation?" *

God listened and instructed Moses to have Korah, Dathan, and Abiram return to their tents, and all others to leave this holy area.

The three men and their families reluctantly complied, encouraged by the crowd that followed them. Moses shouted for all to hear, "Get back lest you be swept away in their sin." As the crowd receded, Moses said. "If these men die the death of all men, then the LORD has not sent me. But if the ground opens its mouth and swallows them, then you will understand that these men have spurned the LORD." *

A sudden earthquake occurred, the ground split open, and Korah, Dathan, Abiram, and their families were flung screaming, deep into its crevasses. Within minutes, the earth closed[11] back over them, to the horror of those who then watched as multiple bursts of fire cremated each of the 250 conspirators. Then God instructed Moses to have Eleazar make a large hammered plate from the 250 censers to serve as a covering for the bronze altar as a warning to the people. While Eleazar collected the censers, he reminded the people there that none but a priest should ever burn incense before the LORD, lest he become like Korah.

It was dusk as Moses and Aaron walked toward the edge of the camp, past groups of stunned and terrified people scrambling aside to let them pass. The brothers left the camp and walked silently into the night alone, still shaken by the ravages of God's swift vengeance.

As they walked on and on, deep in their thoughts, they spoke occasionally. Moses said, "Had my anger not provoked God to deal with Korah and his followers, the earthquake may not have occurred."

"They rebelled against God, not you," Aaron said. "Their deaths were justified."

After a while, Moses said, "Many of those burned had been our supposed friends and supporters, even Shimron. What a loss." Then he asked, "Was Korah known to you in Rameses?"

"I hardly knew him," said Aaron, "but he had a reputation as a gifted instigator. Too bad he misused his talent. Did you know that two of his sons who had been on a hunting trip survived?"

"We will welcome them back."

As night wore on, the exercise and conversation calmed them. Finally, as the sun rose, they discussed various ways to restore the people's trust, deciding to take a firmer hand with them.

During that same night, many of the frightened congregation convened with their leaders. Tensions had grown to the breaking point.

Kemuel said, "I thought when we finally left the bulging cemeteries around Mount Sier that God's wrath would have been satisfied. But now He has destroyed 250 more, including Shimron."

"Eleazar said it was partly because they all burned incense in censers before God. And who drew them into that sin but an angry Moses?" asked Samuel.

The outspoken Tasun from Benjamin stood with his hands on his hips. "All Korah and the others did was express ideas that many of us share—that Moses and Aaron have too much authority and are too much coddled by God. In Egypt, Moses walked in presenting himself as God's handmaiden. He has no scars on his back, no pieces of his heart torn out, as our fathers had."

Kemuel nodded. "The deaths we suffered when we tried to return to Egypt were too many to just be an accident. I believe Moses has cursed this entire trip."

"We are here because of Moses and Aaron, the people were killed because of Moses, and we will all die because of them," said Samuel.

"If Moses and Aaron were dead," said Tasun bluntly, "God would have to deal with us with greater compassion."

All were of one accord. The spoken convictions of these men found a ready audience in the hearts of the Hebrews, and the word spread, as flame through dry leaves.

In the morning, a mass of dissatisfied congregants assembled, many in the courtyard and more outside, when the weary Moses and Aaron returned. Zipporah, who had been sleepless and worried by Moses' absence, joined the crowd, hanging back anxiously at its edge.

Tasun and Samuel stepped forward and accused the brothers. "You are the ones who have caused the death of the LORD's people." As the crowd closed in menacingly toward the two, the attention of all was drawn toward the tabernacle, where there appeared again not the cloud but the brilliant light. *"Get away from among this congregation,"* God again ordered Moses and Aaron, *"that I may consume them instantly"* (Num. 16:45). The brothers approached and fell prostrate. Moses did not plead for clemency, sensing that God had indeed had His fill of these Israelites, as he himself had also.

Lying face down before God, Moses and Aaron heard the wailing as people began to choke, gasp for breath, turn blue, and within minutes, to die. Moses, drawn once more by duty, told Aaron to take fire from the altar, put it in his censer, lay incense on it, and carry it to the congregation, for surely a virulent plague had begun. Aaron, obedient but still fearful of the angry mob, hurried into the midst of them and wove his way between the living and the dying, extending his path outside of the courtyard.

In less than two hours, after Aaron had completely circumscribed and isolated the dead, God stopped the punishment.

Zipporah and her family had been spared. She hastily wended her way up through the crowd. When Moses saw her, he grasped her outstretched hand. "The boys?" he asked.

"They are safe."

"Walk with me," he requested as they moved through the sorrowful courtyard and outside to view yet another expanse of carnage and a growing flock of mourners. Moses felt drained. "The people cannot all be wrong. Perhaps there is one among them who could lead better than I."

Zipporah reassured him, "It was just through these horrors that God endorsed your authority. Persevere, my husband."

"If only they would appreciate what I am trying to do."

In the short-lived plague, 14,700 men died, including Tasun and Samuel. But there remained seeds of doubt about the right of Aaron to his authority; several times his actions had revealed his weaknesses. He did seem to stop the plague, but he had acted only under Moses' direction and power. God decided it was time to protect Aaron from further accusations and confirm His high priest.

Following divine directions, Moses instructed each tribal leader to bring him a dead branch.[12] He would write the name of its leader on each and deposit them in the tabernacle that night. A thirteenth rod was to be added for the tribe of Levi, with Aaron's name inscribed on it. *"The rod of the man whom I choose will sprout,"* said God (Num. 17:5).

Aaron felt unsure, while the leaders were hopeful, as they offered their branches to Moses. Under the eyes of all leaders, Moses placed the rods in the tabernacle and left. Two leaders volunteered to stay up all night to guard the entrance.

The next morning, Moses found the thirteen sticks still on the floor, but Aaron's branch was alive, budded, and bore blossoms and ripe almonds! Moses showed the rods to the disappointed leaders, who reluctantly accepted Aaron as high priest. God instructed Moses to place Aaron's budded rod into the ark of the covenant next to the Ten Commandments and the portion of manna already there. Thereafter, the rod would be Moses' own responsibility. *"Put back the rod of Aaron … to be kept as a sign against the rebels,"* said God, *"that you may put an end to their grumbling against Me, so that they should not die"* (Num. 17:10).

After Moses placed the rod, the twelve tribal leaders bartered with him, saying they would accept Aaron's priesthood if Moses would help protect them. "According to God's decree, if anyone but a Levite walks next to the tabernacle of the LORD, except by invitation or to sacrifice, he will die![13] The toll of our careless intruders is mounting. Are we to perish completely?" they asked.

Moses consulted God. To solve the problem, God held the Levites responsible to prevent any common person from accidentally approaching the tabernacle, except to make a sacrifice. If they failed, the Levites were to take the trespasser's punishment, becoming their brothers' keepers.

The duties of the Levites toward the laity and the priests mounted. For that, their compensation was outlined by God: one-tenth of the animals, flocks, fruit, grain, and money owned by the twelve tribes must be paid to the Levites every third year. Of these tithes, the Levites would give one-tenth in thanksgiving to Aaron, who also received the part of the most holy sacrifices that is kept from the fire, and, after entry into Canaan, the first fruits of the harvest, the oil, the grain and wine.

The Levites and priests were both told by God, *"You shall have no inheritance in their land. I am your portion and inheritance among the people of Israel"* (Num. 18:20). Unencumbered by concerns of property ownership, Aaron and his sons were to lead a sequestered life, associating only with their families, Moses, and the Levites. *"An outsider may not come near you"* (Num. 18:4), declared God.

It was time again to travel, and the congregation moved south from Hormah toward Kadesh-barnea. Along the way, Miriam became ill, and the next morning she was found dead in her bed, having lived thirty-seven years in her healed leprous state. On the rare trips she had made out in public, her body was well covered, only a stark white face peering from beneath her cowl. Women had visited her often, bringing gifts of food and sewn goods. Aaron had spent many hours with her, trying to ease her depression and to make her life bearable. Moses had long since forgiven her, and their visits had afforded him the opportunity to repay her early care of him. The burial was a simple, private affair attended by Moses, Aaron, Hur, and a few of her close female friends.

Endnotes
1. "scapegoat," Lev. 16:10.
2. "wasting," Ps. 106:15.
3. "Rithmah…," Num. 33:18-22.
4. "sandals and shoes," Deut. 29:5.
5. "Mount Shepher…," Num. 33:25-28.
6. "circumcisions had been abandoned," Joshua 5:7.
7. "not lacked a thing," Deut. 2:7.
8. Num. 15:24
9. Num. 15:27
10. The story of Korah is told in chapter 16 of Numbers.
11. "earth closed," Num. 16:33.
12. The story of Aaron's rod is told in chapter 17 of Numbers.
13. "he will die," Num. 1:51, 17:13, 18:7.

Chapter 16

Moses Fails

After four days of plodding along, baking in the searing sun that reflected off the rocks, the people's water bags were empty, their lips shriveled. The leaders accosted Moses. "You and your God find us water to drink!" they demanded.[1]

"The oasis of Kadesh is but a short distance ahead," Moses replied.

"There had better be water there."

When they reached Kadesh, the formerly lush oasis was dry. The leaders complained, "If only we had perished when our brothers perished. Why have you made us come up from Egypt, to bring us to this wretched place? It is not a place of grain or figs or vines or pomegranates as you had promised, nor is there water to drink." *

Moses knew that God was listening, and he thought, *Let God deal with them.* He walked with Aaron—whose frustration exceeded even that of his brother—to the tabernacle. They fell down on their faces, fearing the worst would befall the crowd.

"God," Moses railed, "listen to their complaining. Do not pity them. You gave me Aaron's rod to prevent this, but I chose not to use it. Deal with them."

But God did not punish the people. *"Take the rod and you and your brother Aaron assemble the congregation and speak to the rock before their eyes, that it may yield its water"* (Num. 20:8), God directed.

The cloud hovered over a huge boulder. *"You shall thus bring forth water for them out of the rock and let the congregation and their beasts drink"* (Num. 20:8).

Moses said to Aaron, as they walked a few steps away, "God wants me to just talk to the rock! What if I stand there, speaking to the rock, and nothing happens? I would be ridiculed. I will do what worked before."

Moses' face flushed as he grabbed Aaron by the forearm and strode toward the leaders, saying, "Bring the people together before that rock," as he pointed to the boulder.

The people shuffled slowly to the rock, where Moses shouted, "Listen now, you rebels: shall we bring forth water for you out of this rock?" *

"Yes!" yelled the doubting crowd.

Moses approached the rock. For a brief moment, he considered standing back from the rock and speaking to it, as God had commanded. Instead, he raised his staff over his head for all to see. Aaron encouraged him with a whispered, "Go ahead, hit it."

Crack! Nothing happened! The crowd tittered. "Your tricks aren't working," someone called. Moses felt the hairs on his neck standing up. He dared not face the crowd. He approached the rock again, raised the staff, and struck it harder. To his great relief, the rock split, water gushed forth, and the people and their animals drank their fill. "Thank you, Moses," was heard from a few. "It's about time," said Kenan.

From the cloud, God said in a grieving voice, *"Because you have not believed Me, to treat Me as holy in the sight of the sons of Israel, therefore, you shall not bring this assembly into the land which I have given them"* (Num. 20:12). It had taken two whacks to break the rock—and God's heart.

"No, God!" cried Moses. "Have I not served You well on this trip, only to lose all for this simple act? Does it deserve death?" Then, looking at his hand, he argued, "Why did You tell me to bring this staff if not to use it?"

Aaron asked of the cloud, "Am I condemned also, LORD?"

God's silence swallowed their hopes.

Devastated, the brothers walked silently away from the crowd. After some minutes, Aaron said, "All those years of leading and now this!"

"I didn't trust Him enough. I wanted to show them, to get the praise," admitted Moses.

Aaron entered Moses' tent the next day and said, "All night I was trying to understand God. At Rephidim, He wanted you to strike the rock so that the people's trust in us would grow. Here, it was time to give Him all the glory.

"But later, I understood differently. What has happened in the last weeks? God has promoted us through Korah's punishment and my budded rod. Then He told us to speak to the rock and we—we, Moses, would bring forth water.

"God offered us His very word to use, the word by which He created all things. A wondrous, unique gift—that we wasted."

Moses dropped his head. "I did not see it that way."

Moses had called the people "rebels," using God's label for them. At a leaders' meeting four days later, Moses would tell them, "You provoked me. The LORD was angry with me on your account and swore to me that I should not cross the Jordan."[2] But the leaders felt no personal guilt for Moses' fate.

The site at Kadesh-barnea, where the waters sprang forth, was named "Meribah," from the Hebrew word meaning "to strive."[3]

Endnotes
1. The story of Moses' failure is recorded in Numbers 20:1–13.
2. "The LORD was angry with me…," Deut. 4:21.
3. "'Meribah,' from the Hebrew word meaning 'to strive,'" according to the footnote for Numbers 20:13 in the Ryrie Study Bible.

Chapter 17

A New Journey; A New High Priest; A New Faith?

God instructed the brothers, *"You have circled this mountain long enough. Now turn north ... through the territory of* [Edom] *... do not provoke them, for I will not give you any of their land, even as little as a footstep, because I have given* [Edom] *to Esau as a possession"* (Deut. 2:3–5).

Although God had originally planned for the Israelites to invade Canaan due north from Kadesh-barnea, where the spying trip had originated, He changed His tactics and opted to make the assault from east of the Jordan River. Moving the Israelites there required travel through Edom, whose border was nearby. The land of Edom, south of the Salt—or the Dead—Sea, was composed mainly of rolling hills interspersed with many deep ravines. God intended His people to go quickly through this infertile land, using it merely as a thoroughfare. *"You shall buy food from them with money so that you may eat, and you shall also purchase water from them with money so that you may drink. For the LORD your God has blessed you"* (Deut. 2:6–7).

Moses sent messengers to Edom's king. "The LORD brought us out from Egypt. We are at Kadesh; may we pass through?" they asked.

"Your request is denied!" said the king.

Moses sent his leaders for a second attempt.

The king accompanied this "No!" by moving his army to his western border to assure compliance, apparently foiling God's plans again. The Israelites were not to engage the Edomites.

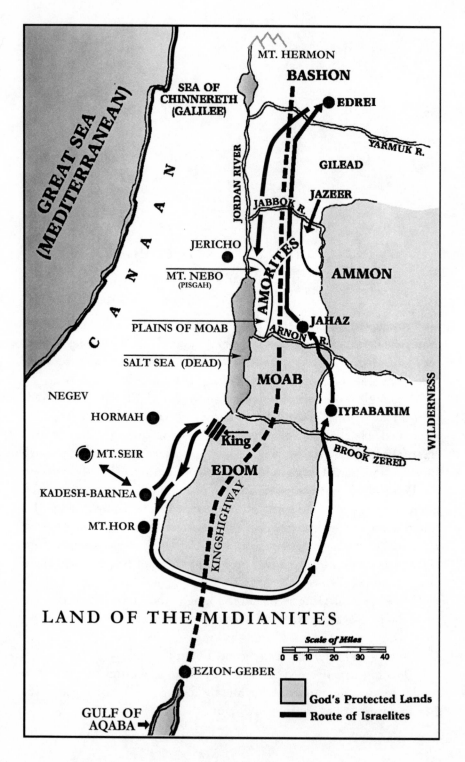

MT. HERMON

BASHON

EDREI

SEA OF
CHINNERETH
(GALILEE)

GREAT SEA
(MEDITERRANEAN)

YARMUK R.

GILEAD

JORDAN RIVER

JAZEER

JABBOK R.

C A N A A N

JERICHO

AMMON

MT. NEBO
(PISGAH)

A M O R I T E S

JAHAZ

PLAINS OF MOAB

ARNON R.

SALT SEA (DEAD)

MOAB

NEGEV

IYEABARIM

HORMAH

King

BROOK ZERED

WILDERNESS

MT. SEIR

KADESH-BARNEA

EDOM

KINGSHIGHWAY

MT. HOR

LAND OF THE MIDIANITES

Scale of Miles

0 5 10   20   30   40

EZION-GEBER

God's Protected Lands

GULF OF
AQABA

Route of Israelites

212

Because entry into Edom was blocked, God told Moses to go north and then travel east through the land of Moab, then north through the land of the Amorites, to the east bank of the Jordan River. But God warned His people, *"Do not harass Moab nor provoke them to war, for I will not give you any of their land ... because I have given it to the sons of Lot as a possession"* (Deut. 2:9).[1] When a contingent of Hebrews was sent to Balak, the king of Moab, he likewise refused them permission to traverse his land.

That left God only one other less favorable option: to lead the people south and then east beyond the land of Edom, and finally north, through the land of the Midianites, adding over one hundred miles to the journey. The people broke camp, took down the tabernacle, and headed south, maintaining their orderly march. They soon reached the lone, large Mount Hor.

There, God told Moses that Aaron must now be gathered to his people because of his role at Meribah.

The congregation assembled at the foot of Mount Hor. Aaron, wearing full priestly regalia, climbed the mountain path ahead of Moses and Eleazar. Moses looked at his brother with compassion and love. "Brother, what we are about now is God's doing, you know; I only act as His intermediary."

"I understand," said Aaron.

"We have been through an epic march together and you have served God and the people well. Now you must die—before me—though it was I who struck the rock."

"I encouraged you to do it." Aaron touched his arm. "My brother, you and I know that it is more than just the rock. The golden calf cost a number of lives. Also, it was because of vicious envy that Miriam and I challenged your authority. Miriam is gone now, and it seems that God has had His fill of me."

"God loves you, brother. Remember it was your rod that budded and you stopped the plague."

"It's no use," Aaron answered. "God's decisions are irrevocable. Do what you must. At least Eleazar will come into the priesthood with clean hands."

"Take hope for what is ahead for you," said Moses. "Remember that, at the burning bush, God told me that He is, not *was,* the God of Abraham, Isaac, and Jacob. Although physically dead, they must live with Him. I believe that you, as His high priest, will live with Him in some way or the other.[2] God also said twice that you shall be gathered to your people. There may be quite a reception awaiting you."

On reaching the summit, they embraced. "We shall look after your wife," promised Moses. "Be strong."

There, Aaron—a recluse by decree—stood in full view of the congregation while Moses performed his difficult assignment. He stripped his brother of his cherished priestly garments, leaving him only in his breeches, and methodically put the holy raiment on a hesitant, tearful Eleazar who thereafter would be recognized as the high priest and accorded the respect due his office. Then God took Aaron's life from him. He was 123 years old. Moses and Eleazar climbed down the mountain, and the congregation mourned for Aaron a full month.

At Aaron's memorial, Moses' prayer concluded: "As God turns all men soon back into the grave, into mere dust, with each death He cries out to the living, *'Return, O children of men,* [to Me]' (Ps. 90:3). O Lord, as we do, make us glad; satisfy us with Your lovingkindness; teach us to number all our days that we may present to you a heart of wisdom. Let the favor of the Lord our God be upon us, confirming the work of our hands."[3]

While at Hor, Hebrew sentries reported to Moses and Joshua that they had seen two towns to the northwest. On closer inspection, they had found several stables of horses near one town, but the inhabitants of the cities did not seem to host an army.

At dawn, under clear skies on the day they were preparing to leave Hor, a cavalry, brandishing swords, swept down from the northern hills, butchering many as they advanced toward the tabernacle.[4] Sentries blew the alarm, but the Israelite soldiers responded haphazardly, unlike the Levites, who quickly surrounded their tabernacle.

Bezalel was polishing a handcrafted chair in his tent, close to the path of the advancing army, when he heard their shouts. Fearing for his beloved tabernacle, he hobbled over and impulsively ran headlong in front of the lead horse with outstretched arms, shrieking. The horse reared when startled by the odd man, and a hoof struck him in the head. The next rider leaned over, and in a quick jabbing motion, thrust his sword in and out of the tottering Bezalel's neck, tumbling him beneath the trampling hoofs.

Heavy dark clouds suddenly covered the camp, and increasing numbers of armed Hebrews slowed the advance of the attacking army. The invaders, surprised by the darkness, retreated with small losses, carrying off choice items from the tents and a number of female captives.

Moses picked up the dying Bezalel and carried him up to the tabernacle, followed by Joshua and an apprehensive crowd. As his breathing faltered, Moses placed him before the doorway, where the cloud hovered over him until he died. He was buried in a plain grave the next day, as he would have liked, but that grave was moistened with the tears of many mourners and lovingly strewn with flowers.

As the Hebrews tried to regroup, Moses interviewed several wounded attackers. The enemy's leader, he learned, was the Canaanite king of Arad, a small nation nearby in the Negev Desert.

Hanniel called the leaders together. "Caleb, Machir, and I see before us an opportunity," he announced, "the first battle for our generation, the first encounter since our fathers and grandfathers deserted God. Hopefully, we have learned something in these thirty-nine years. Let us first seek God's help, this time without Moses' intercession, for it was our people who failed before, not Moses."

In the silence of the evening, Caleb raised a hand toward the tabernacle and vowed to the LORD, "If You will indeed deliver this people into our hands, then we will utterly destroy their cities." *

The next morning, Joshua and the mobilized army advanced on the two towns. When the Aradite army rode out to battle, the Hebrew army fought with new conviction as God showed them favor. They slaughtered the Aradites, entered their cities, freed the hostages, and destroyed the cities. Just as with the Amalekites, God did not prevent His people from being attacked, but the new word spread that the Hebrews' ferocity had returned.

The victory further persuaded the Hebrew leaders that God fulfilled His promises. But they saw how much better it would have been had the people believed and acted on His promise at Kadesh and prevented the years of wandering.

God told Moses to abandon the Aradic ruins and journey southward toward Ezion-geber on the Gulf of Aqaba. From there, they would turn east to skirt Edom. After several days on that route, the Hebrews grew tired of marching. Hot, dry, thirsty, and bored with living on manna, the people doubted again: "Why have you brought us up out of Egypt to die in the wilderness?" * The tassels on robes had failed to remind them of God's provisions, and Moses again ignored Aaron's rod.

The private complaining grew in intensity until it reached Joshua's ears. "Moses," he said, "you know that God hears the prattle of this people. Has He talked to you?"

"No, and that is worrisome," answered Moses. "He must know that I have asked the leaders to control their people, and some have earnestly tried, but the mood of the village has become rebellious again."

"Will He punish with fire or another plague?" Joshua asked.

"He might. Zipporah worries even now for our own safety." Moses spread out his hand. "Perhaps I may have a new chance to speak to a rock."

Before dawn the next morning, venomous serpents slithered into the camp, biting people at random. The bites were all fatal, the bitten dying within two hours. In a panic, the people cried to Moses, "We have sinned because we have spoken against the LORD and you; intercede with the LORD, that He may remove the serpents from us!" *

Moses pleaded to God from his tent, "Remove the serpents, I pray."

For the first time, God refused, leaving the poisonous snakes to terrify the people and remind them of their need for Him. Instead, he told Moses to make a bronze *"serpent and set it on a standard. Everyone who is bitten, when he looks at it, he shall live"* (Num. 21:8). Two of Bezalel's assistants quickly fashioned the bronze serpent and had it erected on a tall post near the perimeter of the Levite camp.

Chaletra, Ruth, and Shum were each trying to gather a skin of water from the scattered puddles of a wadi bed near the camp. As they knelt, intent on their tasks, four crimson snakes shot out from the mid-afternoon shadows of the creek-bed wall. One struck Ruth on the thigh, and another bit Shum on the ankle. Chaletra grabbed a crook, killed one snake, and drove the others back into the shadows. The two teeth marks of each wound caused searing pain, and Shum cried out. To keep from sobbing, Ruth bit into her fleshy thumb.

Chaletra shouted, "Don't move; I'll go for help."

Still shaking, Ruth relaxed her jaws enough to say, "The poisonous serpents of God! Let's hurry to the bronze snake."

Shum was immobilized with fear and pain. Between sobs, she cried, "I will wait for a physician. Chaletra, get a doctor for me!" Chaletra ran to the tents, calling for help. Her brother responded quickly and soon arrived at the wadi with a village doctor. Ruth rose and hobbled toward the brother. The doctor warned, "If you walk, the venom will spread faster."

Ruth replied, "Come with me, Shum; it is your only chance. The doctor cannot cure you."

"You and your superstitions," said Shum. "I'll trust the physician." Ruth left, assisted by Chaletra's brother, while the doctor applied poultices to Shum's wound.

As Ruth stumbled along, supported by the brother, she began to vomit and felt weak as the burning pain from the bite persisted. Her mind whirled, and soon she was delirious. However, as soon as she gazed upon the bronze snake, the confusion began to clear, the pain subsided, and during the next hour, her strength returned. She and the brother ran back to the wadi and found Shum dead in the arms of the physician.

The Hebrews soon dismantled their camp and struck northward through the hilly land of Midian. The miraculous healing of believers by the bronze serpent finally put an end to their murmuring. Trust was growing. (See map #9)

In order to reach the land of the Amorites, at God's direction, they forded first the Brook Zered, camped at Iyeabarim, and then crossed the Arnon River, entering the extreme northeast corner of Moab. Although the Moabites were committed to other gods, God tried to influence them through visions and revelations to provision the hungry and thirsty Israelites whose supplies were low.[5] The Moabite king had heard of the recent slaughter at Arad and refused God's request, thwarting His plans again. The king did, however, permit the Hebrews their limited passage.

God did not leave his weary people to suffer from thirst. When they arrived at a place named Beer, He did not instruct Moses to strike a rock or to speak to one, but simply told him to assemble the people and that He would give them water. Another marvel occurred when the leaders easily dug a well without shovels, and the people sang: "Spring up, O well! Sing to it! The well, which the leaders sank, which the nobles of the people dug, with the scepter and with their staffs."[6] Moses understood that his role as an intermediary in miracle production was ended.

The Israelites made the short trip across the corner of Moab, again forded the Arnon River that had turned ninety degrees to the west, and entered the land of the Amorites. Determined to gain access to a better road, they sent a message to Sihon, king of the Amorites, requesting permission to travel north through his country on the King's Highway. They promised to disturb nothing.

217

Sihon not only refused but gathered his entire army and attacked the Israelites in the Battle of Jahaz in southern Amorite country. God had long hated the evil deeds of the Amorites, who practiced child sacrifice, sorcery, and witchcraft, and engaged freely in adultery, incest, and sodomy like their Canaanite neighbors. This was God's opportunity, and He said to Moses, *"I have given Sihon ... into your hand. This day I will begin to put the dread and fear of you upon the peoples everywhere ..."* (Deut. 2:24–25). The Israelites won a resounding victory.

Afterward, from a nearby hill, the Hebrew leaders surveyed the battlefield littered with dead soldiers.

Kenan said, "I see no Amorite survivors; each of our brave soldiers took twenty of theirs." He turned to Bukki. "Bukki, you have become a noble leader since Tasun died in the plague. We mourn with you over the death of your cherished son. And Caleb, to have lost that strapping grandson! They fought valiantly, and we will carry their names in high honor."

Bukki, cradling his left hand in his right, said, "It was a vicious battle, but victory came sooner than expected—at a heavy cost to our family."

"God fulfilled His vow to give us victory, as he had thirty-eight years earlier," reminded Kemuel.

"Perhaps our future protection will be proportional to our degree of trust in God," said Kenan.

"A troubling thought," replied Kemuel.

Bukki

Thirty-eight-year-old Bukki was elected to replace Tasun as Benjamin's leader, a position he felt he had deserved earlier. For years he had believed himself to be wiser than Tasun, advising Abidan repeatedly in decisions affecting their tribe.

Confident, heavily muscled, fearless, even boisterous, he had been wounded battling with the attacking armies of the King of Arad. While he was pulling riders off of two horses and killing them with an axe, three fingers of his left hand were carved off by a sharp sword. Bandaged up, with a useless left hand, he led the Benjaminite regiment the next day in victory, swinging a heavy sword, one meant for two strong hands.

As people spoke of him they reminded others that, earlier, he had designed the graveyards, even wielding a shovel himself when needed: exposed himself repeatedly to the lethal insects, setting up dung pots with Ahira: subdued a bull once, crazed and dying of disease, with only the help of his brother. They even knew that this passionate man had pleaded with Tasun and Samuel not to make their accusations against Moses.

He was a strict disciplinarian and a domineering father to his four sons. His wife, a tall and wise lady, patiently reared the sons, who loved her dearly yet secretly idolized their father.

The Israelites occupied the Amorite land, killing her inhabitants on the way. Their spoils included the excellent grazing land of Jazeer to the northeast, and the arid Arabah Desert to the west that encompassed the Plains of Moab opposite Jericho. Under God's direction, they later moved northwest and crossed the Jabbok River, which lay at the bottom of a deep valley,[7] entering the lush grazing land of Gilead. They conquered part of it with relative ease and advanced northward to the Yarmuk River, bordering the land of Bashan.

Og, the king of Bashan, reputed to be twelve feet tall, had learned of the Hebrew advance. He mobilized his army, stationing them around the city of Edrei, located on a northern bluff of the Yarmuk River. The Israelites forded the river, climbed the hills, and engaged in a fierce battle. God had said to Moses, *"I have delivered him and all his people ... into your hand. Do to him just as you did to ... the Amorites"* (Deut. 3:2–3). The Bashanites were utterly destroyed, and no [living] remnant was left,[8] while the Israelites suffered only light losses.

Despite the victory, the sweetness was tragically marred for Moses and Zipporah. While leading a charge, their son Gershom sustained a fatal arrow wound to the chest. His death fulfilled their long-held fears, although they had prayed for his exclusion from God's decree.

The Israelite army captured the sixty cities of Bashan—many high-walled and well-fortified—before returning over the Yarmuk to conquer the remainder of Gilead. Several tribes settled in Bashan and on the fertile, grassy slopes of Gilead, while the main body of the Israelites moved southwestward. They retraced their steps for sixty miles, finally erecting the tabernacle in the valley on the east bank of the Jordan, across from Jericho, a land with a tarnished history.

Endnote

1. Lot's sons, Moab and Ben-Ammon, conceived through incest under extraordinary circumstances, had been blessed; their lands were protected.
2. "live with Him," Mk. 12:26-27.
3. Psalm 90, paraphrased.
4. Attack against Israel, Numbers 21:1-3.
5. "provision the Israelites," Deut. 23:4.
6. "scepter and staff," Num. 21:17-18.
7. "bottom of a deep valley" Merill Tenney. *The Zondervan Pictorial Encyclopedia of the Bible.* 1975, p 381.
8. "no living remnant," Num.21:35.

Section V
Plains of Moab

Chapter 18

Parching the Jordan Valley

Many scattered rivulets, born of the melting snow and enlarged by rains, ran down from the summit of nine-thousand-foot Mount Hermon, high in the north of Canaan, finally merging to form a river that raced southward away from the mountain base. Its course was studded with rapids and cataracts as it progressively fell eight hundred feet before flowing into the Sea of Chinnereth fifteen miles away. This fourteen-mile-long freshwater lake, teeming with fish, drained southward as the snakelike Jordan River.

Several miles down the Jordan River Valley, a sizable tributary emptied into it from the east, the Yarmuk River, whose waters in springtime equaled or exceeded the upper Jordan's. Other rivers drained into the Jordan as it wound sixty-five miles[1] south into the Salt Sea.

This is the valley where, five hundred years earlier, Lot chose to live when he and Abraham parted ways. "The valley of the Jordan was well watered everywhere ... like the garden of the LORD,"[2] Lot had observed. In the adjoining hills were several cities, including Sodom and Gomorrah. However, the valley's fertility had been ruined—becoming a "burning waste and no grass grows on it"—when God destroyed those wicked cities by pelting them with fire and sulfur from heaven "in His anger and His wrath."[3]

It was on the parched lowlands north and east of the Salt Sea, the Plains of Moab, with mountains to the east, where Moses established the Israelite camp. To the west, dense thickets, the little remaining greenery, guarded each bank of the Jordan.

Endnote

1. "65 miles": Harold Brodsky, "The Jordan, Symbol of Spiritual Transition." *Bible Review,* June 1992. p. 42.
2. "The valley of the Jordan…," Gen. 13:10.
3. "burning waste…," Gen. 19:24; Deut. 29:23.

Chapter 19

The Magician[1]

After learning the fates of the Amorites and the Bashanites, the leaders of Moab feared they might be next. "This horde will lick up all that is around us, as the ox licks up the grass of the field," * said Balak, their king. He had forgotten God's promised protection of their country, a promise He honored even though they had turned away to worship other gods. Therefore, Balak formed a military alliance with the Midianites who lived to the east and south of them.

Balak also sought more than military assistance. "I need magic!" he said. He knew of a man named Balaam, who lived far to the northeast in Mesopotamia. Balaam's unique powers were legendary: those whom he blessed became blessed indeed, and those whom he cursed were cursed. Balak sent messengers from Moab and Midian to Balaam, offering to pay his usual fee. "Behold, a horde of people came out of Egypt, and they are living opposite me. Please curse this people for me, since they are too mighty for me; perhaps I may be able to drive them out of the land." *

Balaam enjoyed a cherished relationship with God. He invited the messengers to spend the night while he humbly sought God's advice. God replied, *"Do not go with them; you shall not curse the people, for they are blessed"* (Num. 22:12). Balaam sent the messengers home with a curt response: "The LORD has refused to let me go with you."

Other distinguished leaders soon came, urging Balaam to reconsider and promising him great honors and riches. Balaam stood firm. "Though Balak were to give me his house full of silver and gold, I could not do anything, either small or great, contrary to the command of the LORD, my God." * But then he made a costly error. "And now, please, you also stay here tonight," he said to the messengers, "and I will find out what else the LORD will speak to me." * Perhaps, he thought, God would reconsider. God did return that night, and sensing that Balaam's feelings and desires were at odds with His, He approved of the trip but cautioned, *"Only the word which I speak to you shall you do"* (Num. 22:20).

Overnight, Balaam's heart became filled with thoughts of riches. In the morning, he saddled his donkey, and while he rode with the leaders, his daydreams were read angrily by God, who stationed an armed angel, visible only to the donkey, in Balaam's way. As the angel thrust its sword, the donkey protected its master by dodging first off the road and then against a wall, trapping Balaam's foot. Finally the donkey backed up and fell into a crevice. Balaam beat the donkey each time it jostled him until finally, in anger, he dismounted the beast.

"What have I done to you that you have struck me these three times?" * wailed the donkey. As a wonder-worker himself, Balaam had grown accustomed to hearing God speak to him out of nothingness, but not out of a donkey! And this was not God's voice.

Balaam looked around at the other men, and finding none near, walked close to the donkey, frowned, and stared into the beast's left eye. "You have made a mockery of me," he raged. "If there had been a sword in my hand, I would have killed you by now!" *

The donkey answered, "You've ridden me all my life. Did I ever injure you?" *

Balaam forced himself to consider the unique question. "No, I suppose you haven't," he said.

With that, God opened Balaam's eyes to see the sword-bearing angel dressed in white, standing next to the donkey. Balaam's bewilderment changed to fear. Believing the angel knew about his greed, he admitted, "I have sinned." The angel said nothing. "I will turn back if you wish," * he added.

"Go with the men," admonished the angel, who repeated God's warning. *"But speak only the words which I shall tell you"* (Num. 22:35).

Balaam mounted his donkey and rode on. Fording the Arnon River, he entered Moab, where an impatient Balak scolded him for the delay. "Only the word that God puts in my mouth, that I shall speak," * said Balaam.

Balaam

Balaam was born in southern Midian, the fourth son and the seventh and youngest child in his family. His father, Beor, was the chief diviner for the king. Balaam was drilled in his father's craft and how to use divination tools, reading thrown dice, the reaction of a suspended severed tail of a pregnant two-year-old cow to the winds at dawn, the random draw of his picture cards, and the layering of ashes after being swirled in a beaker of water. However, Balaam proved useless in their deliberate manipulation, whereas his oldest brother, Bela, became proficient and was appreciated in the court.

One day, at age seven, beaten and bloodied by a local bully, Balaam cursed the boy in anger before a group of his peers. Four days later, the bully drowned in a swimming accident. Thereafter, Balaam was treated with wary courtesy. A year later, a dying uncle, blessed by Balaam, surprisingly recovered in a week. The young boy began to realize that his powers exceeded the family's secret potions and objects.

As Bela rose in the king's sight, he felt threatened by his younger brother's budding powers. Two years after their father's death, when Balaam was thirteen, Bela drove him away, supplying him with donkeys, three manservants, and bags of supplies.

Balaam traveled north and east to the land of Mesopotamia, the city of Pethor, to the house of an aunt. God appeared to him one night in a vision and warned him of a planned attack on the life of the king of Mesopotamia. He informed the king, who foiled the plot and offered a great reward for his warning, but Balaam refused it, crediting God with the revelation.

God appeared to him many times over the years, to advise and empower him. Occasionally God even came at Balaam's invitation, an invitation frequently fortified by animal sacrifices. Balaam's reputation for magical powers spread widely.

He married and reared a family in modest surroundings, appearing humble before God. He made a satisfactory living as a diviner. As the years went by, however, he often secretly rued his rejection of wealth from the king, hoping always for a second chance at riches.

Early the next morning, Balak took Balaam to a site where the Moabites worshipped their god, Baal—a hill overlooking a portion of the Israelite camp. Balaam required seven large altars, seven bulls, and seven rams, before he would speak to the king. A bull and ram were sacrificed on each altar as burnt and peace offerings to God. Then Balaam climbed a small rise alone, seeking divine guidance.

He returned to Balak, who was standing with his armed leaders, anticipating the curse on the Israelites. With courage instilled by God, Balaam pronounced, "God does not curse the Israelites, and since He does not, I cannot. They are a people who live alone and are not like other nations. They are so numerous that one cannot count even a fourth part of them. " Then, in appreciation of their mission, Balaam added, "Let me die the death of the upright and let my end be like his." *

Stunned, Balak said, "What have you done to me? I took you to curse my enemies, but you have actually blessed them!" *

"Must I not be careful to speak what the LORD puts in my mouth?" * Balaam responded.

In the afternoon, the furious Balak led Balaam and his retinue to the top of the tall Mount Pisgah, overlooking another section of the Israelite camp, and demanded that Balaam curse them. After the ritual of burnt and peace offerings was repeated, Balaam went off to pray and then returned to Balak.

"What has the LORD spoken?" Balak asked.

"God is not a man that He should lie, nor a son of man that He should repent," replied Balaam. "He can be counted on to do exactly what He says He will do.

"I must bless all of these people, because God had just informed me that it is He who leads them and He is their own special God! He has brought them out of Egypt and prods them as with the horns of the wild ox." He surveyed the vast Israelite encampment below. "Even the Israelites do not yet know all the good things God has done and will do for them. They will yet rise. As a lion, it lifts itself; and it shall not lie down until it devours the prey and drinks the blood of the slain." *

Balak shook with distress. "Do not curse them or bless them at all." * He took several deep breaths to calm himself, stared at Balaam, and led the way back to his nearby encampment.

The next morning, Balak led Balaam to the top of Mount Peor, overlooking another wasteland where additional Israelite tribes camped. "Perhaps," said Balak, "it will be agreeable with God that you curse them for me from here." * He ordered the same seven altars rebuilt and the sacrifices repeated. As Balaam looked down over the wilderness, God poured out His Spirit upon him.

Balaam, thus inspired, reminded the king that the Israelites were God's own special people. Balaam foresaw that the tents of this horde of homeless people would become like long valleys and riverside gardens, like valuable aloe trees and strong cedars by the waters. They would prosper. Their king would become great, their kingdom exalted, and they would crush unfriendly nations. "Blessed is everyone who blesses Israel, and cursed is everyone who curses her," * finished Balaam.

Balak could stand it no longer. He told Balaam to return home without the riches he had promised. "The LORD has held you back from honor," Balak said. But Balaam stood firm, saying, "What the LORD speaks, that I will speak. I'll tell you what this people will do to your people in the days to come," * Balaam continued.

He told of the later coming of a great king, descended from Jacob, who would crush Moab and also Edom to the south. Moab would be allowed to exist until that time—a small consolation for Balak. The Amalekites, the most powerful among the nations, would finally be destroyed. "Alas, who can live except God has ordained it?" * Balaam said.

With these words, Balaam and a disappointed Balak parted company. Balak's military forces would have to suffice.

Meanwhile, the Israelites were flush with pride from their recent military victories. To the south of their camp was the country of Moab, and its eastern neighbor was Midian.

While the Israelite soldiers, married and unmarried, patrolled the outskirts of their camps, young Midianite women began to cross the border from the land of Moab.[2] They had been trained by clans to please men in every way. They approached the soldiers to offer them silks, colored cloths, aromatic spices, delicious dishes of food, and gums that, when chewed, invigorated the men. Day by day, growing numbers of these women, joined by Moabite accomplices, walked among the men, coyly displaying glimpses of ankles and legs, sensual movements of their hips, the invitations and suggestions of their veiled, proud breasts, the fullness of their painted lips, and the warmth of their dark eyes. They enticed many battle-weary young men to cross over into Moab and into their bedrooms. There the women indulged the men, greatly satisfying their desires, while listening to stories about their Israelite God. They described their own god, Baal, as a more lenient god who fertilized the soil with his rains and showered the animals and people with his benevolence. Many of the men made gifts to Baal and soon were wholeheartedly worshipping him, even bringing some of their animals to sacrifice to him.

As word of this garden of lust filtered back to the Israelite camp, more young men volunteered for patrols, eagerly trading the God of Abraham for this god of vibrant sexual pleasures offered by enchanting women.

Some of the Israelite leaders looked the other way. "Harmless," they said. Others, among whom were Caleb, Hanniel, and Machir, condemned this behavior and reminded the men that God had told them to have no other gods before Him. What was more, God had specifically said in the second covenant of Sinai, *"Watch yourselves lest you make a covenant with the inhabitants of the land … and play the harlot with their gods and sacrifice to their gods"* (Ex. 34:12, 15–16).

But the men ignored the warnings, as did Zimri, the handsome son of a Simeonite leader, recently assigned to an evening shift on the patrol.[3] He was quickly singled out by Cozbi, the short, dark youngest daughter of a chieftain of a northern Midianite nation. Her older sisters were all taller and more willowy, so she had to work to attract the young men. She became proficient at her craft, and when she saw Zimri, she cast her net for him. She flounced in front of him and soon captured his interest. One day, arousing him with kissing, she coyly asked, "How much do you love me?"

"More than anything," he said.

"Prove it to me, Zimri. Make love to me for the first time in your tabernacle."

"No! God forbids us from even walking into that building," he said.

"Do you believe that, silly one? He wouldn't hurt a man as brave as you. You just don't really love me enough."

Zimri had never cared much for God's overpowering restrictions. Overcome with emotion, he said, "Cozbi, I do, I do. And I want you so much. I have a day off again in three days."

When God realized that the tribal chiefs would not intercede and punish their own licentious soldiers, His anger erupted. *"Take all the [guilty] leaders of the people and execute them in broad daylight before the LORD so that the fierce anger of the LORD may turn away from Israel"* (Num. 25:4), He commanded Moses.

The next day, a furious Caleb opened the council meeting. "We have permitted these orgies, this flagrant betrayal of our faithful God! At least three times we swore, 'All the words which the LORD has spoken, we will do, and we will be obedient.' We all deserve to die. However, God selects only our lustful, betraying leaders, and Jazallun, the respected son of Ahira is one of them! Prepare them to die day after tomorrow."

Hanniel added, "This is only the second time that we have been called on to execute our own, the first time since the golden calf. God refuses to even touch such sinners! We are to know just how sickening it is for Him to kill."

"When will we learn?" groaned Machir. "If God doesn't provide a miracle today, we shun Him tomorrow and reject Him the next. We paint our lintels with grape juice, and self-discipline departs by noon."

Moses and a mass of spectators gathered outside of the courtyard, watching as hoods were placed over the heads of Jazallun and seventeen of the lieutenants, who were lined up bare-chested. Eighteen trained foot soldiers, holding long, sharp spears, faced them. On the signal from Moses, each soldier, seizing his spear with both hands, took a jump-step forward and thrust it with full force into the offender before him, aiming just to the left of the breast bone, where the rib is soft. The men crumpled as the spears were withdrawn. In the silence that followed, all lay dead or dying on the reddening soil.

After the executions, God completed the penalty by sending a plague that killed the other guilty soldiers, and it spread quickly to many other sons of Israel.

A number of the unaffected, weeping in fear, followed Moses and the priests as they hurried into the courtyard and gathered around the bronze altar, praying that God would stop the plague.

At that moment, Zimri nervously walked into the crowded courtyard, arm in arm with Cozbi. The skies darkened as Cozbi and Zimri proceeded all the way up to the entrance of the tabernacle. What little respect he retained for the tabernacle crumbled under Cozbi's coaxing. They slipped through its doorway. Once inside the tabernacle's holy room, Cozbi quickly disrobed, giggled, and squirmed to the floor, pulling Zimri after her. He pulled up his tunic and lay on her.

While Moses and Eleazar rose in surprise to stop them, Phinehas, one of the sons of Eleazar, wrenched a spear from the hand of a soldier. He raced after them, although without the protective attire of a priest, pursuing them into the tabernacle. There, in the holy room, he quickly raised his spear and pierced both of them through their chests with one stroke. Zimri splayed forward, dead, and Cozbi, choking up blood, died in a few moments. Phinehas pulled the spear out and walked to the door, surprised that he himself was unharmed. When he emerged, holding his bloody spear, the sun broke out from the clouds, and suddenly the plague on the sons of Israel was checked.

Although shaken by the events, Eleazar stepped up and put his arm around his son. As they left the courtyard, he gazed out at the fields of the dead, knowing that God's manner was to increase the penalty if a sin, once paid for, was repeated.

Later that day, God's cloud appeared to Phinehas and praised him for his courage. As a reward, he and his descendants after him would inherit the perpetual priesthood from his father, Eleazar, because he was jealous for his God and made atonement for the sons of Israel.

But Phinehas' mind could not rest. The incursion of the harlots had been too orderly, too orchestrated to have happened without some master plan.

He entered the land of Moab with six armed men to seek answers. Because he was feared and respected by all, he found a few women willing to cooperate with him. In just three days, the trail of information led to the higher echelons, and the orders for the deeds were finally traced back to Balak himself.

Phinehas used money he had taken from the treasury to bribe one of Balak's aides, who had overheard several private conversations. It had been Balaam himself—the God-fearing, God-guided Balaam—who advised the Moabites and Midianites to seduce the Israelites. Abandoned by God after his extraordinary stand before Balak, Baalam had been left alone with his avarice, seeking to profit from Balak's power and wealth. He had been prohibited by God from directly cursing the Israelites, so he cleverly suggested to Balak the harlotry plot, knowing that God would punish His lustful people.

Despite an intensive search, Phinehas returned empty-handed to Moses. The magician remained at large.

Endnotes
1. The contents of this chapter, widely quoted and paraphrased, are based on chapters 22 through 24 of Numbers.
2. The story of Baal worship is recorded in Numbers, chapter 25.
3. The story of Zimri and Cosby, Numbers 25:6-15.

Chapter 20

An Army at the Ready

Twenty-four thousand Israelite men died as victims of the plague. After their burial, God determined to attack the Midianite nation in retaliation for the seductions and for Cozbi's sacrilege. But first, Moses would need to organize his troops, beginning with a new census. Like the one taken at Sinai, the census would enroll all men over twenty years of age, establish the size and military strength of each tribe, and provide data by which to allot present and future conquered lands.[1]

Moses dispatched the tribal leaders, and in two weeks they returned with their tabulations. Judah's tribe, the largest, numbered 76,500, whereas the chastised Simeon's had dwindled to a mere 22,000. The total count of the tribes was 601,730 males, 1,820 fewer than on the first census. Over 1 million people had died during the forty-year march.[2]

The figures also confirmed that only six men survived who had been over twenty years of age when they left Egypt: Moses, Joshua, Caleb, Pagiel, and Aaron's sons, Eleazar and Ithamar. Many had died in the battles, but for most, as Moses said, "The hand of the LORD was against them to destroy them from within the camp, until they all perished."[3]

A new problem arose[4] after the census was taken. One of the male descendants of the tribe of Manasseh was Zelophehad, who died on the march, prior to Korah's uprising. He left five daughters but no sons. The daughters were distressed by a law stating that only sons could inherit family land, so they decided to appeal it. They approached Moses and the priests and members of the congregation in the courtyard, not far from the doorway of the tabernacle, an act of surprising boldness that was tolerated by God. "Why can't we have the land that belonged to our father?" they asked.

Moses brought the question before God, and as usual, He patiently addressed even this problem in some detail. *"The daughters ... are right"* (Num. 27:7), God said, establishing a law that a man's property should go to his daughters if he died without sons. If he had no daughter either, it would fall to his brothers; if no brothers, to his uncles; and if no uncles, the nearest relative.

But there was a further problem. If a daughter of Zelophehad married, her husband would acquire her share of the land. If she married outside of her tribe, the land would go to another tribe. God, to whom the ownership of land was very important, decreed another law that henceforth, all daughters should marry only within their own tribe: *"No inheritance of the sons of Israel shall be transferred from tribe to tribe"* (Num. 36:7), He said. Satisfied, the daughters ended the meeting.

God had been so compassionate in dealing with the daughters' problem that Moses, considering his own plight, returned to God to plead for himself. "I am broken, my God. When miracles are needed, mine are no longer the hands, the feet, the tongue for their accomplishment. You speak to me still, but as to one condemned. The love I have for You seems one-sided, not as a glass but as a mirror. Did one mistake doom me?

"You had warned me, *'You shall not turn aside to the right nor to the left ... that it may be well with you, and that you may prolong your days in the land which you shall possess'* (Deut. 5:32–33). And although I rebelled, is the blame mine alone? From a glob of clay You molded and baked me. Am I too hardened to be reshaped by You? I would pay a ransom or sacrifice a prized unblemished animal, but You seem inflexible. I would even march as an underling in Your army to enter the glorious land of Canaan. Do not turn Your face from me."

God responded, *"Speak no more to Me of this matter"* (Deut. 3:26). Moses recalled God's words, *"I will be gracious to whom I will be gracious ..."* (Ex. 33:19). Moses wept.

God mercifully said, *"Go up to this mountain of Abarim [Nebo] and see the lands which I have given to the sons of Israel. When you have seen it, you too shall be gathered to your people as Aaron, your brother, was"* (Num. 27:12–

13). After years of leading, Moses was to be denied the final conquest of Canaan. The glory of victory would rightfully go to God.

Moses would still be allowed to be the people's guardian for a while longer. He knew they needed a strong leader to succeed him, and he asked God to appoint a responsible man so that the congregation of the LORD may not be like sheep that have no shepherd.[5]

There were two obvious candidates, and God selected Joshua over Caleb to be his captain. He told Moses to bring him before Eleazar, the high priest, and the congregation. When he did so, Moses placed his hand on Joshua and publicly commissioned him, ensuring that the congregation would follow him after Moses died.

The strength of the army was now catalogued for the invasion. God promised Moses and Joshua that He would plan all of the strategies, send the ark and priests to lead, and provide the victories, if the Israelites devoted the time before they invaded Canaan to worship. God said, *"Command the sons of Israel and say to them: 'You shall be careful to present My food for My offerings by fire at their appointed time'"* (Num. 28:2). The priests must no longer omit any ritual.

The "appointed times" included all daily, weekly, and monthly sacrifices and the specified feasts. Feasts would be joyful times, except for the solemn Passover and Atonement.

God surprised Moses by announcing that the Israelites would observe the upcoming Passover in Canaan, because they were to cross the Jordan and invade just before that celebration. Lambs would still be the offered animals for Passover, but during the week following, the Feast of Unleavened Bread, a new set of sacrifices must be offered daily, the same as offered on the first day of each month.

Joshua, Caleb, Kemuel, and Bukki were at their midday meal outside the council tent, watching small clouds gather on the northern horizon, when Machir and his herdsmen passed by with two bulls.

"What goes, Machir?" Bukki asked.

"The first day of the month's sacrifice. It's our tribe's turn," yelled Machir.

"The first of the month? God must have lighted a fire under you, eh?" teased Bukki.

"You'd better round up the sheep. We'll need eight," shouted Machir.

"Guess we should," said Caleb, swallowing a bit of manna. He turned back to his friends. "And, speaking of sacrifices, God prescribes yet another festival, the one-day Feast of Trumpets[6] on the first day of the seventh month. Eleazar and Phinehas will have to blow their trumpets loud and long on that first day of the civil new year, while animal sacrifices are being offered, to remind the people that only nine days remain before Atonement."

"And Kemuel," Joshua chided, "we won't let you go after the scapegoat to save it on that Day of Atonement!"

"You fail at humor," responded Kemuel. "Not all of us approve of the many sacrifices!"

"The relief we will feel after Atonement should trigger a great celebration during the following week, the Feast of Booths,"[7] said Joshua.

"Talk of a slaughter! One hundred and ninety-nine animals during that week," groaned Kemuel.

Caleb said, "And seventy-four of those are to be our prized bulls. But God seems to equate joy with sacrificing—the greater the one, the greater the other."

"So you say," grumbled Kemuel.

"In future years, during the Feast of Booths," said Joshua, "our descendants will have a taste of the way many of us have had to live on this journey as they gather palm branches, boughs of leafy trees, and willows to make booths to live in that week."

Days of Rememberance; (Festivals)

Springtime;

Passover (one day, initiating the week-long,)
Feast of Unleavened Bread. (The day after
    Passover was the Feast of the First Fruits).
Pentecost (fifty days after Passover).

Fall;

Trumpets, (beginning of the civil new year.
    Then, nine days later, the)
Day of Atonement (followed by the week-long,)
Feast of the Tabernacles, Booths.

Endnotes

1. Census, Numbers chapter 26.
2. "over one million died." This information is found in the footnote for Numbers 26:4 in the Ryrie Bible.
3. "perished," Deut. 2:15.
4. Story from Numbers chapter 27.
5. "sheep that have no shepherd," Num. 27:17.
6. Feast of Trumpets, Lev. 23:24.
7. Feast of Booths, Lev. 23:34.

Chapter 21

A Stain Stamped Out by Grace

"It's time to go to war against the Midianites!"[1] Moses announced to Joshua, Caleb, and Phinehas. "This will be a different kind of war—a holy war. God is sending us to administer His vengeance against the Midianites, not to conquer their land. I will need a thousand warriors from each tribe to attack their army—one that is larger than ours. Phinehas, you, as the priestly representative, will lead the soldiers with the ark."

Joshua said, "At sunup, we will march southeastward into the hill country, where our scouts have seen their cities."

Moses interjected, "Remind the men that God has promised, *'Before all your people I will perform miracles which have not been produced in all the earth ... for it is a fearful thing that I am going to perform with you'* (Ex. 34:10). Therefore, encourage the men to fight with assurance."

Balaam did not return to Mesopotamia after being rewarded for making his cunning recommendation to Balak, but settled in a northern province of the land of Midian, living in the sumptuous style afforded by Balak's gifts. He felt secure under the protection of King Reba of Midian and was unaware that knowledge of his deceit had been circulated in the harlots' bedrooms and then among the Hebrews. He had broken his bonds with God by his betrayal, and dialogues between them had ceased.

As the Israelites approached the first Midianite city, surrounded by a four-foot-high wall, they saw the tops of flag-bearing standards in the midst of a group of milling soldiers. They stormed the city gates, climbed the walls, and engaged the enemy. They routed them with ease, killing every man[2]. Scattered dead hornets speckled the dust about the largely undernourished victims. The victorious army advanced to the next town, finding its defenders disorganized, weak, and easy prey.

One Hebrew officer, moving from street to street, encountered a fleeing Balaam dressed in fine robes. The officer pursued him and soon overtook the magician. Balaam desperately proffered a handful of gleaming jewels. "I am Balaam," he panted. "Do you not know me?" The officer thrust his sharp sword into Balaam's upper abdomen.

As he withdrew his blade out of the slumping body, the wise soldier flared his nostrils in disgust. "How many thousands of lives would have been spared had you just stayed home in Mesopotamia!"

In two weeks, the army easily conquered the entire northern kingdom of the Midianites and slew her five kings, including King Reba.

Moses went out to greet the conquering army, but observing the captives, was instantly disturbed. He turned on the captains. "Have you spared all the women? Behold, these caused the sons of Israel to trespass against the LORD so the plague was among the congregation. Now, therefore, kill every male among the little ones, and kill every woman who has known man intimately. But spare all the virgin girls; the older ones you may marry as you please." He added curtly, "Purify yourselves, you and your captives, outside of the camp on the third day and the seventh day."*

When they tallied up the booty, their human captives totaled 48,000. Each was examined, and 16,000 doomed non-virgin women and male babies were segregated in a separate compound. The captains organized their 12,000 men, fresh from battle, assigning them to the marked prisoners. One night, while the captives were sleeping in their tents, the soldiers crept up on their victims and killed them by hatchet, sword, or knife. Many short, muffled cries arose from the compound.

The next morning, the slaughter of the night was revealed as masses of bodies were heaped up for burial by civilians. The soldiers began their seven-day process of purification, their weapons to go through fire, they themselves to be washed with water filtered through the ashes of the red heifer.

Hanniel, Machir, Kenan, and Benjamin's Bukki walked out together among the bodies. "How could Moses have ordered our soldiers to kill all those male babies?" asked Kenan.

"Males must represent a great eventual threat to our still-fragile faith," replied Machir. "We have not proven trustworthy."

"But Moses also ordered the execution of the women. Some squeamish soldiers vomited because of what they had to do," said a grimacing Kenan.

"Perhaps God again wanted our soldiers to feel some of His agony during mass killings," answered Hanniel. "God did the killing at the Red Sea and during the plague, but we did not understand. Now we do."

"Don't fault Moses too much," Machir defended. "Didn't God tell him, *'Take full vengeance for the sons of Israel upon the Midianites after which you will be gathered to your people'* (Num. 31:2)? As Moses ordered the war, so he also ordered his own death."

"But don't kill those pretty, defenseless women," said Kenan angrily. "God gave us two laws that said, if a soldier in a foreign land, *'shall see among the captives a beautiful woman,* [he could] ... *take her as a wife'* (Deut. 21:11). Also, *'the women and children ... you shall take as booty for ourselves'* (Deut. 20:14). Moses overstepped God's law in ordering this massacre."

"Remember, they were some of the same women who enticed our soldiers," said Bukki. "All had to suffer for what a few did."

Hanniel nodded. "This was also a rehearsal for us, because God told us to leave no one alive when we invade their land, no one to contaminate what faith we have.[3] If only we'd shown greater loyalty, God might have been more lenient toward our enemies."

"That law of total annihilation applies only to Canaan, where we will eventually live, not to Midian," retorted Kenan.

"Yes, Kenan, but Moses did spare the young girls," offered Bukki.

"I was told that Moses did not sleep last night," Machir added. "Others heard him weeping off and on, and heard Zipporah's words of comfort from their tent. I would not wish that man's office on any other."

Soon the time came to divide up the live booty. There were 675,000 sheep, 72,000 cows, 61,000 donkeys, and 32,000 virgins, all captured by 12,000 Israelite soldiers. God instructed Moses to divide them equally among the warriors and the remainder of the congregation, a practice that rewarded those who had stayed behind to provision the army and maintain the camp. From the warriors' allotment of girls, women, and animals, a tax was levied—one in five hundred was to be given to the priests; and from the congregation's, one in fifty went to the Levites.

Then the captains approached Moses and Eleazar. "We have taken a census of the men of war, and amazingly, no man is missing. Not one of ours died! In thanksgiving for God's protection, and as atonement for stealing and for killing, each soldier has brought the captured earrings, necklaces, bracelets, and rings to you—16,750 shekels of gold. Please accept them for God."

Moses looked at Eleazar, deeply moved. "Evidence of God's trustworthiness mounts before them." They took the gift and put it in the tabernacle's holy room as a memorial for the sons of Israel.[4]

The soldiers' courage and generosity contrasted with the selfishness of the tribes of Reuben and Gad—cattlemen who had accumulated large herds—and their attitude threatened the long-awaited invasion of Canaan.

One day Bohan, the new leader of Reuben, and Kenan of Gad, asked Moses if their cattle might remain in the lush pasturelands of Jazeer and Gilead, freeing their owners from the obligation of crossing the Jordan River and fighting the Canaanites. Moses was stunned by their proposal, counting on each of the twelve tribes to provide manpower for the invasion.[5]

"Shall your brothers go to war while you yourselves sit here?" Moses asked, glaring at them. "Why are you discouraging them from crossing over into the land that the LORD has given them? This is what your fathers did when I sent them from Kadesh-barnea to see Canaan. They discouraged the sons of Israel so that they did not go into the land. And the LORD's anger made them wander until that generation was consumed. Now, behold, you have risen in your fathers' stead, to add still more to the burning anger of the LORD against Israel! For if you turn away from following Him, He will once more abandon us in the wilderness." Moses' apprehension grew. "And you will destroy all this people!" * he warned.

The two chagrined leaders countered with a compromise. They would begin to build up cities for their families and fenced-in areas for their cattle in Jazeer and Gilead, and then accompany their brothers across the Jordan into battle. "We will not return to our homes until every one of the sons of Israel has possessed his inheritance," * promised Bohan.

Moses accepted, but changed the conditions; they must arm themselves and cross over the Jordan before their brothers, spearheading the invasion, or their inheritance would be denied them.[6] If they failed to do that, God would punish them. Hesitantly, they accepted this agreement.

The following day, Moses returned to Bohan and Kenan to assign them the lands east of the Jordan for their inheritance. The tribe of Reuben received the southern portion, most of the former kingdom of the Amorites; Gad was assigned the central portion, most of the area of Gilead, and a part of Bashan, the former kingdom of Og. Moses also gave some of the land east of the Jordan to half of the tribe of Manasseh because of their large cattle holdings, granting them most of Bashan and part of Gilead. Each tribe soon began to build more fortified cities and enlarged the existing ones on their land.

Endnotes
1. Midianite war: Numbers chapter 31.
2. "killing every man," Num. 31:7; Deut. 20:13.
3. "no one alive," Deut. 20:16.
4. "memorial," Num. 31:54.
5. The request of Gad and Reuben to be excused from the attack is based on chapter 32 of Numbers.
6. spearhead the invasion, Josh. 4:12.

Chapter 22

God's Command: Destroy Their Gods

At this, the Israelites' forty-first campsite, east of the Jordan and opposite Jericho, God called Moses to His tabernacle and gave a message for the people. *"The LORD, your God, is bringing you into a good land, a land of brooks of water, of fountains and springs, flowing forth in valleys and hills, a land of wheat and barley, of vines and fig trees and pomegranates, a land of olive oil and honey, a land in which you shall eat food without scarcity, in which you shall not lack anything, a land whose stones are iron, and out of whose hills you can dig copper. When you have eaten and are satisfied, you shall bless the LORD, your God, for the good land He has given you"* (Deut. 8:7–10).

God set borders for the lands He had promised them. They began at the southwestern extremity of the Salt Sea, followed the eastern border of Edom southwest, and then turned westward below Kadesh-barnea, curving up to the Great Sea. Follow that shore up north to a city that was at about the same level as Mount Hermon. The line curved southeastward to the eastern shore of the Sea of Chinnereth and then southward along the Jordan River to the Salt Sea.

The land was to be divided among the nine and one-half tribes remaining after Reuben, Gad, and half of Manasseh were given the lands east of the Jordan. Eleazar and Joshua would apportion the land and disperse it by lottery—presumably God-directed—with the leader of each tribe assisting in the distribution. Each leader would subdivide his allotted area among his people in proportion to the size of their families.

The Levites could not own land, but would scatter themselves strategically into forty-eight separate cities of the other twelve tribes, where they could continue to serve the people in their designated roles.

Six of those cities—three east of the Jordan and three west—were designated as "cities of refuge"[1] to which a person who killed another might flee and obtain safe haven until a trial could be held. God's law stated *"a life for a life"* (Deut. 19:21). If a man killed another, he could expect a family member of the victim, or "blood avenger,"[2] to legally pursue and kill him. God said, *"Blood pollutes the land and no expiation can be made for the land for the blood that is shed on it, except by the blood of him who shed it"* (Num. 35:33).

If the verdict of the trial was murder, the offender was cast out to the blood avenger. However, if the verdict was only manslaughter, the perpetrator must still stay in the sanctuary city because, outside its gates, he was still legal prey to the avenger. He would be released to safety only upon the death of the current high priest who, by his death, symbolically paid the ransom for all accidental homicides. While the death of the high priest brought mourning for the congregation, it brought joyful reunions for others.

In Canaan, each Israelite, except for the Levites, would have his own parcel of land to use as he saw fit, and he had freedom to choose his spouse, vocation, and leisure activities. The people would govern their own cities. But as they enjoyed His blessings, they should recognize God as Provider and obey the laws made for their own good, to assure their safety, peace, and joy. It would be another chance—almost another Garden of Eden.

Although the land of Canaan was good, God sternly warned Moses that its occupants were not. The Israelites should be ruthless toward them, showing no mercy, because all the peoples of Canaan, *"a nation greater and mightier than you"* (Deut. 9:1), carried on the same vile practices as did their neighbors, the Amorites.

"You shall utterly destroy all the places where the nations whom you shall dispossess serve their gods, on the high mountains and on the hills and under every green tree," God commanded. *"You shall tear down their altars and smash their sacred pillars and burn their Asherim with fire, and you shall cut down the engraved images of their gods, and you shall obliterate their name from that place"* (Deut. 12:2–3).

He warned of the consequences. *"But if you do not drive out the inhabitants of the land from before you, then it shall come about that those whom you let remain of them shall be as pricks in your eyes and thorns in your sides, and they shall trouble you in the land in which you live. And it shall come about that as I plan to do to them, so I will do to you* (Num. 33:55–56).

"You shall not leave alive anything that breathes" (Deut. 20:16).

Moses left the tabernacle, his mind weighed down with God's messages.

Two days later, Moses shared this information with the leaders at the council meeting. "I will be unable to carry this out," he said. "That will be Joshua's task. Now, prepare your soldiers. If they are to obediently destroy these places of worship, they must first discard their own idols, idols that many still cherish and worship."[3]

Moses reminded them that God was bringing the Israelites to the land of Canaan to fulfill a longstanding promise: "It is not for your righteousness or for the uprightness of your heart that you are going to possess their land … for you are stubborn people. It is because of the wickedness of these nations that the LORD your God is driving them out before you, … in order to confirm the oath which the LORD swore to your fathers, to Abraham, Isaac, and Jacob."[4]

The leaders silently filed out of the meeting. Their proud, joyous feelings of promised victory to occupy this bounteous land had been tempered by God's personal reproof.

Endnotes;
1. "cities of refuge," Num. 35:6-15.
2. "blood avenger," Num. 35:19.
3. "idols worshipped," Amos 5:26; Acts 7:43.
4. "It is not for your righteousness…," Deut. 9:4-6.

Chapter 23

Crucial Decision Time

Moses was troubled by a deep concern for the future safety of his wards after his death. He had just reproached his leaders for the stubbornness of the people, that they had done nothing to deserve the might of God that would procure upcoming victories for them. Now it was time to address the larger body of people. Therefore, on the cusp of the invasion, he assembled a large number of the congregation in the courtyard, both to warn and encourage them once more.

He reminded them of how God had destroyed his own, those who sacrificed to Baal. "But you who held fast to the LORD your God are alive today." Calling for obedience, he said, "And now, O Israel, listen to the statutes and the judgments that I am teaching you to perform, in order that you may live and go in and take possession of the land that the LORD, the God of your fathers, is giving you. When you reach Canaan, if you act corruptly and serve other gods, you shall surely perish. But if you seek the LORD your God, with all your heart and soul, you will find Him. For what great nation is there that has a god so near to it as is the LORD our God whenever we call on Him?"[2]

He looked out over the people. "The LORD your God is a compassionate God; He will not fail you. Indeed, ask from one end of heaven to the other. Has anything been done like this great thing, or has anything been heard like it? Has any people heard the voice of God speaking from the midst of fire, as you have heard it, and survived? Or has a god tried to take for himself a nation from within another nation by trials, by signs and wonders, and by war and a mighty hand, and by an outstretched arm and great terrors, as God did for you in Egypt before your eyes?"[3]

He told them that if they hold fast to God, no man can stand against them. They should show their love for Him by teaching their children the words of God, talking of them when they sit, when they walk, when they lie down, and when they rise up. They should even write His words on their hands and their doorposts.[4]

If any Israelite should become their king, he must write a copy of this law on a scroll and read it everyday so that he remains humble and obedient to the commandments.[5]

Moses concluded by saying that if they obey, they will be His people, a treasured possession, and He will set them high above all nations for praise, fame, and honor.

Kemuel, Bukki, Machir, and Hanniel sat together after the meeting in the late afternoon. "God told Moses that there are witches and sorcerers living in Canaan," said Bukki, "casting spells in concert with the devil, even spiritualists who call up the dead and who divine the future."[6]

Hanniel said, "God also said that He will drive them out before us so that we will not be tempted to believe their false teachings."

"But God knows our own desire for true understanding," said Machir. "He promised that one day He will send us a special man, one of our own countrymen, through whom He will speak His truths."

"We already have two good men, Moses and now Joshua, through whom God sends us messages," said Kemuel.

"The man will be more than a leader," said Machir, "more than Moses. God refers to him as a prophet."[7]

Kemuel said, "With God among us, what need do we have for a prophet? Only if He disappeared, as He did for forty days, would we need one. Do you think He will ever leave?"

"If we persist in being disobedient, God warns," cautioned Machir.

"Then we had better obey Him," Bukki nodded in assent. "I wonder if we will fear the prophet as we sometimes do God?"

"God said," said Machir, "that we will be able to listen to him without fear."

"How do you think he will be recognized?" asked Bukki.

"I guess that God will arrange that," said Hanniel. As he peered outside, Hanniel noticed a change in the weather.

Moses also was watching from his tent as a barely visible darkness gathered over the northern horizon. Although the clouds probably would not reach them, rains upstream would raise the Jordan beyond the reported current flood stage. He summoned a driver and a captured chariot and set off to inspect the river.

While crossing the plains, they passed a group of Hebrew archers on the right, target-shooting at a wooden figure mounted on a small three-wheeled platform pulled by a galloping horse. Farther on, to their left, an officer was drilling a formation of soldiers.

Upon reaching the river's edge, Moses looked out at the swift current swirling past largely submerged but well-anchored thickets. "The flood waters are higher than the scouts reported," he observed. "Crossing will be difficult."

Nearby were two groups of men who were binding logs and small trees with dried reeds and hemp ropes. "What are you doing?" Moses asked.

"We have retrieved these logs from the river and are building rafts," replied one man. "It will be the only way for us to get across."

Moses became angry. "I do not know how God will arrange our crossing, but if He wanted us to build rafts, He would have ordered it. Cease your labors!"

"We will complete these two but build no more."

Moses sighed and turned toward home.

On returning to camp, he found Joshua, and the two men entered the tabernacle to present the flood problem to God.

To their surprise, God's concerns focused mainly on the continued waywardness of the people. In an attempt to capture their obedience, God revealed part of His invasion plan to the two men.

The next morning, Moses and Joshua called a meeting of Levites, selected soldiers, tribal leaders, and the elders to share God's message. "Unlike the war against the Midianites, you men had to fight your way into the lands of the Amorites and the Bashanites," said Moses. "This time, however, you will not be met by such an expectant army in Canaan. God has planted a great fear of you in them.

"Four days before Passover, when the sacrificial lambs will be selected, you are to cross over the river. The priests, carrying the ark, will lead you, followed by the soldiers, and then the people. As you cross, God says that somehow you must pick up a number of large stones from the riverbed and carry them with you, then move northwestward and climb into the hills until you reach two adjacent mountains, Gerizim and Ebal.[8] At Mount Ebal, you should place other stones together in a row, coat them with lime, and the priests will copy all the words of God's new laws upon them. You will fit other stones together to form an altar, without cutting or shaping them with tools, and there we will perform peace and thanksgiving sacrifices."

Kemuel turned to Machir and said, "We are craftsmen and can shape the stones to make a perfect altar."

Machir answered, "God cursed the ground when Adam ate the fruit. Perhaps we are not to try to remove the curse with our chisels; only the sacrifice can do that."[9]

Moses continued, "Some of the Levites will station themselves between the two mounts. A large contingent of people from each of six tribes will stand on Mount Ebal, and a number from the other six tribes will climb Gerizim," he added. "The Levites will shout, 'Cursed is the man who makes an idol or a molten image, an abomination to the LORD!' The people on the mountains will respond in unison, 'Amen!' The Levites will shout again, 'Cursed is he who dishonors his father or mother!' The people will give a booming 'Amen.' The Levites will cry out the laws, one after another—laws concerning boundary marks; care of the blind, the alien, the orphan, and the widow; malicious gossip; bribing; and sexual sins. Then one last curse encompassing all of the others will be shouted out: 'Cursed is he who does not confirm the words of these laws by doing them.' And the people will say 'Amen.'"

Moses said, "You are to spend the first two weeks in concentrated worship of God, strengthening your faith, because He knows that the temptations ahead of you will be powerful.

"Even though we have broken God's first two covenants and lived thirty-eight years without a binding agreement," Moses continued, "He now offers the opportunity and assurance of a third covenant. It is a simple one. If the people promise to perform this series of rituals after the crossing and do not turn away from God later, He will bless them in everything and they need have no fears."

Kemuel was puzzled. "Why is it so important that we, a people who vacillate in our thoughts and actions, make a binding pact with this powerful, vast, yet dreadful God? We already know that He will lead us into Canaan, and He has promised us eventual victory."

"By the covenant, He promises to bless all of us beyond belief in all that we do," explained Moses.

"And if we are disobedient?"

"*I declare that you shall surely perish*' (Deut. 30:18) is God's reply to that," said Moses. "We will be cursed in everything we do."

"In that case, the priests must set an example of obedience for us," said Kemuel. "They have skipped many of their prescribed duties."

"Indeed they must," agreed Moses. "But you, you consider this covenant thoroughly before you agree, the blessings, but also the curses. If you and your people enter into this covenant with Him, He will establish you anew as His people and He will be your God. But on this day, you must choose whether or not to love the LORD your God, to walk in His ways, and to keep His commandments. It is decision time for you, individually and collectively!" *

"Our choice is not 'follow God or leave,'" said Machir. "The choice is 'be faithful to Him or suffer,' for we are eternally adopted."

"It seems that way," Moses continued, repeating God's warning. "I have set before you life and death, the blessing and the curse. So choose life in order that you may live, you and your descendants by loving, obeying, and by holding fast to Him."[10]

Finally, the assembly soberly pledged obedience to all of God's conditions. Moses concluded: "The LORD has today declared you to be His people, a treasured possession, and He shall set you high above all nations which He has made, for praise, fame, and honor."[11]

Moses gave the book of laws to the high priest, who placed it in the tabernacle beside the ark, to be read to the people every seventh year, so that those who have not known would hear and learn to fear the LORD, their God.

In his tent later that day, Moses heard God telling him that the time for his death was approaching, and he should bring Joshua to Him.

Moses found Joshua inspecting a makeshift armory with Hanniel and Machir. "Come, Joshua, God wants to see you," Moses said. "And you two accompany us to the gate."

Moses said as they walked, "God knows that our men are more committed than their fathers. However, He sees that future prosperity after the war will cause even them to defect to other gods.

"Should that happen, God will finally *'hide* [His] *face from them'* (Deut. 32:20), the curses will be dispensed, our people will suffer and be dispersed. Finally, when they are brought back to Egypt as slaves, no one will even buy them."[12]

The three men were aghast. "Moses, would God really do all of that?" Hanniel asked.

"That and more, Hanniel," Moses assured him. "God says that *'He would turn the land of Israel into a burning waste, unsown and unproductive ... like the overthrow of Sodom and Gomorrah'* (Deut. 29:23). Only God can see the horrible state to which mankind might sink, and He will do whatever He can to prevent that, even if chastisement of the Israelites becomes necessary."

Joshua added quickly, "Can't I, can't we, start to prevent this now? I wish that God would, for once, impose obedience on us and not just try to earn it—this Enormous Power earning our obedience!"

Machir said, "I doubt that we are necessarily doomed. I believe that God can be flexible. Didn't Moses cause Him to change His mind? Didn't God change a few of His sacrificial laws on this trip? Didn't He have to change His plan when the kings of Edom and Moab prevented our passage through their land? If He projects the future from our current thoughts and actions, can't we change? Joshua, you must keep us vigilant."

They reached the gate and only Moses and Joshua entered the courtyard.

God appeared before them as the cloud. "Joshua!" His name rolled out of the cloud, and Joshua's eyes widened. *"Be strong and courageous, for you shall give the people possession of the land which I swore to their fathers to give them"* (Josh. 1:6).

Joshua's doubts vanished and his spirit was lifted by God's words, while Moses' shoulders sagged under the morsel of envy he harbored and the finality of God's censure.

The two men then fell into a deep sleep, and God gave them each a vision portraying the future development of the Israelite nation as it conquered the nations of Canaan. Through an extraordinary provision, Moses and Joshua were allowed to sense in some small measure God's love and His true anguish. On awakening, the two men discovered their visions were identical.

As a lasting legacy, God commissioned them to compose a song based on their insights. It would describe a future in which the Israelites would renounce Him. Memorized by the people, as a rote melody, they and their descendants would sing it in years to come during times of discipline so they might understand the cause of their plight and its only remedy.

"Be strong and courageous in your trials and leadership," Moses said to Joshua. "Do not let the people's errancy undermine your relationship with God as they have mine. They have been a pebble in my sandal for forty years. But now, Joshua, I must prepare to die. My son is independent and can take care of Zipporah. Come, let us write the song."[13]

"Give ear, O heavens, and let me speak," Moses began. "Let my song nourish you as the droplets on the fresh grass, and as the showers on the herb. God's work is perfect, for all His ways are just. A God of faithfulness and without injustice, righteous and upright is He."

"Add this," said Joshua. "You people will have acted corruptly toward Him, as a perverse and crooked generation. Is this how you repay the LORD? Is He not your Father who has brought, made, and established you?"

"Remember the days of old when God blessed you wondrously," said Moses as he wrote. "If you do not know, ask your fathers, your elders, and they will tell you. God found Jacob in a desert land, in the howling waste of a wilderness, and He protected him and guarded him as the pupil of His eye. The LORD alone guided him and there was no foreign god with him."

Joshua picked up the thought. "And He took his descendants into the land of Canaan, which was everything that God had promised, with abundant honey, oil, curds, milk, fat of lambs, wheat, and of the blood of grapes for wine. But in time, the Israelites grew fat and forsook the God who made them, scorning and ignoring Him, provoking Him to jealousy by worshipping other gods."

"Finally," said Moses, "when God's patience was drained, He heaped misfortunes on His people, the sword wounding outside but terror tormenting from within. Enemies would overcome them."

"But soon the corrupt foes of the Israelites would falter and, as they succumb, God will ask, *'Where are their gods? ... Let them rise up and help you!'* God will declare to all, *'See now ... there is no god besides Me. It is I who put to death and give life. I have wounded and it is I who heal ... I will render vengeance on My adversaries, and I will repay those who hate Me. I will make My arrows drunk with blood'*" (Deut. 32:37–42), quoted Joshua.

Moses envisioned, "Finally, in spite of their waywardness and lack of repentance, He will still preserve His people, making the necessary payment for their sins Himself."

Moses and Joshua came before the people the next morning to teach them the words to the song. "Take to your heart all you have heard this day, the laws, blessings, curses, and the song," Moses pleaded. "These are not idle words for you. Indeed, it is your life."

After the song was concluded, Joshua led Moses away from the crowd. When they were alone, Joshua said, "Moses, how can we convince others that God is not a cruel tyrant, but a wise, forgiving, and indeed a feeling God?"

"Soon that will be one of your most important tasks—and yours alone," said Moses.

After dinner that night, Moses, Hanniel, and Machir visited Pagiel, who was weakened by a month-long illness. They sat around his bed, sharing stories and reminiscing. After a while, Moses looked at his friends affectionately and said, "God has told me that I must die soon, probably long before you, Pagiel. Death is still an unknown to me, even after watching many die. I wonder if we will become merely corpses in a grave or will we be 'gathered to our people' as Aaron was, perhaps deemed worthy to live with Him as Abraham does?"

Hanniel, turning to Moses, said, "You are worthy to live with God, Moses. As to why you must die and not be permitted even a sacrifice, the way I see it, God invested too much of Himself into you. You became almost a part of Him, and He could not tolerate even your brief defiance. Even by His great mercy, He could not let you live."

"You have been loyal to God all along," said Machir. "I believe He saw that the frustrations, failures, and perhaps a re-awakening pride, were allowing another power to draw your loyalties away. To save you, His great love will jealously and mercifully take you to Himself."[14]

Pagiel said, "I share your concerns, Moses, but the hour fatigues me. Good night, all of you and—thank you for your visit."

Three days later Pagiel died, and Heber became leader of the tribe of Asher.

Endnotes
1. The retelling of the Exodus journey by Moses is based on Deuteronomy 4.
2. "And now, O Israel, listen...," Deut. 4:1f.
3. "The LORD your God is a compassionate God...," Deut. 4:31-34.
4. "Write these words...," Deut. 11:19-25.

5. "become their king…," Deut. 17:14-20.

6. "witches, sorcerers, cast spells," Deuteronomy 18:11ff, Leviticus 19:31, and Leviticus 20:27.

7. "prophet," Deut. 18:15-19.

8. The retelling of the ceremony on the mounts is based on Deuteronomy 27.

9. "curses, chisels": This point was made by J. H. Kurtz in his book, *Offerings, Sacrifices and Worship in the Old Testament,* 1998, p. 45.

10. "I have set before you…," Deut. 30:19.

11. "The Lord has today declared…," Deut. 26:18-19.

12. "no one to buy them," Deut. 28:68.

13. The song composed by Moses and Joshua is a paraphrase of Deuteronomy 32. Lyrics adapted from the New American Standard Bible. ©Copyright 1960, 1962, 1963, 1968, 1971, 1972, 1973, 1975, 1977 by The Lockman Foundation. Used by permission. (www. Lockman.org)

14. See Isaiah 57:1, 2.

Chapter 24

A Call from God

After Pagiel's funeral, Moses called the congregation together, unwilling to leave them with only dire prophecies, and gave them blessings[1] like those given by Isaac to Jacob[2] and by Jacob to his sons.[3]

Moses addressed each tribe individually for the last time. He foresaw a different occupation and blessing for each tribe; there would be tribes of seamen and farmers, writers and warriors, gardeners and judges, priests and miners; and he pictured one tribe, in particular, the Benjaminites, who would simply walk closely with God. The greatest blessings were given to the descendants of Joseph and Levi.

For Ephraim and Manasseh, through Joseph: May his land have the best the sun, the earth and the mountains can bring forth. They will be warriors blessed by God.

For Levi: They will continue to serve God as the priestly tribe, teaching the law and judgments and offering sacrifices for the people. God will protect them from their foes.

Moses ended his blessings with his arms stretched lovingly toward his people. "God rides the heavens to your help, and through the skies in His majesty. He drove out the enemy from before you.... Blessed are you, O Israel; who is like you, a people saved by the LORD?"[4]

Later that night, Moses drew his family around him. They knew God would call him in the morning. They spent a somber evening reminiscing and sharing future plans, finding comfort, at times, in reviewing Moses' life, while some still hoped that God would rescind His decree. Laughter mingled with tears.

In the morning, there were warm hugs and soft, tearful goodbyes. Moses' hand lingered in Zipporah's as their eyes held each other until the final moment.

The time came. At God's bidding, Moses left the plains of Moab and climbed Mount Nebo to the peak called Pisgah. His energy and vision were good, despite his 120 years. He had served God and the people well, seeking as his only reward to see his task through to the end. He had asked little for himself.

God met him on the mountain and showed him all of the land that was to become Israelite territory—from the northern border to the southern border, and all the way to the Great Sea. *"This is the land which I swore to Abraham, Isaac, and Jacob, saying, 'I will give it to your descendants,'"* God said to him. *"I have let you see it with your eyes, but you shall not go over there"* (Deut. 34:4). The lingering waves of disappointment that had lapped at Moses were suddenly replaced by a surprising peace, a confident calm.

Moses died there, and after a struggle for his body between the devil and God's angel, Michael,[5] God Himself buried the body.[6] His family and the other Israelites searched but found no grave or body; there would be no gravestone to visit and revere. Moses was God's alone. The people grieved for Moses, weeping for him for thirty days. Then they turned to Joshua, listened to him, and obeyed his word.

Endnotes
1. "blessings," Deut. 33.
2. Isaac to Jacob, Gen. 27:27-29.
3. Jacob to his sons, Gen. 49.
4. "God rides the heavens…," Deut. 33:26-29.
5. devil and God's angel, Michael, Jude 1:9.
6. "God buried the body," Deut. 34:6.

Chapter 25

The Invasion

On the day following the end of the mourning period for Moses, God called Joshua to the tabernacle and met him at the doorway. *"Cross this Jordan, you and all of this people, to the land which I am giving to them ... No man will be able to stand before you, all the days of your life. Just as I have been with Moses, I will be with you; I will not fail or forsake you.*

"Be strong and very courageous; be careful to do according to all the law which Moses My servant commanded you; do not turn from it to the right or to the left, so that you may have success wherever you go. This book of the law shall not depart from your mouth, but you shall meditate on it day and night, so that you may be careful to do according to all that is written in it; for then your way will be prosperous, and then you will have success.

"Have I not commanded you? Be strong and courageous! Do not tremble or be dismayed, for the LORD your God is with you wherever you go" (Josh. 1:2–9).

As Joshua left the tabernacle, whatever self-doubts he had were ebbing away under God's encouragement and reassurance. Reading the book, thanks to Moses' tutelage, would keep those convictions going in him.

He dutifully assembled his leaders. "Tell all the people that we will move out in three days toward the Jordan River. Prepare provisions for its crossing." To the leaders of Reuben, Gad, and Manasseh, Joshua announced, "Although your soldiers will lead us over—after the ark, of course—your wives and children and animals may stay in your lands on this side of the Jordan until we conquer Canaan. Then you may return to them."*

The leaders of the three tribes responded as one, "All that you have commanded us, we will do. As we obeyed Moses, so we will obey you." Then, to his surprise, they added, "And we shall also become your aides, killing anyone who rebels against your command." *

On the morning of the third day, the people departed the plains of Moab and traveled to the vicinity of the raging Jordan, where they set up camp again.

Ithamar entered the tent of his brother, Eleazar, the high priest, and his son, Phinehas. "The Levites grumble that we prepared no rafts to get them over this swollen river," Ithamar said. "They fear for their lives. You have assigned several of them to carry the ark into the water, ahead of the people, but the torrents will carry them away!"

"They are concerned!" scoffed Eleazar. "It is I who must lead the whole procession, I who cannot swim, who must enter those swift currents first. I am fearful for my life! Let us go talk to Joshua."

They walked the twenty paces to Joshua's tent, where he was sitting on the floor reading the Book. "Come in," he said.

"Is this foolishness?" Eleazar asked Joshua. "We are supposed to try to wade across those strong waters. We might as well walk into a lion's mouth. Even Moses would not have asked this of us. And besides, we no longer have Moses' miracle-working staff. It disappeared along with him."

"I also wish that we had his staff, but we don't. God has told me simply that all are to be ready," Joshua said. "You, Eleazar, must lead, followed by the ark, and a thousand paces behind you, the soldiers, then the people. God said that you are to walk into the water, and that is all."

Phinehas cleared his throat. "Joshua, would it be all right if I tie a rope around my father's waist, to pull him to safety, if things do not go well?"

"I suppose so," said Joshua. "God has told me to be courageous, and so must you be. This time we cannot fail Him."

At dawn on the fourth day at camp, Joshua shouted the command, "Cross the Jordan!" Only after the Levites had taken up the ark and followed the priests toward the water's edge, with the mass of people following the specified distance behind them, did God speak to Joshua again. *"This day I will begin to exalt you in the sight of all Israel that they may know that just as I was with Moses, I will be with you. You shall, moreover, command the priests who are carrying the ark of the covenant, saying, 'When you come to the edge of the waters of the Jordan, you shall stand still in the Jordan'"* (Josh. 3:7-8).

Joshua walked up to the priests and the Levites carrying the ark and pronounced God's message. "Come here and hear the words of the Lord your God. By this you shall know that the living God is among you, and that He will assuredly dispossess from before you the Canaanite, the Hittite, the Hivite, the Perizzite, the Girgashite, the Amorite, and the Jebusite. And ... when the soles of the feet of the priests who carry the ark of the Lord ... shall rest in the waters of the Jordan, those waters ... shall be cut off, and the waters which are flowing down from above shall stand in one heap."[1]

Hesitantly but obediently Eleazar approached the lapping waters. He forced himself to place one foot into the water—and the waters above stopped! Those below flowed out toward the Salt Sea, leaving an empty riverbed that God dried up with a fierce wind. The awe-stricken priests and the Levites who carried the ark cautiously entered the riverbed. Following God's instructions, the priests stopped in the middle of the Jordan with the ark, while all of the wary, incredulous nation crossed over safely before them with their chosen animals.

On the way through, one strong man from each tribe picked up a large stone from the river bottom and carried it out. Others collected smaller stones. When the last person had crossed and the priests joined them on the riverbank, the waters burst back in a torrent into their accustomed channel.

The men carried the stones inland to their first camping spot at Gilgal, just east of Jericho, and near the mounts, Gerazim and Ebal, where they set up a memorial to God for the amazing crossing. The rituals that God had prescribed to be performed on those mounts, though delayed, would occur.

"On that day the Lord exalted Joshua in the sight of all Israel; so that they revered him, just as they had revered Moses all the days of his life."[2]

With just four days to go before Passover, the families bathed their chosen lambs in preparation.

The next morning, the sentries announced to the camp that no enemy had moved against them. God indeed must have melted their resolve. That day, God ordered Joshua to take flint knives and circumcise those males who had been born along the journey, for none had been circumcised since they left Egypt.[3] So Joshua and the priests did so, marking them irrevocably as God's covenant people.

Three days later, the people celebrated Passover. The following day, they ate the grains from the captured fields and God ceased the production of manna. After the Feast of Unleavened Bread, the invasion began—the first conquest aimed at the high-walled, seemingly insurmountable city of Jericho.

God warned that the victories would come, but slowly. *"I will not drive them out before you in a single year, that the land may not become desolate, and the beasts of the field become too numerous for you ... [but] I will drive them out ... little by little, until you become fruitful and take possession of the land"* (Ex. 23:29–30).

And later, they will abandon Him, worshipping other gods. God's patience will be stretched for an agonizingly long time while He waits in vain for their repentance. Finally, He will reach out to them in the ultimate act of grace, offering the sacrifice Himself to bring about their redemption.

"His anger is but for a moment,
"His favor is for a lifetime;
"Weeping may last for the night,
"But a shout of joy comes in the morning."
Psalm 30:5.

The people would again prosper and multiply, and God would "rejoice over them."[5]

Endnotes;
1. "Come hear the words of the LORD...," Josh. 3:9-13.
2. "On that day the LORD exalted Joshua...," Josh. 4:14.
3. "none had been circumcised...," Josh. 5:2-5.
4. "rejoice over them," Deut. 30:2-9.

Postscript
Where Are You?

How do you apply this story to your own life? God did everything possible to secure the trust of a people. Today He desires all to come to Him.[1] Listen—is He trying to win your trust?

The Israelite trek is much like the walk of believers; some seemingly follow God from early in life, others believe only later, and some never. Are you choosing not to believe, to be left behind in Egypt? Are you in the wilderness, trying to obey with differing amounts of faith, fluctuating day to day? Or are you east of the Jordan, already disciplined and molded, undergoing final preparations to move into what God really has planned for you?

The journey was a trying one for Moses. He grumbled and questioned God but acted faithfully as His servant. Whenever troubles arose, he called and God delivered him out of one difficulty after another—examples of God's increasing availability to those committed to Him.

When the people rebelled, they lost a great opportunity. Do we ignore similar opportunities to follow His novel course? If so, might we—as they—be cast aside, only to hope that the next generation will do better?

The Promised Land was truly lush and certainly worth the trip! Can we trust that what He plans for us is better than we can even imagine?

Moses was largely obedient for forty years, yet he did not realize his ultimate goal. Can we persevere in faith to the end, even if we also are denied the final fruits of our labors?

What should our response be to our God who has plenty of reasons to be angry with us? Can we learn obedience and contrition from the Sinai experience? God needs committed human hands, hearts, minds, and voices, many of which may have been tempered by difficult journeys through their own wildernesses.

Animal sacrifices were the only way by which the Israelites could atone for sins. However, the New Testament Letter to the Hebrews tells us: "For it is impossible for the blood of bulls and goats to take away sins." [2] Only the Lamb of God does that. F. B. Meyer wrote, "Moses represented the law ... but the law can never lead us into rest. It can conduct us to the ... threshold, but no further. Another must take us in, the true Joshua-Jesus." [3]

The focus has been on the Israelites and their journey. And what was to become later of Egypt? Isaiah prophesied: When Egypt will come upon hard times, God will "send them a savior and defender and rescue them … .They will turn to the LORD and He will respond to their pleas and heal them … . Egypt … [will be] a blessing on the earth. The LORD Almighty will bless them saying, 'Blessed be Egypt my people … .'" [4]

This book, which may help a few people to know God better, is merely an example of what God can bring out of a pen from one who wishes to serve Him.

Endnotes
1. "all to come to Him," 2Peter 3:9.
2. "impossible for the blood of bulls…," Heb. 10:4.
3. F.B. Meyer, *Moses, The Servant of God*. London: 1960, p. 177.
4. Isaiah 19:20-25.

Bibliography

Brodsky, Harold. "The Jordan, Symbol of Spiritual Transition." *Bible Review,* June 1992. Cheyne and Black, Encyclopedia Biblica. Wikipedia.

Crim, Keith ed.,*Interpreter's Dictionary of the Bible, Supplementary Volume,* "Atonement," Nashville, Abingdon Press, 1991.

Crim, Keith ed., *Interpreter's Dictionary of the Bible, Supplementary Volume,* "Philistines," Nashville, Abingdon Press, 1991.

Daiches, David. *Moses: Man and His Vision.* Praeger Publishers, New York, 1975.

Edersheim, Alfred. *Bible History: Old Testament,* "Wanderings in the Wilderness," William B. Eerdmans Publishing Co., Grand Rapids, MI, 1949.

Edersheim, Alfred. *Bible History: Old Testament,* "The Exodus," William B. Eerdmans Publishing Co., Grand Rapids, MI, 1949.

Egypt: Gods of Ancient Egypt—*Egyptian Mythology http://www.touregypt. net/gods1.htm*

Gods and Mythology of Ancient Egypt http://www.touregypt.net/godsofegypt/

Horowitz, Edward MA., DRE. *How the Hebrew Language Grew,* KTAV Publishing House, 1960.

Josephus, Flavius. *The Antiquities of the Jews,* translated by William Whiston, A. M., Hendrickson Publishers, Peabody, Massachusetts, 1987, book 2, chapter 10.

Keller, Dr. Werner. *The Bible as History: A Confirmation of the Book of Books.* Translated by Dr. William Neil. New York. William Morrow, 1964.

Kurtz, J. H. *Offerings, Sacrifices and Worship in the Old Testament,* Hendrickson, Peabody, Mass., 1998.

Meyer, F.B. *Moses, The Servant of God.* London: Marshall, Morgan and Scott: 1960.

Neuser, Jacob_*The Mishnah, A New Translation.* "Pesahin 2:1, 2, 3" New Haven. Yale Univ. Press, 1988.

Packer, J.I. *Knowing God,*. Intervarsity Press, Downer's Grove, IL 1973.

Palmer, Edward Henry. *Desert of the Exodus,* Vol. 1, Harper and Bros., New York, 1872.

Peck, M. Scott. *The Road Less Traveled, A New Psychology of Love. Traditional Values and Spiritual Growth.* New York, Simon and Schuster, 1978.

Raban, Avnr and Stieglitz, Tobert R. "The Sea Peoples and Their Contributions to Civilization." *Biblical Archeology Review,* Nov.-Dec. 1991.

Rawlinson, George. *Moses, His Life and Times,* Anson D.F. Randolph and Company, 1887, New York.

Reeves, Nicholas. "Pithom" and "Rameses," *Ancient Egypt: The Great Discoveries,* Thames and Hudson, New York, 2000.

Robertson, Reverend George W. Ph.D., senior minister, First Presbyterian Church (PCA), Augusta, Georgia.

Saenz-Badillos, Angel. "New Hebrew alphabet" *A History of the Hebrew Language,* Cambridge University Press, 1993.

Tenney, Merill. *The Zondervan Pictorial Encyclopedia of the Bible.* Grand Rapids, Michigan: Zondervan, 1975.

Velikovsky, Immanuel. *Ages in Chaos,* Vol. I., Garden City, NY, Doubleday, 1952.

Wood, Bryant G. "The Philistines Enter Canaan: Were They Egyptian Lackeys or Invading conquerors?" *Biblical Archaelogy Review,* Nov.-Dec. 1991.